BOSS ME

A BOSS-ASSISTANT ON VACATION STANDALONE ROMANCE

SYNERGY WORKPLACE ROMANCE
BOOK 4

MICHELLE MCCRAW

Cover by Qamber Designs

ISBN: 978-1-7368294-7-9
BN ISBN: 979-83692366-6-6
D2D ISBN: 979-82235433-1-2

BOOKS BY MICHELLE MCCRAW

40 and Fabulous

Fashion and Passion

Frenemies and Lovers

Books and Hookups

Conspiracies and Chemistry

Advances and Retreats

Synergy Series

Work with Me

Friend Me

Trip Me Up

Boss Me

Forget Me

Tempt Me

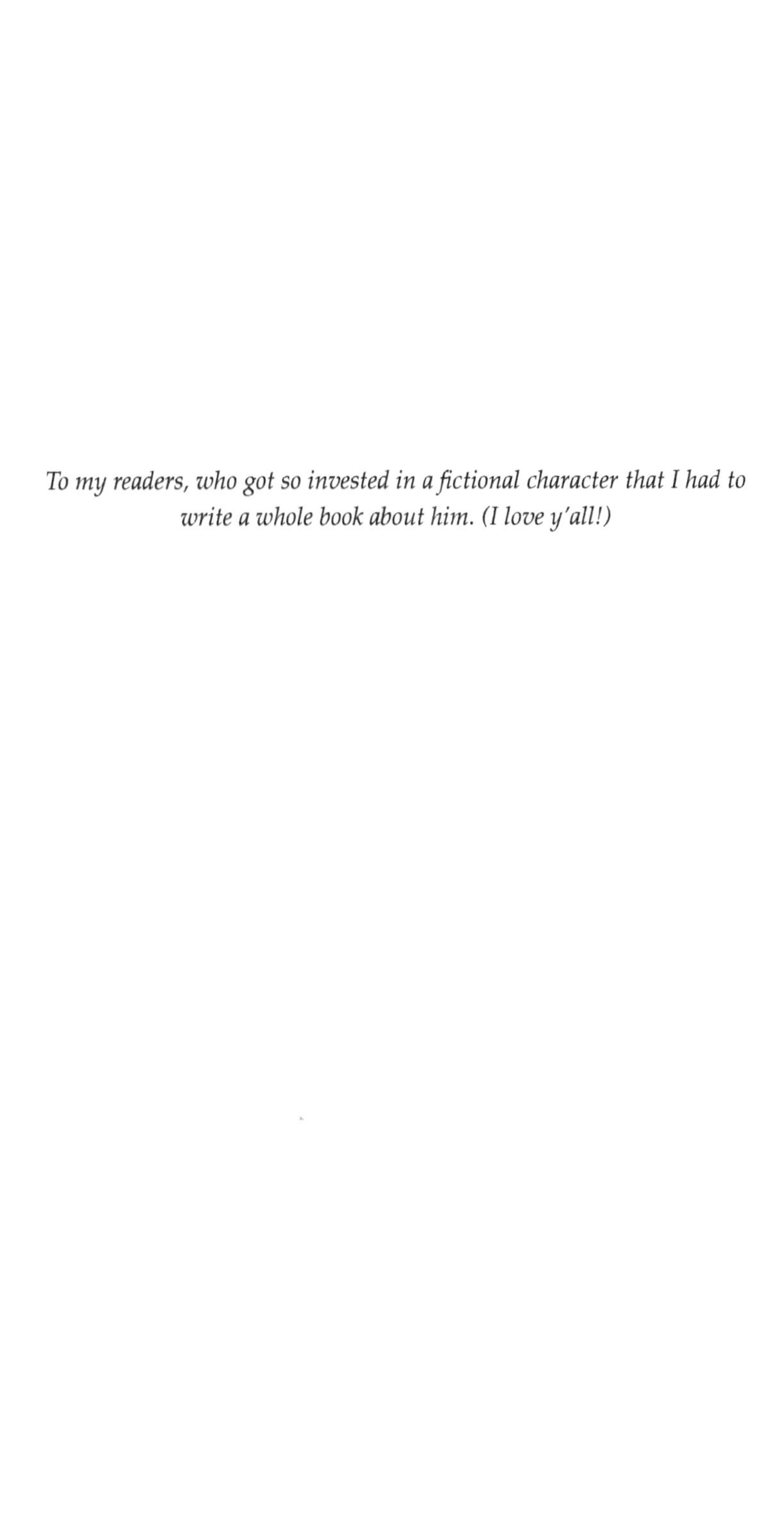

To my readers, who got so invested in a fictional character that I had to write a whole book about him. (I love y'all!)

1

BEN

TROUBLE CAME in the shape of a pair of broad shoulders.

Even hunched forward, bracketing his drooping head, they were wide and muscled, his biceps barely contained in a paper-thin vintage Rolling Stones T-shirt tucked at his narrow waist into a pair of jeans. His ridiculous Austin, Texas, belt buckle was as big as my hand.

When I hung out with the other admins at coffee breaks, they swooned over Jackson Jones's rakish good looks and flirtatious personality.

Not me. I left that for my boss.

Wait, sorry, did I say that? Regardless, I knew Jackson Jones was trouble.

He scuffed to my desk and turned a pair of bloodshot eyes on me. "He in?"

God, I wished he wasn't. Or that I could lie and save my boss from whatever fresh hell Jackson was about to drag him into.

"Something I can help you with?" I stood and smoothed down my navy merino wool sweater. I wasn't a tall man, but standing, I didn't have to crane my neck up at Jackson.

He chuckled. "Not unless you've got a miracle cure for whatever baby bug took down my kid, my wife, and the nanny."

"Sorry, I'm fresh out—oh. You're supposed to go to Boston today."

"Yeah. About that…"

I winced. My boss had just gotten back from a trip to Asia the week before. He hadn't had time to recover from the jet lag. And Jackson was about to ask him to get back on a plane to fly across the country and screw up his body clock again.

But Jackson thought Cooper Fallon was Superman, that he could do it all—his own job as the Chief Operating Officer and Jackson's job, too.

It didn't help that Cooper did nothing to dispel that notion. When Jackson asked him to jump, he asked how high. According to the executive assistant who supported Synergy's board, who'd been there almost since the beginning, it had been their dynamic since they'd founded the company over a dozen years before. They were partners, but it was nothing like 50-50. More like 80-20. And Cooper always ended up on the wrong end of that ratio.

"So can I go in?"

I hadn't realized I'd moved in front of the glass door to Cooper's office, blocking his partner from entry. I wished I could tell him no to protect Cooper from Jackson and from his own overcommitment, but Cooper didn't want to be protected from Jackson.

Even though he needed it.

Deliberately, I lowered my shoulders from where they'd crept up by my ears. I turned and rapped on the door before I pushed it open and stuck my head into the opening. "Mr. Fallon?"

When he turned from his monitor, the blue light lit his face, turning his normally golden tan skin greenish pale. His eyes were red, too. Not as bad as Jackson's, but I could tell he'd spent too much time staring at spreadsheets. He lifted a hand to the juncture of his neck and shoulder and kneaded the muscle there. I wished I could do that for him, but that would've violated our unspoken no-touching rule.

"Ben, how many times have I asked you to call me Cooper?"

I let one side of my mouth curl up. "About once a day since I started working here six months ago, Mr. Fallon."

"So approximately one hundred twenty times. And how many more times do I need to tell you before you listen?"

The snap in his tone might have scared someone else. Cooper Fallon was famous for his relentless drive and his quick temper. I knew he'd never follow up that bark with a proper bite. Maybe with an executive like Jackson, but not for someone at my level. I'd watched him, probably more than was healthy, and I knew from many hours of careful observation that even though his tone was sharp, he usually kept a leash on the fury that flashed in his blue eyes.

"Oh, I listen," I said.

Behind me, Jackson cleared his throat, and the smile melted off my face. "Jackson is here to see you. Do you have a minute?" *Please say no.*

He ran a hand through his sunkissed hair and stood, his six-foot-four frame unfolding with athletic elegance. "Send him in."

I held in a sigh and pressed the door all the way open, stepping into the office, and said more formally than I needed to, "He can see you now."

Jackson shuffled past me. "Hey, Coop."

Cooper strode around his desk and clapped Jackson's shoulder. They were about the same height, two gorgeous physical specimens, but only one of them turned me inside out whenever I was in his presence.

I stayed there, pressed against the door. "Can I get you anything? Coffee? A sandwich?" Had Cooper eaten lunch? I'd gone to the cafeteria with Jackson's assistant, Marlee, but I wasn't sure if Cooper had left his desk.

"Would you get me a coffee, please?" Jackson asked.

"Sure. How about a green smoothie, Mr. Fallon?" He'd need

the antioxidants to keep up his strength if he was going back out on the road.

His gaze flicked to me, and heat washed over my skin. But his words were crisp with frost. "Yes, please. Thank you."

And then, as much as I hated to do it, I walked out of his office and closed the door on Jackson Jones and Cooper Fallon.

———

I RUBBED at my throbbing temple and edged forward in line for the coffee kiosk in Synergy's soaring lobby. My gaze trailed up the glass elevator shaft to the sixth floor.

If I was any judge of the tightening around Cooper's eyes, he was suffering through his own headache. Not that he'd ever admit to being human enough to experience pain. Maybe I could slip him a pain reliever along with the revolting green smoothie.

Smoothies: my small but important contribution to the company. Cooper drank at least one a day. It was quick, efficient fuel for his duties as Chief Operating Officer of Synergy Analytics. Cooper kept Synergy running, and by fetching his smoothies, I did my part.

I scrubbed my hand over my face and stared out across the lobby. Who was I kidding? I didn't do it for Synergy. I did it for him.

I did it for the flare in those cool blue eyes when I handed the cup to him and said, "Your smoothie, Mr. Fallon."

I did it because of the infatuation that fluttered in my stomach the moment I shook his hand on my first day on the job six months ago. And as we'd worked together, as I'd gotten to know the driven executive who'd do anything for his partner and best friend, who'd grown the company from a business plan he'd written in a spiral notebook in their dorm room, who supported foundations that helped at-risk kids, those flutters moved right into my heart and never left.

My sister, Mimi, said I lived with my heart on the outside, and I'd fall for anyone who gave me a hint of returning my attraction.

Not true.

Cooper Fallon had given me no hints. He was always cool and polite. He said, "Thank you, Ben," at the end of each day. He'd given me an expensive but impersonal cheese basket for the holidays. He asked me about school sometimes, but he probably had to since the company was paying my tuition.

Yet I gobbled up those flares of heat when I handed over his smoothies.

A woman took her coffee and strode away from the kiosk, and I stepped forward, still two people from the front of the line. I checked my phone. Ten minutes since I'd left Cooper alone with Jackson.

Why had I tried to save time by coming downstairs to the kiosk? The place down the street knew our order. But I'd wanted to stay close enough to rescue Cooper if he needed it. Ha. Cooper Fallon would never admit he needed rescuing. Or a goddamned break from saving the world. I inched forward in line and tapped the toe of my chukka boot against the floor to relieve the nervous energy that made me want to shake someone.

Jackson, who was supposed to be Cooper's best friend, pulled this shit all the damn time. There was always a reason he couldn't take a trip or present to the board.

When I was first hired, Cooper handled it, no problem. But since Jackson's baby was born in February, Cooper seemed paler somehow. Not just his skin, but the whole of him. Like some of his actual life essence had been sucked out of him by that machine in *The Princess Bride*. His movements were smaller. His smile—rare at the best of times—was nonexistent now. Even that famous Fallon temper had cooled, like nothing was worth getting upset over anymore.

Maybe it was just a seasonal thing, and Cooper would spring back to life when the days got longer and brighter in the summer.

But I had a feeling it wasn't. It was a Jackson Jones thing. I dug a knuckle into my temple. Fucking Jackson Jones and his bullshit.

"Hey, Ben." The barista's voice snapped me back to reality. Finally, I was at the front of the line.

"Hey." I didn't come to the kiosk often, but I guessed the barista made it his job to know everyone's name.

"It's Kris." He winked at me, his dark hair flopping over one eye.

"Oh, right, I knew that. Sorry, Kris." Did I know that? "Do you have blueberries?"

Kris blinked. "Um, sure."

"Can you add a handful of them to a kale smoothie, please?" I checked my phone. Fifteen minutes, and no SOS text. That had to be a good sign. "And can I also get a black coffee and a skinny latte? Plus a caramel macchiato for Marlee. Please."

"Got it." He scooped fresh grounds into a French press. "You don't come here that often. Not as often as I'd like."

I flicked my gaze from his hands, which I'd been mentally urging to move faster, to his face. He had a Harry Styles look going with that floppy hair and those to-die-for cheekbones. Totally my type.

Except he wasn't. Not anymore. My type, apparently, was emotionally unavailable, blue-eyed billionaires. Fuck. My. Life.

My phone buzzed in my hand.

Marlee: 911. Need you NOW.

"Shit, sorry, 86 all that." I shot Kris a quick smile. The corners of his mouth turned down just before I sprinted across the lobby to the elevator bank. I pounded the button and whirled to scan the elevator doors behind me. *Open, open, open.* I hopped on my toes like that would make the elevator come faster.

At last, a door pinged, and I rushed to stand in front of it. The elevator was full, and it took every ounce of self-control I had not to shove past my fellow employees and then push them out.

When the car finally emptied, I darted inside and pushed the button for the sixth floor, then I slammed my palm over the close-door button. It wasn't the first time I'd had to rush back to my desk for my demanding boss. But I had a bad feeling today. Goddamn Jackson Jones.

I watched the floors light on the screen above the door and breathed deep. Maybe I was being unfair to Jackson. Marlee liked him. Everyone liked him. Including Cooper. In fact—

I rubbed my hand over the too-familiar burn in my belly. I needed to stop caring about Cooper. Like most people I'd fallen for, he was out of my league. Besides, his heart was otherwise engaged, and the sooner I got over my ridiculous crush, the better.

At last, the doors opened on the sixth floor, and I stepped out, my heart in my throat.

Raised voices assaulted the usual calm of the executive floor. They were coming from Cooper's office. A crowd of people gathered near the door.

Marlee trotted toward me on her pink kitten heels. Wringing her hands, she whispered, "Great galloping Galileo, Ben. They're fighting. Like, actually yelling at each other, and they wouldn't answer when I knocked. You've got to go in there and make them stop. Everyone's staring."

"Is Weston in there?" The CEO was Jackson's archnemesis, and neither man pulled any punches when they disagreed.

"No, just Jackson and Cooper. But I'm sure someone will tell Weston."

The tension in my chest eased. Jackson and Cooper got loud sometimes, but it never lasted long. At least the CEO wasn't witnessing it firsthand. Cooper could explain it away later. He had a magic touch with his boss.

I needed to capture some of that boss-magic for myself. "Back to work, everyone. Nothing to see here," I announced as I made my way to Cooper's office. Some people returned to their desks. Weston's assistant, Julie, more brazen, lingered nearby.

I raised an eyebrow, and slowly, she turned and plodded back to her desk. She didn't sit behind it but stood, staring, ready to witness whatever would erupt when I opened the door.

I knocked, but they were yelling too loudly to hear anything. I pushed the handle, but it didn't budge. Why was it locked?

Reluctantly, I flicked my badge in front of the sensor. It was keyed to only Cooper's ID, Jackson's, and mine. The light turned green. I sucked in a deep breath, pushed the handle down, and opened the door.

Cooper, his face red and his eyes bulging, roared, "I'm not putting up with your bullshit anymore!" He slammed his hand onto his desk.

It all happened so fast. When I replayed the scene later in my mind, I thought I remembered hearing a ping as if that big, ugly ring Cooper always wore had hit the glass top that protected the wood.

Regardless of what caused it, there was a crackle like fireworks popping and then silence. After a second, a shard of glass tumbled off the edge and jabbed into the thick carpet. A few smaller pieces followed it. Cooper stared at the surface of his desk. Then he looked up and scanned his best friend from head to toe.

Jealousy ignited in my gut. Why, even when Jackson was dumping his responsibilities on Cooper, was Cooper's first instinct to protect Jackson? What I wouldn't give to have that concern, that care, directed at me.

Shit, this was no time for me to moon over my boss. I had to do something to fix this. But my feet stuck to the floor. I was intimately familiar with his temper, but as far as I knew, he'd never hit anything.

"Coop—you all right?" Jackson's voice was funeral-quiet. It was the first time I'd seen him motionless.

"I—I'm sorry, Jay. It was an…"

I wanted to run to him, check that he wasn't hurt, but the

tension in the room was solid enough to keep me rooted at the door. I closed it behind me. "Everything okay in here?"

Clearly it wasn't. The top of Cooper's desk sparkled with shattered glass. His face was as white as the papers stacked neatly in his outbox. When a drop of blood plopped onto the desk, he raised his hand and gazed at it like he wasn't sure it belonged to him.

"Sh—I mean, here. Let me help." My feet unstuck from the carpet, and the next second, I stood beside my boss. His palm was crisscrossed with cuts, blood welling in each one.

I dug in my front pocket for my handkerchief and shook out the creases. I hesitated for a moment—that no-touching rule—but this was an emergency. He'd hate it if I had to disrupt his work to remove a bloodstained rug.

I folded the handkerchief in thirds and gently pressed it against his palm. His jaw tightened.

"Does it hurt?" The cuts didn't look deep, but I hadn't gotten a good look at them.

"No." The word held none of his usual crispness. Was he in shock?

"Sit down." With the hand I wasn't using to apply pressure to his wound, I reached up and pushed on his shoulder until he folded into his chair.

Finally, I looked at Jackson, whose mouth still hung open, staring at his friend. "What happened?" My tone wasn't as respectful as it should've been around the company's cofounder, but anything involving blood was extenuating circumstances.

Jackson leaped toward the desk and scooped the shards of shattered glass into a pile. "Cooper was making a point a little too forcefully. I guess he should've sprung for the tempered glass."

Fuck, if he kept doing that, I was going to have two bleeders on my hands. "Jackson, stop. I'll get maintenance up here—"

"Dammit!" When Jackson stuck his thumb in his mouth, his elbow caught the conch shell on Cooper's desk. The one I'd dusted once a week, each time wondering why he kept that one decorative item on his desk. I didn't have to wonder anymore. It tumbled off the desk, bounced once on the carpet, and shattered when it smashed on the wood floor.

The silence after was even louder than when Cooper broke his desk.

"Sorry, Coop, I—"

Pain flashed across Cooper's face. It was the same look he'd gotten the day Jackson wore his baby to the office in one of those backward backpacks. "Forget about it. I—I need to go."

"Now?" I lifted a corner of my handkerchief. The bleeding had slowed. "You can't go to a meeting like this." Only Cooper Fallon would continue his workday like nothing had happened after he'd sliced himself open. I wrapped the ends of the cloth around the back of his hand and tied them into a knot over his palm.

"People are used to me showing up as a hot mess. Not you." Jackson raked his hand through his dark hair. "Listen to Ben. Sit and rest a minute. I've got some whiskey in my office. We can—"

As soon as my fingers left the knot on the handkerchief, Cooper ripped his hand away. His blue eyes weren't as icy as usual when he turned them on me. Probably because of the blood loss.

"I need—out." He rose and stepped around me on his way to the door. His hand on the latch, he turned back.

Thank God, he was going to sit down and be reasonable. I took a half step toward him in case he wobbled on his way back to the chair.

But he stayed there, gripping the handle. "Ben, let the New England Entrepreneurs' Society know I'll be taking Jackson's place as the keynote speaker. And switch his hotel reservation to me."

Jackson popped his thumb out of his mouth. "Coop, you don't have to do that."

Cooper gave his best friend a wry smile. "Isn't that exactly what you were telling me I had to do before—before this?" He waved his handkerchief-wrapped hand at the mess in his office.

"But—"

He held out his palm. It trembled. He must have been exerting an enormous amount of control over himself. "Move all my meetings to next week."

What the absolute fuck was happening? "Yes, Mr. Fallon."

He opened the door and walked out, closing it gently behind him. No gym bag, no coat, no laptop. Was he staying in the building? Did he have a secret, primal-scream room downstairs?

"It's okay." Jackson hung his head. "You can say it. I'm the worst friend ever."

I couldn't help it. I smiled at the jerk. He was irritatingly adorable. "You totally are. But he loves you anyway."

He whipped his head up and grinned. "He does, doesn't he? I'm the luckiest guy in San Francisco."

My smile melted off my face. He fucking was. What I wouldn't give to be on the receiving end of one percent of that love. Jackson was too full of himself to notice, but I'd seen it from my first days at the company. Cooper was pining for his best friend. His obliviously straight best friend.

"You should get out of here," I said, my tone flat. "I'll call maintenance to clean this up."

"Thanks, Ben. I'll give Coop an hour or so to stew, and then I'll talk to him."

If I knew my boss, he needed more than an hour. And I guessed he'd get it on his last-minute trip to Boston. Which I now had to schedule.

Fucking hell.

I'd figure out a way to check on him, even in Boston. Because maybe Jackson Jones didn't give a shit about how much he'd fucked up Cooper's life, but I did.

2

COOPER

WHEN I'D APPROVED the open-plan design of the sixth floor of our building, I never anticipated needing somewhere other than my office to get my shit together.

I worked hard to make my office a place of calm, a place where I could recall the peace and safety of the island and where none of the bad memories, memories of the man who'd given me my name, could intrude.

Nevertheless, my office was where I'd just lost my shit.

Despite the ache from the cuts, my palm itched for a stress ball or a punching bag, some way to get the tension out of my muscles, to cool the anger bubbling in my veins. If I had the courage to look in a mirror, I was sure my reflection would remind me of my father's face, scarlet with rage.

Somehow I ended up in front of Weston's office. It made sense because from the early days when we'd taken Synergy public, he'd acted almost like a father to me, giving me the kind of advice my own father wasn't wise or sober enough to give.

"He in?" I paused in front of Julie's desk.

She stared at me, wide-eyed, before dropping her gaze to the bloody handkerchief wrapped around my hand.

"He's on a call."

"I need him." I strode past her desk and straight into Weston's office.

"But—"

I closed the door on her protest.

Weston glanced over his shoulder. His impeccable loafers rested on the credenza in front of the window. Unlike mine, his view of the bay was unobstructed by the neighboring building. Gray water churned under the hovering clouds.

He held up a finger and lowered his feet. "I'm going to have to call you back." He tugged out his earphone and laid it on the desk.

His eyes fell to my handkerchief-wrapped palm. "What happened?"

I covered it with my other hand. "An accident."

"I see." And he did. His clear eyes saw right down to the roiling core of me. He stood and gestured at the studded leather sofa.

I perched on it. Weston's furniture wasn't comfortable enough to sink into. Besides, my body still vibrated with the adrenaline that roared through my blood.

He sat in the high-backed wing chair next to the sofa and crossed his legs. A few inches of plain black dress sock were visible under the hem of his wool pants.

My voice was too calm, even in my ears. "I'm going to the New England Entrepreneurs' conference. For Jackson."

"You volunteered to go?" His dark eyebrows winged up over eyes that matched the deep blue of his silk tie.

"Not exactly. His wife and the baby are sick. He needs to take care of them and their other kid." It sounded perfectly reasonable when I said it. Why had I blown up on him when he told me? I gripped my cut-up hand with my other one.

"Didn't you just get back from Asia?"

"I did. I don't suppose you want to go to Boston?"

He chuckled. "Sorry, I've got Phoebe this week."

I glanced at the photo on his desk. Weston stood next to his daughter in her riding helmet and coat, his arms around her shoulders and her small hand holding the leather reins of the chestnut horse on her other side.

"You could always cancel," he said.

My jaw clenched. "Synergy doesn't cancel on its commitments. Not to customers, not to our employees, not to fellow entrepreneurs. And not at the last minute."

"They'd understand. Have Jones call them."

That was just what Jackson needed, another dent in his already fragile reputation. "No, I'll do it."

"You'd do anything for him, wouldn't you?" The words were light, but his stare was heavy with meaning.

I wished I could unburden myself to him. That I could tell him how I felt about Jackson Jones since almost the first moment he walked into our dorm room at Stanford. About keeping my ridiculous crush bottled up for years, knowing Jackson was straight and not wanting to ruin our friendship with a confession. About how my heart had ripped in two when he'd gotten engaged—my commitment-phobic friend who'd refused to sink money into anything that didn't have wheels he could drive away in, engaged! And then it crumbled to dust completely when he told me his fiancée was pregnant.

I knew he'd never be mine, but that kidney bean on the ultrasound he waved in my face was the final buzzer on the game of delusions I'd played with myself.

The night she was born, I was the one left standing in the hospital hallway when the nurse barred my way and said, "Family only."

Jackson was my best friend, but he'd never be my family.

I didn't need Dr. Pradhi to psychoanalyze it for me. The reminder he'd given me earlier today—choosing his family over the company we'd built together—was what made me explode.

Like he could see my thoughts written on my forehead, Weston said, "I think you could use some time away."

"But I—"

"Think about it. I'll take care of things here. You should consider what you want. For yourself and for Synergy."

What did I want? I'd wanted Jackson for so long, there was a void inside me where all that want used to live. Even Synergy felt empty. He'd abandoned it, just like he'd abandoned me.

"Do you want to talk about it?" He leaned his elbows on his knees, earnestness wrinkling his forehead. He looked like the father I wished I had when I was Phoebe's age. Like one of my tíos back on the island.

I trusted Weston, ever since he saved Synergy when Jackson let me down. The night before we met with the investment bankers, Jackson and I went out for drinks to celebrate the fact that our seven-year partnership was finally about to pay off in a big way. After I went back to the hotel, Jackson got into it with a cop. He showed up to our meeting rumpled, a mouse under his eye, smelling like holy hell.

The bankers insisted we replace Jackson as CEO with Weston. And with Jackson looking like my father the mornings I'd gone to pick him up from the drunk tank, I agreed. Jackson, being Jackson, ditched me for a yacht full of bikini models, but Weston stayed. He guided Synergy—and me—through the process to become a publicly traded company. And helped grow it into the software powerhouse it became.

Even though we'd worked together for the past seven years, I never told Weston what I felt for Jackson. I hadn't told anyone. Ever. Though my other best friend, Jamila, had guessed it on her own.

"No, I'm good."

"Are you? I worry about you, Fallon."

My last name, the one I shared with my father, made me blink. His name wasn't the only thing I'd inherited. I proved that today.

Like I was replaying it from a video recording, I pictured

myself, my face red, spit flying from my mouth as I smashed the glass of my desk. I hadn't felt any of it, the impact or the cuts. When my father used to come home smelling of cheap whiskey, he never remembered why his knuckles were red until he saw the matching bruise on my cheek.

Despite the fact that Weston looked like a stock photo of an expensive psychiatrist with the gray hair sparkling at his temples and in his close-cropped beard, I couldn't tell him what I'd done or why I'd done it. Those blue eyes would turn hard or, worse, soften with pity.

"I'm good," I repeated. Cooper Fallon was always good. Reliable. Hardworking. "Ben's moving my meetings. Can you keep an eye on things while I'm in Boston?"

"Of course. Is Ben going with you?"

"Ben…going with me?" I blinked. That was a terrible idea. When he'd joined the company right after Jackson's wedding, I'd been vulnerable, cut-open. That was the only thing that could explain the zing I felt when I shook his hand for the first time. The warmth in my chest where my heart used to be before it went cold and dark. Traveling with Ben would be too much temptation. "No."

"You could use the support. You don't have to do everything yourself, you know."

"Don't I?" I bared my teeth in a grim smile.

He mirrored the expression. "You're right. And it might get worse if Jones decides to get out and focus on his family."

My muscles went as rigid as the leather chair. "Get out?"

"We both see the writing on the wall, Fallon. His heart isn't in it anymore. He has other priorities."

Priorities other than me and the company we'd built together. Why hadn't I seen it? Maybe I had, subconsciously, and that was why I'd lost it in my office.

Fuck.

Without Jackson, Synergy would be a painful reminder of everything I'd lost. It wouldn't be fun anymore. It would be work.

Weston's eyes bored into mine like a drill, mining for my secrets. Then he reached over and clasped my shoulder. "Think about it. Take some time if you need it. After Boston."

I stood. "I will."

I strode out of his office and straight to the stairs, not meeting anyone's gaze, afraid I'd crack the faux-stone veneer I'd plastered over my volatile emotions. For the first time in months, I left the office while the winter sun still hung above the horizon.

———

WHEN I WALKED in my front door, Norma took one look at me and crossed herself. Rolling up her brown eyes, she muttered something—a prayer, I was sure, since she was always praying about something—then held out her hand.

It was no use resisting, so I laid my hand in hers, palm-up.

"Boxing again?"

"Jiu-jitsu," I reminded her. "And no. I—" I couldn't tell her. She'd say something to my mother at church. "I cut myself at work."

"You work at a desk." She clucked her tongue as she took in the bloody handkerchief. "Not a factory."

"It's a paper cut?"

She didn't so much as smile at my weak joke. But I'd never tell no-nonsense Norma—my employee for whom I was responsible —that I'd slammed my hand onto my desk because my best friend had slipped under my defenses and hurt my feelings. Feelings I didn't think I had anymore.

She bent her head over my hand. Not one hair escaped her tight, gray bun, but her fingers were gentle when she tugged at the handkerchief.

I flexed my hand around it, gripping the cloth. "It's fine."

Her lips pressed into a pale line. "We need to wash it out. And put on a fresh bandage. It's not deep enough for stitches, is it?"

"No." Still, I followed her to the kitchen and let her unwind Ben's handkerchief over the sink. Briskly, and not gently, she washed my hand with stinging soap. I gazed at the bloodstained handkerchief she'd dropped so carelessly beside the sink. It wasn't anything special, just the kind you bought in packs at a department store. Yet, it *was* special. Because it was his. I had to return it.

"You'll get that laundered for me?" I tilted my chin at the cloth. "I borrowed it from someone."

"Yes, yes. Just like all your stinky workout clothes and the sheets you barely sleep on."

She was patting my hand dry, so she didn't see me roll my eyes. She released me for a second to pull the first aid kit from under the sink. "You burn yourself out, you can't work anymore. And then what happens to this place?" She waved a hand at the gourmet kitchen she used to prepare my meals, at the elegant, adjoining dining room I used only for catered business dinners. "You must take care of yourself first, Lito."

I didn't bother explaining that if I resigned today, I'd still be a wealthy man due to my Synergy stock holdings and other investments. Like all the housekeepers and cooks and gardeners Mamá sent me from church—hardworking, down-on-their-luck women —she understood cash flow but not much else.

Norma, who'd lost her husband of twenty-five years six months ago in an accident, was better than most. She made my house hum like a Ferrari's engine, unlike her predecessor who'd forgotten to pay the light bill and left me in the dark for one chilly January weekend, which happened to be my birthday weekend. But I could never fire one of Mamá's people. Unlike at work, I was at the bottom of the church-lady hierarchy. I put her in charge of the laundry and hired Norma as my housekeeper.

After Norma slapped a piece of tape over the gauze to secure it, she picked up the bloody handkerchief and shoved it into her apron pocket. I eyed the bulge. It wouldn't be clean until tomorrow, and I'd be in Boston.

Which reminded me… "I'm leaving tonight for a trip. I won't be back until the weekend. Take some time off."

She frowned, halfway to the laundry room. "Another trip? You just got back from Asia last Friday."

"I know." I traced the gauze on my hand, willing the surge of anger back down. "Something came up."

"I worry about you, mijo. You work too hard."

It was what I'd been telling Jackson when I broke the desk. The anger pulsed again, quietly. I needed to call Dr. Pradhi.

"I'll heat up your dinner for you before I go."

"Thanks, Norma. And thanks for this." I gestured with my bandaged right hand.

She waved away my thanks as she set one of my pre-portioned meals in the oven. "You need a vacation, not another work trip. A massage. Some sleep."

"Mamá and I went to the island over Christmas."

"That was months ago, and you've worked almost every weekend since. Evenings, too. You need a break."

She wasn't wrong. Today proved it.

"Someday," I said. Though not while Jackson had a newborn, apparently.

She pursed her lips and lifted her handbag to her shoulder. "Have a good trip. And don't forget to eat."

I gave her a weak smile. "Don't you forget, either. And don't spend your days off working in the soup kitchen."

"What I do on my days off is none of your business, Miguelito. If I want to spend time at church or even here, it's not your concern."

I held up my palms. "Sí, señora. Good night."

She nodded once and walked out the door to the garage. Her headlights swept away down the street.

After my solitary meal, I trudged upstairs to my bedroom. The suit bag in the walk-in closet was still half-packed from my trip to Asia.

Boston in early April. I shivered.

I slid a couple of wool sweaters into the pockets, then clipped in my suits and shirts on their hangers. Just as I was considering adding a pair of jeans on the off-chance I'd have the energy to go out after the conference, my phone buzzed on the chest of drawers in the center of the closet.

Was it Ben, calling to check on me? No, he didn't call me after hours. But I'd never hurt myself at work before. My stomach gave a hopeful flutter.

When I checked the name on the display, my gut settled for a second and then clenched. She must have heard what I did.

"Jamila."

"Hey, now. No need to be so growly. You know I don't fall for that shit. I'm calling to see how you're doing." Her honey-dipped Texas accent softened the consonants.

I checked my right hand. The bandage was free of blood despite the packing I'd done. "I'm fine."

"You sure about that? Because people who are *fine* don't Hulk out at the office."

"What the fuck did Jackson tell you? I didn't Hulk out. I was making a point, and my ring caught that glass on my desk." Why was I lying to her? She was my best friend, after Jackson. She had to know why I did it.

"You mean the glass you put on it after you argued with one of your temps and she keyed the wood?"

I winced. Not my finest moment. But the temp had been the one to damage the desk that time, not me. "You know how Jay is. He got on my last nerve."

"I know how you are about Jay. Ever since—"

"It had nothing to do with that." Another lie. They just kept flying out of my mouth. Had my father died and possessed me like the jumbee from my tías' stories? I could only hope Mick Fallon was dead. As Jamila often said, that man was too mean to die.

"You sure? You've been in a horn-tossing mood since Valentine was born."

"I've always picked up his slack, but he's hardly been in the office since the birth. I've been doing my work and his, too."

I crossed to the built-in shelving that held my watches. Next to my Breitling was the fragile, dried calla lily boutonnière I'd saved from his wedding. When I touched it, the edge of a petal flaked off. That night had broken my heart in two. Thank God Jamila had been there to save me. I shuddered to think about what I could've said—or done—if I'd gotten drunk.

I returned to stand in front of my suit bag. "I'm packing right now to give his speech to the Entrepreneurs' Society in Boston."

"No, Coop. You just got back from Singapore."

"Someone's got to do it," I growled, scanning the closet for my dress shoes. What had Norma done with them?

"There are other people who can take up the slack, you know. Get Weston to do it. The CEO ought to step up."

"He can't." He'd told me to cancel. And I'd been tempted. Especially after he made me see how Jackson was disentangling himself from the company we'd built together, the one that symbolized our friendship.

"No one else can pivot at the last minute like I can. They've got spouses. Kids. Families." All I had was an enormous, empty mansion in Pacific Heights. I didn't have as much as a fucking goldfish to care for. And if I did, Norma could have fed it while I was in Boston.

After a moment's hesitation, she said, "Not having those obligations doesn't mean you can do everyone's work, Cooper. You need some downtime, too. Don't you think what happened today proves it?"

I felt in my trouser pocket and pulled out the ring that had started all the trouble. It was a big, ugly signet-style ring with a light-blue stone set in the center. The silver ring was flattened slightly from the impact, and the stone now cracked down the middle. Larimar. For enlightenment and healing, Mamá said when she gave it to me. If it worked, I doubted I would've used it to smash my desk. I wouldn't have acted like *him*.

"I don't want to talk about it."

"You need to talk to someone. Have you called your therapist?"

"Not yet." The words ground out between my gritted teeth.

"Don't get your tail up. I'm trying to help you."

"I know. I know." But knowing Jamila was in my corner didn't put out the fire blazing inside me. "I have to get to the airport. I'll call you this weekend."

"Okay, honey. Take care." Concern tinged her voice. Add her to the list with Norma and Ben.

I checked the heavy Rolex on my wrist. The car would be outside in ten minutes. Where were my fucking shoes? I pitched the phone through the door toward the bed so I'd have both hands free to tear apart my closet. I spun on my toe and—

When I looked down, I spotted my shoes. On my feet. I'd been about to wreck my closet over a pair of shoes I'd forgotten I was wearing.

My hands shook, and when I caught my reflection in the mirror on the back of the door, my eyes were wide and wild. My hair stood up in sandy spikes.

Next time, it might not be a desk I hit. It might not be a sheet of glass I destroyed.

Add myself to that list of concerned people.

I strode across the closet, snatched the boutonnière off the shelf, and crushed it in my fist. I dropped the pieces in the trash. I was done with him. Done with it all.

My fingers were almost too shaky to find the contact in my phone, but at last I hit the call button. "Emily?" I said when the pilot picked up. "I need you to change our flight plan. We're not going to Boston."

3

BEN

MARLEE SMILED as I passed her desk. "You're in a good mood."

I paused and pointed up at the huge skylight. "The sun is shining, and I got an A on my econ paper last night." I felt like crowing when I saw it. I almost wished my ex, Trey, and I were still on speaking terms so I could've told him.

"Good job! But remind me why you're taking econ?" She grimaced. "You hate spreadsheets."

"This is just an intro class, and it's more about theory than actual formulas. The accounting class I took last semester?" I shuddered at the memory. Numbers had always been so difficult for me. Unlike my sister, Mimi, who was an accountant downstairs and a total boss at math. "Nothing but spreadsheets. But it's required for my business major."

"Should've majored in programming like me." She flipped her light-brown hair.

"I should've done a lot of things different." Like going to counseling after my boyfriend broke up with me my freshman year instead of dropping out. Maybe then I'd have what Trey considered a real job, and I wouldn't be the oldest student in my econ class and getting my degree so slowly I'd be lucky if I graduated before I turned thirty.

"Hey." Marlee reached across her desk to squeeze my hand. "I think it's great that you're getting your bachelor's." She smirked. "One of Cooper's degrees is in business. Maybe you'll be as rich as he is someday."

"Ha, ha. By the time he was twenty-eight, he'd taken Synergy public and was already a multimillionaire." I glanced toward his office out of habit, but of course it was dark. He was in Boston. "I hope he's okay after all that shit Jackson pulled yesterday."

"Jackson?" She released my hand. "He wasn't the one who smashed his desk."

"Yeah, but he—never mind." Marlee was best friends with Jackson's wife and thought of his kids as her nephew and niece. None of them worried about the burdens Jackson put on Cooper.

"I'm sure he's fine. Cooper always takes it in stride."

He did. Right up until yesterday. He was a pressure cooker, holding all that steam inside. We'd seen some of it escape yesterday, but what would happen if it continued to build? Would he go off on someone who wouldn't immediately forgive him? Weston, maybe? God help us all if Weston fired Cooper.

"What are you going to do with all your leisure time while he's away?"

"Leisure time? I've got to make sure they put his office back the way it should be." The cleaning crew had removed all the glass, but when I inspected it, I'd found tiny scratches in the cherry finish from the broken glass. Someone like Jackson would never notice, but Cooper would. "The furniture refinishers should be here any minute. The new top will be delivered tomorrow." I'd been sure to order the tempered glass in case of another accident.

But what would I do without Cooper there? It sounded perfect: no strain of holding myself back, holding myself in, around him. No temptation to caress his back through those deliciously soft-looking tailored shirts. Not until next Monday. I deserved a flipping break from the daily torture.

I could get a head start on my next assignment for school, I supposed. Though writing another dry economics paper was a different type of agony. "Let me know what I can do to help you, okay?"

"Sure, sure." She bit her lip. "Do you think they're okay now? Jackson and Cooper?"

"You've known them longer than I have. They argue all the time." Never like yesterday, though, and we both knew it. I glanced around to see if anyone else was near enough to overhear. We had to pretend everything was normal, or a rumor would reach Weston. Something sinister lurked just below that cold, stylish exterior.

"But"—Marlee leaned closer and lowered her voice—"they've never gotten physical before. He was like…like the Beast."

"You mean from the X-Men?" Had Tyler given her a proper comic-book education?

"No, from *Beauty and the Beast*. Though the Beast was really gentle, you know." Marlee twirled a lock of hair around her finger. "Until Gaston attacked him."

Of course she'd think of one of her fairy tales. "Didn't you ever read an X-Men comic or see the movies? He's totally Beast. His eyes are the same color as Beast's blue fur. And they're both geniuses."

Marlee tipped her head to the side. "I've always thought of him as a Thor, myself. Blond hair, blue eyes, the stubble, those muscles—" She shivered.

"Hey, now." The stairwell door banged behind Tyler. "You'd better be talking about me."

"Of course." She winked at me before she turned, arms out, to welcome her fiancé to the executive floor. She only pecked his cheek, but I turned my face away. The love shining on Tyler's face was too obscene for an office setting.

"Jay's not here yet?" He tipped his chin toward the dark office.

"No, poor Valentine's got a fever, and she's been keeping them both up at night. That's why he didn't go to Boston. He's working from home today so Alicia can rest."

And that meant Cooper couldn't rest. He always picked up Jackson's slack. I put out the irritation burning in my chest with a swig of my lukewarm latte. "Morning, Tyler. See you later, Marlee."

"Later," Marlee murmured, still grinning at Tyler like they'd been apart days and not hours.

That flare of irritation went cold and heavy. I would never experience love like that. Not as long as I kept falling for the wrong guys. I trudged across the floor to my desk just outside Cooper's office. As soon as I set down my satchel, the red blinking light on my phone drew my attention. Had the furniture guys arrived? Why hadn't José called my mobile? I picked up the handset and pressed the button to retrieve the messages.

The first one was from six a.m., nine a.m. on the East Coast. "Mr. Levy-Walters, this is Shauna from the New England Entrepreneurs' Society. Mr. Fallon hasn't checked in yet, and I haven't been able to reach him. I'm hoping you can confirm that he's still able to give the keynote speech today at noon."

Give the guy a break, lady. He couldn't have gotten there any earlier than midnight. He was a man, not a machine; he was probably just grabbing an extra espresso to fuel him through the jet lag. Still…Cooper acted more like a machine than a man, and I'd never known him to be late. To anything.

The second message played immediately, timestamped thirty minutes ago. "Mr. Levy-Walters, it's Shauna again. From the Entrepreneurs' Society? I'm starting to get a little anxious. Mr. Fallon still isn't here. Can you call me back?"

I picked up my Synergy-issued mobile and dialed Cooper. It went straight to his voice mail. Usually, listening to his outgoing message made me feel all swoopy inside, but my stomach clenched with nerves. What could've happened to him? I left him a terse message asking him to check in as soon as he could.

The desk phone rang with a Boston caller ID. "Cooper Fallon's office. Ben Levy-Walters speaking."

"Oh, Mr. Levy-Walters. I'm so glad I finally caught you. I'm sorry to call so many times, but we still haven't seen Mr. Fallon. Is he on his way?"

If he hadn't arrived yet, I doubted it. Cooper Fallon followed through on his obligations.

Something was wrong.

"I'm sorry for the late notice, Shauna, but Mr. Fallon is unexpectedly ill. Fever. Chills. Vomiting." I cut myself off there before I could give Cooper any more disgusting symptoms. "Sudden onset. He's probably contagious. He'd like me to pass on his apologies. He'll be making a large donation to the Society as soon as he's recovered."

"Oh. Thank you." I'd learned from working with Cooper that cash always helped smooth things. Shauna didn't sound as mollified as I'd hoped. "But what about the keynote?"

"I'm sorry, Shauna," I said, as gently as possible. "I can't help you with that. But you have a roomful of entrepreneurs. Can't one of them step in?"

"I—I guess I'll try—"

"Perfect. Have a fantastic day." I hung up quickly before she could make it my problem again.

My phone rang almost immediately, and I sighed when I saw it was the security desk. After a brief chat with José, I stepped into the elevator to escort the refinishers.

Where was Cooper?

After I let the furniture team into Cooper's office and they got to work, I walked back to Marlee's desk. She squinted at her screen, probably doing her morning code-check. How open could I be with her about my Cooper problem? We'd been friends since my first day, and we laughingly complained to each other about our bosses almost daily. But this was different. Stomach-sinkingly different.

Clearly, whatever was going on with Cooper was his secret since he hadn't told me. And he was allowed to have secrets. At least in his personal life. His professional life was my business. He should have told Shauna he wasn't going to show. And me.

I'd never known him to bail like that on an obligation. So whatever his secret was, it must have been a big one. One he didn't want anyone to know about.

Although it wasn't mine to share, I needed to know because it affected Synergy. Cooper was the heartbeat of the company, and if rumors reached the media, the stock would tank like Thor had smacked it with his hammer. And then the company would tank, too, just like at my last job.

I cleared my throat. "Hey, so I know I said I'd help you today, but Cooper assigned me to a special project." I watched her face for any signs of recognition or disbelief.

She glanced at me quickly and shrugged. "No problem, then. Project away."

"He, ah, he didn't say anything to you or to Jackson about... the project?"

Her gaze was already back on the screen. "No. Need help?"

"No. Not right now, anyway. Thanks." I trudged back to my desk.

I called Cooper again. Straight to voice mail.

I called the hotel in Boston. He hadn't checked in.

I called Emily, the jet's pilot. She didn't answer, but I left a voice mail. Why hadn't I insisted Cooper give me access to the jet's flight tracking? I'd know if they'd left the airport.

Julie, Weston's executive assistant, scurried past, clutching papers to her chest above her pregnant belly.

Maybe she knew what was going on. "Hey, Julie."

She turned back, her mouth set in an impatient line. She and I weren't as friendly as Marlee and I were, but we got along. Normally. Clearly, something was up today. "Yes, Ben?"

"Sorry to bother you. I was wondering if Mr. Weston had heard from Cooper today. I know he's in Boston, but I have a question for him."

"Isn't he giving a keynote speech this morning? He'll probably call you after."

So she didn't know anything, either. "That's right." I smiled. "Thanks."

She nodded and continued her dash toward the CEO's office.

I picked up my mobile phone and cradled it for a minute. My company phone had Synergy's tracking app on it in case it was lost or stolen. As the COO, Cooper guarded the company's secrets, and the devices that held those secrets, like treasure. Which they probably were, in the wrong hands.

I bit my lip. I wasn't exactly tracking a lost device. I was tracking a lost person. An executive. It was an invasion of privacy. An unauthorized one.

But what if he was actually sick? Or injured? What if the jet had crashed? My heart raced. Someone would've called if the plane had crashed, wouldn't they? Shit.

I opened the tracking app and clicked Cooper's name. The wheel spun. At last, a message popped up. *Unable to find device. See map for last known location.* He must have turned off his phone.

My heart pounded as I squinted at the map. The landmarks resolved. San Francisco. What? He hadn't left? I zoomed in on the icon that showed the last known location of Cooper's phone. His house in Pacific Heights.

I stood so fast my chair went spinning off and hit the wall. Grabbing my satchel and my jacket, I sprinted toward the elevators. He hadn't gotten on the plane. Was he sick? Like, actually sick, not the pretend thing I'd made up for the Entrepreneurs' Society? Maybe Jackson had infected him with whatever baby virus Valentine had. I imagined Cooper lying in his bed, alone, burning up with fever. Or groaning on his bathroom floor, clutching the rim of the toilet.

"Gotta go, Marlee," I said as I passed her desk. "Project emergency."

"Good luck," she called as I stepped into the elevator.

How long since I'd seen him? Eighteen hours? Had he been sick and alone for that long? I tapped my boot all the way down to the ground floor.

I didn't bother with the bus. I used my corporate card—if this wasn't company business, I didn't know what was—to take a ride share to Cooper's swanky neighborhood and straight to his hilltop mansion, all Doric columns, white stone, and well-groomed environmentally friendly native plants. I asked the driver to wait for me in case we had to rush to the hospital. I wished I'd thought to grab a nondisclosure form before I left the office, but I could deal with that later. The important thing was ensuring Cooper was okay.

Jogging up to the fancy, carved-oak door, I rang the bell. A screen next to the door lit up and showed a woman's face. Her gray hair was scraped back into a severe bun. Her face, golden brown and lightly lined, was an expressionless mask. "Can I help you?"

"Hi," I panted. God, if just running from the car had gotten me this out of breath, I needed to start doing some cardio. "I'm Ben. Cooper's assistant. I'm looking for him. Is he okay?"

Recognition flared in her brown eyes. "He's not here."

"He's…not here? He's not sick?"

"He left last night on a trip. But he left a package for you. I meant to send it to the office this morning, but the laundry was delayed." She frowned. "One moment." The screen went black.

A minute later, the door opened. From the woman's tight bun, I expected her to answer the door in one of those old-fashioned black uniform dresses with a white apron. But she wore yoga pants and a dust-speckled T-shirt. She smoothed the hem of her shirt. "I was cleaning the chandeliers since Mr. Fallon is gone. Here." She shoved a small box at me.

I took it automatically. "But he—he never showed. He didn't go to Boston."

Her eyes narrowed. "He's not here."

"Please." I stepped closer. "Do you have any idea where he might've gone?"

She did. I could tell by the gleam in her eyes. But she said, "No. Sorry." She hesitated for a moment. "The best thing you can do for Mr. Fallon is to give him a few days to himself."

"Please, I—"

"Good-bye. When he comes back, I'll let him know you were here." She shut the heavy wooden door in my face.

I pressed the bell another dozen times, but the door didn't open. Finally, I leaned back against a column and scanned the box in my hands. It was longer than it was wide and flat, made of glossy cardboard. It felt too light for one of Cooper's fancy silk neckties.

I slid my thumb under the lid and opened it. A regular business-sized envelope lay on top of a crisply folded white handkerchief. Mine? I stroked the starched cotton. My handkerchief had never been so clean or…stiff. I sniffed it and caught the smell of Cooper's laundry detergent. I snatched the envelope then crushed the box closed to lock in the scent. I tucked it under my arm and turned my attention to the envelope.

He'd scrawled my name across the front. *Ben.* Just my first name. It was almost intimate. I shivered as I turned it over to slide out the contents.

A gift certificate to a spa. A very generous one that'd cover a full day of treatments, even the decadent Dead Sea mud bath.

And a handwritten note.

Ben – I'll be out for a few days. Take some time off. – Cooper

That was it. Eleven words, plus my name and his. No apology. No explanation. What the hell was going on?

"I need to find him," I muttered.

But did I?

I turned back toward the car, still clutching the note he'd written. He'd left, according to his housekeeper. Most likely, he wasn't sick. He'd turned off his phone. That meant he didn't want to be found. Maybe she was right and what he needed most from me was time alone. To cover for him until he was scheduled to be back in the office on Monday.

I could do that. I could do what would help Cooper—and the company—the most.

He'd be back on Monday, and everything would be back to normal.

Right?

4

COOPER

IT TOOK me five tries to type the text to my financial adviser.

Dell 25$ Class A shares

Normally, I'd have talked through it with Luis, but he wasn't working tonight. That was probably why I composed the text. I was lonely. Missing Jackson, but also angry at him. Wallowing in the feels I usually kept boxed up inside. Surrounded by happy vacationers. And drunk.

The bartender was some kid I didn't know. I turned to the beefy guy on the next barstool. He wore a hat that reminded me of Marlon Brando in *Guys and Dolls*. Who the hell wore a fedora in this heat? Still, he seemed more sober than me.

"Hey. Does this text make sense?" I showed it to him.

He frowned at the screen. "I thought Dell wasn't publicly traded anymore."

"Dell? What the fuck?" I squinted at the screen. "Oh, shit. Typo." Fighting my recalcitrant fingers, I changed the *D* to an *S* and held up the phone. "Better now?"

"Did you mean to sell twenty-five dollars' worth of stock? Or maybe you mean percent?"

"Jesus fucking Christ." I stabbed at the dollar sign, backspaced over it, and then flicked through screen after screen to find a percent sign. The characters swam in my vision.

"Want me to help?"

"Would you?" I tried to flash him a winning smile, but I'd numbed my face with whiskey. Jackson never had that problem. Even drunk, his grin could charm the pants off anyone. But he didn't do that anymore. Not now he had a wife and a goddamn kid. And a baby. Fuck. I wiped my prickling eyes on the sleeve of my dress shirt and left a wet smear on the droopy cotton.

Jackson would never be alone in a bar like a loser. Not for long.

Me, on the other hand? I'd be alone forever.

The guy nudged my arm. "All fixed."

I glanced at the screen.

Sell 25% Class A shares

"Thanks, man." Carefully, I zeroed in on the tiny arrow and mashed it.

"If you don't mind me asking," the guy said, "why're you doing that now? You don't look like the kind of guy who has to sell something to stay in a place like this."

I looked down at my rumpled suit pants and my shirt that had gone soggy in the island's humidity. I looked like—like my father. I swallowed. He'd never had clothes as expensive as mine, but when he'd come home from the bars, his work shirts had lost the crispness my mother had so carefully ironed into them.

What had he asked me? My phone's screen flashed. Another call from Ben. Dismissing it, I remembered: the stock.

"Bad associations," I said. Even I wasn't sure if I meant the stock reminded me of Jackson or if it reminded me of my own bad behavior in my office yesterday. Either way, the memory had to be purged, and the booze told me selling stock would do it.

I sat for a minute, staring at the lone ice cube in my whiskey glass. Did I feel any different? Any lighter, with fewer ties, fewer burdens?

No. I still felt heavy and morose.

Selling Synergy stock hadn't helped. The whiskey hadn't helped either, though now the bar had a soft-focus glow like Carole Lombard in *My Man Godfrey*. It was a good bar. I smoothed my hand over the glossy wood top. A nice bar. I'd visit it again tomorrow. Maybe another day of drinking would help me forget.

I slid off my stool and wobbled for a second.

"You okay, man? Need help?" The husky guy with the hat spread his hands like he'd steady me.

"I've got him." A shorter bulk hovered behind me. Ramón.

"You're a porter," I said, like that was relevant to anything. "I don't have any bags for you to carry."

He laughed. "I'll just make sure you get to your room. Safely. And alone." Glaring at the other guy, he grasped me under the elbow.

After we'd descended the steps and started down the gravel path to my bungalow, he asked, "How's your mama?"

"She's fine. I called her when I got here yesterday." A warm feeling filled me when I remembered I'd added a couple guys to her security detail. She'd be safe even though I was thousands of miles away.

"She is joining you?"

"Not this time." She couldn't see me like this. Wallowing. Drunk.

"What about the rest of your family? Are you going to see Isobel?"

"Fuck, no." My tía abuela was worse than Mamá. She'd cook for me and chatter and drag the whole sordid story out of me. And the last thing I wanted was to rehash how I'd gone Mick

Fallon on my best friend, to remember his wide, frightened eyes, and Ben's shocked expression.

I never wanted to think about that again.

"You need someone," he said. "You shouldn't be alone."

"Shouldn't I?" For some reason, Ben's face swam into my vision. I blinked my eyes hard. No. When I couldn't trust myself, alone seemed best. Maybe I could rent a cabin on the mountain and become a hermit.

What I needed was another drink.

Thankfully, I had a full liquor cabinet in my bungalow, and as soon as Ramón dropped me off, I poured myself another whiskey.

If I drank enough, I could forget what I'd done. What I'd lost.

5

BEN

THE NEXT MORNING, just as I was about to ping Cooper's phone again, Julie parked herself in front of my desk. I blanked my phone's screen and flashed her a smile. "What can I do for you, Julie?"

"Mr. Weston says Mr. Fallon is taking some time off. Does that mean he won't be calling into the media conference about the research partnership?"

Fuck, that was today. Synergy had assigned a small team to customize our software for a climate-change research organization, like they'd done last year for a genetic research group. The hope was that Synergy's analytics engine could streamline and accelerate the research for faster results. Cooper had fought hard for the donation, and he should've been the one to talk about it.

"No, sorry."

"I'll let Mr. Weston know."

I released my breath. "Thanks, Julie."

"Have him email an update, will you? Mr. Weston is looking for the latest numbers for his big project. Also, he wants Cooper's network password."

"His password?"

"Since Cooper won't be back for a while, Mr. Weston wants to be sure he can get into his files. He needs his password."

"I—I can't give him that." In my new-employee training, I'd signed a paper that I'd never, ever share my password with anyone else, not even my sister. That had to apply to Cooper's password, too.

Julie frowned. "Of course you can. It doesn't belong to Cooper. It belongs to Synergy. And Mr. Weston is the CEO."

Numbly, my lips formed the word, "Okay."

After she walked away, I dropped my head into my hands.

I should've taken the damn spa day.

Weston knew about Cooper's time away. I supposed it made sense for Cooper to have told his boss. Couldn't he have taken the time to tell his assistant? Fucking note. Fucking gift certificate. My belly burned.

But I was a professional, even if Cooper had decided to stop acting like one. I'd email him—

Email! Why hadn't I thought of that? If Cooper was sending email, maybe I could figure out where he'd gone.

I flipped from the calendar app to the email app and logged in to view Cooper's. The unreads were staggering; I'd have to triage them later. I checked the Sent box.

One email had been sent since Cooper disappeared Tuesday night. The time stamp was late Wednesday, less than eight hours ago. I scanned it, hungry for details.

It was a message to Synergy's compliance officer, confirming an email from his financial adviser. Cooper planned to sell some Class A shares.

What. The. Fuck.

I searched for a reply in Cooper's inbox. There it was. The compliance officer sent a friendly response reminding Cooper we were currently in a blackout period, but he could sell as soon as it ended in a week.

Cooper was selling shares. Not just any shares. Class A, company-controlling shares.

What the fuck did *that* mean?

I knew what it had meant at my old company, but only in hindsight. The founders had dumped their shares a few weeks before it all went down. One said he was buying a place on the beach; the other was getting a divorce and needed the cash. There was no place on the beach. The divorce happened, though. And after they had their money, they called me into the conference room, their faces full of apology and a smidge of guilt, and laid me off.

With the small amount of severance they'd given me, I'd had to choose between paying rent and paying tuition.

When I'd asked my boyfriend, Trey, if I could stay with him for a month or two, just until I got my life back together, he'd gotten a terrified look on his face. Okay, maybe I had a smear of Häagen-Dazs Triple Chocolate Fudge Cookie ice cream on my T-shirt and I hadn't shaved in a few days. But when he started making excuses, I knew we were done.

I deserved someone who supported me when I needed it. Who didn't run at the first sign of trouble. Who was willing to work through life's problems together. I moved in with Mimi the next day and stopped taking Trey's late-night calls and texts.

And when I found a great job at Synergy that paid my tuition, I promised myself I wouldn't get caught unaware again. I'd be ready next time, on the lookout for trouble.

Did Cooper know something about Synergy's future? Was he getting out while he could? Sweat trickled down my back and stuck my shirt to my skin.

I opened a browser window and searched. It wasn't all of his Class A shares. About a quarter of them. Not even close to a sell-off.

Still, what did it mean?

"Are you okay?"

I looked up from the screen, blinking. I hadn't heard Marlee's heels clicking across the old wood planks. A tiny frown line divided her eyebrows.

I minimized the browser window. "I'm good. What's up?" I tried and failed to smile.

"You're really pale. Are you sure you're feeling okay?"

Marlee had worked at Synergy a lot longer than I had. She knew Jackson and Cooper better than I did. And she was discreet about Jackson's shenanigans. I could talk to her.

"Do you have a minute?" I nodded toward the empty conference room behind her.

"Sure." She led the way into the room, which looked out over the busy street and the tall buildings surrounding the converted factory that now housed Synergy. I closed the door.

I knew something about stock from my finance class last year. The compliance officer's job was to ensure that what Synergy did was kosher with government regulations. She'd probably already sent public notice of Cooper's plan to sell his stock, so I wouldn't be telling Marlee anything confidential.

Still, it wouldn't hurt to be circumspect. "When was the last time Jackson sold Synergy shares?"

The little frown line was back. "You mean, exercised his stock options?"

"No, I mean actually sold stock."

"I've worked for Jackson for four years, and I've never known him to sell shares. Not when he bought his house, not when he got married, and not when they had Valentine. He and Cooper are going to hold on to this company until they pry it out of their cold, dead hands. Why do you ask?"

I checked that the door was closed behind me. "Cooper's selling some of his Class A shares. That seems weird, right?"

Marlee's eyes widened. "Super-weird. The Class As are the ones that give them extra voting rights, aren't they?"

"Exactly."

She scrunched her nose. "I thought those got passed on to people's heirs. Like the Fords. Can he even sell those?"

"Not in the regular stock market. But Synergy's charter lets the holders convert them to a larger number of regular shares."

"Look at you and your fancy business degree."

My cheeks burned. "Business degree in progress."

"What did he say when you asked him about it?"

I winced. Before, I didn't want to let on that Cooper was missing. And he hadn't been gone forty-eight hours yet. But Marlee could help me track him down. Plus, I was desperate to share the burden.

"Cooper left. Vanished. Didn't show up in Boston." I spilled out words, telling her about Cooper's phone, his housekeeper, the unreturned messages to the pilot, the email. Even the note telling me to take a few days off, though I couldn't meet her eyes when I told her about it.

By the time I finished, Marlee held her hands over her mouth. "That's not right," she mumbled between her fingers. "We have to track him down."

"I've been trying for the past day and a half, but no luck."

Marlee let her hands fall to her sides, and she straightened her skirt. "The good thing is, we know he's alive and at least reasonably well if he's sending email to the compliance officer."

I hadn't thought of it that way. The tension in my body eased the tiniest bit. "What a Boy Scout. He checks the boxes even when he's M.I.A."

Marlee snorted. "Boy Scout. Still, we have to find him. Someone's going to find out at some point, and having your COO go missing isn't a good look."

"Okay, so what's the plan?" Marlee always had a plan.

"I'll talk to Jackson. If Cooper told anyone where he was going, it would've been him. And I'll use some of my Jackson-tracking techniques to find out where Cooper went."

"Jackson-tracking techniques?"

She smirked. "Jackson's favorite coping technique for stress is to disappear. I can't even begin to tell you all the places he's tried to hide. Let me work on it for a couple of days. Today is Thursday.

If I haven't found out anything and he's not back by Monday, we'll reevaluate."

That fit into the few days he thought he'd be away. "Maybe he went to a spa."

"One of those silent monastery retreats?"

I chuckled at the thought of Cooper Fallon remaining silent for a week without bossing anyone around. "God help those monks."

"Don't worry. We'll find him."

Clutching my friend's hand, I felt the tiniest bit better.

6

BEN

THEY WAITED until dessert to ambush me.

Dad had just brought out his homemade lemon pound cake with raspberry sauce when the doorbell rang.

"Want me to see who it is?" Mimi set down the coffee carafe.

"No, no." My mother fluttered her hands nervously. I narrowed my eyes at her. Mom, an environmental lawyer, was never nervous. "I asked an associate to bring me some papers tonight. Remember, I told you about him. The new one. David." She scurried off toward the door.

My mother never scurried.

I raised my eyebrows at Dad, but he focused his attention on cutting thick slices of cake. So I turned to Mimi. She twisted her lips to the side.

"What do you know, Mimi?"

"Nothing." She got down another china cup from the old-fashioned hutch. Even the back of her curly hair looked smug.

Mom bustled back into the dining room, making the Shabbat candles flicker. "David was so nice to bring me the papers I needed from the office, I asked him to stay for dessert."

Behind her, a white guy about my age walked into the room. He wasn't too much taller than my mother, so around my height. Dark-haired with a close-cropped beard and a good, strong nose, he had that sun-starved look all her associates did from spending too much time in the office.

I rolled my eyes at my sister. Mom had done it again.

"David, you met my husband, Adam, at the party last month. This is my daughter, Miriam, and my son, Benjamin. Ben is finishing his degree in business."

Mimi didn't even get a profession. There went my last hope this setup was for her. He was for me. Wonderful.

He shook Mimi's hand, then mine. Good, strong grip. Long eyelashes fringed his dark eyes. "Shabbat shalom," he said.

"Shabbat shalom," I repeated. Jewish, too. Mom was swinging for the fences with David.

She directed him to the seat next to mine. Over cake and coffee, we made small talk about where he grew up, where he went to school, how much he liked environmental law.

Mom pretended to be absorbed in Dad and Mimi's conversation about the latest stock market scandal, but I could tell she was listening from the way she twitched when David talked about his stellar undergraduate university.

Finally, she jumped in. "Ben took a nontraditional approach to his education. And now he's working and going to school. He's going to follow his father into business."

"Really?" David frowned when I'd told him I was an executive assistant, but now his brown eyes sparked to life. Trey had been the same way. When we first met, he asked me why I wanted to be a secretary.

"Well, not exactly. My dad taught for twenty years before he started his tutoring business. Once I have my degree, I'll apply for a different job at the company where Mimi and I work. Maybe in marketing."

"Marketing is a solid choice, Ben." Mom must've seen the way I couldn't help wrinkling my nose when I talked about my career path. "You know you can't support yourself doing social work."

"I know." We'd gone over and over it until I changed my major. Marketing wasn't the most thrilling career, but it'd get Mom off my back and launch me off Mimi's couch.

And I'd leave the sixth floor, Cooper Fallon, and his tempting blue eyes behind me.

David tipped his head. "You don't sound excited about marketing."

I refocused on him. His eyes really were pretty with those long lashes. Not as stunning as Cooper's, but Mom had gone to all this trouble. I pasted a flirty smile on my face. "What do I sound excited about?"

"Well"—he smoothed his hand next to the crisp pleat of his trousers—"you've talked a lot about Cooper Fallon."

I grabbed for my water, wishing it had more ice to cool down my cheeks. I gulped it down and set the glass on the table. "He's my boss. And he's amazing. He rose from nothing to create a Fortune 1000 company in less than ten years."

"Stanford isn't nothing." My mother couldn't stay out of our conversation. "You can do anything with a degree from Stanford. You could—" She pursed her lips. "Why are we talking about Cooper Fallon? You two have so much in common! You both like…"

When she paused too long, I exchanged a glance with David. What did we have in common?

"Causes!" She finally supplied the word. "David cares about the environment—thus, the environmental law. And Ben…"

She'd backed herself into a corner again. She didn't want to bring up my particular cause because it hit too close to home.

David didn't know about the minefield he'd sauntered into. "What's your passion, Ben?"

"I volunteer most weekends at the community center. With at-risk kids."

David leaned forward. His deep voice and the steady focus of those brown eyes should've made me tingle. But, dammit, there was no tingle. No nothing. "Why the community center?"

I shot a glance at my parents, who'd stilled. Better not disclose that sordid history to a stranger, especially one who worked for my mother. So I shrugged like I'd never been handed a threadbare blanket at a shelter. "I'm passionate about homelessness, especially because it disproportionately affects LGBTQ people."

"Oh. That's noble of you."

My mother's shoulders relaxed. Dad started gathering the empty plates.

I stood and took David's plate. "Oh, I'm the farthest thing from noble. But a lot of times, shelters are the only things standing between those kids and harm by themselves or others."

"No, Ben, I'll take care of the dishes." Mom half-stood.

I waved her down. "I need to stretch. Why don't you tell David about the day last year the whole firm volunteered at the soup kitchen? You know, David, it's only three miles from here. Hunger is a real problem in our communities."

Not that he'd ever experienced it. Cooper, on the other hand, gave me that vibe. He didn't seem to feel the signals from his stomach. Maybe it was his fitness regimen that had done it to him, but that was another sign of a troubled past—trying to exert control over one's body. It was why I brought him all those smoothies and sweetened them with blueberries.

No, the blueberries weren't just because they reminded me of his eyes.

"I like that passion, that fire," David said, ripping me from my musings on Cooper Fallon.

"Thanks," I said, smiling. How I wished I could get passionate about David. But my stubborn heart wanted only one man. One I couldn't have.

In the kitchen, I set the stack of plates next to the sink and loaded the ones Dad rinsed into the dishwasher.

Dad leaned against the sink. "She's trying to help, you know."

I sighed. "I know. And he's perfectly nice, but..."

"But?"

"I'm not ready."

He peered at me from under his gray eyebrows. "It's been months since you broke up with that—that—"

"Trey, Dad. His name is Trey."

"He's an ass." He whispered it. "Not good enough for you."

"No." I smiled. I couldn't help it around my protective dad. "He wasn't right for me. But that's my whole dating history: guys who didn't think I was good enough for them. And guys like that don't deserve me. That's why I'm taking a break." I shut the dishwasher.

"But what if—"

"No." I folded my arms. "Not even if…if Jonathan Groff showed up on my doorstep and begged to take me out for coffee. I'm focusing on school. And my job. I'll make you proud. I promise."

"Benny, you know we're proud of you, regardless. You've pulled yourself up, made something of your life." He dried his hands and set one on my shoulder. "But you don't have to do it alone. I think you'd be happier with someone at your side. Someone deserving." He squeezed my shoulder.

I patted his hand and blinked back the tears burning in my eyes. "I'm not alone. I have you guys. And Mimi. I don't need anyone else. I'm fine on my own."

"You don't have to prove anything to us. In fact, we'd be happy to help—"

I held up a hand. "No, Dad. I'm paying my own way. Synergy's paying my tuition now, and I'm saving up for my own place."

"Benny—"

I shook my head. We'd had this argument too many times.

"Still," he said, "life is more fun with a special someone in your life."

I smiled. "Maybe it is. You and Mom should know. I just haven't found that special someone yet."

"So it's a no for David?" One corner of his mouth lifted.

"Today, it's a no."

"Your poor mother. She's been working on this for weeks."

"I'm sure he'll find a lovely guy."

"And someday"—he speared me with his gaze—"so will you."

That was my dad. Always seeing the best in people. Even me. I was glad he couldn't see the real reason I didn't find David attractive. That was my highly inappropriate crush on my unavailable boss.

Who was currently missing.

7

BEN

COOPER WASN'T BACK on Monday.

Worse, Weston himself called me into his office to ask me for Cooper's network password. I'd hoped he'd forget about it, but I should've known better. Our intense CEO didn't forget anything.

"I'll submit an IT ticket today," I promised.

He frowned. "We have to involve IT? You don't know it?"

"No." Even if I did, I wouldn't tell him. It was hard to get fired at Synergy, but fucking with security? If Cooper found out, I'd be back in the unemployment line.

"Check his desk. Maybe he's written it down."

I could've cataloged the items on Cooper's immaculate desk from memory, and there was no way he'd written his password on a sticky note and taped it under his phone like some Boomer. But to get out of Weston's office, I said, "Sure, I'll check now."

I bypassed Cooper's office and went straight to Marlee's desk. Glancing over my shoulder to ensure Weston wasn't watching, I hauled her into a nearby conference room and told her what Weston had asked me to do.

Marlee blinked her big, brown eyes. "You didn't give him the password, did you?"

"No, I don't even know it. Do you know Jackson's?"

"Not anymore. Though I did when he was"—she winced—"going through his less responsible phase. He needed a lot of help back then. I used to set them for him. I always used the titles of my favorite romance books."

"You—never mind." Cooper had never asked that of me. Did it mean he didn't trust me? Or that he could get his own shit done, unlike Jackson? "I guess I'll ask the IT guys."

"Don't."

It felt good to have Marlee confirm the itchy feeling Weston's request had wedged under my skin. "I shouldn't, should I? It's weird."

"No one should share passwords. I wouldn't have done it for Jackson back then if it wasn't a dire situation. Cooper would put your head on a stake and use it as a visual aid in his next cybersecurity speech."

"Right." God, I wished he were there to explain what was going on. Even if he yelled at me for not instantly refusing Weston's request. "Any luck with your Jackson-tracking techniques?"

"Not yet." She lowered her voice. "Did you check the phone-tracking app?"

"Yeah, every day, but no pings."

"He probably turned it off. He built it, you know."

I winced. "Ah." I should've remembered Cooper was a business genius and a decent programmer. "Now what?"

"Now we move to Phase Two of the plan."

"Phase Two?"

"Weston knows he's gone. And if he's asking you for Cooper's password, he's up to something. We need to escalate. Find out what Weston knows."

I didn't know Weston all that well. He was gorgeous in a silver-fox kind of way, but the cruel twist to his lush mouth turned me right off. And those sapphire-blue eyes of his were always watching. Creepy. I looked back over my shoulder, but no one hovered outside the conference room's glass door.

"What do you think he's up to?"

"No idea, but it can't be good. Jackson doesn't trust him."

There went that dropping sensation in my stomach again, like I was on a roller coaster and we'd just started flying down the big hill. But Marlee would figure something out.

"Thanks, Marlee." I hugged her, enveloped in her rose-scented perfume.

"Don't thank me yet." She tightened her grip on my back and spoke in my ear. "You haven't heard your part of the plan."

———

MARLEE MADE me memorize the three steps of the deceptively simple-sounding plan, which she'd named Operation Finding Nemo. Who'd have thought a woman who looked and spoke like a Disney Princess had such a devious mind?

The next day, Tuesday, one week since I'd seen Cooper, she paused at my desk, her arm slung around Julie's shoulders. They both had their raincoats on, Julie's gapping around her protruding belly. When was she scheduled to take maternity leave, again? It looked like soon.

"Hey, Ben. Julie and I are going to hit that ice-cream truck down the street. They have these amazing flavors, but it's only there for another twenty minutes."

Julie's eyes widened. "Marlee says they have a sweet potato and bacon one. And maybe a scoop of sriracha gelato on top?"

I suppressed a shudder. "Sounds yummy." Casually, I added, "Anything I need to cover while you're gone?"

"Ohmygod, I almost forgot. I can't go, Marlee. Mr. Weston has a call with the Chairman in five minutes. He always makes me dial the call and connect them like it's 1960." She rolled her eyes.

I gave a fake snort. "I can do that for you, no problem."

"Really?" Her eyes widened.

"Of course. I wouldn't want you to miss that sriracha gelato."

"Ohmygod, I'm drooling. I owe you big-time, Ben. All the info's in my calendar."

Marlee winked. *Step One—check.*

"I'm on it. You two have fun."

"Thanks. You're the best, Ben," Julie called over her shoulder as Marlee guided her toward the elevator.

Now for Step Two. I pulled up Julie's calendar and found the information for the call. When the clock ticked over to the hour, I called the Chairman and asked him to hold for Weston. Then I called Weston.

"Mr. Weston, I've got the Chairman holding."

"Ben? Where's—? Never mind. Put him through."

I connected the call, but instead of dropping off, I stayed on, ensuring I'd muted my line. Marlee had promised me Weston wasn't tech-savvy enough to know. Still, I watched his closed office door from my desk, my sweaty palms making the handset slip in my grip.

"Good afternoon, Charles." Weston launched into small-talk, asking about the Chairman's new granddaughter, his wife, and his own business. In return, the Chairman proposed a golf outing in a few weeks when the weather warmed.

While they shot the shit, I waited, my pencil poised over my notepad, perspiration prickling across my forehead. I breathed as little as possible, even though I was muted and they couldn't hear me.

Finally, Weston asked, "Did you read my proposal?"

"I did, and I have some concerns." The Chairman sounded… uncomfortable? That couldn't be right. I'd met him only once, and he'd been all ease and confidence. "I don't think Cooper or Jackson will sign off on some of your cost-cutting measures. The tuition-reimbursement plan, for example—"

I gasped. Then I triple-checked I was still on mute. I'd never finish my degree if Synergy didn't pay for my classes and books. But the Chairman wasn't done yet.

"The real no-go is this ten percent across-the-board staff cut. Neither one of the founders has ever supported a reduction in force, even during the last recession."

I stiffened. Layoffs? Who would they cut? Someone in a big department like my sister, Mimi, or the most recent hires? I'd been hired only six months ago.

"What's the update on Cooper?" the Chairman asked. "Jackson won't sign off if he opposes it."

"I don't think Fallon will be a problem much longer."

An honest-to-God chill clawed down my spine when Weston said that. He was a dick, but he wouldn't do anything to hurt Cooper, would he?

"What do you mean?" I rolled my eyes up to the skylight and thanked God for making the Chairman ask the question burning on my lips.

"He's put in a Class A conversion notice."

The Chairman didn't say a word for a few seconds. "How much?"

"About a quarter."

"Could be he needs the cash."

"Could be. Or it could be a sign he's done. Burned out. He wouldn't be the first founder to become disillusioned with his company. To want to move on. Which supports the opportunity I told you about last week."

"Have you talked to your contact?" the Chairman asked.

An opportunity? A contact? What was going on?

"If he sells another five percent, he and Jones will lose their voting bloc. Synergy becomes much more attractive."

Attractive to whom? Customers? The market? What were they talking about? I'd gone so still I couldn't feel my feet. I gripped the handset like a lifeline.

"That's what I'm concerned about." The Chairman's voice rumbled in my ear. "What if there's a hostile takeover? Gurusoft—"

"Charles, Charles," Weston cooed. "I've got it handled. I

worked with the compliance officer. The company is safe from unwanted advances."

The Chairman was silent. I stared at my computer screen, unseeing. Weston said he had the situation handled. How? And would the shift in shares—and power—mean Jackson and Cooper would find it harder to resist Weston's cost-cutting measures? Those measures directly impacted me.

If I got laid off, I'd be out on my ass again for the second time in less than a year. No tuition plan, no college degree. If Mimi lost her job, too, we'd both be homeless.

I hung up the handset. I didn't need to hear anymore. I had to find Cooper, make sure he didn't sell any more shares, and do whatever it took to make him come back.

8

BEN

THURSDAY, ten days since I'd seen Cooper, Marlee's secret tracking method hadn't turned up a single clue. And when she asked Jackson about where Cooper might be, he was just as confused as we were.

Cooper hadn't called him, either.

Cooper's phone was still unpingable, and his voice mailbox was full. I went back to his house, but his housekeeper stonewalled me again.

I went to class Thursday night, but I didn't hear a word of the lecture, too busy worrying about the summer session. I couldn't afford it if Weston cut the tuition program. And if I got laid off, I'd be that guy with another hole in his résumé, living on his sister's couch, desperate enough to scramble for a minimum-wage job.

Friday, in the sixth-floor employee breakroom, I munched a bite of my turkey sandwich. I swallowed hard to get it past the lump in my throat. How many more lunches would I eat in Synergy's office? How long until I had to deal with the unemployment office again?

Marlee burst into the breakroom, her cheeks as pink as her blouse. "I have news!"

I dropped my sandwich onto my napkin. "Good news?"

She shrugged. "Isn't any news good at this point?"

"You're right." If we had a clue about where Cooper had gone, we were one step closer to getting him back. Leaving my lunch on the table, I followed Marlee to the nearest empty conference room.

She closed the door and leaned against it. In a low voice that vibrated with excitement, she said, "You know that island where he goes for vacation?"

"In the Caribbean, right?"

"Yeah. He's there." She slipped her hand into her skirt pocket and pulled out a sticky note. I took it from her. In her loopy hand-writing was the name of a resort, a phone number, and an address.

A Caribbean island. He was on fucking vacation, sipping umbrella drinks and turning his skin that golden shade that looked so good on him. While all of us worried about him.

Ignoring the sinking feeling in my gut, I waved the note. "How did you find him?"

She grimaced. "He isn't using his corporate card. I may have called his personal card company and pretended we thought it was stolen. Don't tell him, especially if they cancel his card."

Like I said, devious.

"Your secret's safe with me." I stared at the note. "So I, uh, call them and ask for Cooper?"

She grimaced. "Sorry, already tried. They're just as bad as his housekeeper. Wouldn't even confirm he was staying there. You'll have to go."

"Go?" I blinked. I'd never been on an airplane. Never even left the state of California. I'd never needed to. Everything I cared about—my job, my family—was here.

"Yeah, you know. Fly out there. Find him. Kidnap him. What-ever it takes."

Whatever it takes. She was right. The stakes were too high not to try it. Without Cooper, I wouldn't have a job or any hope for my future. And neither would Marlee. Although she was a part-time member of the development team, if they forced out Jackson, they wouldn't want to keep his most loyal supporter around.

"I've already reserved your flights for tomorrow morning. Sorry I can't swing the company jet, but we need to keep this on the down-low, you know? You've got your corporate card? And a passport?"

"Cooper made me get one when I was hired. In case I had to travel with him." I'd shivered when he'd told me, thinking about strolls along the Champs-Élysées or snapping a selfie in front of the Petronas Twin Towers with Cooper. But he'd never asked me to travel with him. And now, maybe he never would.

"Then you're all set. Call me as soon as you find him, okay?" She rubbed at her eyelid, smearing mascara over the purple smudges that had lived for the past week under her eyes.

I whipped out my handkerchief—not the one that smelled like Cooper, but a regular one—and wiped away the mascara. "Okay. And you'll call me if you hear anything else?"

"Yep." She stared at me, hard. "There's a lot riding on this. I know you can do it."

I nodded, feeling like Spider-Man taking an order from Iron Man. Though Iron Man didn't usually wear so much pink. The weight of the world—at least the company—sat heavy on my shoulders.

"And?" Her eyebrows rose.

"And…what?" I blinked at her.

"Go home! Pack. Sleep. Your only job now is to find Cooper. Focus, Ben." She put her hands on her hips.

"Yes, ma'am."

She nodded, opened the door, and strode out. I went back to the breakroom and tossed the remnants of my lunch. In a daze, I packed my satchel and left. This time tomorrow, I'd be on my mission: Operation Finding Nemo. I couldn't come back without him.

———

WHEN MIMI CAME HOME, I was staring into my duffel, piles of my clothes surrounding it on the couch that doubled as my bed.

"What are you doing?" She toed off her shoes and set her laptop bag on the floor next to them.

"Packing."

"Obviously. What are you packing for, Benjamin? You're not— You're not leaving?" Her voice rose to a squeak.

"No! I mean, of course I'm *leaving*. But not permanently."

"Good." She flopped down into the armchair.

"Don't you want me to leave, though?" I scanned the apartment we'd been sharing since I'd lost my old job. Fortunately, it was a one-bedroom, not a studio, so she still had a room to herself. And I tried to stay out of her way as much as I could. But when she'd moved in, she hadn't planned to share it with her brother. There wasn't much space beyond the small couch where I slept, the armchair, and what passed for a kitchen in Potrero Hill. As neat as I tried to be, as often as I cooked dinner for us both, she had to be ready to have her space to herself again.

She reached out and cuffed my shoulder. "Eventually. But I haven't hated having my little brother around. I've liked having you where I can keep an eye on you." She scanned the duffel and the piles of my clothes that usually lived in a pair of packing boxes in the corner.

"Did you finally give up on your crush on Cooper and meet someone?" Her eyes rounded. "Did you actually like David?"

My face went hot. "I do not have a crush on Cooper."

Her lips flattened. "Yes, you do. Your eyes go all soft when you talk about him."

"He's a good guy! And my eyes do not go soft."

"They're soft right now. Squishy, like caramel."

"Are not!"

"Okay, fine. You don't have a crush on your boss. You just like him. A lot. Professionally. So did you like David?"

"No! Of course not! I mean, he was fine. Just not for me."

"Why *of course not?* You are the champion of meeting someone and instantly falling in love. You can't go to the grocery store without coming home practically engaged."

She was exaggerating. Mostly. So what if I'd slept with Trey the day I'd met him, and we'd been inseparable for the next month?

I tossed a pair of swim trunks into the duffel. "This is work-related. I—I—" I hadn't shared anything with her. I didn't want her to worry about her job. But now, considering I was about to get on an airplane and fly to another country to find our COO, I figured it was time to tell her. In case I died, you know.

The whole story of Cooper's disappearance and Weston's mysterious conversation with the Chairman poured out of me.

By the time I was done, Mimi leaned forward in the armchair, her elbows resting on her knees. "What are you going to do about school?"

"It'll be fine. I'm leaving early tomorrow, and I can probably get back in time for class on Tuesday. But just in case, I told my prof I had to travel for work, and he said I can keep up with the assignments remotely if I need to. But I won't need to. I'll find Cooper, tell him about Weston's evil plot, and come back. Maybe I'll have one umbrella drink while I'm there." I tried to reassure her with a smile, but my cheeks refused to cooperate.

"Benjamin." Mimi's tone was full of big-sister warning. "Look at me."

I met her gaze. Her eyes were darker than mine, the color of a porter instead of an amber ale.

"You go there. You convince him to come back and take care of his company. And then you come back. No falling in love with your boss. You are not Pepper Potts. Understand?"

I nodded. Cooper Fallon was exactly the opposite of Tony Stark. He made the rules and never broke them. He was Captain America, standing up for what was right and good. And falling for his assistant was against the rules, no matter how much I yearned for it.

Though it had been a total Tony Stark move to run off to a fucking island vacation without telling anyone, leaving me—all of us—to worry about him.

"Still," Mimi said, reaching into the bowl under the coffee table and pulling out a strip of condoms, which she tossed into my duffel, "you never know what might happen with the pool boy."

I snorted. If I followed her plan—go in, convince Cooper, get out—there'd be no time for island flings.

Her dark eyebrows winged up. "Keep a lock on that fragile heart of yours, Ben. And come back soon, okay?"

I lunged across the space between us and hugged her. "I promise, I will."

9

BEN

I THOUGHT FOR A SECOND, as the ancient Ford Escort wheezed up the side of a small mountain in the center of the island on the way from the airport to the resort, that we might not make it over. But I didn't care. At least we were on land. After the turbulent propeller-plane flight from Charlotte Amalie, my stomach heaving and my fingers trembling on the barf bag, nothing on land would ever scare me again.

The ocean-scented island breeze warmed my cheeks as the taxi puttered slowly up the circle drive, past palm trees and masses of big, red tropical flowers.

The driver stopped the car in front of a pair of wide-open, carved wooden doors. A man in a poppy-pink guayabera and a pair of khaki Bermuda shorts opened my door.

"Welcome to paradise, señor." His tanned face creased in a smile, showing straight, white teeth. His nametag read *Ramón*.

I ducked out of the car and stood, stretching. Ramón grabbed my duffel from the driver and flourished his hand toward the doors of the resort.

I shuffled in the direction he'd pointed. "Thank you. I mean, gracias."

The humid air stuck to my skin and softened the creases in my golf shirt. I shouldn't have bothered ironing it that morning back at home. One of my dark curls caught my peripheral vision, and I smoothed it back onto the top of my head. It sprang back instantly and stuck to my forehead. My hair product was not designed for this climate.

Ramón followed me to the front desk, where he stood a discreet distance away, my bag between his feet, while I checked in.

After the clerk described their accommodations—private beachfront bungalows, a penthouse with an infinity pool, luxurious suites, spa rooms with whirlpool tubs—I asked her for her cheapest room. I'd have to ask Cooper to approve my expense report, and I didn't want to have to justify an in-room massage table, no matter how much I needed it after the armrest-gripping flight.

They'd stonewalled me over the phone, but now that I was a guest, I hoped they'd be more cooperative. As I handed over my corporate card, I leaned in. "I'm meeting another guest. Cooper Fallon. Do you know where he's staying?"

The front desk clerk pursed her red lips and jabbed my card into the reader. "I'm sorry, I can't give out that information."

"He's on the property...somewhere," I pressed her. If I were a spy in a movie, I'd slip her a crisp hundred-dollar bill. But I was fresh out of hundreds and also not an asshole. Instead, I gave her my brightest smile.

"Sorry, sir. I can't tell you that."

Shit. I'd have to wait for Marlee to let me know he'd spent money in a local bar or shop. Assuming she hadn't gotten his charge privileges suspended. Meanwhile, I'd hunt him down at the resort's restaurant or the pool.

The pool. I let myself imagine it for a moment. Cooper would be reclining in a lounge chair, reading the *Wall Street Journal* or the

Financial Times. He'd wear a short-sleeved cotton shirt, open in the front, over a—I gulped—a Speedo? No, I'd never be that lucky. He'd wear regular, long trunks like I'd packed. I'd stand by his chair, the way I often did in the office, waiting for him to finish his article and acknowledge me. He'd lower the paper over the washboard abs I'd daydreamed about and lift his sunglasses to perch on top of his sandy-blond hair, ruffling in the breeze. And he'd say—

"How many nights?"

I refocused my gaze on the clerk. She blinked at me expectantly.

"Oh, just tonight, I think." Though it was already late afternoon. Would I be able to find him that quickly? "Actually, better make it two." In case I didn't locate him right away and had to look for him the next day. Besides, I was in no hurry to get back in that rusty-can propeller plane at the island's tiny airport. After covering for Cooper for almost a week, hauling my ass across the continental U.S., and puking up practically my entire digestive tract over the Caribbean Sea, I deserved two nights in a real bed at a fancy resort. And an umbrella drink or two.

Right after I found Cooper Fallon, told him what was happening back at the office, and reminded him that his place was there. I'd send him on his way on the fancy Synergy jet, and then I'd sit by the pool, sip something fruity to celebrate a job well done, spend one more night in a private bedroom without my sister tiptoeing past the couch in the middle of the night for a glass of water, and head home, patting myself on the back.

The clerk slid me a paper folio with two key cards inside and circled the far end of the main building in pink Sharpie on my copy of the resort map. "Bienvenido. Enjoy your stay."

"Thank you." I took the folio and map and turned toward Ramón. He led the way toward a long hallway to the left. After we passed the elevator bank, he said softly, "Are you a friend of señor Fallon?"

A friend? Not exactly. But *friend* would probably get me farther than *employee.* "He left home and didn't tell anyone where he was going. I'm concerned about him." All true.

Ramón stopped and set my duffel on the Spanish tile. He scanned me, a speculative glint in his dark irises. "We are also his friends. We are concerned, too. Señor Fallon hasn't been himself since he has been here."

"Not himself?" Then I remembered he came here once or twice a year. The people at the resort knew him, at least a little.

"No. He's—" He narrowed his eyes at me like he could see right through me to my heart. Then he nodded once. "Come. I'll show you." Shouldering my bag, he spun on the heel of his shoe and strode back the way we'd come. But instead of returning to the lobby, he turned off down a narrower hallway that ended at a glass door. He pulled open the door for me, and I stepped into the hotel's bar.

The near half looked like a regular bar with bamboo floors, a low-pitched roof with exposed, dark wood beams, and high-top tables surrounding a central, square bar. A blender growled behind the glossy wood top. A dark-skinned bartender in a teal guayabera poked an umbrella into a tall glass of something pink —my mouth watered—and set it on the tray of a server, who carried it out to the far end of the bar.

The far end opened out onto the beach. The roof shaded the deck, but a few umbrella-topped tables stood directly on the beach, where people could drink with their toes in the sand and sunshine on their skin. I wiggled my own toes in my loafers. Maybe I deserved more than two nights to fully enjoy the island's amenities. A gentle, warm breeze tickled my cheeks.

Ramón nudged my shoulder. "There." I followed the jut of his chin toward the near side of the bar, which was occupied by a woman in a floral sundress and a huge straw hat, a man slumped over his drink, and another man who ogled a nearby table of college girls wearing thin cover-up dresses over their bikinis. My stomach sank like I was back on that prop plane. The dude had blond highlights in his hair like Cooper's, but he wasn't my boss.

I looked back at Ramón. Maybe I'd misunderstood him earlier, and we weren't talking about the same person. But he nodded at the bar.

I checked it again, and this time, I caught the familiar shape of the forearm the man in the middle had slung onto the bar to clutch his whiskey. The same golden-hair-dusted forearm I'd salivated over on the few occasions Cooper had rolled up the sleeves of his dress shirt in the office. It was wrapped with muscles and tendons and slightly freckled, especially if he'd spent the weekend on a bike ride. And now it was resting on the bar top, twenty feet in front of me, attached to a man who was sliding-off-his-stool drunk.

"What the—" I darted forward, inserting myself between the brim of the woman's straw hat and my boss. I gripped his shoulder and tipped him straight. My hand, sticky with humidity, came away with tiny fibers stuck to it. Cooper wore a paper-thin charcoal gray sweater over a pair of black trousers. Shiny black dress shoes completed his ready-for-the-office look.

He shuddered and looked over his shoulder—the wrong one —and then turned to face me. His mouth slackened. "Ben?" A wave of alcoholic breath hit me. His cheeks were pink, and sweat slicked his forehead.

The bartender slid his gaze from me to Ramón. He nodded and took half a step back, pretending to wipe out a margarita glass but keeping one eye on Cooper and me.

"Cooper." *Mr. Fallon* seemed out of place when my boss was drunk off his ass at an island bar in the Caribbean.

"Wha— Why—?"

Work talk—anything serious—would have to wait until he'd sobered up. I let one corner of my mouth turn up. "You look...hot."

"Thankssss." His red, unfocused eyes met mine. "Wait. Was that a come-on? Ben would never do that. You can't be Ben. You're a fanta—phantas—dream." He shook his head, and one lock of his hair fell between his eyes and stuck to his brow.

"No, I'm real, and that wasn't a pick-up line." I grabbed a cocktail napkin and blotted the sweat from his forehead. "I'm wondering why you're wearing a cashmere sweater when it's eighty degrees out."

His words came out crisper than I expected. "Wardrobe malfunction."

I raised an eyebrow, and he had the strangest reaction: he smiled. Not the tight-lipped one he gave me in the office after he said, "Good job, Ben." A real smile with an honest-to-God dimple in his left cheek. I was dressed appropriately for the heat, and still, warmth rushed to my cheeks.

The smile was gone a second later, and he turned to the bartender. "Another, Luis."

The bartender's gaze met mine. I shook my head, and he nodded. He scooped ice into a tall glass and filled it from his soda gun. He slid the water to Cooper, who stared at it.

"This isn't whiskey."

"Drink up, then I'll take you to bed." Shit, that came out wrong. "I mean, your bed." Dammit, that still wasn't right. I hadn't had even one drink, and my cheeks felt like the surface of the sun.

Cooper's blue eyes went hazy again. "Now I know you're not Ben. Who the fuck is this, Luis?"

Luis grinned, showcasing two dimples. "Dunno. But I'd let a guy this cute take me to bed." He winked.

Whoa. I took in Luis's muscled forearms and flawless, dark skin. Maybe I would use Mimi's strip of condoms. After I sent Cooper back home.

Cooper stared into his water. "You know I don't do that, Luis. Not in a long, long, long, long time."

"I know." Luis's lush mouth pinched. "But like I'm always telling you—"

"I know, I know. Everyone deserves love. You're so full of shit, Luis." Cooper stared hard at the water again like he could turn it into whiskey through sheer force of will.

I stared at my boss. In the office, he was a block of marble, impenetrable and with ninety-degree angles sharp enough to cut you. Here, in the bar, he sounded suspiciously like me: squishy-soft, vulnerable, and aching for someone to love him.

No. That couldn't be right. That was the whiskey talking. My boss and I had zero in common.

"Me, full of shit? No more than you are, old friend." He reached out and patted Cooper's shoulder. Cooper didn't flinch away, not like he did when I touched him. "Now, go home and rest." Luis beckoned with his fingers at someone behind me.

The next second, Ramón stood on Cooper's other side. He no longer had my bag. "Time to go, señor Fallon." He wedged a broad shoulder under Cooper's right arm. I did the same with Cooper's left, and together we lifted him off the stool and to his feet.

Ramón directed us not through the glass door and into the hotel but toward the deck and carefully down a couple of steps to a crushed-shell path. The sun had started to sink over the water, its orange glare dazzling.

Kicking up shells, we shuffled along the path. The setting sun flickered between the trunks of palm trees, making the experience surreal as dancing at a club with a strobe light. Or maybe that was my jet lag.

I stumbled at a dip in the path, and Cooper's palm, dangling over my shoulder below where I gripped his arm, seized over my left pec. I shivered at the sensation. What would it feel like to have him do that on purpose? To touch me, to caress my skin the way no one had since Trey?

Trey. I tightened my grip on Cooper's arm. He said he loved me but then dumped my ass when I needed him. To Trey, I was only good enough for the occasional hookup. Nothing more.

On this, I agreed with Cooper. Luis was full of shit. Love wasn't right for everyone.

I gave my love freely—too freely, according to Mimi—and never got anything in return. My purpose here was to return

Cooper to San Francisco where he belonged. Then I'd forget about my stupid crush on him and pick up some rando at a club. One hundred percent lust, zero percent love. That was what I needed. What I deserved.

Though when would I get another chance to be this close to my boss? I turned my head toward his neck and took a good sniff of him, opening my nose to the cedar of his expensive cologne and the minty undertone that made me shiver when I got too close in the office. But tonight, alcohol seeped from his pores, covering up his irresistible scent with the sickly smell of fermented corn.

Cooper turned his head, his nose an inch from mine. "Whadd're you doing?"

Fuck, I'd just sniffed my boss, and he'd noticed. I hoped he was too drunk to remember it. I faced the path ahead. "Dragging your sorry ass to your room."

He chuckled. "Can't be Ben. Ben doesn't swear."

"I can say what I want when I'm going above and beyond my job responsibilities," I muttered. For real, Cooper was heavy. And neither an international manhunt nor personally dragging my boss out of a beachside bar were anywhere in my job description.

"Above and beyond," he repeated. "Ben always goes above and beyond. Best assistant I ever had. I love him."

I stumbled again and almost face-planted into the shell path. Luckily, Ramón's solid weight served as an anchor, keeping Cooper upright. Grimacing, I tucked myself under Cooper's sweaty armpit, and we continued down the path.

He loved me? He meant he loved my work. Loved having me as his assistant. That was all. And I was a fool to dream it meant anything more.

"How much farther?" I asked Ramón. We'd lost sight of the main part of the resort, and it'd been a couple of minutes since we'd passed one of the beachfront bungalows.

"Almost there," he grunted. He shouldered most of Cooper's weight.

Ahead, a white stucco wall came into view. The path turned sharply away from the beach, but a smaller path led to a metal gate in the wall.

"Your card, señor."

"Hmm?"

When Ramón released Cooper, I staggered under his weight. He patted my boss's pockets, and from his right trouser pocket pulled a key card. Not white like mine but gold plastic that glittered in the red rays of sunset.

He waved it in front of a sensor at the gate, and we dragged Cooper through. The property in front of us was breathtaking. The back of the single-story stucco house was all windows overlooking a landscaped private pool and, beyond a low wall with another gate, the beach. We approached the house from the back deck among hibiscus and bougainvillea. Sweet jasmine mixed with the sea breeze as we weaved between a round patio table and chairs and a wicker sectional.

When we reached the house, Ramón waved the key card at another sensor, and the glass door slid open into a living room with furniture turned toward the view of the pool and beach.

Like he knew the place, Ramón turned down a hall to the right and opened the door of a bedroom. Its enormous window gave us a heart-stopping view of the sun setting over the beach. But I was too sweaty and exhausted to admire it. We let Cooper flop onto the foot of the bed. He bounced once and then sank onto the mattress, his dark sweater and trousers a contrast to the white sheets.

"This's nice," he muttered. "I'm gonna give you all stock shares. Ssssynergy ssstock." His eyelids fluttered shut.

Ramón and I exchanged a look.

"You got him from here?" Ramón asked, wiping perspiration from his brow with his sleeve.

"Yeah, I—I guess so?"

Cooper sighed, already asleep. But I couldn't leave him there alone after drinking that much.

"I had them take your bag to your room," Ramón said. "Want me to bring it here?"

I thought of my clean clothes. My toothbrush. The face lotion I used before bed. But I served others for a living, and I wasn't about to make someone—certainly not Ramón, who'd also gone above and beyond—schlep it to me.

"No, I'll be fine tonight. Thank you. For everything."

"De nada. See you around, Ben." He winked and then disappeared down the hall.

A light snore buzzed from the bed, and I turned my attention back to Cooper. He'd be hot sleeping in that sweater. And pants. But even above and beyond didn't cover undressing my boss. Touching his bare skin. Checking him out in his boxers…or briefs? I shivered. I'd turn down the air conditioning so he'd be comfortable.

His dress shoes hung off the end of the bed, dusty from the shells on the path. I eased off one and then the other, then I took them into the en-suite bathroom, where I wiped them, along with my Chucks, with a damp cloth. Didn't he have a pair of flip-flops?

I went to his closet, where, as I'd expected, Cooper had unpacked his bag and hung up his clothes. Another wool sweater in soft camel. A trio of rumpled dress shirts, each of them worn at least once, and two suit coats and a blazer, unworn. Two pairs of wrinkled suit pants hung limply on separate hangers. Folded on the top shelf of the closet was a silky pair of basketball shorts and a high-tech workout shirt. A pair of sneakers stood rigid beside them. No flip-flops, no T-shirts, not even a pair of jeans.

I found the resort's laundry bag and filled out the order sheet. I stuffed the trousers and shirts into it and followed the instructions to call the front desk and leave the bag outside the front door.

The bungalow's kitchenette, stocked with upscale appliances, was open to the living room. Everything was decorated in beachy neutrals: white, sand, and pale blue with the occasional coral accent. Not a glass or plate was out of place, and I couldn't tell if that was because Cooper was as much of a neat-freak on vacation as he was in the office or if it was because he'd only slept here and spent every waking hour getting drunk in the bar.

On the other side of the living room were two smaller bedrooms. One was decorated in neutrals like the rest of the house. The other was clearly intended for a woman. The hibiscus-print bedspread, the lacy cover on the nightstand, and the pair of suspense novels stacked on top of it tightened my throat. Which woman stayed here so often he'd decorated for her?

Though…the bedroom was separate from Cooper's. He'd set it up for a woman he didn't sleep with?

I cast one more longing glance at the other guest bedroom and then used the guest bath. I found a new toothbrush and tooth-paste, so I had that small comfort. Finally, I shuffled back to Cooper's room.

He'd turned onto his side, tucking his knees up and cradling the pillow. He looked peaceful, innocent. I tamped down my urge to brush the damp hair from his sweaty forehead.

Instead, I turned the thermostat down to sixty, grabbed the spare blanket and pillow from his closet, and flicked off the light. Curling up on the small sofa in the bedroom, I let pure exhaustion carry me off to sleep.

10

COOPER

AS USUAL, I woke up with an eyepopping headache, a mouth that tasted like the bottom of a dumpster, and a hole in the center of my chest.

Nothing I could do about the hole, but I could take care of the other two.

I cracked open an eye, and there, on the bedside table, was a tall glass of water and a couple of aspirin. Had I been sober enough last night to put that there? I tried to remember, but thinking made me want to claw my own eye out of its socket, so I gulped down the pills, drained the glass, and slowly sat up.

When my head stopped spinning, I stood and made my way into the bathroom. After I emptied my bladder and brushed my teeth, I made the mistake of looking into the mirror. Puffy, bloodshot eyes. Pasty skin. Whiskers that were starting to look more like a beard than stylish scruff. And was that a gray streak right next to my mouth? Holy fuck, was I glad no one on the island cared what I looked like. Or my professional image. My sweater and pants were beyond wrinkled after sleeping in them. And this was my last set of clean clothes.

I rubbed my chest where it ached. It didn't matter. This was my life now. Hanging out in paradise where I didn't have to do anything but drink until I forgot what I'd done in the office and what that meant I'd become.

At least here, there was no one I loved enough to hurt.

I took the glass from the bedside table and headed down the hall toward the liquor cabinet. Might as well start now.

The glass doors were open, the sheer curtains blowing in the warm breeze. Jesus Christ. No one would fuck with me on the island, but did I really have to tempt fate by leaving the doors open all night?

Bypassing the kitchen, I went straight to the liquor cabinet.

And froze.

The bottles were missing from where I'd left them on top of the low cabinet. Only a pitcher of water sat there.

I ripped open the cabinet doors. All empty.

Shit. Someone had stolen all the booze. Ironic, since I'd apparently been too drunk to lock the doors.

They'd replaced the booze with water. And were those orange slices floating on top? What. The. Fuck?

Gripping my hair to counteract the pounding inside my skull, I whirled to face the back deck and spotted a figure sitting on the outdoor sectional. The blowing curtains partially obscured him, but if I were anywhere else other than an out-of-the-way, minor island in the middle of the Caribbean, three thousand miles from where I'd left him, I'd say that slight figure and those dark curls belonged to Ben Levy-Walters.

I should know. I'd been staring at him every chance I got for the past six months.

I strode out through the curtains into the blinding sun on the deck. Slapping a hand over my eyes, I waited for the stabbing pain behind my eyeballs to ease. Finally, I separated two fingers enough to peer through the gap.

"Ben? What the fuck are you doing here?" I'd done everything I could think of to ensure he wouldn't find me—the note suggesting he take a few days off, turning off the tracking on my phone. Because if there was one thing I'd learned about my assistant, it was that he was as persistent as I was.

"Good morning—um—afternoon." He stood, his hands fluttering from his shorts pockets to his hips. The bright tropical sun glinted on his hair. Sunglasses concealed his eyes, but I knew they sparkled like single-malt whiskey under bar lights. He'd grown a day or two's worth of scruff, and I liked it. Wanted to run my fingers over it.

No, I didn't!

I couldn't.

I fisted my hands at my sides and kept my gaze on his sunglasses, not daring to tempt myself with the sight of my assistant's legs in shorts.

He looked out toward the beach for a second like he'd read my thoughts and wanted to run away. "How about some coffee?" He pointed at an insulated carafe on the coffee table next to a plate of sandwiches.

My stomach flipped over, anticipating what the coffee's acid would do to my already abused stomach lining. "That wasn't a rhetorical question," I growled. "Why are you here?"

"Let's get some food into you before we talk about that."

"Fuck food. Where's the whiskey?" I snarled. I couldn't let him see what he'd done to me, how glad I was to see him.

"Fine." He folded his arms over his chest. "It's gone. And we need to talk."

"Talk?" I hit him with my full glare, the one that made negotiation opponents cower and slacking junior staffers avoid me in the halls.

He took a half-step back and bumped into the sofa. After windmilling his arms for a second, he straightened and squared his jaw. "Yes, talk. About Synergy."

I scrubbed my face. All my angry energy drained out through my feet. He was just a lackey, loyal to someone else now that I'd been gone over a week. I'd hoped for more from

Ben. I thought we understood each other. That he understood me.

It wasn't the first time someone had let me down. Maybe it'd be the last.

"Who sent you? Weston? Or Jackson?" When I said my partner's name, my empty stomach seized. His abandonment was the other thing I'd been trying to erase with the booze.

Ben's mouth tightened. "No one sent me."

A bitter laugh barked out of me. "No one sent you? You came all the way out here on your own to—to talk to me about Synergy?" He had to be working for Weston. I thought Weston understood I needed a break, but maybe he'd sent Ben to check up on me. There was no way Ben had chosen to come out here. Not after he'd seen me blow up at the office. Not after he'd had to clean up the mess I'd made.

Ben was too kind, too bright, too beautiful. He was the sunny, tropical, blue-sky day to my black-cloud hurricane. He was the gentle breeze and the soft, soothing lap of water on the Caribbean side of the island. I was the whipping wind and pounding surf on the Atlantic side. He nurtured; I destroyed. My desk back at the office was proof.

He must have been horrified to witness my loss of control. He should have resigned. He shouldn't be standing there on my deck offering me coffee.

Had he come to tender his resignation? That didn't make any sense. I shook my head, and that only made a new pain erupt between my eyes. I rubbed it with my fingertip.

"I came here for you." His voice was so gentle I almost couldn't hear it over the sea breeze. "I was worried, Mr. Fallon."

It felt like a feint followed by a shovel punch to the liver. He was worried. About me. And then he'd reminded me of our relationship. I was his boss. He worked for me, and that made me responsible for him. For his well-being. Which meant the attraction I felt was completely inappropriate. Not to mention I was a danger to people I was supposed to care for.

I needed a drink. A strong one. Fortunately, my house wasn't the only place on the island with a stockpile of alcohol.

I turned on my bare feet and stalked back to my bedroom, where I found my last clean pair of socks and, in the bathroom, my dress shoes. What the fuck were they doing in the bathroom? They were suspiciously clean, too, not coated in dust from the shell path. Had Ben—? Impossible.

I slipped on my shoes and strode to the front door. Ben stood in the kitchen and held out a cup of steaming, black coffee.

I waved it off. "I'm leaving. Good-bye, Ben."

His jaw dropped open, and with a satisfying slam of the door, I left.

11

BEN

I STOOD FROZEN, mindlessly gripping the cup of coffee, after Cooper stomped out. Then I slammed the mug on the counter, the coffee sloshing over the smooth granite. Now that I'd found him, I couldn't let him out of my sight. Not until I asked him about the stock sale. And asked him about what I'd overheard on Weston's call with the Chairman.

Scrambling to the back door, I slipped on my Converse then hopped off the deck and sprinted through the back gate. Cooper, with his long-legged strides, was already well ahead of me. I speed-walked to keep him in view.

I wasn't shocked when he headed right back to the bar where I'd found him last night. He trudged up the steps and disappeared behind the wall. I sped up to a full jog—what if there was some private room I didn't know about?—and bounded up the steps to the bar.

Cooper sat on the same stool as last night and said something to the bartender. It wasn't Luis but a fresh-faced kid, no older than twenty, with a pixie cut and a *they/them* button. Instead of a teal guayabera, they wore a white tank top, knotted just below their ribs. They leaned over the bar, shapely ass and thighs on display under their cut-offs. Damn, did Cooper return here year after year for the eye candy? Had he tasted some of the treats on offer? My neck heated under the collar of my polo shirt.

When the bartender turned to make Cooper's drink, I caught their eye and shook my head. They bit their lip and nodded.

I slipped onto the stool next to Cooper. "You can't get rid of me that easily."

He kept his gaze on the bartender's back. "How much?" he asked, too low for them to hear.

Was he talking to me? "How much what?"

"How much is Weston paying you to bring me back?"

I recoiled. "Weston's not paying me!"

"Jackson, then." The look he gave me was a heartbreaking mix of hope and anguish.

"No," I said softly. I'd seen the way he looked at Jackson in the office. It was the same way Mimi looked at chocolate, even though she was allergic. The same way I looked at every dog we'd passed on the street when I was a kid. Mimi was allergic to dogs, too.

It was the way I looked at Cooper every damn day.

His jaw hardened, and he stared at the drink the bartender slid in front of him. "What the fuck is this?" he growled.

"Today's special. Banana daiquiri. Virgin." They perched a tiny blue umbrella on top of it and winked at him.

"I asked for whiskey." His voice had taken on a gravelly rumble.

I nodded at the bartender, and they scurried to the other side of the bar. I set my hand on the sleeve of Cooper's sweater where it covered his forearm. "I need you sober. We need to talk."

He stood. "I don't want a goddamned virgin daiquiri, and I don't want to talk." A man in a straw fedora at the nearest table glanced up at Cooper's raised tone. "I want to talk to Luis," he called to the bartender.

They stayed where they were, twisting their finger in the knot of their tank. "Luis isn't scheduled until four."

Cooper glared at his Rolex, spun on his toe, and strode out of the bar and onto the shell path.

With one last, longing look at the jaunty blue umbrella, I jogged to catch up.

"I guess I can check cardio off my list," I said when I reached his side.

Cooper grunted and continued at the same ground-eating speed. It was okay. I was used to his pace at the office. And unlike him, I had the proper footwear for speed-walking on an uneven surface.

I hesitated for only a moment. I'd rather not start the conversation out in the open, where anyone could hear us, but I needed to get his attention before he tried to shut me out again. "So, what's up with selling your stock?"

He stared straight ahead. "You read the compliance disclosures?"

"I didn't have much else to do when you disappeared."

He glanced at me, his thick eyebrows furrowed. "You were supposed to take time off. Did Jackson send you here?"

"No!" I bit my lip to keep from telling him I'd come because I was worried about him. I was pretty sure he could still fire me even when we weren't in the Synergy building.

He spoke through his clenched jaw. "Company executives buy and sell stock all the time. Weston sold some last year when he got divorced."

"But not you." *And not Jackson*, I didn't say. I couldn't stand to see that look again.

"There's a first time for everything."

"Is there"—*suck it up, Ben*—"is the company in trouble?"

He frowned. "Of course not. Why would you think that?"

"It's just that...my old bosses did that. Sold off stock just before the company cratered."

He scowled. "I hope the SEC put them in prison. No, it's nothing like that." His house—more a compound, really—was in sight. Instead of going straight toward the back gate, he veered left toward the path to the front door.

"Then what is it?" I ran a few steps to match his accelerated pace. "Something to do with the—"

Cooper bounded up the steps to his front porch. "Just doing a little simplifying. Cutting things out of my life I don't need. Good-bye, Ben. Go home."

And for the second time in less than an hour, he slammed the door in my face.

I didn't have a key to his house, so I pounded on the door for a few minutes. He didn't respond. I circled the house to the gate and peered through. He wasn't on the back deck.

I hadn't had a chance to ask him about Weston's cuts. And I couldn't go home until I'd asked him about what I'd heard.

It was a good thing I'd already decided to stay an extra night. Too bad I wouldn't be getting that umbrella drink.

12

COOPER

A CHIME STARTLED me from a nightmare.

I'd never worked a marionette in my life, but I'd watched *The Sound of Music* about a hundred times. In my dream, I held the puppet's control bar and made it perform a complex dance on the stage below. The audience of small children cheered, and I grinned as I twitched the strings.

Then I noticed a string attached to the back of my own hand. I followed it up and saw that it was attached to a rod. The puppeteer leered down at me. "Dance, Mikey!"

He was my father.

I sat up, sweating, when the chime sounded again. Sobriety fucking sucked. So did talking to Dr. Pradhi. She'd known instantly why I'd run away from Synergy. She said smashing my desk didn't make me my father. That it was an accident. That I needed to forgive myself the same as I'd forgiven Jackson all those times he'd hurt me. That I needed to talk to him, ask him if what Weston said was true, if he was looking for his own escape from Synergy.

I didn't need to ask. What Weston said resonated with my own read of the situation. Jackson was a wealthy man. He didn't need the income from Synergy. He was ready to focus on what was important to him, which wasn't the company we'd built together. He'd turned his focus to his family, which he'd built all on his own. With a fence around it that kept me out.

Dr. Pradhi said running from my problems didn't solve them. But the whiskey made me forget them.

Until Ben showed up, dumped the booze, and brought the memories back.

The chime rang once more, and this time I heard pounding from the front of the house. The door. Had Luis come to check on me?

Barefoot, I padded to the foyer. What time was it? I must have slept for a few hours after I'd sent Ben home and called my therapist. Through the back windows, the sun was setting over the water.

Just as the doorbell chimed again, I flung it open. Ben stood there, holding a brown paper shopping bag. His smile was tight, nervous. "Evening, Mr. Fallon."

"Why are you still here?"

"Can I come in?"

"Why?" He always followed my orders perfectly. He should have been landing in San Francisco by now. Was there an issue with the jet?

"So we can talk."

"I don't want to talk." I was still shaky and vulnerable after talking to Dr. Pradhi. After the nightmare. I might say something I didn't mean.

"What do you want?" He cocked his head and pursed his full lips. The pink rays of the setting sun speared through the back windows and tinted his dark curls in fiery rose gold.

Not that. I could want it, but I couldn't have it. "What do you mean?"

"Why'd you come here, to the island? From the clothes in your closet, it didn't look like you'd planned on it. Why the last-minute change? What were you looking for? Or running from?"

My head spun with his questions and a few of my own. "You were in my closet?"

He rolled his eyes, just barely. "Ramón and I brought you back from the bar last night."

"Oh." I kept my face neutral, but self-disgust roiled just below the surface. He must have seen me at my worst. "I didn't…um… take a swing at you, did I?"

His eyebrows scrunched together. "You don't remember?"

"No, I—" I searched back, but the last week after arriving on the island, after calling Mamá, was a blur of sweat and the burn of whiskey and waking up on the floor more often than in my bed. "I don't."

"You said you'd give Ramón and me shares of Synergy."

Oh. He'd asked about selling stock earlier. I was drunk when I'd placed the first sale order. I could've canceled it the next day, but I'd let it stand to see how it felt. So far, it didn't feel like anything. Maybe I'd feel something once it executed. If not, I'd try another order in a few days. Giving away shares was the same as selling them. "I'm a man of my word. How much did I say I'd give you?"

Ben snorted and leaned against the doorframe. "You were plast—not thinking clearly. Neither of us took you seriously."

"Is that what you wanted to talk about?" If Weston or Jackson hadn't sent him, why had Ben come? And why was he still on the island? Usually, I was the one with all the answers, but my head ached again, and my thoughts refused to knit together.

My legs were suddenly noodle-like. Leaving the door open, I turned toward the living room. "Need to sit down."

Ben was there the next moment, wedged under my arm. Fuck, I'd been wearing the same clothes for two days, and I was rank, but I couldn't muster the strength to push him away. He guided me to the sofa and urged me to sink into it. Gently, he pushed my head between my knees then rubbed circles on my back. It felt nice, like when Mamá used to tuck me into bed at night.

"When's the last time you ate?" he asked from high above me.

The blood rushed into my ears and throbbed in my brain. Thinking was hard. "Don't know."

"Did you eat anything today? I left the sandwiches in the fridge for you."

"No. Luis usually serves me my meals at the bar, but you made me leave."

The circles stalled for a second and then resumed. "Would you rather eat a sandwich right now or go with me to the restaurant for dinner?"

With me sold it. "Restaurant. But I need to shower and change first."

"About that—"

"Give me ten minutes." I launched to my feet and wobbled for a second, but this time my knees held. I strode into the bedroom, flung the door shut behind me, and slid open the closet door. Only suit coats and empty hangers greeted me. Plus my workout clothes, unused on the top shelf. Just like the liquor cabinet.

"Ben!" I roared.

Ben poked his head into the bedroom. "Mr. Fallon, I—"

"Did you also throw away my clothes? Each one of those suits costs more than I pay you in a month."

"No! I sent them to the laundry. I spoke with the manager, and they sent them to a very high-end dry cleaner in Miami. They'll be back the day after tomorrow. Meantime, I got you these." He held out the shopping bag.

I took it from him with two fingers and peered inside. "Is this a joke?"

"It's island-appropriate clothing. You'll be much more comfortable."

I pulled out a collared shirt. The lemon-yellow cotton was printed with pink seashells. "Really?"

"That yellow is going to look fantastic against your...your skin tone." Ben's cheeks blazed red, and not from the sunset this time. "There's shorts, too. I'll just wait out on the deck." He was gone before I could respond.

Shorts. And a tropical shirt. I'd look like a tourist. I stared at the ridiculous printed fabric I clutched. Then at the empty hangers in the closet. I wore shorts all the time when I came here. And sometimes, in the privacy of my own pool, far less. But somehow, exposing my arms and legs to Ben, my assistant, was different.

I stroked a finger over one of the printed shells. The unwashed cotton was stiff, the sizing still in it. But he'd bought it for me. Thinking of me.

A few minutes later, I stepped onto the deck, my hair damp, wearing the seashell shirt and khaki shorts. When the ocean breeze hit my exposed skin, it pebbled, making the hairs on my arms and legs stand straight up.

Or maybe that was Ben. Caught up in my nightmare and hunger-tunneled vision, I hadn't looked at him before. He wore a rose-pink golf shirt and white Bermuda shorts. Before yesterday, I'd never seen his legs. I hadn't looked then, but I did now. His olive-toned skin was pale under thick, dark hair. His lean thighs and calves had just the right shape and definition.

When he saw me, he stood, his lavender Converse slapping onto the wood. "Ready?" His voice was high and thready. He cleared his throat.

"Yes." I gestured him through the slider ahead of me and locked it from the inside. We went out the front, and I locked that door, too. As far apart as I could manage, we walked along the path to the main resort.

"It's really beautiful here," Ben said, his sneakers crunching over the shells. "Is that why you come? The—the scenery?"

He was my assistant, I reminded myself. Not my friend. So I gave him part of the truth. "I have some connections here on the island. It feels comfortable."

"Connections...like Luis?" He watched the path ahead. Smart, as sometimes a turtle or a hutia wandered onto it.

"Sure, Luis. And others." Luis had been my best friend on the island when my mother brought me here as a kid. And Mamá's family—at least the ones who hadn't gone to the U.S. like she had—lived nearby. I couldn't walk into town without seeing at least three cousins and being invited for coffee or a meal. So I hadn't gone into town.

"Others?" Ben stole a glance at me. Was it the sunset, or were the tips of his ears red? Maybe he'd gotten sunburned.

"Others." I never talked about my family. The business press would have a field day with it, sending reporters to the island to talk to the people who knew Cooper Fallon best. Then they'd dig up my father, and that was the kind of publicity no one needed.

Ben bit his lip and scanned the darkening path. We crunched along in silence for a minute until the resort's main building came into view.

"If you, um, meet one of those *others* and want me to, um, give you some space, just let me know. I understand this isn't a social thing, Mr. Fallon." He waved between us but carefully didn't look at me.

"Ben." I finally understood what he was saying. I stopped walking, and after a second, he stopped and faced me. "You graciously invited me to dinner. Of course it's a social thing. And I wouldn't leave you alone to hook up with someone else."

The thought of hooking up at all was laughable. I wasn't sure I remembered how.

But Ben and his *Mr. Fallons* tempted me to think about it. Why was that *Mr.* in his mouth so fucking sexy? It had to stop or I'd do something I'd regret, like caress his hand. "Look, we're not in the office. You might as well call me Cooper."

Slowly, a smile spread across his face and lit up those whiskey-brown eyes. "Okay. Cooper."

My chest twinged. Maybe it hadn't been such a great idea to

have him call me by my first name. My name—in any form—on his lips lit up nerve endings I thought had died long ago.

"Come on." My voice was gruffer than I'd intended. "Let's eat."

I took him to the less formal of the resort's two restaurants, the one where families tended to go. Where my ridiculous shirt would be acceptable. Taking him to the formal restaurant would've felt dangerously like a date. And Ben and I were *not* on a date.

Which was clear from the moment we sat next to a family of five.

Ben eyed the pair of toddlers, crayons clutched in their fists, and the baby napping in her carrier. "Is this okay?" he muttered.

"It's fine." I picked up the menu. No danger of getting caught up in Ben's whiskey eyes while the children babbled away at the next table.

I didn't bother trying to order a bourbon or even a beer, but I wished I had when an earsplitting squall erupted from the next table. The baby had woken up. The mother tried to soothe her while the toddlers, no longer entertained by their crayons, whined at their father. The noise partnered with the throbbing in my head, and I rubbed at my temple.

"Can you get our waiter's attention? I need a drink."

"No, but give me a minute." Ben pushed back from the table, and seconds later, silence dropped like a blanket.

I looked up to see the toddlers holding Ben's hands as he led them away from the table to the fountain in the middle of the restaurant. He dug in his shorts pocket and produced something that lit up the kids' eyes. Then he knelt down beside them and let them pluck the items off his palm. Coins. The girl closed her eyes for a few seconds then extended her fist over the pool under the fountain. Then she opened her hand, and the coin dropped in. The boy repeated her actions. Ben smiled, delighted.

The restaurant's lights glinted off the dark waves of his hair, contrasting with the kids' fluffy blond curls. They plucked more coins off his palm and tossed them into the fountain, giggling. I'd never seen such an expression of pleasure on Ben's face. At the office, he was all serious respect. With those kids, he was free.

For a second, I imagined Ben with a pair of kids of his own. Pushing a stroller at The Presidio back in San Francisco. Or on the beach, holding their hands as they danced in and out of the waves as I'd seen so many families do. That, over there with the kids, was what Ben was supposed to be doing. Not stuck in an office managing calendars and meetings for me while I hid my longing behind my crusty, cranky exterior.

I squeezed my eyes shut. Ben needed to go home. If—when—I cut ties with Synergy, I'd ensure he ended up somewhere safe and secure. Which was as far away as possible from me.

13

BEN

WHEN WE STEPPED outside the resort, the rhythmic song of the surf called to me. "Can we walk back along the beach?"

Cooper frowned. "You don't have to walk me back."

I saw the way his gaze cut to the bar. "But I want to."

He bent to untie his running shoes. "You have a room at the resort, right?"

"Yeah." I set down my paper bag of leftover steak to toe off my Chucks and pull off my socks. Stepping into the sand, I wiggled my toes.

It was a lot different from the last time I'd been to a beach, when my friends and I had driven down to Half Moon Bay. Warm sand stretched as far as I could see, and the surf murmured like a lullaby. I glanced at Cooper and the muscled calves I'd never seen before tonight. Just the right amount of hair. Smooth, golden skin underneath. I wanted to lick right up that calf, behind his knee, and—shit! I had to stop staring at my boss's legs.

"Ready?" I didn't wait for his answer. I trudged across the sand, past the line of lounge chairs and umbrellas, all the way to where the sand was packed and damp under my feet. I stared out over the dark water. The moon hadn't risen enough to shine on it yet, but stars sparkled above, more than I'd ever seen at one time.

"It's peaceful, isn't it?" Cooper stood beside me, and I felt him breathe in the salty air.

I did the same and sighed out a breath full of the strain of the past two weeks. "Yeah." The breeze fluttered my hair away from my sticky skin. I lifted a hand to smooth down my curls, and it snagged in the untamed mess. The steamy Caribbean air had utterly defeated my product. Good thing the night was dark.

Cooper turned and walked toward his bungalow. I hurried to catch up so I wouldn't be tempted to watch the way his ass moved in those shorts, the strain of his hamstrings as he powered through the sand.

But I couldn't resist sneaking a glance at his face. I tried to tell myself it was to check his color—he was detoxing pretty hard— and not to ogle the sharpness of his cheekbones.

Something moved in the shadows behind him.

I froze like I was its prey. "What's that?"

"What?" He followed my gaze.

"There." I pointed. "Behind that last lounge chair. Something moved."

He squinted. "People are walking on the path. Maybe you saw that."

Sure enough, there was the glint of something shiny—glass, or someone's phone—and a scuff on the shell path just visible through the trees. But I didn't think that was what caught my attention. I'd seen something, and it wasn't human.

"Are there wolves here? Coyotes? Bobcats?"

"No. Could've been a rodent. Or a peccary."

"A peccary?"

"It's like a wild boar."

I peered into the darkness, but I saw nothing. I looked down at my hands. One held my shoes, and the other held the takeout bag. Neither would be a good weapon against a whatsit. A wild boar. Did it have tusks?

Now even the surf sounded menacing. "Let's go." I'd take the well-lit shell path back to my room after I dropped off Cooper.

I walked as quickly as I could on the beach's uneven surface. Cooper easily kept pace with his longer legs. I glanced back a few times but saw nothing. I'd almost relaxed when Cooper spoke.

"We're being followed."

"By one of those boars? Or a Bigfoot? Do they have those here?" My heart was already skipping in my chest, but it started to jog then.

"No." He chuckled. "By a Coconut Hound."

"Is that like the *Hound of the Baskervilles*?"

"That's just what they call feral dogs here on the island. Keep walking and look back. Eight o'clock."

I slowed enough to glance back over my shoulder. A dog skulked behind us, keeping to the shadows, but its eyes glinted in the starlight.

"He probably smells your dinner."

The dog wasn't even that big. It was smaller than a Labrador, the dog I'd always wanted. It was light-colored in the starlight, yellow or tan, with a dark face. When I stopped and turned around, it stilled.

"Hey there," I said softly. I squatted and dropped my shoes onto the sand. Then I set down the bag with my leftovers.

The dog lifted its nose to sniff. Its enormous ears made it look like an overgrown, wingless bat. It took a tentative step toward us, and that's when I noticed how skinny it was. Its ribs showed even in the starlight. It was about the size of a beagle, but it couldn't have weighed more than twenty pounds.

Slowly, I reached into the bag and pulled out the foil-wrapped package inside. The kitchen had twisted it into the shape of a swan, with a long foil neck rising over the bundle of steak. The foil crinkled as I began to unwrap it.

"What are you doing?" Cooper's voice startled the dog, and it shimmied back into the shadows.

"Shh. I'm feeding that poor dog."

"It's feral. Wild. It could have a disease. It could bite you."

I crooned at the dog. "You're not going to bite me, sweetie, are you?" When I opened the package, the meat scent wafted out. I set it on the sand and scooted back a few steps.

The dog took one hunched, tentative step toward the food, then another.

"That's right, honey. Come on and have some dinner."

"You're just going to teach it to pester tourists, and someone's going to lock it up for being a nuisance."

The dog froze again at Cooper's voice.

"Shh. Walk a few steps away. You're scaring him."

I didn't have to look to see that Cooper did what I'd asked. I felt his absence behind me. "C'mon, sweetie. No one's gonna hurt you."

The dog skulked closer and closer until it snatched one cut-up bite and ran back to the shadows.

"That's right. Good boy. Now come have some more."

He repeated the process, grabbing a bite and running away, until it was all gone. I wanted to reach out and scratch those huge, triangular ears, but I didn't want to scare him. I wadded up the foil and stuffed it into the bag. "All gone," I called.

Those big, dark eyes glinted at me from the shadows.

"Happy now?" Cooper said. But his voice didn't hold the bite of sarcasm. It was softer than I'd ever heard it.

He stood tall and straight on the sand against the gurgling surf. His hair fell in perfect, beachy waves over his brow. He probably didn't even need to use product to achieve hair perfection. And tonight, he was all mine to admire. "Yeah, I am."

Like he'd somehow read my thoughts, he ducked his head. "Let's go before any other hungry dogs find out what a soft heart you have."

I picked up my shoes, and together we continued toward his house. There were so many things I wanted to ask him, needed to ask him. About the stock sale. About why he'd come to the island. About why he hadn't gone to Boston. But every time I looked at him and saw the softness in his eye, his jaw loose and unclenched in a way I'd never seen at the office, I forgot what I'd been about to ask. The moon lifted above the trees and gilded him in silver, and the only thought left in my brain was about tracing those lines of moonlight with my fingers.

But I couldn't. I was his assistant, and he was my cold, stern boss. Cooper Fallon would never have a relationship with an employee, and certainly not his direct employee. Besides, my heart was still bruised and battered from Trey. I couldn't give it away to someone like Cooper. Hell, I didn't know for sure he was out. According to the tabloids, he dated women. The more-than-friends feelings I sensed he had for Jackson might have been a shameful secret. He might not have accepted his bisexuality; not everyone did. I could've been imagining the tenderness I thought I'd seen in his angular face when he looked at me.

By the time we reached his gate, I'd built up an emotional hurricane in my chest. I had to get away from Cooper and chill out. I'd wasted the day; I couldn't afford to waste another. I'd sleep in a real bed and in the morning, I'd be prepared to ask Cooper the questions I needed to ask. I wouldn't be distracted by his cheekbones or the touchable waves of his hair or the fondness in his tone.

"G'night," I said, already turning toward the shell path.

"Good-night, Ben."

Everything inside me stilled at the low thrum of his voice. I dared to look up at his face.

It was a mistake. Some trick of the moonlight warmed his blue eyes. And when he flicked out his tongue to wet his lower lip, he was just tasting the tang of the ocean spray. Something touched my knuckle, and I looked down as Cooper's hand brushed by mine and then tucked into the pocket of his shorts.

My knees loosened under me. "Good-night."

"You already said that." The glint of his teeth—an actual smile from Cooper Fallon—was the last thing I saw before the gate closed behind him.

I stood there for a moment, gasping in the sea air. Then I slid on my shoes and crunched back toward the resort along the shell path. Actually, I floated.

When my phone rang, I didn't even glance at the caller ID, still locked in Cooper's dreamy smile.

"Hello?"

"Ben, are you okay?" Marlee's voice dropped me out of the dream.

I cleared my throat. "Fine. What's up?"

"What's up with you? Any progress?"

I winced. "Not yet. I'm trying to ease into it."

Her voice crackled. "You're out of time for easing. That sell order executes tomorrow."

14

COOPER

ON MONDAY when I woke up sober again, I shoved the bag with the shirts Ben had bought me into the back of the closet and put on my workout shirt and shorts. I wasn't going to work out, but I wouldn't wear clothes that reminded me of Ben, either.

I'd been as foolish about Ben as he'd been about that dog last night. I'd let him get close even though I knew we had no future together. I had no future with anyone. Better to be alone than to hurt someone I cared about.

I had to stop it, cold.

I ignored Ben's knocks and his texts and his phone calls. When he called through the gate, I went inside. If I didn't answer, he'd go away. He'd go home.

On the couch, I read the email from my financial adviser that summarized the stock sale. I checked my account balance. My foundation director would be thrilled. And each of the fifty or so women's shelters in the Bay Area would receive a sizable but anonymous gift. They'd be ecstatic.

And how did I feel?

Empty.

I'd hoped to feel something. Relief that I was disentangling myself from Jackson at last. Regret that I'd broken my promise to my friend. Excitement about the possibility of doing something new, something I didn't have to fight Weston for, something I didn't feel I was forcing Jackson to do.

All I felt was tired.

So, like one of the island lizards, I took a nap on the couch under the sun shining warm through the windows.

Blasting rays against my closed eyelids woke me. Lowering toward the horizon, the sun shimmered on the ocean and on the pool and threw golden sparkles onto the living room ceiling. I sat up and rubbed my face.

I was less tired…and famished. My stomach growled.

But I couldn't go to the bar or the restaurant. Ben would stalk me there. So I called room service.

Half an hour later, my doorbell buzzed, one short ring the way Ramón always did it. I padded to the door in my bare feet and swung it open. But it wasn't Ramón.

It was Ben.

And he had Ramón's cart.

"What did you do with Ramón?" was the smartest thing I could think of to say. I grimaced.

Ben nudged the cart across the threshold until I moved out of the way. "I think we should eat on the patio, don't you? It's a beautiful evening."

"We?" I trailed him through the slider and out onto the deck.

He stopped the cart and whirled toward me, hands on his hips. "I brought you dinner." He gestured at the cart. "The least you can do is share it with me."

"Why are you still here?" Anyone else would have gone home. With no executive to support, Ben could play Animal Crossing all day at his desk. Or take a week off like I'd suggested. No one would question it.

"Really?" His jaw, clean-shaven again, jutted out. "You've come out here to rest and relax, but you don't know how. I think it's pretty evident that you're depressed. You need someone to talk to. To make sure you eat. Maybe you don't want that person to be me, but I'm all you've got right now."

He turned toward the cart. With jerky movements, he flung a cloth over the patio table and skillfully but not quietly clattered the dishes and place settings on top.

Was I depressed? Maybe that explained the void inside me. I'd ask Dr. Pradhi about it next week.

While he wheeled the cart back inside, I checked out the table. There were platters of fish and vegetables. A bowl of salad and another bowl of a grain dish. It was exactly what I'd have eaten if I'd come to the island for one of my regular visits, nothing like the crap I'd been eating at the bar. There was even a small arrangement of native orchids. And a trio of candles in the center.

With the rosy sunset over the ocean turning the waves to molten gold, the rhythmic crashing of the waves on the beach, it all seemed so…romantic.

"What's wrong?" Ben stepped out onto the patio.

"I feel underdressed." I tried to put all my thanks, my apology into the quick smile I shot him.

He scanned my compression shirt and athletic shorts then cleared his throat. "You're fine." His voice came out husky, and despite the blazing sunset, goosebumps rose on my arms.

I rubbed them down. "Shall we eat?"

I didn't know what made me do it, but I pulled out the nearest chair and waited for him to sit in it. Then I took the chair across the table.

"This is nice. Thank you." I waved at the table. "But you didn't ambush Ramón, did you? He's not lying in the bushes somewhere?"

"No." His cheeks pinked as he picked up the platter of fish and passed it to me. "Ramón did me a favor."

I took a piece of fish and passed the platter back to him. A favor? And that blush. I knew well what a flirt Ramón was. Were he and Ben having an island fling? I checked out Ben's throat but didn't see any of Ramón's signature hickeys. Though maybe he'd put them somewhere hidden by Ben's polo and shorts.

I tugged my shirt collar away from my heated skin, suddenly less hungry than I'd been before.

Ben flicked his eyes to the gate and then back to me. "How are you feeling?"

"You mean, did I drink today?" I let one corner of my mouth curl up.

"No, I mean, you look good today." He circled his fork to indicate my face. "Though you always look good. Better rested."

I let the compliment soak in and warm my belly. It was almost as good as bourbon. "I took a nap."

"That's great. Did you, ah, exercise?" He stared at my tight shirt.

"No. This was what I had."

He bit his lip, and when he released it, it was shiny and pinker than before. I wanted to lean across the table and taste it. But that delectable lip belonged to Ben, my assistant, so I kept my ass in my chair.

"We should get you more exercise. It'll do you good. How do you normally work out while you're here?"

I didn't usually need to. Between all the walks into town and the construction projects, I burned plenty of calories. But I wasn't about to share my real connection to the island with Ben. He'd find some way to use the people I cared about as leverage to get me to do whatever Weston had sent him to do. And if I went to town, my family would get into my business, especially if Ben told them I was depressed.

"I don't need you to manage my workouts," I growled.

He flicked his gaze to the gate but then focused back on me. "Okay, then, we'll get down to business. I understand you went ahead with your Synergy stock sale."

Disappointment crushed the tiny flare that had ignited in my heart. The food, the candles, the flowers were all a ruse. Not what I'd let myself dare to hope for: a romantic evening with Ben. He wanted to talk about Synergy. Fine. I sat up straighter. "I did. Though it's none of your business."

"Not my business?" His thick eyebrows disappeared under the curls that flopped on his forehead. "Cooper, if you're leaving—"

I poked at my fish. "I'm not going anywhere." *Yet.* If I did, I'd find Ben another position within Synergy so he could finish his degree.

"Um…I heard some things. At the office."

When he didn't continue, I asked, "What did you hear?"

"Weston has some ideas about the company. Ideas for cuts."

I snorted. "Weston is always wanting to cut something. He's a numbers guy."

Ben set down his fork. "Staff cuts. And—and the tuition program."

"Ridiculous." I leaned back in my chair. "Weston wouldn't do that. And even if he wanted to, someone would talk him out of it."

"Who, Cooper?" Ben tilted his head. "Who's going to talk him out of it? The CFO? Jackson? You're not there to do it."

Jackson's name and the reminder that I'd left my company pinged my chest like a pair of BB shots. But Weston had promised he'd see to things. "Weston wants what's best for the company. I trust him."

"Do you? Because he said some stuff that worried me."

"He did?" I rubbed the sore spot on my chest. "What?"

"I overheard him telling the Chairman about you selling your shares. And then talking about an opportunity."

Suddenly, the fact that Charles knew I'd sold my shares made it all seem real. Jackson's stepfather Charles had always supported us, so it made sense for us to ask him to be Chairman of the Board back in Synergy's early days. And now I'd sold my shares without warning him. Reducing my ownership of Synergy stopped being a concept as light and transparent as the island breeze and became concrete, guilty reality. It felt like I'd lost part of myself. Part of my soul.

But that was me being selfish. Ben was worried about his job and his education.

"Weston has been part of Synergy for half its existence. He'll do what's right by it. And by the employees."

Ben's lips twisted to the side like he didn't buy what I was selling. "The Chairman said something about a hostile takeover?"

"I'm sure Weston's taking steps to prevent that. He's got the best interest of the company at heart. I promise."

Ben's eyes narrowed for a second, but then he nodded. "Okay. If you say so."

"I do."

"But what about Jackson?"

My lungs seized, forcing me to cough. I swigged some water. "What about Jackson?" My voice came out as a growl through my constricted throat.

"He's there alone to stand up to Weston. If Weston needs standing up to."

I saw it then. "Did Jackson put you up to this?" Leave it to Jackson to send someone in his place to beg me to come back to work. Fucking Jackson, always wanting, needing something from me. The scraps of friendship I got in return weren't enough anymore.

Plus, I'd foolishly hoped Ben had come out here for me. He was just a tool Jackson had picked up, clueless that it was exactly the right one to break me.

"No!" The sunset flashed in his eyes. "I came here because I was worried. About you."

"I don't need you to fucking worry about me. I'm fine!" I heard that my voice had risen, but I seemed to hover over my own body, separate from the red-faced asshole shouting at the nice man who'd brought him dinner. The nice man whose face had gone from smiling to stony.

During the silence that stretched between us, I heard a rustle down by the pool, and my consciousness slammed back into my body, swimming in the liquid heat that filled it. Who the fuck had Ben brought with him? Who else was joining the pity party? I shoved away from the table, my chair's legs screeching across the deck boards, and stomped down to the gate. When I yanked it open, a brown flash darted past me.

I whirled around to see a Coconut Hound raised on its hind legs, licking Ben's face. A fucking dog. Was it the same one as last night, the one he'd fed with his leftover steak? Or had he attracted an entire colony of them while I'd napped? Was I just another stray dog to him, one who needed feeding and walks?

Ben's eyes widened when he saw the expression on my face, a split second before the anger erupted out of me.

When I strode closer, the dog turned and growled, showing its teeth.

"I came here for me. Because I wanted to. It's not anyone's fucking business what I do." Wildly, I pointed at the pool, the house, the beach. "This isn't a fucking vacation for anyone except me. You're not staying. You're going home tomorrow or you're fired." I glared at the dog through a red haze. It bared its teeth and growled louder. "And you can't keep feeding that fucking feral dog. It's not a pet. It could bite you!" I slammed my hand on the table, making the dishes jump. A glass of water fell over with a crash.

I stilled. That was what had started this whole mess. Separating myself from Jackson, numbing myself with booze, and spilling my guts to my therapist—none of it had fixed anything.

Ben stood. I put my hand over my eyes so I wouldn't see him run out through the gate. My throat was raw and tight, and even swallowing didn't relieve it.

A featherlight touch landed on my arm just below my T-shirt sleeve. "I'm—I'm not leaving."

The anger drained out, leaving me wobbly like the blaze of it had been the only thing keeping me upright. Despite myself, I leaned into Ben's touch. He rubbed my arm, up and down, like he'd pet a dog.

But in that moment, I didn't mind. I didn't care that I was just another stray dog to him, needing care and affection. And that when he left the island, he'd leave me just like he'd leave that damned dog.

"I'm sorry. Sorry I yelled," I mumbled. It wasn't nearly enough, but it was all I could think to say. If I opened my mouth again, I might say something I'd regret even more. Beg him to stay. With me. I couldn't want that. Couldn't have that. Not even when sparks jolted me every time he touched me, like they had from that first day, shocking my heart into a new rhythm: *Ben-Ben, Ben-Ben.* I rubbed my other hand over my chest.

"It's okay. Do you want dessert, or would you rather go to bed?"

I knew he didn't mean with him, but my heart wasn't nearly as smart. It thudded, and Ben probably saw it through my spandex shirt. "Bed."

"Okay." He stroked my arm one more time, and when he stopped, my arm felt cold. "I'll clean up out here. See you in the morning."

"Okay," I murmured, still under his spell.

It wasn't until I'd stepped inside that I realized he'd set me up. What the fuck were we going to do in the morning?

Even though I'd taken a nap, my feet dragged. I needed more sleep. The last thing I heard him say before I shut my bedroom door was, "Coco, how about some tasty fish?"

15

BEN

WHEN I KNOCKED on Cooper's door the next morning, dry cleaning in one hand and a tray of coffees in the other, I knew it was too early. Well, it should've been too early. But I knew two things: my boss was an early riser—when he wasn't drunk or hungover—and he needed exercise. Last night, when I'd touched his arm, I'd practically felt the excess energy zipping through him.

Sure enough, he answered the door. I had no idea if he looked sleep-rumpled or awake because I could. Not. Stop. Staring. At his chest. His naked chest. Muscled, all the way from his thick, flat pecs down to his six-pack abs. A tropical jungle of dark-blond hair across his upper chest and down, down, down below those athletic shorts. My fingers twitched to stroke his golden skin, the mole on his left pec, right above his nipple. That tan nipple strained toward me as if it liked that idea, too. Thank God I clutched his clean suits in one hand and the coffees in the other. Wouldn't do to be touching my mostly naked boss.

He cleared his throat. "What the hell, Ben? It's barely seven." But he took the heavy dry cleaning from me and stepped aside when I moved forward.

I set the coffee on the kitchen counter and fixed my gaze on the plastic-covered clothes in his hand. "Want to put those away and put on a—a shirt? You need exercise, so I figured we could take a run together." I carefully didn't wince. I hated running. Too many memories of laps around the high-school track with Coach shouting, *"Move, it, Walters!"*

Not unlike Coach, Cooper scanned me from my *Guardians of the Galaxy* T-shirt to my purple Converse. "You can't run in those shoes."

"These are the only athletic shoes I've got. They'll be fine. They're court shoes."

"Court shoes," he scoffed. "You're not running in those. We'll walk instead."

Walking sounded much nicer than running. "A walk would be great. In fact, Ramón told me we should walk into town and see Tía's Garden. What's that? I didn't see it on the sheet they gave me of things to do."

"Ramón," he growled. At last, he took the dry cleaning from me. "It's one of those locals-only spots."

"Ooh! Will you take me? I love seeing places like a local does."

"Give me a minute."

It took more than a minute. I was halfway through my coffee when he emerged from the bedroom, showered and shaved, wearing the second shirt and shorts I'd gotten him. The shirt was white with sun-basking green lizards printed on it. I'd thought it was cute, but from Cooper's thunderous expression, he didn't.

I held out his coffee to him, carefully averting my eyes from his smooth, bare, chiseled jaw that was somehow even sexier, more touchable, than his naked chest had been. "Ready to go, or did you want to eat something first?"

"Let's go. I'm sure we'll find something to eat in town."

"Ooh, another secret, local spot?"

Cooper only grunted.

It was a good thing I'd drunk half my coffee because I would have spilled a full one at the half-jog I had to maintain to keep up with Cooper's long strides. We took the shell path to the main resort building and a paved path around it until we reached the circle drive that led onto the road. I knew it wasn't far to town, a little more than a mile, but I was almost too out of breath to talk. And we needed to talk.

"Can we slow down?" I huffed out.

He stopped so suddenly I almost smacked into his back. Glancing behind me, he said, "We're being followed."

I turned and spotted Coco, skulking in the bushes about twenty feet behind us. "It's okay. It's only Coco."

Cooper's heavy eyebrows lifted. "Coco? You named it?"

"He's a boy, and of course I named him." I whistled, and Coco trotted toward us. He slunk the last few feet and cowered behind me.

Cooper wrinkled his nose. "Is that…chamomile?"

"It's better than what he smelled like before. It's just the shampoo they had in my room. I used the whole bottle on him." I reached down and ruffled Coco's fur.

"He was in your room? What about fleas?" Cooper's lip curled.

"He had plenty of fleas, all right. A couple of ticks, too. But Ramón helped me give him a flea bath in one of the outdoor showers. It smelled absolutely disgusting, and that's why I bathed him with the chamomile shampoo. He didn't like the dryer, though, and I couldn't let him sleep outside when he was still wet." I snapped my mouth shut and steeled myself for Cooper's blow-up about how I wasn't staying and how it made no sense to make friends with a stray dog.

But he didn't. He just watched me stroke Coco's yellow fur for a minute before he turned and continued marching toward town.

"Good boy," I muttered. Then I jogged to catch up with my boss, Coco trotting at my heels.

The first few homes we saw were small, no bigger than my modest room at the resort, but sturdy-looking and painted in sherbet colors. Early as it was, a few people puttered in their gardens, collecting ripe, red tomatoes and golden squash.

A little boy streaked out of a turquoise-painted house and barreled into Cooper's legs. His skinny arms wrapped around Cooper's waist, and he buried his face in Cooper's hip. A pregnant woman slowly descended from the porch, ambled down the path, and planted a kiss on Cooper's cheek. There was nothing slow about the Spanish she fired at Cooper. All I caught were the words for *build* and *school.*

Cooper mumbled an answer in Spanish.

The woman cocked her hip and scanned me, then asked Cooper a question. He didn't answer but reached down to gently disentangle the child from his legs. Then he tipped his chin in the direction we'd been going and said something about the garden we planned to visit.

After Cooper patted the kid's head and kissed the woman's right cheek, she looked me up and down once more. They returned to the turquoise house without so much as a glance at Coco. Cooper resumed his long-legged stride.

"Who was that?" I asked when I caught up.

"Just someone I know."

"You know her?" I turned around to reassess the turquoise house. "How? Does she work at the resort?"

"You ask a lot of questions," he grumbled.

"That wasn't an answer." I stepped into his path so he had to stop and crossed my arms.

He let out a frustrated sigh. "Fine. She's a family friend. They wanted to thank me for some work I did in the community last time I was here."

"Work? Like, a software program?"

"No." He tipped his chin at something behind me. "That."

I turned and saw a small stucco building painted a cheery sunflower yellow. "What's that?"

"A school. For the village kids."

"You donated money for it?"

"Yes." He resumed his march toward town. "And I helped them build it."

I scrunched my nose. "Like, with a hammer?" Before I'd found him on the island, I couldn't have imagined Cooper in anything but starched business casual, his phone pressed to his ear. I struggled to imagine him doing manual labor.

"I have skills, you know. I wasn't always a COO. I had summer jobs once." His jaw clamped shut, and I knew not to ask him about those summer jobs.

We continued down the road, passing the school, a grocery store, a drugstore. A few men hung out in front of the tobacco store talking, their clouds of smoke drifting into the clear, blue sky.

Alleys branched off from the main road, leading to more houses. Cooper turned onto one bordered by a white-painted picket fence. Vines crawled over it, their violet buds just unfurling in the morning sunshine. In other places, tall flowers leaned over the fence, blooms bobbing in the light breeze as if to tell us good morning. Sunflowers curved toward the street, their heads too heavy with seeds to lift.

On the other side of the fence, a small woman wearing a hat as big as a bicycle wheel used a dangerously sharp pair of shears to snip off a sunflower head and dropped it into her basket. She startled at the scuff of my sneaker on the pavement. "Lito?"

I looked up at Cooper, who was…grinning. "Tía Camelia."

Pulling Cooper down to kiss his cheek, the woman spoke so quickly my high-school Spanish couldn't keep up. Cooper didn't try to interrupt her. I caught the words for *visit* and *too long* and *hungry.* My stomach growled.

"¿Y él, quién es?" she asked.

"Tía Camelia, this is Ben, my assistant."

She shot off another string of Spanish that made Cooper's cheeks redden.

"También es un amigo."

Amigo. I understood that one. He was calling me his friend? My cheeks warmed, too.

Finally, she spoke in English. "Come inside. For breakfast." Without waiting for a response, she lifted her basket, turned, and walked inside.

"So, it's not Tía's Garden, secret spot for locals. It's *your* tía's garden."

The grin disappeared from his face, and he was back to my jaw-clenching boss. "It is. Remind me to have a chat with Ramón later."

"On it. Boss."

He narrowed his eyes at me. And then at Coco. He held open the gate to let us walk through.

We didn't need to go inside Camelia's house. A vine-woven pergola shaded her back porch, which housed a long wooden table with mismatched chairs, each painted a different bright color. I took the purple one, and Cooper took the blue one that matched the sky and his eyes. Coco flattened himself along the lower step, one eye on Cooper and the other on his escape route.

Camelia already had fresh bread, mango slices, and a hash she called mangú set out on the table. The coffee cups were as mismatched as the chairs, and she poured coffee into a Delft cup so thin I could practically see through it. She handed it to me.

When she sat in an orange chair across from us, I lifted the cup to my lips. The robust scent curled into my nostrils. It was hot and bitter-strong with a little sweetness to it. Sipping it, my eyes widened.

"Tía Camelia makes the best coffee on the island," Cooper said, setting his own cup back on its saucer.

"You could make it, too," she said, passing over the breadbasket. "Alfonso down the street roasts the beans. He'll give you as many bags as you want."

He waved his hand. "I've tried. But when I make it at my house in California, it doesn't taste the way it does here, with your flowers and the ocean breeze."

Like he'd paid it, the breeze wafted through the garden and ruffled his sun-kissed hair. I wanted to do that, too. Run my fingers through those soft-looking waves. Rub his scalp and see if he closed his eyes, savoring the sensation the way he had his coffee.

Fuck. I stared into my cup. What was in this stuff, anyway, making me think I could casually touch Cooper, my buttoned-up boss? I took a hunk of fresh-baked bread from the basket Cooper passed me and slathered it with butter and jam. I hadn't eaten yet, so it wasn't the coffee, it was low blood sugar that had given me the totally unwelcome thought.

"So, Ben, are you Miguelito's assistant, or his friend?" She raised her eyebrows, deepening the wrinkles on her forehead. Now that she'd taken off the hat, I could see her deep-brown eyes were clear and sharp.

Wow. Tía Camelia didn't pull any punches. And why was she calling him Miguelito? Was it a nickname? "Not a friend. I like him, of course." I set down my coffee. Too hot. Everywhere. "He's a great boss." I wanted to slide under the table.

Tía Camelia narrowed her eyes at me, then at Cooper. "And you like him, too."

I sat up and watched him like he was about to spill the secrets of the universe. But he didn't look at me. He stared at Coco on the porch step. "Ben is very likable. And the best assistant I've ever had."

My chest expanded at the compliment. Then I remembered the string of truly terrible temps who'd preceded me. The best assistant he'd ever had wasn't a high bar. And he'd called me likable. Like a concept. Not that he actually liked me. I slumped.

Tía Camelia's eyes became slits. "Ben followed you here. He is worried about you." Then she tilted her head at me. "And you're still here."

Finally, her gaze landed on Cooper's lizard-print shirt. She clapped her hands. "I see! Tendrás la boda aquí ¿sí?"

Cooper shook his head, but his lips quirked like he was trying to keep from smiling. "Tía, you're incorrigible."

I wished my high-school Spanish had stuck better in my head. Maybe tía Camelia would tell me her joke in English later. What was la boda?

"Miguelito, why are you here on the island? We weren't expecting you until July."

I busied myself with buttering another piece of bread.

I felt Cooper's gaze land on me before he said quietly, "I had an incident at work. I knew I needed a break."

She nodded. "And how long is this break?"

I stilled, the piece of bread halfway to my mouth.

"As long as it takes. Maybe a long time. Maybe forever." He mumbled the last part, but I heard it.

Tía Camelia did, too. "You can't run from your problems. Especially if they're inside you." She reached across the table and grasped his hand. "But this is exactly where you need to be to figure things out. Surrounded by la familia." She raised both arms as if she were in a group hug.

I looked around, half-expecting to see a family of Fallons gathered around us. But there were only the buzzing bees and the flowers and the salty breeze. She must've meant metaphorically. Unless…she included me as part of Cooper's family? Warmth filled my belly. I did care about him. Not because he signed my paychecks. And not only because I'd been crushing on him since my first day on the job. He was a good man. He helped people at home in California through his foundation, and he helped people at his secret vacation hideaway by building schools with his fucking *hands*. I'd help him figure out his shit if I could.

Cooper didn't say anything. Instead, he gazed at his hands and rubbed at the scab on his palm from when he'd broken the desk.

Coco growled, the hair spiking up along his back. He stared through the thick greenery at the alley beyond.

"What is it, Coco?"

Not breaking his stare, he growled louder. A shoe scuffed in the alley, and footsteps receded toward the street. With one last whuff, Coco shook himself and resettled on the step.

"I hear strangers have been asking questions." Tía Camelia stood, the coffee carafe in her hand.

"It wouldn't be the first time," Cooper grumbled. "And it won't be the last."

"Still, I don't like it. Be careful, Miguelito."

"I'm always careful." They exchanged a glance, and I didn't like the way his jaw clenched or the way she bristled. What did he have to be careful about in this island paradise?

Cooper reached for Camelia's empty plate and stacked it with his. "All done, Ben?"

I shoved the last, delicious bite of bread into my mouth and passed over my plate. Standing, I gathered the jam jars and the empty breadbasket.

"Cariños, don't worry about it. I'll clean up," Camelia said.

"I'll do it," Cooper said with a glare so forceful I almost sat back down.

I jutted out my chin. "I'll help."

Years of cleaning up my parents' kitchen made me a champion dishwasher, and Cooper surprised me as a capable dish dryer. The kitchen was tiny, but everything had its place, and Cooper seemed to know it as well as if he lived there.

Under the clatter of scrubbing the flatware, I asked, "Do you want to talk about it? About the break from work?"

He wiped out a coffee cup. "You were there. You saw it. I need to work through my..."

"Your shit?"

One corner of his mouth quirked up. "My shit."

"Are you"—God, I was smashing through that professional wall like the Kool-Aid Man—"talking to someone?"

His smile gone, he rubbed an invisible speck off the cup. "I am."

"Good. That's good." Though I wished he'd talk to me, too.

And then I remembered what I needed to talk to him about. "I know you said there was nothing to be worried about at Synergy. But I'm worried. About Weston's plan. About you selling your shares. About this break you're on. Are you—are you leaving Synergy permanently?"

He set down the cup and answered the question I'd been too afraid to ask. "Ben, nothing will happen to you. Even if I decide to step away from Synergy, your job is secure. I promise."

My stomach unclenched a little. But not all the way. Because if Cooper *stepped away*, did I want to have a secure job at Synergy? Sure, the pay and benefits, especially the tuition reimbursement, were great. And I liked Marlee a lot. I'd even planned to apply for a different job once I got my degree. But after a couple of days with unbuttoned Cooper on the island, I knew if Cooper wasn't there, it wouldn't be the same. It'd be…empty.

I was in trouble. So. Much. Trouble. My heart raced.

"Ben, are you okay?" Cooper curled his hand around my shoulder. I froze, still gripping the cutlery. "You're pale. Need to sit down?"

"No, I'm good." My voice was too high, and I cleared my throat. "I'm fine." I rinsed the flatware and set it on the towel for Cooper to dry. I pried out the plug and let the water drain out of the sink.

"Maybe you need a break, too. You should—you should stay."

I really needed to sit down. I gripped the edge of the sink. Breathed. Tried to brush it off with a joke. "You said I was fired if I stayed, so I guess I'm already in garbage time."

He squeezed my shoulder and released it with a chuckle. "You should know by now I don't always mean what I say."

My heart stopped, and the words tumbled out. "So you didn't mean it just now? About staying?"

His blue eyes softened. "Of course I did. You should enjoy the vacation."

He didn't move to pick up the flatware to dry it. He just stared at me, like he meant more than he'd said. What was the meaning behind those impenetrable blue eyes? Did he mean that I needed a break after working my ass off for him for the past six months? Or that he wanted me to stay because he enjoyed my company? Or that—I swallowed past my suddenly dry throat—I could enjoy *him*, in this temporary respite from the real world?

"O—okay."

"Good." He scooped up a spoon and rubbed it dry.

"Ah." Tía Camelia stood in the doorway, hands on her hips. "I knew you'd figure out a way to make it work. Together." She waved a hand at her clean kitchen, like that's what she'd meant.

I narrowed my eyes at her. Tía Camelia's innocent act wasn't fooling anyone.

Still, when we got back to the resort, I talked to Maria at the front desk and extended my stay for a week.

16

BEN

THE MORNING after I met Cooper's tía Camelia, Coco and I showed up at his place early. So what if I did it two days in a row? Cooper was an early-morning guy. It didn't necessarily mean I wanted to start my day seeing his face…and maybe his bare chest again. Besides, Coco seemed thrilled to visit again, despite my boss's lack of enthusiasm for my four-legged companion.

Plus, Marlee's call last night haunted me. Apparently, while I'd been chowing down on mangú, strangers had appeared in Synergy's boardroom for a meeting with Weston. Strangers who had that oily Gurusoft look, at least according to Jackson and Marlee. Did corporate raiders come visit the targets of their hostile takeovers?

I had to up my game. So I brought a sack of pastries Luis said were Cooper's favorites. I couldn't imagine Cooper eating anything with that many carbs, but they smelled heavenly enough that if I were him, I'd break a years-long diet to eat them.

I knocked on the door. No response.

I banged louder. Only the stillness of an empty house answered me.

Coco trailed me around the side to the back gate, and I peered through. Not a ripple disturbed the pool. The chairs were all empty.

Had he left? Had Cooper gone home to California? As much as that aligned with what I was trying to get him to do, disappointment twinged through me. He wouldn't leave without telling me, would he?

He'd done it before.

I trudged toward the beach and scanned it. No Cooper. Only a couple of joggers and a family with a golden-haired toddler playing in the surf.

I dropped onto the sand. With a sympathetic whine, Coco sat beside me.

"He doesn't owe me anything," I said.

Coco pawed at my shorts.

"He isn't accountable to me. He proved that by coming here in the first place. Weston's his boss, and that's the only person he owes an explanation to."

Coco scooted a little closer.

"Yeah." I couldn't ignore the heaviness in my belly. "You're right. I'm full of shit. I knew he couldn't care about someone like me." I opened the pastry bag and pulled out one of the sticky spherical pastries. When I popped it into my mouth and crunched through the fried outside, the fluffy inside melted on my tongue.

"O.M.G., Coco. Where have these things been all my life?" I bit into a second one and handed half to Coco. He inhaled it and licked the syrup off his snout.

The third one was all mine. "I guess we can sit here and stuff our faces all day. Though these would go better with a cup of—"

"Coffee?" The voice behind me was achingly familiar and gruffly amused.

I scrambled to my feet and whirled to find Cooper, dressed in his form-fitting workout clothes again, standing behind me with a pair of to-go cups.

"Oh, hey. I mean, good morning." I kept my eyes on his face.

The sun glinted on it, turning his stubble golden. And as irresistible as I found his jawline, that was nothing to the muscles his compression shirt revealed. *Do. Not. Look.* I'd melt right onto the sand if I did.

"I was on my way to…out…and then I thought you might be coming here." He cleared his throat. "So I bought you a latte." He handed it to me.

I took it, speechless for once.

"It's what you like, right? With skim milk?"

"How did you know? I bring *you* coffee. It's, like, almost in my job description."

He scuffed his high-tech sneaker in the sand. "I pay attention."

"Oh, right." Of course. One of the secrets to Cooper Fallon's success was his attention to details. He had to have a million of them flitting through his genius brain at that very second. "Thank you."

"You have, ah, something on your shirt."

I looked down. Shit, there was a drizzle of syrup over my right pec. I couldn't even eat my feelings without looking like a toddler. I held out the bag. "I got these for you."

"For me." His lips twitched like he wanted to smile. He took the bag and peered inside. "Buñuelos! These are my fav—" He trailed off when he looked up at me, and his eyes went hot like they did when I called him "Mr. Fallon" in the office. "You have some miel—some syrup—on your lip."

When I licked the corner of my mouth and found the sweetness there, my face blazed. It wasn't all from the sun creeping up into the sky. Some of it was from those blue laser beams of his eyes that followed the path of my tongue.

I rolled my lips between my teeth. If I didn't say anything, didn't eat or drink anything, maybe I could salvage my dignity.

He cleared his throat. "I have somewhere I need to be. You should try out the spa here today. Or relax by the pool." He nodded toward the resort.

I narrowed my eyes. This again? "You can't get rid of me with your hot-stone massage temptation. I go where you go. Until you go home."

He didn't look angry. He looked almost...pleased? Though his gaze cooled a little. "All right, then. Come on." Without waiting for me to respond, he turned and headed back toward the resort.

———

BY THE TIME we made it to the jobsite, the buñuelos were gone, and I had a stitch in my side from Cooper's brisk pace.

The building stood in a cleared space with pickup trucks parked haphazardly around it. It was coated in that plastic wrapping I'd seen on additions to homes in my parents' neighborhood. The roof was bare plywood. A few brave souls in orange hard hats stood on the roof, and a machine on the ground lifted materials up to them. God, it was like my favorite Village People fantasy come to life.

"What are they building?" I asked.

"This will be the new community center. The hurricane damaged the old one." Cooper set one hand on his hip and shielded his eyes with the other to peer up at the roof.

"¡Oye!" Cooper shouted to the men on the roof. In Spanish, he asked something about metal.

The guys nodded, and one of them shouted something in response and pointed at the materials slowly rising toward them.

Cooper strode to the nearest ladder and was a quarter of the way up before I realized what was happening and scurried to his side. Coco followed me, barking his head off. He might be as worried as I was, or else he thought chasing Cooper was a fun game.

The guys on the roof shook their heads, and the guy who'd talked to Cooper waved his palms in a clear don't-come-up-here signal. One guy wearing jeans and a white hard hat reached the ladder at the same time I did.

"¡Lito, no!"

Cooper stopped and looked down. He shot off a string of Spanish and waved up at the roof. White-hat guy planted his hands on his hips, shook his head, and responded. My high-school class hadn't given me any building vocabulary, but I caught the word *peligroso*—dangerous. I agreed.

The guy tapped his helmet and pointed at Cooper's hands. Cooper rolled his eyes and then gestured at the man's hat. He shook his head, his expression serious except for the twitch at the corner of his mouth.

The guy in the white hat, apparently a supervisor, shouted at another guy on the ground who brought over a pair of work gloves and a couple of metal trowels. With a full-body sigh, Cooper trudged back down the rungs of the ladder until he stood at my side. Reluctantly, he took the trowels and the gloves. The supervisor didn't move until Cooper tugged on the gloves and waved them in a "happy now?" gesture.

He squinted at Cooper and then pointed him to the side of the building, where a couple of guys tacked metal mesh over the plastic. Then he turned and walked away.

"What was that about?" I asked.

Cooper gazed up at the guys on the roof like he wished he had wings. "I was the one who recommended the metal roofing. It's more resistant to strong winds. And I wanted to help install it. But"—his cheeks went red—"the foreman won't let me. He says he doesn't have any spare hard hats, and my brain and my hands are too valuable to risk in a fall. Jesus Christ! I worked in construction when he was learning his ABCs!"

"Hey, now." I rubbed his biceps. "It's not a reflection on your ability. But you're more valuable here on the ground. Any schmo can install roofing. You're the only one who can run Synergy and keep writing checks to support the rebuilding here."

He didn't deny it. Still, he stared hard at the roofers as they rolled a dark material onto the roof and tacked it down with nail guns.

"Did you really work construction?"

"Yeah. When I was in high school. Even before that. My dad —" He shuddered and looked at my hand, which still rested on his sleeve.

I jerked back like he'd burned me. I'd forgotten about the no-touching rule.

"Never mind," he said. "Take that dog under those trees. I don't want him to get in the way. And watch where you step. Roofing nails are a bitch if you're not wearing work boots."

"I can help," I protested. Weakly. I was the son of a lawyer and a teacher. When things needed fixing around the house, they hired a contractor. I'd never built so much as a birdhouse in my brief career in Cub Scouts. I quit the program after I found a spider as big as my hand in my sleeping bag during our first campout.

"You can help by keeping that dog out from underfoot. And make sure you stay hydrated. I'm not carrying you back."

He stalked away toward the side of the building, loaded up one trowel with a mudlike substance, and smeared it over the mesh like it had insulted his mother.

Me? I did what he told me to do. I sat in the shade with Coco. Well, and I brought the rest of the guys bottles of water from the cooler as the sun rose high overhead. And if my gaze didn't leave those sculpted muscles of Cooper's as he bent and lifted the heavy mud, as his arms arced across the side of the new community center, as he squatted to scrape the metal bar that smoothed the surface of the stucco, who could blame me?

17

COOPER

I TOILED on the community center until my muscles ached and the crew brought out a cooler full of celebratory beers.

I could practically taste the bitter coolness numbing the back of my throat. But I thanked the guys and left, saying I needed a hot shower.

Make that a cold shower. I'd felt Ben's gaze stuck to me all day like a caress, and I'd practically pressed myself against the tacky side of the building to hide the bulge in my basketball shorts.

I sent him to the resort bar with a request for something refreshing. Whatever he brought back was sure to be disappointingly nonalcoholic, but it would give me time to settle myself and remember that Ben was still my assistant and not someone I wanted to taste.

But when I returned to the house, it wasn't empty. Someone was on my deck. A tall someone.

I rolled my shoulders, then I unlocked the gate to the back and stepped through. "Security is shit around here."

Jamila whirled from where she'd been studying the trellised

bougainvillea, her white skirt flaring out around her brown thighs. A grin broke out on her face.

"You're right. All it took was a little of this"—she demonstrated with a hip-swinging sashay toward me—"and one of these"—she fluttered a wink—"and I was in your compound. With lunch." She gestured at the spread on the patio table. Two plates for a tête-à-tête. "Or maybe it's dinner. After traveling all day, I have no idea what time it is."

I winced. She was worried about me. I knew well what a CEO would have had to reschedule to spend a day away from her business. "Mila, you didn't have to—"

"The fuck I didn't. Last we spoke, you were on your way to Boston. My friend Cooper goes on an unplanned vacation exactly zero times in the fifteen years I've known him. I've got to check that you haven't been body-snatched. What's something only the real Cooper would know?"

I snorted. "You have a yellow-rose tattoo on the inside of your—"

"Okay, fine. Though a surprising number of people know about that tattoo."

"Surprising?" I raised my eyebrows. "This from the woman who, the first time I met her, was sitting in my dorm room in her underwear?"

"I didn't know then that Jackson could count cards."

Jackson. My face must have shown some of the bleakness that had blackened my insides because she U-turned off Memory Lane.

"Tell me you're not glad to see me."

I kissed her cheek, and her familiar jasmine scent flooded my nose. "Of course I am. But I texted you, I'm fine."

"Fine?" Her brows arched up. "I suspect you're anything but. Now. Sit your ass down and tell your BFF Mila all about it."

I glanced at the gate. Ben would arrive any minute with drinks and that flirty smile of his. And Jamila would see it all. I didn't need to give her any more ammunition for the stern talking-to I saw in my immediate future.

"Normally, I would—"

"Normally? What's going on? You're not drinking again?" She sniffed me, wrinkled her nose, then shook her head. "A secret, then." She tapped her lips, darkened with deep violet lipstick. "A secret affair! Where is she? Or he? Or they?"

I ignored her sky-high eyebrows. "I just meant I could have used a little warning. Advanced planning."

"Whatever for? You know you don't have to clean the place for me." Beneath her flirtation, beneath the softness of the Texas accent that clung to her like honey, gumming up the California accent she'd adopted, she watched me with those dark eyes. Scanning. Cataloging. Assessing, like she'd do with a rogue bit of code.

"Let me go clean up. I stink." I'd catch Ben at the front door, send him away. He'd be hurt, but it'd be better than sitting under Jamila's scrutiny for an hour.

"Cooper?" Too late.

Jamila peered around me at the back gate. "Well, what have we here?" she murmured.

"Behave," I warned her before I turned and strode to the gate to let Ben in. He held a pitcher in one hand and a stack of plastic cups in the other.

I opened the gate. "Jamila Jallow dropped by for a surprise visit. If you don't want to stay—"

"Of course he wants to stay." Jamila was right behind me. "Ben. We've met before at Cooper's office."

Did she land a little harder than she needed to on *Cooper's office?* And did she flick those big, dark eyes at me? Or was I seeing things?

"Right," Ben said. "You don't make appointments there, either."

Jamila's eyes flared for a moment, then she threw back her

head and laughed. "Not so punctilious outside the office, are you?" She stuck out her hand. "Good to see you again."

Ben, still hovering at the open gate, tucked the cups under his arm and shook her hand. "Good flight?"

Fuck, was this what we were doing? Pretending it was perfectly normal for me to be at a Caribbean resort *with my assistant?* I tugged my compression shirt away from my sticky skin. That was a mistake. The odor of sweat and lime wafted into my nose.

Jamila scanned Ben from the pink sunburn on his nose down to his dusty Converse. Then she arrowed her gaze at my stucco-smeared workout clothes. God only knew what she thought the crusty white stains were. A smile curled her purple lips. "Hungry, Ben?"

"N—I—Am I? Hungry?" He blinked at me.

I closed my eyes and sighed through my nose. "Come in, Ben. Let's have a drink, at least." I eyed the fruity concoction in the pitcher. I'd bet my mother's favorite rosary—the one Pope John Paul II had touched himself—that it didn't contain a single drop of alcohol.

But Ben wasn't the first to come through the gate. That dog, the one that followed him everywhere, slunk through, low to the ground, straight toward Jamila.

"And who do we have here?" She squatted gracefully, like a feather descending, and held out her hand. The dog sniffed it and then butted his head into it, seeking her caress. Jamila scratched his chin and behind his ears before he flopped to his back so she could scratch his belly.

"I call him Coco," Ben said.

"Coco," Jamila crooned. The dog wagged his tail.

While Jamila lavished attention on the dog, I took the pitcher from Ben and tugged him a few feet away. "Sorry, I—she doesn't usually stay long." Why was I apologizing to Ben? Jamila was my friend and had more right to be here than he did. Still, I said, "You can leave whenever you'd like."

He ducked his head. "Do you want me to go?"

Did I? Jamila had already seen and deduced more than I liked. More than there was, probably. It couldn't get any worse if he stayed. And as soon as he left, Jamila would launch a line of questioning I wasn't ready to answer. "It's up to you." I crossed one arm, the one that wasn't holding the pitcher, over my chest.

"She has a room here in your house, doesn't she?"

He'd seen the frilly guest room. "Sometimes my mother stays there, but it's mostly Jamila's."

"Does—" He pressed his lips together and shook his head. "I'll stay. For a drink. I'm thirsty." And he jutted out his chin. For some reason, I wanted to tweak it between my fingers and pull his lips to mine. But I couldn't. Not in front of Jamila. Fuck! I couldn't kiss Ben regardless of who else was there. He was my assistant. Off limits.

He brushed past me, and that casual slide of his bare forearm against mine set me on fire. I rubbed it, and when I looked up, Jamila was watching me, a knowing smile playing over her face. Did I say it couldn't get any worse? I was wrong.

"Cooper," Ben said, "could you hand me the pitcher, please?"

"Right. Sorry." I trotted to the table and set it down.

Ben removed the plastic from the top and poured it into the cups he'd filled from the ice bucket. He handed one to Jamila, another to me, and lifted his own. "To surprise visits."

"To friends, old and new," she countered.

I couldn't look at her. Instead, I downed the oversweet drink. I ran my tongue over the sticky film it left on my teeth. "What is this?"

"Guava punch. Tasty, isn't it?" Ben licked a drop from the corner of his mouth, and I had to look away before I thought too hard about what guava punch would taste like on his skin.

Jamila took a cautious second sip. "Maybe I can cut it with a little tea. Though I think it'd still be too sweet for you, Coop."

I felt Ben slump even though he was across the table from me. "It's fine." I took another gulp and tried not to wince. The headache and nausea from the sugar would come later, but I could keep up the pretense for an hour or so.

"I don't know about you two, but I'm starved. You wouldn't believe the ungodly hour I had to leave California." She produced a plate from somewhere on the overloaded table and set it in front of Ben. Then she filled up her own plate with fruit and a pastry. "Aren't y'all hungry?"

"I'm not. Cooper, what about you? You worked all day with hardly a break." Ben sipped his drink.

"No." I didn't know what to do with my hands, so I took a piece of cheese from the platter.

"What have y'all been up to here on the island?" Jamila scooped fruit onto a plate and passed it to Ben.

I answered for him. "Oh, you know. Umbrella drinks on the beach. Steel drum lessons. Line dancing with the other tourists."

Jamila ignored my flippant comment. "How's the community center coming along?"

"Fine." I picked at a spot of stucco on my shorts.

"He's thrown himself into work here, just like he would in the office, hasn't he?" Jamila tapped her short, polished fingernails on the table.

"Eh—I guess?" Two spots of color bloomed on Ben's cheekbones. He scooped a slice of banana from his plate and tossed it to Coco, who swallowed it whole.

In the office and on the island, Ben protected me. He thought he was doing me a favor by not telling Jamila what a sad sack I'd been for a week on the island. He was so kind. So caring. Even after I'd almost lost control again two nights ago, he'd come back. He had that in common with Coco the dog.

Jamila knew my coping mechanisms too well to be fooled. She tilted her head at me.

"Not the first few days," I admitted. "But Ben convinced me to pull my head out of my ass. You know I always need something to do. And there are enough construction projects around here to keep me busy for a while."

She buttered a roll. "Or"—she drew out the word—"you could relax, spend some time on the beach. You don't always have to be proving your worth to people."

I snorted. Dr. Pradhi told me that at least once a month. "Don't I?"

Jamila set down the roll and grabbed my hand. "No. You don't. People care about you." Her deep brown eyes were fierce. "I care about you. And so does Ben." The squeeze she gave my hand guaranteed she had more to say when we were alone.

I glanced at Ben and froze. His lighter brown eyes weren't fierce like Jamila's, but the expression in them scared me even more. They were gentle, soothing, and full of delicious promise. An offering I was desperate to accept. But I couldn't.

"Ben came here to check up on me. Same as you. I wish you'd all believe that I'm fine. I can take care of myself. I just needed a break." And for lack of something better to do with my hands, I took another gulp of the punch. I grimaced.

"We'd have been more likely to believe you're fine if you'd turn on your damn phone and talk to us." Jamila's lips pressed into a thin, purple line.

The whole mess started when I talked to Jackson. I'd gone off on him. I'd done the same to Ben just the other night. I couldn't trust myself not to hurt the people I cared about. Not then. Maybe not ever.

"Do you want my number?" Ben asked. "I'm staying for a few days, and I'd let you know he's okay."

The growl erupted from me, unbidden. "What are you, my fucking babysitter?"

With a cool glance at me, Ben handed his phone to Jamila, who added herself as a contact and then called her own phone to get Ben's number.

I dumped my guava punch into the potted hibiscus behind me and refilled the glass with water from the other pitcher. The icy liquid snuffed out the flare of anger in my chest.

"I think I'll go now. Let you two catch up." Ben stood, and something pulled in my belly. *Not yet.*

I should have let him go. Let him walk right out of my life. But my traitorous knees pushed me to my feet.

"I'll go with you to the gate. It sticks sometimes." A lie. Luis's staff ensured the gate never stuck.

We strolled in silence to the gate, the dog trotting at Ben's heels. When we reached it, I rested my hand on the metal. My voice came out sulky and gruff. "You could come over later. For dinner. If you want."

"She's not staying?" He flicked his gaze to the deck and Jamila.

"No. She only came to check on me."

"That was nice of her. But really, don't kick her out on my account. I have some work to do. For school. I took a couple days off, and now I have to catch up."

"Bring it over?" Why couldn't I just let him go, let him have an evening to himself? Avoid the temptation?

Because he'd followed me here. Taken care of me. Hadn't treated me like the monster I was. And because I wanted him. Needed him. Even though that made me a beast.

A little line creased between his eyebrows. "Okay. See you around nine?"

"Eight. I'll send her off early."

A tiny smile. "See you then."

He ambled back toward the resort, Coco trotting at his heels.

When I returned to the table, Jamila had pushed away her plate. "So how are you really?"

"Better." My chest didn't squeeze all the time, and I'd slept almost eight hours straight the previous night.

"Good. You know we're all worried about you. Especially Jay."

My mouth tightened. "And yet, you're the one who came to check on me."

"I don't have an infant at home and a wife trying to keep her business afloat. Jay has new responsibilities. You're going to have to get used to them, you know." Her voice was gentle as the distant surf.

"I don't know that." I tried to breathe through the tightness that was back in full force. "Weston said Jay's considering getting out."

She cocked her head. "Weston said this? Not Jay?"

"He didn't have to fucking say it," I snarled. "He's had one foot out the fucking door since he got married."

Jamila spoke even more slowly than usual, feeling her way through my emotional minefield. "I know his marriage last fall was a lot for you to accept, feeling the way you do."

"Did. I don't…not anymore."

"You sure about that?"

"Of course I am! He's got a fucking family. I'd never—" I tried to swallow, but my throat had sand in it. I gulped from my glass of water.

"I know, honey. I know. But." She took her time folding her napkin next to her plate. "I thought maybe when you yelled at him, it meant…"

"It meant I miss my best friend."

Her eyes went liquid. "Coop, he—"

"No. She's his best friend now. He's moved on. He's a husband and a father first. And that's—that's the way it should be." I stood and strode to the edge of the pool to recapture my breath.

"And you think selling your shares will make you feel better?" She stroked the center of my back and stared with me into the blue depths of the water.

"I don't know. I made the sale when I was drunk. It didn't feel terrible when it went through." It felt like nothing at all. Ben was probably right about my depression.

"If you're going to sell more, you should tell him first. You guys had that agreement."

I stepped out of her reach. "I—I can't. Talk to him." Every time

I did, the ice inside me turned to fire. When I'd smacked the desk almost two weeks ago, I'd really wanted to punch him, right in the solar plexus, so he'd hurt as much as I did.

"Have you talked to Dr. Pradhi lately?"

"Yeah. Earlier this week."

"Okay. I'm sure she said you've got to do what's right for yourself. For your mental health. If that's saying an Irish good-bye to Jackson and Synergy, so be it."

I let my gaze drift to the beach and the ocean beyond my fenced-off pool. Could I stay on the island? Let my responsibilities in California drop away? Working on the community center felt good. Fulfilling. And there was plenty more to do.

Could I convince Mamá to move back? She'd be safer this far away from my father. She'd miss her friends at church and at the senior center, but on the island, she had family.

I sucked in a deep breath of the salty air. Let it out. If Jamila hadn't been there, I'd have walked through the gate onto the sand and dug my toes in. The island always felt like home, soothing me, reassuring me, embracing me in a way my childhood home never had and in a way I could never recreate in California in the big, cold mansion in Pacific Heights.

"Though that Ben—" Jamila slid me a sly look. "It'd be a shame to tell him good-bye."

My mind spun, and for once, no words came.

"Thought so. A little island fling might do you some good. Get you past all that mess with Jay. Let you move on."

I snorted. "A fling with my assistant? That'd be a terrible idea. I'd have to write myself up."

"Good lord, Cooper. Everybody fucks on vacation. Hell, you and I—"

I cut her off with a sharp shake of my head. "The COO doesn't fuck his assistant."

"What if Ben wants to fuck the hot guy he can't keep his eyes off, who happens to be his boss when they're an entire continent away? As long as it's consensual, it doesn't seem like an issue to me."

"So when I write his performance report at the end of the year, do I rate him on how well he fucks, in addition to his other responsibilities?" But it wasn't just a fling with my assistant I was protesting. It was a fling with Ben. Ben, savior of children and animals. Ben, with his soft brown eyes and softer skin. Ben, who'd come all the way out to this tiny island to care for me. Ben deserved so much more than a fling. So much more than me.

She propped her fists on her hips. "You're both adults. I think you can figure this out. Clearly, y'all need to get it out of your systems."

"No, I don't. I've dealt with it for six months, and—"

"Six months? You mean since he started at Synergy?"

I winced. "Yes?"

"Oh, honey." She put her hand on my arm, and it didn't tingle the way it had when Ben had done it last night. "You need to work this out. Besides…"

I took the bait, hope flickering in my belly. "Besides?"

"If you don't go back, he won't be your assistant anymore."

Holy fuck.

18

COOPER

IT WAS HIS WRISTS. The delicate curve of them over his laptop's keyboard as he typed, sitting six feet away from me on the sectional. The bones and tendons shifting as his fingers moved. That was the part of him I most wanted to touch, to explore.

After his lips, of course.

As he'd done a dozen times already, he tensed and turned his head to look at me, somehow sensing I was staring. He sat straight, feet on the floor, his laptop on his knees, all business. His expression said, *Why are you trying to distract me from my work?*

Or maybe, *Stop staring at me, creeper.* I was his boss, and I had to stop ogling my employee's wrists.

I was half-sprawled in the corner of the sectional, my legs stretched toward him. My bare feet hung off the seat. I buried my nose in my beat-up paperback, pretending to read the thriller. When I flipped the page, it fluttered away from the spine. Books didn't hold up well in the Caribbean humidity, especially those I'd read as many times as I'd read this one. I smoothed the page back in place and then, without moving my head, cut my eyes to Ben.

He was still watching me. "Good book?"

"Yeah, I love this one. Twisty."

Why the fuck had I said "twisty"? Because now all I could think about was the curl at the center of Ben's forehead that I wanted to twist around my finger. I'd never been so glad for the island's humidity. It had thoroughly vanquished Ben's haircare regimen, and his curls sprung free and loose at the end of the day.

He ran a hand through them, but the one at the front flopped back over his forehead. I clenched my hand to keep from reaching for it. I couldn't touch him. I was his boss. What Jamila said about staying together on the island was a dream. He cared about me, but not like that.

I smoothed the page, pretending to read. "Getting good work done?"

"Yeah, I'm almost finished drafting this paper for my econ class."

Econ? Ben didn't seem like the business type. He was a fantastic assistant, but he never seemed curious about the inner workings of Synergy. I'd figured he was studying something more people-focused. "Is that your major?"

His cheeks pinked at the tops, and he hit a couple of keys on the keyboard before he set the laptop on the coffee table and turned to face me, one knee bent on the seat cushion. "I'm majoring in business. For the job prospects." He stared at his knees.

"For the job prospects?" I echoed. "It's a great field. But it's not what you love, is it?"

He didn't look up. "Not really."

I leaned toward him. "What, Ben? What do you love?"

I watched him swallow, his Adam's apple bobbing. "I love… working with kids. I want to help them. I'll never be able to do it the way you do, with your foundation and your programs and all. But maybe I'll have a little spare cash I can give. And time to volunteer. I work at the shelter on the weekends, but…" He shook his head. "I like working with individual kids. Kids who are in trouble, like I was." He closed his mouth tight, like he hadn't meant to say it.

"You were in trouble?" I couldn't imagine cool, buttoned-up, stylish Ben ever in trouble. Then I remembered my own youthful troubles, the black eyes I'd had to explain to my teachers, the bruises I'd hidden during gym class by changing in the toilet stall. Heat rose in my chest. No one had hurt Ben like that, had they? My heart kicked into a faster rhythm, and my hand curled into a fist.

"I—" He let out a nervous chuckle. "My sister says I keep my heart outside my body, where anyone can hurt it. And freshman year of college, I let someone—my boyfriend—hurt me. Emotionally," he rushed to say, laying his hand on my fist.

The touch cooled my blood and sent it back to my heart, where it slowed the angry pounding. I loosened my fingers under his.

"I flunked all my classes, and then I was too embarrassed—too fucked-up—to go home and tell my parents. So I couch-surfed for a while, but then I ended up on the street. And I—shit, why am I telling you this?"

I flipped my hand over and clutched his. "I want to hear it, Ben. If you don't mind telling me."

He stared at our joined hands. Fuck, I was holding my assistant's hand. I released my hold on him, but he tightened his grip.

"I got into trouble. With the cops. But instead of sending me to jail, the judge sent me to a program. They let me live there, and they—well, the director, a guy named Victor—helped me get back on my feet. Found me a job in a diner. If it hadn't been for him, I don't know what would've happened to me. I mean"—he looked up at me, his eyes big—"I have great parents. Supportive. They wanted me to come home. But I—I couldn't. Not then. Anyway, I wish I could be like Victor. And help other kids who've gotten themselves in trouble and need a hand up."

"That's—" I stared at our joined hands, his paler, smaller one in mine. "That's—" My brain was stuck in neutral. I heard every word, but his grip on me made everything slow. Easy. Peaceful.

"That's beautiful." I meant everything he told me. And more. The lamplight gleaming in his dark locks. The seriousness of those golden-brown eyes that absorbed every concern of mine and vaporized it. All I wanted to do was hold Ben with my hands, with my gaze, forever.

But I couldn't. He was so much more than I'd known. Resilient. Strong. Too strong for me to hurt? No. My smashed desk was proof.

Besides, he was still my employee.

I ripped my hand from his. "I—I'm going for a swim."

I strode out onto the deck and took a couple of breaths of the sticky air. The pool looked cool and inviting.

Damn it, I'd come out here with no suit. Mine was in the house. But I couldn't walk past Ben. I'd never withstand the temptation to take him in my arms and kiss the hell out of him.

"Fuck it," I mumbled. I stepped out of the puddle of light coming from the house and stripped off my shirt and shorts. Wearing my boxer briefs, I dove into the pool and stayed submerged as long as I could. The pressure of the water, the coolness against my skin, even the burning in my lungs grounded me. Reminded me that I was Cooper Fallon, and I didn't deserve anyone's love. Certainly not Ben's. Jesus Christ, he wanted to work with at-risk kids. Even that damned hound knew Ben was gentle and good, not dangerous like me.

At last, the squeeze in my lungs forced me to the surface. Gasping, I shook the water out of my eyes and tipped to float on my back. I gazed up at the moon, white and serene. That was how I needed to be. Cold. Hard. Separated from life by thousands of miles and the emptiness of space.

"Mind if I join you?"

I curled into myself and spun to face Ben, who stood on the side of the pool.

"What?" I shook water out of my ear.

He fingered the hem of his golf shirt. "Mind if I join you in the pool?"

"But you're not—" I gestured at his shirt and shorts. "You don't have a suit."

One corner of his mouth curled up. "Neither do you."

Fuck, I was out here in my underwear. I supposed this situation could fall under the dress-code exceptions Synergy had for pool parties. I'd have overlooked it for just about any other employee. Except myself. "I—I don't think—"

"Don't think," he said. He pulled off his shirt, and I couldn't help it. I stared. At the dark hair scattered across his chest, the paleness of the skin his shirt covered and the darker skin on his arms where the Caribbean sun had kissed it.

Then his fingers went to the button of his shorts, and I turned away to stare past the fence to the ocean beyond. I let out my breath when I heard the splash of his entry into the water.

Suddenly, the pool seemed too small. I breast-stroked to the deep end where there was a submerged seat and parked my ass on it. I gripped the ledge. Nothing would move me from this spot. Not until Ben left.

He paddled toward me but stopped where the floor started to drop away. "Did I make you uncomfortable in there?" He tilted his head toward the house.

"No." The only uncomfortable thing had been the pressure in my shorts. But how did it look that I left right after he shared that very personal information with me? Jesus, I'd acted like an ass. I ran a cool, wet hand over my face. "Thank you for sharing your story with me. I like that you feel comfortable enough to talk to me."

His shoulders slumped, and he paddled away from me to the steps in the shallow end. He sat on a low one, most of his body below the water.

"I thought we were talking. I thought maybe you'd talk to me." The words were barely audible across the length of the pool.

My stomach contracted. "I—Ben, I—" Shit. I couldn't shout this across the pool.

I swam toward him and stopped a few feet away from the steps. No, it was still wrong. I pushed through the water and sat on the far end of his step. A pool raft could have squeezed between us.

"I was moved by what you said. I didn't have the greatest teenage years. I wish I had a Victor to go to." Not that I would have. Fallons didn't ask for help. They struggled until they drowned—or learned to swim.

Ben scooted closer. "You do?"

I dragged my gaze off him and stared over the fence at the ocean. Here on the island, time and the tide always eroded away my problems. And I didn't want to conjure him here. My father had no place in this beautiful refuge. "If you don't mind, I'd rather not talk about it."

"Okay. But if you ever want to talk about it…"

I wouldn't. But I nodded once.

A cool, wet hand landed on my shoulder, and it startled me enough that I looked at him. Ben was close, too close, his brown eyes dark and those full lips tempting. I longed to reach out a finger and touch them. But I couldn't. I—

"Fuck it," Ben muttered.

When he leaned across the distance that separated us, ripples lapped between our bare chests. I fixated on them. They'd touched his skin, and now they touched mine. Where did he end, and where did I begin? The water had washed away our barriers. My barriers. His gaze burned into mine, and I was lost.

After the briefest of hesitations, he brushed his lips across mine.

That slide of his lips was everything I'd imagined and more. His skin was soft and smelled of the honey-scented lip balm he kept in his desk drawer. His warm breath skated over my cheek. I kept my eyes open—I must have known at an instinctual level that I couldn't miss a single detail of this experience because it could never, ever happen again—but his dark eyelashes fluttered down over his cheekbones. This close, I smelled his aftershave, and it made me think of lazy mornings, sunlight streaming across the bed, the tip of his hipbone just visible over the edge of a rumpled sheet.

I must have made a noise because he froze. I stilled, too, hoping if I didn't move, I wouldn't break the spell.

He stayed there, his lips an inch from mine, for three of my ragged breaths. The ripples caressed my chest when he tensed, readying to pull away.

I couldn't let him do that. Now that I'd tasted him, I needed more. Like that fucking dog lying under the patio table, once I felt Ben's caring kindness, I knew better than to let him out of my sight.

I'd wanted to do it for the past four days—hell, ever since he'd walked onto the sixth floor of my building—so I buried my hand in his hair to steady him while I crushed my lips against his.

Our second kiss wasn't featherlight like the first. No, this one was mine, and it carried my need, my want, even my barely contained violence for anyone who'd ever hurt Ben. I thrust my tongue against the seam of his lips until he opened. I took and pillaged everything. I devoured the evening bristles around his mouth. I raked my tongue against his sharp teeth. I fisted his curls and tugged.

Ben didn't pull away. Instead, he sagged against me, his bare chest sliding against my skin. He met each attack on his mouth with an easy counteroffense, sliding his tongue against mine, nibbling at my bottom lip, and resting his palm on the center of my chest, not to push me away but as if he needed to feel how my heart raced for him.

At last, as I knew he would—as he should, for his own preservation—he pulled away, gusting heavy breaths into my ear. "God. Damn."

I wiggled, trying to sit up straight, but when he kissed my jaw, I froze.

"You're so hot," he murmured, "and wild." His lips descended to my neck, and chills raised goosebumps on my skin.

I released my hold on his hair and clamped my fingers onto the pool step.

"No, no." He licked my earlobe and sucked it. The sensation went right to my balls, drawing them up tight. "Pull my hair again. I liked it."

I lifted my trembling hands to his hair and stroked the curls. "I—I shouldn't."

"Shouldn't you?" he breathed into my ear.

My dick turned to steel.

"Shouldn't you—instead of always doing what's right, just for once, do what feels good?" He nuzzled against my neck and gently sucked on the pulse point.

I couldn't help it. I curled my fingers into his hair. His mouth on me, the weight of his body on mine, felt so fucking good. I was losing control, and it was amazing.

His breath hitched as I tightened my grip, and he shifted into my lap, his hip just grazing the tip of my dick in my shorts. A desperate urge seized me, and my fingers were already tugging him toward the side so I could reverse our positions, so I could be in control, so I could make him feel as good as he was making me feel.

Then I sucked in a breath, and the oxygen reached my brain at last, reminding me that Ben was my assistant, and I shouldn't be making out with him. Not even on vacation.

"Cooper?" His voice sounded just as drugged as I'd felt a second before.

"We have to stop."

"You should stop thinking. Just feel." He swayed toward me.

"I can't." As gently as I could, I shifted him to the side and scooted a few feet away on the step. I leaned my elbows on my knees and scrubbed my face. "I need to—"

"Process this?" His voice caressed my taut nerves.

My hands still covering my face, I shook my head. "I need to call Human Resources."

"The fuck you do."

Had Ben ever cursed at me before? "Of course I do. I just kissed my assistant."

"No. You kissed me. Ben." He touched my hand.

Shivers rocketed through me. I was a hair's breadth away from kissing him again. And I couldn't. For more reasons than I could tell him. I had to shut this down.

I lifted my face to look at him and gave him my hardest stare. "This is a pattern of behavior for which I should be disciplined."

"A pattern?" He scrunched his nose.

I kept my voice diamond-hard as the stars glittering above us. "Did Marlee tell you I kissed her last year?"

That was the day I'd realized Jackson wasn't mine anymore. He and I were drunk at his annual Halloween party, the one that differed from all the rest because he'd cohosted it with Alicia, not with me. And then he'd told me he loved his unborn fetus more than he loved me.

When Marlee had rubbed my back and tried to make me feel better, I'd taken advantage of her kind heart and tried to take the comfort I'd needed from her.

I was a fucking asshole.

And here I was, doing it again.

Ben's face went comically slack. I'd have laughed if I weren't drowning in a tarpit of my own self-loathing.

"I'm a predator, Ben. I'll call HR tomorrow. They'll need a statement from you, too."

That lush mouth of his thinned and hardened. "I'll give my statement in person when we get back to the office."

"Fine. You can leave first thing tomorrow morning." I stood, and the water cascaded from me. I didn't have to worry about what I looked like in my clinging underwear. My dick had gone soft, the opposite of my heart.

Ben stood, too. "I'm not leaving this island without you, Mr. Fallon."

Did I say I was soft? Because as soon as the word *Mr.* left his lips, I stiffened. I sloshed out of the pool and kept my back to him. "I'm not going back. I—I can't. I'll email a statement to HR. The jet will be ready to take you back by eight tomorrow morning."

"Is this because of Jackson?" His voice cracked on my friend's name.

"It is." Synergy wouldn't be the same without my best friend. What was the point of all the wealth I'd amassed if I hated going to work every day? "I'll ensure your job is safe." *And that you're safe from me.*

"Fine." His voice vibrated with anger. I heard his whispered, "Fuck you, Cooper Fallon," just before his feet slapped away on the pool deck.

Good.

Perfect.

Just what I wanted.

And the next day, to keep myself from thinking about what I'd lost, I'd go to the next town over where they didn't know not to sell me whiskey.

19

BEN

FUCKING COOPER FALLON.

How dare he? How fucking *dare* he kiss me and then use that gorgeous mouth of his to talk about his feelings for Jackson Jones? I scuffed my Converse, and a shell went pinging off a tree trunk.

Fucking Jackson Jones. He had a brilliant wife and two wonderful kids, a shit-ton of money, a job where he could do exactly what he wanted. And he had Cooper's heart.

He didn't even fucking want it.

But I did.

Fuck me.

My wet underwear lodged in my ass crack. I hadn't noticed it when I'd floated in Cooper's pool and kissed his soft lips and felt the barest brush of his erection against my hip. He tasted like mint, and he smelled like the fulfillment of my every wish. But I noticed the irritation as I trudged along the shell path, humiliation crushing my lungs as my wet clothes clung to my skin.

He'd kissed me. And it meant nothing, just like when he'd kissed Marlee.

He'd kissed *Marlee?* I'd known when I started that she thought she was in love with him. I'd also known he wasn't the slightest bit interested in her.

I loved Marlee, but, God, she could be so dense sometimes. Cooper was all wrong for her. And now I'd been just as dense. I'd thought he cared. He'd proved me wrong.

I was done making a fool of myself. I was going to pack my shit and wait at the airport. As soon as Emily was ready to go, I'd take my ass back to California. Why the fuck did I care what Cooper did with his stock shares? He was a grown-ass adult and could take care of himself.

And even though I'd acted like a teenager with a pathetic crush, I was a grown-ass adult, too. I'd pick up my bruised heart, rub some dirt on it, and be fine.

Eventually.

Coco growled.

I stopped on the path because he'd stopped, too, facing back toward Cooper's place. "No, buddy. We're not going back there. You don't have to growl at him anymore. We're done with him."

In fact—fuck. I squatted on the path and stroked Coco's fur that still smelled like chamomile, no matter how many times he'd tried to roll it off on the sand. "I can't take you with me. There's probably some paperwork and shots and shit, and, besides, Mimi's allergic, and her place doesn't allow pets." I cleared my throat and rubbed behind his ears the way he liked. "You'd better trot off now."

Coco pretended he hadn't heard me and stared back toward Cooper's place. I shouldn't have expected him to understand.

I scanned the dark path and saw nothing. When I listened, all I heard was the sound of the surf. Even the frogs had quieted. I pulled out my phone and flicked on the flashlight app. Nothing but the path and the bushes that lined it.

"See, Coco, nothing to be scared—oh."

There was a text alert. I flicked off the flashlight and opened the text.

Mimi: How's it going?

Fucking terrible, especially after I kissed him. But I couldn't say that. She'd flip out. Remind me of all the reasons I shouldn't have followed him out to the pool, ogled him in his underwear, and then *actually joined him* in the pool. Much less kissed him. She didn't have to point out that I'd lost my heart again. To my boss. I winced.

I hadn't come to the island to kiss Cooper; I'd come to convince him to return to Synergy so people like Mimi could keep their jobs. And I'd failed. My stomach tightened.

Not so good. On my way home.

But Mimi had known me all my life.

Mimi: YOU FUCKING FELL FOR YOUR BOSS,
DIDN'T YOU?

It was an accident. But it's over now.

Mimi: WHAT'S over?

Everything

I could almost sense the I-told-you-so in her typing bubbles. But in the end, she was the big sister I'd always relied on.

Mimi: I'm sorry, sweetie. I'll stock up on chips
and chocolate, and you can watch as many
superhero movies as you want when you get
home.

Not even superhero movies could help this. I'd made a superhero of Cooper Fallon, but he'd shown he was exactly like all the other ordinary men I'd given my heart to, who'd tossed it right back at me.

I'd forgotten everything when I'd leaned so close I could smell the mint and his cedar cologne, see the bristles on his chin glowing silver in the moonlight. His blue eyes hadn't been icy. They were the color of the shallow water at the edge of the sand where minnows darted. The water that was warm against my skin, that sucked me out toward the depths.

I never should've followed him out to the pool. I should've known he'd go frosty on me. Clearly, I wasn't worth breaking HR rules for. I'd known it since that first day I'd walked into Synergy and shaken his hand. That flare of blue that had flickered in his eyes before he shut me out. When he finally came back to Synergy, we'd go back to normal and pretend I didn't know he tasted like mint and the syrupy remains of my crush.

When I got home, Mimi would cuddle me close, handing me salt, sugar, tissues. For someone who never let herself do anything as ridiculous as fall in love, she had an uncanny sense for what would cure my broken heart. I couldn't wait to see her.

See you soon

Before I even swiped away the text app, Coco erupted in barking a second before something heavy crashed into me.

My ankle twisted, wobbled, and gave out, and I collapsed, my cheek digging into the shell path with my attacker weighing on my back. He—it was definitely a man, not an extra-large iguana or a peccary—pinned me with his arms.

I'd managed to fall on top of my bag. Was my laptop okay? Was I going to lose a semester's worth of coursework? My heart jackrabbited. What if he wanted to steal it? I'd never pass my class then, and if I didn't pass, Synergy didn't pay. *Fuck.* I tried to shield the bag from the big guy.

When he spoke, the scent of rum hugged my cheek like a wet washcloth. "Go home," he growled.

What the hell?

I could hardly speak, unable to get a full breath with the huge guy on top of me. "I was. Going home." I tried to point with my chin toward the other wing of the resort, past the busy restaurant that was still too far away to hear me shout and too loud to hear Coco's frantic barks.

"No." He felt down my arm to my wrist and grabbed it, twisting it behind my back. Pain jabbed through my shoulder and my wrist. "Go back. To California. Or else."

How the ever-loving hell did he know I lived in California? My heartbeat sped to a hummingbird tempo. What else did he know about me? Did he know Mimi was alone at her place now? Did he know Cooper was back in his bungalow with some very expensive tech and a watch that cost more than a car? Suddenly, my laptop seemed like a fair exchange for this guy to get off me and trundle back to whatever bar he'd come from.

He twisted my arm again, and I gasped at the stab of pain.

But so did he. And then he howled, and the weight on my back rolled to the side, one last lance of pain stabbing my shoulder before he released his grip.

I scrambled to my feet—or tried to. My ankle ignited when I put weight on it. I leaned against a tree for relief, but pain shot through my shoulder. Fuck!

Still, I was in better shape than the dude on the ground. He flailed his arms toward Coco, who had a death grip on his leg. One of his ham hands smacked the back of Coco's head, but the dog didn't budge. If we didn't get out of there, both of us were going to end up seriously injured.

I pushed off the tree and limped a few feet toward Cooper's bungalow. "Coco, let go. Come."

Did feral dogs know commands? Did Coco speak English? I hobbled another step and gestured with my not-aching arm. "Come, Coco."

Releasing the man's leg, he leaped over him and bounded ahead of me on the path to Cooper's, barking an alarm. The man moaned, but no way was I going back to check on him. I limped behind Coco as fast as I could. Why hadn't I thought to pick up some mace after the TSA confiscated mine at the airport?

The island had seemed so safe. The resort staff looked out for me. And I hadn't seen so much as a panhandler since I'd left the city with the airport. This beautiful island where even the wild dogs were friendly had lulled me into a false sense of security.

Either I hadn't realized how far I'd gotten from Cooper's or my slow pace made the path stretch out into eternity. It seemed to take hours to get back to his place. Every few steps, I turned my head to peer over my shoulder to see if the attacker was following, but I saw nothing. Heard nothing but the sound of the surf and the chirp of the coquis.

At last, Cooper's house came into view. Coco scratched at the front door, and it opened just as I dragged my aching leg up the step.

"Ben!" Cooper had changed into pajama pants, leaving the golden skin and the dark-honey hair of his chest exposed. "What's wrong?"

I glanced behind me one more time and, seeing no movement from the path, hobbled the last few steps toward Cooper. My ankle, having gotten me this far, finally gave up, and I fell forward into him. He caught me, scooped an arm under my knees, and carried me inside.

I may have swooned.

20

COOPER

"BEN!" My heart hammered in my chest, beating through my ribs to get to the man on the couch. "Ben!" I knelt on the floor beside where he lay.

"I'm here," he said, like I was the one who needed reassurance.

I did need reassurance. When he blinked open his eyes, I started to breathe again.

His cheek was red and abraded, and pieces of crushed shell stuck to his skin. When I touched his shoulder, he winced. I shoved both hands between my knees. "What happened?"

"Big, burly guy jumped me. No idea why. My laptop?"

"It's here." I nodded at the coffee table where it lay.

"And Coco?"

The damned dog had sneaked inside and now sat on the other side of me, his chin resting on Ben's knee. "He's here, too."

"He saved me. Bit the guy." Ben's eyelids fluttered closed.

I glanced back at the dog. He had the nerve to raise his eyebrows, accusing me of negligence while he'd leaped to Ben's rescue.

"Good dog," I muttered.

"Ice?" Ben asked.

"Of course." I stood and strode to the kitchen, glad to be useful. "Does your face hurt?"

"Not as much as my ankle or my shoulder."

I froze in the middle of finding a dishtowel. "Your ankle and your shoulder?"

"Twisted them."

Fuck. All my attention had been on Ben's face. I hurriedly folded ice into two towels and carried them back to the sofa. I eased off Ben's sneaker. His right ankle swelled. I laid one ice pack over it and the other on the shoulder that had pained him when I'd touched it.

"Okay? Need anything else for a minute?"

His eyes fluttered open, and he squinted in the lamplight. Jesus, did he have a concussion?

"No, I'm okay."

"I'm just going to make a couple of calls." I didn't dare leave him. What if he passed out and rolled off the couch? What if he needed to throw up? I paced a few feet away and called Sara.

She answered in Spanish. "Lito! Tía Camelia told Mamá you were here! Why haven't you come to see us? Sunday. After church —you're coming to Mass, yes?—come for dinner. Papa wants to ask you—"

"Listen, Sara." My Spanish was low and urgent. "I need you. My friend is hurt. Can you come check on him?"

"Hurt? How?" In the background, I heard rustling. If I knew my cousin Sara, she was already grabbing her medical bag.

"Shoulder and ankle injuries. I haven't looked at them yet. And cuts on his face."

"Got it. I'll be there in ten."

"Thank you."

I walked back to Ben. The dog moved closer and sniffed his face. Just as I reached them, the dog's pink tongue snaked out and lapped Ben's cheek.

"Ugh!" I nudged the dog with my knee until he scuttled a few feet away. "I'll get a washcloth and clean you up."

Ben's lips pressed together. Fuck, he was in pain, and it was my fault. I'd sent him out alone in the dark. Shooting a warning glare at the dog, I went to the bathroom for a washcloth. I let the water run until it warmed and thought about my next call.

A minute later, I shoved the dog off Ben again and kneeled at his side. As gently as I could, I patted at the cuts on his cheek. "Did you get a good look at the guy?"

"No. He came at me from behind. He'd been drinking, though. Rum. And he sounded American. I couldn't hear an accent. Though he didn't say much. He was big. He had to be twice my size."

"Tall?"

"Not as tall as you, just bulky. Knocked the wind out of me when he fell on me."

"Do you feel up to talking to Luis? He might remember him from the bar."

"Okay, sure."

I called Luis. When he picked up, I heard talking and music in the background.

"No, Cooper, I'm not bringing you any booze."

"Not what I was going to ask. Can you go somewhere quiet? This is important."

I could picture the surprise on his face, but after a few minutes, a door clicked shut and muted the background noise.

"Thanks, Luis. Someone attacked Ben tonight on his way back to his room. I'm going to put you on speaker so he can tell you about it."

I set the phone on the coffee table. As Ben told his story, my fists clenched tighter until my fingernails left red crescents in my palms.

"Wait," I said. "He told you to go back to California?"

"Yeah, that's weird, right?" Ben said. "How did he know that's where I'm from?"

I glared at the phone. "Maybe he works for the resort."

"Without a description, it's hard to tell," Luis said. "I employ a lot of big, burly guys. Listen, I'll call Mateo."

"Not Mateo," I growled. "Send Ramón. Or come yourself."

"Cooper, it's Friday night. We have two bachelorette parties and a gang of overprivileged college kids. And Ramón has the night off. Mateo will take care of you."

I snorted. It wasn't me I was worried about. It was Ben. I didn't want Mateo anywhere near him. "He stays outside. Out of the way."

"Of course. Ben, you'll be all right?"

A rap came at the door, and I scooped up the phone and turned off the speakerphone on my way to answer it. "Sara's here. He'll be fine. But have someone bring his things to my place. In the morning is fine."

"He's staying with you?" A smile curled into his voice.

"He's staying with me."

"Gracias a Dios."

"Fuck off." I disconnected the call.

When I opened the door, Sara bustled in with her bag. She kissed my cheek on her way to the couch.

She squatted next to Ben. "Good evening. I'm Dr. Sara Castillo."

"Ben Levy-Walters." He held out his hand, and she shook it.

"I'm going to wash my hands, and then, if it's okay with you, I'll check your injuries while you tell me what happened."

Ben nodded.

Instead of going straight to the bathroom to wash, Sara gripped me by the arm and led me to the sliding glass door to the deck. "Cooper, wait out here."

"Wait, what?" I glanced back at Ben.

"I need him to feel safe."

"But I—" I snapped open the slider and pulled her out with me. When the door closed, I said, "You don't think *I* did this to him?"

"Intimate partner violence is a very real thing, Cooper."

Didn't I know it. My voice rose. "He was attacked. He came here for help. And he's *not* my intimate partner. He is my employee. You don't think I'd ever—"

"I want to listen to him. And you need to wait out here. With your dog."

I looked down, and she was right. The dog sat at my feet. "Fine." I flung myself into a deck chair. "Just—just take care of him. Okay?"

"Of course. He means a lot to you, doesn't he?"

I glanced through the glass. Ben looked small and fragile on the sofa. His cheek had swollen. The lies I'd told him earlier no longer mattered. "He does."

"I'll take excellent care of him." She turned on her heel and walked back inside.

After she left, I couldn't stay still. I paced around the pool, glaring at the moon's shimmering reflection in the water. My own cousin thought I could've injured Ben. Preposterous. Though… hadn't I tried to push him away for exactly that reason? Out of fear that I would hurt him?

I wouldn't hurt him. Or would I? He'd come to me for protection. He wouldn't do that if he thought I was a danger to him.

Of course, he didn't know my father. No one thought Mick Fallon would hurt anyone, either.

"Psst. Lito."

I whipped my head toward the gate, where my cousin Mateo pressed his face against the metal bars.

My muscles tensed. I forced my feet to carry me to the gate.

"Luis gave me a keycard"—he waved it in the hand that wasn't holding a suitcase—"but I didn't want to surprise you. You okay?"

"I'm fine." I pushed open the gate and held out my hand for the suitcase.

Mateo had the nerve to look hurt. "No hug for your cousin?"

"No."

He passed over the suitcase. "You're not still mad about—"

"No." Of course I was. Just seeing his handsome face and those Caribbean-blue eyes reminded me of how he used to look dancing with my date every time we went out together.

"What about—"

"No. You stay outside. Call me if you see anyone suspicious."

"Outside? I can't even sit on your deck?"

"No."

"He's someone special, isn't he?" Those blue eyes gleamed in the moonlight.

"Yes. Stay away from him."

"Cooper, I'm not sixteen anymore. I'd never—"

I turned on my heel and hefted Ben's suitcase toward the house. Hadn't I said the same thing? *I'd never hurt him.*

I didn't trust Mateo, but maybe I could trust myself. I'd protect Ben with every resource available to me on the island. Down to my last breath.

BEN

AFTER I EMAILED my final econ paper to my professor, I sighed and closed my laptop.

I reached for my phone on the coffee table. I couldn't delay reading Marlee's texts any longer.

> Marlee: Morning, Ben
>
> Marlee: What's the latest on Cooper?
>
> Marlee: Seriously, what's going on?
>
> Marlee: Is he OK? When is he coming back? Everyone's hounding me about it because Weston won't say.
>
> Marlee: There are rumors, Ben. Employee lists being sent around. I'm worried.
>
> Marlee: STOP IGNORING ME

I winced when I read that. Poor Marlee was holding everything together back at the office while I rested on Cooper's extremely comfortable sofa.

She was right. I had to ask him when he was going back. It had been immature of me to consider going home without him, or at least finding out the end date to this vacation of his. Work had to be piling up for him. My hurt feelings shouldn't prevent me from doing my job.

I promise I'll talk to him today

Besides, employee lists? What was Weston up to?

Past the pillows Cooper had used that morning to elevate my tape-wrapped ankle, through the back windows and the bars of the gate, Mateo's cigarette flared. He'd talk to me. Unlike Cooper, who'd disappeared. Again.

I'd stayed in Cooper's bungalow for two days. Three nights. And when I say *in Cooper's bungalow,* I mean *inside* his bungalow. No trips to the restaurant, no walks on the beach. Not even dinner on the deck.

It was like being in prison. A beautiful prison with a kindly warden who brought me water and guava juice while I lounged on his sofa, who handed me painkillers with the precision of the Queen's Guard.

And each night after he helped me to bed in his guest room, he patted me on the shoulder, flicked off the lights, and walked out.

Not even as much as a fatherly kiss on the temple.

At least he hadn't made good on his promise to call HR—yet. And he'd sent the jet away.

I was burning from the inside out from being so close to him and yet...not. It was like being back in the office again, nothing like the closeness we'd shared when we had dinner on his patio or when we went to visit his tía Camelia. Before we'd kissed in his pool. Except for when he accidentally brushed my skin when he wrapped my ankle, our no-touching rule was back in effect.

It was for the best if I was just another Marlee to him, a fleeting bad decision because he couldn't have Jackson.

When Mateo's cigarette glowed red again, I eased myself off

the couch and limped to the sliding glass door. I slid it open and, just like always, Coco sat inside the gate staring adoringly up at Mateo. He was still pissed off at me for telling him I was leaving him here. He was even more pissed off at Cooper for sending me away that night.

But Cooper's cousin Mateo was his new favorite. And why shouldn't he be? Mateo was almost Cooper's match in every way. They were about the same height, though Mateo was a bit bulkier. His bluer eyes and darker hair were like Cooper turned up a notch. Someone else might think Mateo was more attractive. To me, he looked like an Instagram post with the color saturation turned too high. I preferred Cooper's more muted good looks. Coco, on the other hand, adored Mateo because he always had a morsel of ham in his pocket.

I limped to the gate. Mateo stubbed out his cigarette against the metal. "You won't tell Cooper, will you?"

"About the smoking? Depends." I leaned my shoulder—the one that wasn't sore—against the gate.

I hadn't yet figured out the dynamic between the cousins. He'd shown up sometime during the night of my attack. He never came inside the house. Every time Cooper was cold and dismissive toward him, Mateo looked like a kicked puppy. But when Cooper was gone, Mateo flirted in a way Cooper never did.

"Have you seen him? The guy?" I asked.

"Hard to say." One corner of his mouth twitched up. "There's a lot of big, bulky guys on this island with American accents." He gestured at himself.

I bit my lip. "If you'd jumped me, I think I'd know it."

"Would you, now?" He took a step closer, but then he caught himself and shoved his hands into his pockets.

I sighed. Why couldn't I fall for someone sweet and flirty like Mateo? He'd never freeze me out. "Where'd Cooper go?"

"Community center."

Of course he had. Better to toil and sweat at the jobsite than to remain in my presence. Well, fuck that. I was done sitting around like an invalid. My ankle hardly hurt anymore, and it was time to suck it up and do my fucking job.

"Drive me there."

"Not happening. Cooper said you stay here."

I raised my eyebrows. "What if I tell him you were smoking on his property?"

His flirty smile disappeared. "You wouldn't."

"Not if you take me to him."

"And I thought you were nice," he grumbled. He tugged a set of car keys from his pocket. "Lock the slider and meet me at the front door. I'll pull the car around."

I hid my grin. "See you out front."

I limped back inside, locked the back door, and stuffed my slightly swollen foot into my sneaker. The other shoe slid right on. Then I let Coco out the front door and locked it behind me. Mateo held open the back door of a big, black SUV, parked in the circle drive.

It wasn't far to the community center, but Mateo made me promise three times to tell Cooper I'd forced him to take me. I patted his shoulder. "I'll take all the blame. He'll only be mad at me."

"Mad at you?" he scoffed. "Never. You're su novio."

"Novio? I'm not his boyfriend." But my face heated.

"Could've fooled me." He pulled around the trucks parked at the site, right in front of the building.

My gaze arrowed straight to Cooper. They had him applying another coat of stucco. As unhappy as he looked about the stucco, his eyes went even darker when he spotted Mateo reaching into the car to help me out.

"What the fuck, Mateo?" His trowels clattered to the grass as he strode toward us.

I clung to Mateo's shoulder until I was steady. Then I crossed my arms and looked Cooper straight in the eye. He had pink dust on his shirt and in his hair, even stuck to the stubble on his cheeks. "This is on me, not him. We need to talk."

Cooper narrowed his eyes at his cousin. Mateo's cheeks went blotchy red. "I'll, ah, finish that stucco for you," he said. "It has to be done in one application." He skulked toward the building, rolling up the sleeves of his linen shirt.

"Let's go sit in the shade," I said, pointing to the trees where I'd camped out last time. "You probably haven't had a break all day."

He shook his head, and I knew he wasn't admitting he hadn't had a break. He was denying he was human enough to need one.

"Are you all right?" He scanned me from the middle of my chest to my feet, avoiding my eyes the way he'd done since we kissed that night.

"I'm fine. Synergy isn't." I took a few limping steps toward the trees—my ankle was stiff after sitting in the car—but Cooper wedged his shoulder under mine, supporting me until we sat in the shade. He reached into the cooler and handed me a bottle of water, then he took one for himself.

"We have to talk about the company. They need you back there."

He chugged his water, staring so intently at the building he could've burned a hole in the stucco. He wiped his mouth with his fingers. "Who needs me back?"

"Well, Marlee, for starters." But I had to go for broke. "And J-Jackson."

"Jackson does not need me." His jaw twitched.

"Of course he does. He can't stand up to Weston without you."

"He doesn't need to stand up to Harris. He's getting out. Besides, Harris can handle things until I'm ready to go back. And I'm not ready yet."

"Are you sure?" Although Harris Weston gave me the creeps, he'd been around a lot longer than I had. Cooper looked up to him. And Cooper was a smart man.

"Positive. He's been the leader Synergy needed since the early days. He's never led me wrong."

"But Marlee didn't say anything about Jackson leaving the

company." What would she do if he did? Probably spend all of her time coding rather than babysitting fucking Jackson Jones. She'd never admit it, but she'd be better off without him.

He shrugged. "She might not know. I didn't tell you when I sold my shares. There are rules about what insiders can disclose."

A tiny pain erupted in my chest. Finding out from lurking in his goddamn email had sucked. "Would you tell me if you decided to sell more?"

He turned his head to look at me then. Below the flecks of pink dust in his eyebrows, his eyes softened. "I don't think I could give you advance warning. Not without violating some federal laws and our own code of ethics."

"Oh." I scuffed my sneaker against the spiky grass. "Would you tell Jackson?"

He huffed out a laugh. "Maybe I should've since he's my business partner and my friend."

"But that's not all." I winced, wishing I could take back the words.

"What's not all?"

Why had I said that? I'd crossed about a zillion lines. He could fire me for what I'd implied.

He waited.

"I just meant—" Fuck, there was no good way to say it. I might as well type up my résumé. But I'd gone too far. "I meant that you care about him."

His expression blanked. "Of course I care about him. He's my best friend."

The pain in my chest popped whatever had been holding my anger inside me. "Friends? I think it's more than that." If my ankle were stronger, I'd have jumped up and stalked off. Instead, I sat fuming at my Chucks.

Cooper's voice was gentler than I'd ever heard it. "Does that bother you, Ben?"

He didn't even try to deny it. "Yeah, it does! He has everything! A wife and a family and you. Lucky bastard." I hissed the last bit. I was so fired, but I couldn't help it. I'd let my heart get outside my chest again.

"Are you…are you jealous, Ben?"

"Of course I fucking am! I care about you more than he ever will! Why else do you think I kissed you the other night? Did you think I'd make a career-ending move like that if I wasn't head over heels for you?"

"Head over heels?"

Now he was laughing at me. Cooper Fallon was a lot of things, but cruel wasn't usually one of them. I guessed an unwanted confession of love would do that to a person. I could never look him in the eye again.

I could never work in the office with him, either. Not with *head over heels* floating between us like one of Coco's cheese farts.

I scrambled to my feet, ignoring the twinge in my ankle. "You know what? Forget it. I quit."

I took two wobbly steps toward the SUV. Not that I had the keys or any way to get back to Cooper's place. Or to the airport, which was where I really needed to go.

"Whoa." With two good ankles, he was a lot faster than me, and he gripped my arms firmly but also gently. He came around to block me from the car.

"I'm no good for you, Ben. You know that."

"I don't know that. Or I didn't before you—you—"

"Hurt you?" His eyes flicked between mine.

"More like I hurt myself." I slumped. "Wanting something I could never hope to have."

"Never hope? No, Ben. I care about you. More than I should. You deserve so much more than me."

I looked him dead in the eye. "Don't you think I should be the judge of what I deserve and what I want?"

"I—I guess you should."

"Then I want you." Time to go for broke. I drew myself up. "I deserve you."

"Ben, I—" He tightened his grip on my arms and then released me. "Were you really serious about quitting?"

"Absolutely." No matter what happened now, I couldn't go back to my polite *Mr. Fallons* and the no-touching rule. Not since I kissed him. Not after I told him I deserved his affection.

Quitting my job meant there were no more barriers between us. "I could find another job easier than I could find another Cooper Fallon."

"You're officially resigning?"

Hope flared in my chest. "I'll type up an email as soon as I get back to my laptop."

"So, since you're no longer my employee…" Slipping one arm around my back, he tunneled his hand into my hair then crashed his lips onto mine.

My pulse roared in my ears so loud I almost didn't hear the hoots from the crew and Mateo's "Finally!"

But I didn't care about them. All I cared about was the man holding me in his arms and kissing the hell out of me.

22

COOPER

WHEN BEN EMERGED from his room, I couldn't help it. My jaw dropped. I supposed so even my wisdom teeth could ogle him.

He wore a black T-shirt that hugged every lean muscle. His jeans? I gulped. If he'd pulled up his shirt, I could've told you whether he was circumcised. He'd mentioned his family observed Jewish traditions, so he had to be.

Not that I'd seen it. We'd kissed a lot since yesterday on the jobsite, late into the night until we fell asleep cuddled on the couch. Another makeout session after breakfast. But every time his hand wandered to my waistband, I gently removed it. Seeing each other naked was a point of no return. Were we ready for that?

When he'd emailed me his resignation letter, it hadn't felt right. He seemed happy enough about it, but I worried. What would happen if this thing we were trying out together didn't last? Then he'd be out of both a relationship and a job. Would he take money from me to get back on his feet after? I suspected he wouldn't. He hadn't taken money from his parents when he dropped out of college. Ben Levy-Walters was a proud man.

I should have been the one to make the sacrifice, to resign. Though resigning was a bigger step for me. It required succession plans and transitions. No matter how much I'd wanted to do it when I first got to the island, I couldn't simply walk away. The people who worked for Synergy—who were my responsibility as COO—deserved more.

I half-wished Ben were still one of those people. He'd be so much easier to protect as an employee than as my lover.

And that's why, ignoring how much I wanted to explore every inch of his skin, to learn his tastes, his scents, to hear the sounds he'd make when he was desperate with arousal, I'd kept two barriers between us, and one of them was our clothes.

This morning, when his eyes turned molten and golden and he inched his hand up my thigh, I went for a run where he couldn't follow with his sprained ankle. After lunch, I went to the weight room.

But now he'd found me on the couch. And he looked like *that*.

"Get dressed." It was the ever-so-slightly snappish voice he used in the office when I was running behind schedule and needed to make a meeting or a flight. The voice that made me want to delay a bit longer so he'd use it again.

"Dressed?" I set my laptop aside, the one with the second sell order pulled up. Once I executed it, I'd still be a major stockholder, but Jackson would have all the control. He could decide if he wanted to stay or wash his hands of the company—and me. I hadn't been able to click the button to execute the trade yet. Every time my finger hovered over the trackpad, it started to itch.

"We're going out. Wear your suit pants and that charcoal dress shirt. No tie."

My breath stuttered. "Out?"

"You've kept me in this house for three days. As much as I like you, I need to see other humans."

"But what if that guy—"

"Mateo hasn't seen anyone. It was a random attack, and that guy is long gone. Look." He propped his hands on his hips. "I've given you time to process. And if you've decided you don't want to do this with me, that's okay. Just tell me now."

"No, I—I do. You resigned, for Christ's sake."

"I know." His lush mouth compressed into a thin line. "Don't make me regret it."

I stood and paced to the slider on the pretext of letting Coco outside. Dutifully, he trotted through the door to visit the bougainvillea.

My back to Ben, I asked, "Do you regret it? Because I haven't forwarded your resignation letter to human resources yet." The other barrier.

"Why the hell not? I'm all in. Unless you're not?"

I whirled to face him. I hated the uncertainty in his voice. Uncertainty that I'd put there. "I'm in."

"Then get dressed. We're going dancing. With Ramón and some of the other guys here at the resort."

"Dancing?" I stared at his ankle. His skintight jeans flowed smoothly over it, hiding any swelling. "You can hardly walk. How are you going to dance?"

The twinkle in those whiskey eyes was wicked. "I don't dance with my feet, Cooper."

Fuck. Now all I could imagine was the undulation of Ben's hips. My throat went dry and, like a robot, I marched to my room and put on exactly what he'd told me to. I brushed my teeth and shaved for the second time that day.

I nicked my jaw when I made the mistake of remembering how Ben looked in his jeans. He didn't have to wear those tight clothes for me. I salivated over him in his bright golf shirts and Bermudas. I dabbed at the cut with a tissue. Besides, I danced only when I had to. The last time had been at Jackson's wedding in the fall. With Marlee, after our toast. And with Jamila. I couldn't remember the last time I'd danced with someone I was desperate to fuck.

I finished shaving and put some cream in my hair to smooth it. The shaving nick had closed up, and I looked like I was ready for a casual-Friday meeting at the office. Not at all like a man who went to clubs and fucking danced. Were those *gray hairs* at my temple? Thank God I hadn't let this…this whatever-it-was go any further. Ben could still reconsider.

I stomped out of the master suite to stand in front of Ben where he perched on a barstool at the kitchen counter, flicking through his phone. When he looked up, I held out my arms. "Do I meet your approval?" I spun in a circle.

When I faced him again, he was biting his lip. "Absolutely, Mr. Fallon."

I supposed that was one advantage of Ben's tight pants. A snugger fit to mine would have kept my dick from bulging away from my leg. I turned away to hide my reaction and texted Mateo to bring the car around.

Ben must have taken care of it already because when Mateo pulled up a minute later in one of Luis's SUVs, Ramón was already in the front passenger seat. He descended from the car and offered Ben his place. I wedged my long legs into the third row of seats next to Ramón. The middle row was occupied by a trio I recognized as two of Luis's waiters and a bartender.

Mateo met my gaze in the rearview mirror and raised his eyebrows. I didn't like the idea of any of this—Ben sitting next to my flirty cousin, going to a club where I wouldn't drink, and watching Ben dance—but I nodded anyway. If this was what Ben wanted, I'd give it to him.

Twenty minutes later, Mateo pulled up in front of a club in the city, and we all followed Ben inside. I hadn't been to a club in years, not since Jackson stopped inviting me, but it was the same as I remembered. Loud music and lights that flashed to the beat, which settled right at my temples. Ramón led the way to a reserved table near the dance floor. A banquette curved around the round table, and Ben wiggled in between Mateo and me.

The waiter brought an iced bucket of bottled water, a fifth of rum, and seven glasses. When he tipped the bottle toward the glass in front of me, I laid my hand over the rim. "None for me, thanks."

Mateo grinned and shouted, "Does that mean you're the designated driver?"

My flirty cousin, rum, and Ben? No, thanks. I scowled. "No. You're driving."

When he pouted, I added, "This is for Isaac."

"Isaac." He sat back and stared at the pattern of colored lights on the ceiling. "That tiny, yellow Speedo."

"That's the one." I tipped a bottle of water toward him, and he tapped his own to it. We drank to the first date he'd stolen from me.

Ben watched the exchange with avid interest. Then he grinned. "Nope, I'm not sitting between two sober guys." He half-stood and squirmed across my lap.

My fingers stretched toward Ben's hips like they wanted to pin him onto my lap. And for a hopeful second, I thought he paused to perch there. But the next second, he plopped onto the banquette between Bobby the bartender and me.

He didn't stay there for long. Once he'd downed a glass of rum, Ben scooted out onto the dance floor. And he was right. His feet hardly moved. His shoulders, abdominals, and hips did all the work, a hypnotic gyration that drew more than one person into orbit around him.

Tall, lanky guys and stout ones. Fair-skinned and dark. Guys who dressed up in buttoned-up shirts like me and guys who dressed down in T-shirts and strategically ripped jeans. Even a couple of shirtless guys with harnesses across their chests and teeny-tiny latex shorts. Ben danced with them all, but never for more than a song or two.

Jesus, how I wished I could be one of them. That I could stand behind him and sway my hips with his. Trace the contours of his chest.

But that wasn't me. I was the protector, not the party animal. And the person Ben needed protection from most? Me.

I pulled a cold bottle of water from the tub and held it against my throbbing temple.

Ramón slid back into the banquette. I hadn't noticed whom he'd been dancing with; my gaze had centered—still centered—only on Ben, who'd borrowed a lime-green bowler from his current dance partner and was gazing up at him from under the brim.

Ramón poured a finger of rum into a glass and sipped it. "I haven't had a chance to thank you yet. For the stock."

I ripped my gaze away from Ben to look at Ramón. "You're welcome. I keep my promises, even the ones I make when I'm drunk."

He nodded and sipped his drink again. "He's waiting for you, you know."

"Who's waiting for me?"

He tipped his chin toward the dance floor. Ben stared at me from under the green hat. His hips circled, and in my imagination, they pumped against mine. It stole my breath.

Without breaking our stare, he lifted the hat from his head and tossed it to the other man. His dark curls reflected the red and blue of the multicolored house lights. Ben lifted his chin, daring me to join him on the dance floor.

I trailed my gaze over him. His shirt stuck to him now, and the front of it had ridden up to show a sliver of his flat belly above the waistband of his skintight jeans. The club's spotlights flitted over him, revealing flashes of his taut thighs, the curve of his ass, even for a tantalizing second the outline of a ridge that stretched from his crotch toward his hipbone.

Helpless to resist, I slid to the edge of the banquette and swam toward him through the dancers like a fish on a line. I stepped into his space, close enough that he bent his neck to look up at my face. I stood still while he swayed in front of me.

"Aren't you going to dance?" He had to shout so I could hear him over the music, and his voice was already hoarse.

"I don't dance."

"Of course you do. I heard you danced with Marlee at—once."

"Not like this." I flicked my hand at the mass of whirling dancers.

"It's not complicated. I'll teach you." He set his hands on my hips and tried to rock them from side to side. I didn't budge. I was far too solid for that.

He raised his eyebrows. "No?"

"No."

His eyes glinted golden. "Then we'll try it like this."

He turned his back toward me and shoved his ass into my groin, knocking me off balance just enough that I reached out instinctively and grabbed his hips. They swayed, and like we were glued together, mine followed.

He looked at me over his shoulder. "See? Nice and easy."

There was nothing nice about the way my dick hardened against his tight jeans. Or easy about the way my fingers dug into his hips, searching to anchor me in the twirling, confusing club.

It didn't matter that there were new silver threads in my hair. That I was stiff and gruff and wearing fucking business casual to a club. Inexplicably, Ben wanted me. It was evident in every grind of his ass against me, in the way he leaned his back into my chest. In the nip of his teeth against his lip. When I gripped his hips tighter, my right middle finger bumped something hard and heavy at the front of his jeans. Ben sucked in a breath.

He set his sweat-slicked hands over mine and curled his fingers. The next second, he executed a flowing move like he'd done it a thousand times. He lifted my hands from his hips and twirled so that we stood face to face, our hands clasped high above our heads.

His chest bumped mine, and my nipples hardened at the touch. My abs pressed against his stomach the way I wished my fingertips could. The bulge at the front of his jeans brushed against my erection as his hips pitched, and I shivered despite the heat of the club. Grinding his hips into mine, he moved closer and closer until his face hovered just a few inches below mine.

"Want to get out of here?" He spoke low. Even under the pounding rhythm of the music, I heard every word.

My throat too dry to speak, I nodded.

A cab ride and a text to Mateo later, we stepped into my house, my ears still ringing from the club.

Despite Ben's claim that his ankle would hold up to a night of dancing, he winced as he untied his dress shoes and set them next to the door.

"Sit on the couch and put your foot up. I'll make you an ice pack." I washed my hands at the kitchen sink.

"I don't want to put my foot up. I want—"

I speared him with the gaze that meant my word was final. "You will sit on the couch and rest your ankle."

"Yes, Mr. Fallon," he said breathlessly.

When he'd settled on the couch, his foot propped on the coffee table, I handed him a glass of water. I peeled off his sock and found the wrap cutting into his swollen foot. "Okay if I unwrap your foot?"

"Don't touch my foot. It's sweaty."

"I don't mind your sweat." In fact, I wanted to bury my nose in his chest and breathe in the sharp scent of it. Holding onto my control by a thread, I gently pulled the tape off his foot and laid the gel ice pack Sara had brought over his ankle.

"Better?" I asked.

One corner of his mouth crooked up. "Better."

I balled up the tape and took it to the kitchen to toss it in the trash. I washed my hands again and got my own glass of water.

In the living room, I hesitated. I should remove myself from temptation. I should go into my room and lock the door.

But what if Ben needed help to hobble into his room? I couldn't leave him alone.

Ben made up my mind for me. "Come here. Tell me what you thought about the club."

"It was a club, same as any other." I shrugged, trying to be nonchalant about it as I lowered myself to the coffee table in front of him.

"And the dancing?"

Remembering how he'd beckoned me to the floor, how our hips had bucked together, how he'd almost kissed me right there under the spinning lights, made my pants uncomfortably tight. I cleared my throat. "I liked it."

"I liked it, too." He levered forward and set his hand on my knee. Need traveled up my thigh straight to my groin and parked itself there, hot and heavy. My breath turned shallow.

"Those guys at the club were pretty hot. Especially the one with the hat."

He gave an exasperated snort. "Cooper Fallon, you're not as smart as you think you are if you think I was interested in anyone but you. I came home with exactly the person I wanted to." He trailed his hand higher up my thigh until he was a bare inch from my crotch. "Didn't you?"

The last thread of my control snapped. "Yes." I lunged forward, planted my hands on the back sofa cushion, and crashed my mouth into his. It wasn't soft or pretty. Our kiss was full of need, of the clacking of teeth, of the wrestling of our tongues, of the burn of his stubble against my lips. I flung one knee onto the couch outside his uninjured leg and rubbed my erection everywhere—his thigh, his hip—chasing the sensation from our dance.

He gripped the front of my shirt, bringing my chest closer to him. "Need you," he murmured between sucks on my tongue.

I froze. I hadn't done anything with another guy since high school. Since I'd met Jackson. Did I still remember how it worked? I didn't have lube or condoms or—

"Shh." He abandoned my mouth to kiss over to my ear. "We'll take it slow. I'll make you feel good."

I suppressed a shudder that started at the spot he'd kissed and crawled right down to the base of my spine. "You're hurt. I don't want to—"

"Nothing wrong with my mouth." I felt the wicked curl of it

against the skin of my neck. Then he pulled back. "Unless you don't want to?"

"No, of course I do. I—" I had to stop talking, or I'd say something I couldn't take back. Instead, I backed up to kneel between his legs. I rubbed my face across his sweat-dampened shirt and inhaled long to fill my lungs with the scent of him. With my nose, I drew a line down his stomach to his waistband. He smelled of sweat there, too, mixed with musky arousal. I flicked the button of his jeans and looked up into his face. "Can I?"

He chuckled. "I don't know if you can. It might take the jaws of life to get me out of these jeans."

I traced the ridge of his erection with a finger. It twitched under my touch.

"Sorry." He sucked in a breath. "I meant, yes, please."

I tugged down the zipper and found nothing but Ben underneath. "I believe appropriate undergarments are part of the dress code, Mr. Levy-Walters." But my breathy voice undercut the sternness of my words.

"There's nothing work-appropriate about my outfit tonight, Mr. Fallon."

I peeled the sides of his jeans apart until I freed his cock, darkly flushed and cut as I'd known it would be. I flattened my tongue against it and licked up from where it emerged from his pants all the way to the dusky tip.

He groaned. "If this is how you discipline someone for violating the dress code, I wish I'd shown up in the office without underwear every fucking day."

My fingers tightened on his pants. *The office.* There was no going back from sucking his cock.

Like he'd heard my thoughts, Ben curled his fingers into my hair and gently directed my gaze up to him. "Sorry. No more work talk. I've submitted my resignation. Tonight, you're my…lover."

"Lover?" Every inch of my skin tingled.

"It looks to me like you're about to suck my dick. So I think the term is appropriate, don't you?"

"And we're exclusive?"

His brow furrowed. "Of course. I only danced with those other guys because you wouldn't dance with me."

"But I did. Dance with you."

"You did." His expression went soft for a minute, but then he narrowed his eyes. "And now?"

"Now I'm going to suck your dick."

Gold flared in his eyes. "Yes, please."

It took some maneuvering to tug the jeans down his legs and off without hurting his swollen foot, but I managed it, and soon Ben was splayed out on the couch, naked except for his tight T-shirt. I started at the head of his cock, running my tongue along his slit and sucking the tip until I tasted the tang of his precum. I took him deeper, getting him good and wet and delivering long sucks to his shaft. He threw his head back against the cushions and moaned at that.

Power roared through me, better than when we'd hit a billion dollars in revenue. Better than when we'd hit five billion. All because of a moan.

I licked down to his balls, weighing them with my tongue. Gripping his length with my hand, I slid my fist up to the tip, twisted at the top, and descended. His sharp intake of breath showed I'd found something he liked.

I licked as far down as I could, but the couch prevented me from going farther. I'd explore more next time. Fuck. Next time. I ground my own erection against the sofa cushion. I sucked on his balls until they tightened.

"Gonna, gonna—" Ben croaked.

"Not yet." I squeezed the base of his dick, holding off his orgasm.

He bucked his hips. "I need—"

"I know. You're going to come in my mouth." I wanted to taste him, to feel him pulse inside me. To wreck him the way he was already wrecking me.

I swapped my mouth for my hand and took as much of his length as I could. With my hand, I massaged his balls. Then I gave him a long, hard suck.

His back bowed. "Yes, like that," he gasped.

I hollowed my cheeks around him and let him bump my throat until I gagged. Then I sucked again and again. Hard, then backing off, then hard again. He whined deep in the back of his throat, and it made me want to roar. Instead, I clutched his hip, pinning him to the cushion.

His balls tightened just before my mouth filled with his come. I rose along his length, sucking up every drop of his release, until he popped out, and I swallowed him down.

"Fuck," he groaned. One wrist covered his eyes. He looked completely wrecked, his cock softening against his thigh, his T-shirt rucked up over his navel. I wanted to dip my tongue into the divot. To taste every inch of his chest. Next time.

"Come on." I levered to my feet, tucked one arm under his knees, and wedged the other behind his back.

His eyes flew open. "Wait! What are you doing?"

"I'm putting you to bed. You look"—I smirked—"worn out." I lifted him to my chest.

"No, I'm fine. Give me a minute. Then I'll go down on you."

"No." I circled the coffee table and carried him sideways down the hall to avoid bumping his foot. "You're resting your ankle. In bed."

I didn't miss his shiver at the last word. "But I want to—"

"All in good time." I laid him on his bed and pulled the sheet over him. "Good-night."

I meant to leave a chaste peck on his lips, but he grabbed the back of my head and pulled me to him. The taste of him, mingled with the aftertaste of his come, tempted me to straddle him. To roll over and drag him over my face and see if I could make him climax again this soon. To feel his lips on me.

But I pulled away. His eyelids drooped, and I knew his ankle had to be throbbing.

I tapped his dose of painkiller from the bottle by the bed and handed the tablet to him. "See you in the morning."

He groaned but dutifully swallowed the pill and turned on his side. "Night, Cooper. Thanks for…for the dance."

Grinning, I sauntered out. Dancing had been a perfect way to spend the evening. And right then, I didn't care what changes the morning might bring.

$$23$$

BEN

WHEN I BLINKED my eyes open and saw the sunlight streaming in through the sheer curtains, I knew I'd fucked up.

I'd meant to get up at the crack of dawn, slip into Cooper's room, and wake him up with the blowjob I'd been too tired to give last night. Then—I smiled at the vision—we'd go back to sleep with him spooned around me.

Why hadn't my alarm gotten me up? I glanced at the bedside table, empty except for the bottle of painkillers and a glass of water.

Oh, right. My phone was in my jeans pocket, and my jeans were still crumpled on the floor in the living room where Cooper Fallon had blown my mind. I shivered, remembering what his blue eyes had looked like between my thighs, how perfect his sexy lips had felt stretched around my dick.

It was totally worth quitting my job.

After I finally convinced him to go back to San Francisco, back to Synergy, I'd find another. It wouldn't be as good as the one I'd had at Synergy—though working for Cooper Fallon hadn't been a picnic—but all I needed was income to get me to the end of my degree and—

Fuck. The tuition payment. I'd be in the same situation as when I'd lost my last job. Tuition or rent. Though Mimi had said she didn't mind me sleeping on her couch. Maybe I could spend some nights at Cooper's place? Or was that me wearing my heart on the outside again?

Did I have to keep it inside anymore?

Cooper had wrapped and unwrapped my ankle. He'd touched my sweaty foot and made sure I took my pills and drank water. He'd gone dancing with me, and he *actually danced,* which I hadn't dared hope he'd do. And then he brought me home and gave me amazing head, not caring if he got off or not.

And what had I done? I'd dragged him out to a club where he didn't even drink—probably because he wanted to please me—and danced with a dozen guys, hoping he'd notice, stomp over like a caveman, and drag me into some dark corner and kiss the shit out of me.

I'd been a brat.

Cooper didn't need a brat. He needed someone who'd take care of him, who'd keep him balanced so he didn't drop everything and run away.

I could do that. Starting today. And the first step was to get him back to the office where he belonged. So he could take care of people like Mimi and Marlee and everyone else.

And Jackson Jones? I felt the corners of my mouth lift. Cooper had never given him a blowjob. Sure, they were friends, and I'd never begrudge him that, but Cooper was mine now.

Mine.

I pinched myself and grinned at the pain.

After I'd showered and wrapped my ankle, I hobbled out onto the deck, where he sat with his tablet. Coco jumped up from where he lay at Cooper's feet and ran to me, his nails tapping on the wood deck.

When Cooper glanced up from his tablet, his smile rivaled the brightness of the morning sun. He set down the tablet and bounded—no, strode; Cooper Fallon didn't *bound* anywhere—to me. His fingers curled around my clenched jaw and lifted it right before he landed a soft, coffee-flavored kiss on my lips. "Good morning."

"G-good morning." His touch melted me. I pressed up against his chest and breathed him in. Strong island coffee, the crisp cotton of the seashell shirt I'd bought him, and a hint of spearmint.

"Down, Coco!" Understanding Cooper's tone, Coco stopped jumping up on my knees and sat at my feet.

"How's your ankle?" Cooper gripped my shoulders and leaned back to look at it.

"Fine. I—I wrapped it."

"Good." He kissed my temple—God, I was a puddle—and, with a hand cupping my elbow, led me to the table where a spread of fruit and pastries welcomed us. He settled me in the chair next to his and poured me a cup of coffee with cream and a healthy spoonful of sugar.

"After breakfast, I need to go into town. I'd like you to come with me if you're feeling up to it."

"Oh?" I sipped the perfectly sweetened coffee. "What are we doing in town?"

He dug into the fruit bowl and spooned some onto my plate before he served his own. "Shopping. As much as I like the clothes you bought me, I could use a few more shirts."

I plucked at his sleeve. "Don't bullshit me. You hate this shirt."

His lips curved up. "I like this shirt. I hate the one with the lizards."

"I like it, too." I straightened his collar and smoothed a hand down his chest. Shopping was something boyfriends did together. Was that what we were now? "Okay, I'm in."

After breakfast, Mateo drove us to town and followed at a discreet distance as we walked past the tourist shops selling T-shirts and shell necklaces, past the big jewelry store that sold the larimar the island was famous for, past the liquor store that sold rum imported from Puerto Rico and other nearby islands. Coco didn't worry about discretion; he trotted at our heels and turned up his nose at the other Coconut Hounds who slunk in the alleys.

Instead of walking into one of the island-wear shops, Cooper turned down a side street. The sidewalk was rougher here, pushed up by the roots of the enormous trees that shaded the street, and when he gripped my hand, my heart pitter-pattered.

There were no tourists on this street with their tropical-print shirts, blinding-white sneakers, and baseball caps. Here, people in battered straw hats and white linen guayaberas pulled shopping carts behind them or else carried string bags. Shopkeepers leaned in doorways, calling out to the passersby in Spanish.

And they knew Cooper. Some people nodded shyly. Others walked up to him and engaged him in conversation. He smiled— not the sunny smile he'd given me that morning, but a polite one —and chatted right back. When an older lady in a faded floral dress pinched his cheek and raised her eyebrows at me, he gripped my hand and called me his novio. Even my high-school Spanish knew that one. He'd introduced me not as his amigo, but his boyfriend. A grin stretched my face.

When she kissed his cheek and walked on, I squeezed his hand. "So I'm your novio?"

His cheekbones pinked. "What would you rather be called? There's a word here for friends with benefits, but I—" He winced. "That was my great-aunt."

He was right. We'd never been friends. And I doubted the word was polite. "Novio is perfect." I pulled him down so I could kiss his cheek, and he didn't pull away. He put his arm around my waist. He glanced back at Mateo, who was talking with his great-aunt, and gave him a hard stare.

We passed a grocery store, a shoe repair shop, and a barber-shop. On the other side of the bakery, Cooper opened a door, and a bell jingled above us.

"¡Tío! es Miguel," he called out.

The hum of a sewing machine cut off, and a man with sparse gray hair and a neat goatee stood from a table at the back of the shop. He lifted his glasses to the top of his head and squinted at us. "Lito!" He bowed his back until it creaked then shuffled toward us.

He hugged Cooper and stepped back to lower his glasses and peer at Cooper's shirt. Shaking his head, he clucked his tongue. He said something in Spanish, and I caught the words *camisa fea*. He'd called the shirt ugly. Cooper responded briefly in Spanish and then switched to slow English.

"Tío, this is my friend, Ben."

"Buenos dias," I said and stuck out my hand.

Ignoring my hand, Cooper's uncle hugged me. "José María, but you can call me tío."

He stepped back and looked me up and down from my golf shirt to my Bermuda shorts. "You two need clothes."

I'd come with a full suitcase of tropic-appropriate apparel. "No, I—"

Cooper's heavy hand landed on my shoulder. "Yes, please, tío. Casual wear."

"Something for Sunday?"

"No, thank you, we—"

"Sí, sí. You will come to your tía's for dinner."

Cooper winced, but he didn't protest, either. Sunday dinner with his family? His *family?*

José María bustled around the shop, pulling items from hangers. He handed half to me and half to Cooper, then he shoved us toward two cubicles at the side of the store. The curtain snapped shut behind me.

"Put it on, then come out," José María said.

I stepped out of my shorts into a pair of loose-fitting, buff linen pants. I stripped off my polo and buttoned up a brick-red guayabera. I glanced in the small mirror. Although I normally wore blacks and grays, the red looked good against my skin, and the pants felt cool and light, even in the unairconditioned store.

I slipped through the curtain and stepped out. José María nodded his approval. "Turn," he barked.

I turned and felt him grab the fabric at my ass. "I will take it in a little here. It would be a shame to hide this…what do the young people say in English? Booty?"

I grinned at him over my shoulder. "Thanks."

"Ah," he said, his gaze flicking past me. "One moment."

Cooper stepped out of his dressing room. Like me, he wore linen pants and a guayabera, a sky-blue one that matched his eyes. There was no excess fabric around his hips; the pants looked like they'd been made for him, skimming his narrow hips and muscular thighs and breaking right at his ankle, not pooling at the bottom the way mine did.

"I see you still carry my size," he said.

Boy, did he ever. My eyes roamed over Cooper's broad shoulders and tapered waist.

"Don't be silly. When I heard you were here, I made these for you, Lito."

Cooper's cheeks went red, but he smiled. "Gracias, tío."

José María pinned my pants, and I returned to the dressing room to change into the next outfit, which was similar, but the shirt was a pale oyster pink. José María pinned those, too. The final selection was a pair of slim-fitting stone-gray slacks, a French blue dress shirt, and a seersucker blazer.

While José María pinned the pants, Cooper emerged in breathtakingly tight khaki slacks, a blue-check dress shirt, and a navy linen blazer with a jaunty red-patterned pocket square. "Tío, I don't know about these pants… I think you made them for one of my cousins."

"No," I sighed.

"No," José María said at the same time. "Those are perfect. Turn."

Cooper turned, and I had to bite my tongue to keep it from lolling out of my mouth like a wolf's in an old cartoon. The pants squeezed and defined his ass, and if José María hadn't been there, I'd have let my hands follow the curves my gaze traced. *Fuck me.*

José María chuckled through his mouthful of pins. "See? Perfect. Ben approves."

I winced. I'd said it out loud.

Cooper didn't seem to mind. He turned slowly to face me, and the blue jacket made his blue eyes fierce. "Then I'll take it. Just as it is."

"All done." José María stood, his knees creaking. "I'll have one of the boys deliver the garments to your house. Except the first outfit. You will wear that today. Ben, you can wear the red shirt. It does not need alteration."

"Yes, sir." I stepped back behind the curtain and put on the red guayabera with my khaki shorts. I didn't carry it off as naturally as Cooper did his blue shirt, but I looked slightly less like a tourist.

When I walked out with my armful of pinned clothes, Cooper tapped at his phone. He kissed his uncle's cheek. "Gracias, tío."

I dug for my wallet. There was no way I had enough cash to cover handmade clothing.

"I got it." Cooper stayed my hand and held up his phone with his payment app on the screen. "It's my turn to buy you clothes."

I'd put his camisas feas on my corporate card, so, actually, he'd bought them. But I didn't argue. My novio had bought me clothes. My heart tripped in my chest. I'd lost the battle. Not just with Cooper over money. But the one with my too-ready-to-fall heart. "Thank you."

Outside, Mateo stood, arms crossed, in the shade next to Coco, who gave a joyful bark when we emerged from José María's shop. He had a leash. Not a brand-new nylon one that we could've bought in a pet shop on the mainland. It was soft leather, worn with age. Like it had served many Coconut Hounds who'd decided to self-domesticate. Mateo handed me the end of the leash, and Coco trotted by my side like a natural.

We strolled back to the main street toward where the car was parked. As we passed the spotless windows of the jewelry store, I caught our reflection. We didn't look like a couple of Americans doing a little shopping in the cute Caribbean village. We looked like a pair of expats, fully adapted to the island style. With a dog on a leash to prove it.

When we reached the car, my phone buzzed in my pocket. I pulled it out to read the message.

> Marlee: Weston's meeting with some people from Gurusoft again this morning. What the hell are you doing?

My eyes went wide. What the hell was I doing? Buying clothes like we were staying for longer than a few more days. And completely forgetting what I had schlepped to the island to do.

I had to get back on track. Ensure Cooper didn't sell any more Synergy stock. And make him go back to California where he belonged. Where we both belonged.

24

COOPER

ON THE WAY back from our shopping trip, I watched Ben's thumbs fly over his phone.

It had been a good day, walking through town with him, buying him clothes so he'd look like he belonged on the island.

Would it be so bad if we didn't go back? Jamila said I should do what was best for my mental health, including leaving Synergy and Jackson behind me like the outgrown shell of a hermit crab.

Ben had friends and family back in San Francisco. It might be difficult for him to leave them. But I was a wealthy man, and I had many negotiating tools at my disposal.

While he tapped his phone, I planned my strategy.

He had quit his job so we could be together. Then he'd blushed when I'd slipped and called him mi novio. He seemed to enjoy life on the island. He had made friends with Ramón and the others. Maybe he wanted to be persuaded to stay. But this was too important to leave to hope.

One rule of negotiation is to control the environment. Ben would be most persuadable in a romantic setting. I texted Luis to set up dinner for two just outside my property on the beach, where Ben would be in direct contact with the beauty of the island. And although he would be safer inside the locked gate, it would be important to give him a sense of freedom so he'd know he could walk away if he wanted. My chest burned at the thought of him walking away.

Although I'd made plenty of deals in my career—corporate loans, buyouts, job offers—I'd never been in a personal negotiation with such high stakes. Sure, I'd negotiated with plenty of women to be my temporary girlfriends for some event or another. Once or twice for an entire season's worth of events. If they didn't agree to the terms, I could either find someone else—there always seemed to be someone eager to step up—or go alone and build the buzz about my most eligible bachelorhood.

But this was different. I couldn't walk away from Ben. I'd leave my heart behind if I did. For the first time in years, I was happy. And I'd do almost anything to stay that way.

Ben was still working on his phone, so I reached across the seat and rested my hand on his knee. He looked up, startled, but gave me a quick smile. He continued to type with his left hand and settled his right over my fingers.

The tension left my chest. Ben cared. On that last day in the office, he wrapped my bleeding hand with his handkerchief. Then he came to the island to check on me. To try to convince me to go back. Even though I didn't deserve it, he cared about me.

Now we were together, he had to realize that staying here was the best choice for me. Nevertheless, I'd bring out the big guns. Flowers. Champagne. That triple-chocolate dessert they made in the resort restaurant that made Jamila swoon.

As soon as we pulled up to the house and opened the doors, Coco sniffed the air and growled.

"What's the matter, Coco?" Ben asked like the dog would respond in English.

"Cooper." Mateo's tone held a warning.

I approached him where he stood, hand on the front door's handle.

"Door's unlocked," he said. "And I know I checked it when we left. You two get back in the car and lock the doors."

Coco barked at full volume when I pressed Ben back into the SUV. I scooted in behind him and reached into the driver's seat to hit the door-lock button.

"What's going on?" Ben pulled Coco into his lap and stroked his sides until he quieted. The dog stared forward at the front door like he could see through it.

"Mateo thinks someone might be inside. He's checking it out."

"Is Mateo going to be okay?"

"If he's not out in five minutes, I'll go in."

"I'll go with you."

"No." I put a hand on his shoulder and stared into his startled eyes. "You'll stay out here. Where it's safe."

"Take Coco with you."

I scratched the dog's head. "Okay. He can save the day again by biting the bad guy's ankle."

Mateo emerged from the house and jogged to the car. I unlocked it for him, and he poked his head inside.

"All clear," he said. "A mix-up with housekeeping. New guy thought he was supposed to do your place."

A housekeeping cart bumped through the front door. The man who pushed it was almost too bulky for his uniform to cover him. The buttons strained, ready to pop off. He limped behind the cart on the path and gave us an embarrassed wave. Coco growled.

"Luis should know about this. And he should get him a better-fitting uniform." I reached for my phone.

"Don't." Ben put a hand over mine. "It was an honest mistake. And he's new. I wouldn't want him to lose his job over this."

Ben was always so thoughtful about people in service. I slipped my phone back into my pocket. "Okay."

"Thanks." He kissed my cheek. "I think I'll go inside and take a nap."

I lifted my hand to his cheek and redirected the kiss to my lips. "Sounds good. I've got a special dinner planned."

"Mmm." The sound shot straight to my groin. "I like the sound of that."

It had been a long time since I'd made out in a car, but if Mateo hadn't been standing there, and if Coco hadn't been growling and scratching at the window, I might have tried it. But, circumstances being what they were, I opened the door and grabbed Coco around the middle so he wouldn't chase the housekeeper. I tucked him under my arm and helped Ben out. Our walk through town earlier had to have been rough on his ankle.

While Ben napped, I visited the weight room, and afterward, I picked up a few essentials from the personal care section of the gift shop. Essentials I hoped to use later with Ben. I spoke with Luis about the plans for dinner, but as I'd promised Ben, I said nothing about the wayward housekeeper.

Luis clapped me on the back. "Good luck, my friend. I'm glad you've found love at last."

My eyes must have gone wide because Luis laughed. "Don't tell me you haven't told him how you feel."

"I—no. How do I feel?" Besides possessive as fuck whenever Mateo laughed at one of Ben's jokes. Elated when Ben kissed me. I even loved wearing that ugly-as-fuck iguana shirt he'd chosen for me.

"I think you know. You only need to admit it to yourself. And to him."

Was Luis right about how I felt? I turned it over as I jogged back to the bungalow, clutching my bag of supplies. I'd never been in love with anyone except Jackson. And I knew even when it happened that my feelings weren't healthy. The crush in my chest when I was with Jackson wasn't warm and fizzy like it felt with Ben. With Jackson, it was always pain because I knew he didn't feel the same about me. No matter that he'd kissed me a couple times when he was drunk, Jackson was completely straight. I'd known from almost the first day I'd met him that I had no chance with him.

And yet I'd pined over him like a teenager over a rockstar crush. Why? Why had I done it for fifteen years? I'd thought it was because we were as close as brothers. Best friends who were a hop and a skip from lovers if only he'd wake up and see how I felt about him.

When he married Alicia, I figured it couldn't last. He'd never had a serious relationship. Plus, despite all his flaws, I'd still hoped he and I were meant to be together. It was why I'd picked up every bit of work he'd dropped. So he'd know I'd be there when it all fell apart. But the night their baby was born, when I'd seen the exhilaration in his eyes as he held his new family close...

Maybe Dr. Pradhi had been right for all those years.

What I felt about Ben was different. I didn't know all his secrets. I'd known him for only six months. Yet when I was with him, I felt whole.

I called the catering department and asked them to double the size of the floral arrangement.

Back at the bungalow, I showered and spent extra time getting the wave in my hair just right. Ben fixated on my hair. He loved touching it. I'd never been nervous about my appearance before, certainly not on the island where everyone accepted me. But tonight, everything had to be perfect. For Ben.

When he walked into the living room, I sprang up from where I'd been sitting on the couch, an untouched glass of sparkling water on the coffee table in front of me. I consumed him with my eyes. He looked like he did in the office, with a gray-check button-down shirt and dark-rinse jeans looser than the ones he'd worn to the club. His feet were bare, and his hair was still damp from his shower.

I inhaled the honey of his lip balm and the warm scent of freshly ironed cotton. He'd primped for me, too.

"Hungry?" I kissed him, just a nervous press of my lips to his.

"Famished. I didn't think I'd sleep that long." He gripped my hand to hold me where I was and returned my kiss, longer and with a slide of his tongue that made my toes curl into the rug.

When we broke apart, I leaned my forehead on his. I hoped I'd done enough to ensure we had dinners on the beach together for a long time. That I could have his kisses every night.

"Dinner's ready. Al fresco." I led him by the hand through the patio and out the back gate that led directly onto the beach. My feet sank into the warm sand, and I paused to roll up my pants legs.

Ben did the same, and when he straightened, he spotted the table. Or what he could see of it beneath the enormous arrangement of tropical flowers. He gasped.

"You like it?" Maybe it was too much. The champagne. The flowers. The waiter standing by a prep table with chafing dishes.

"Are you kidding? A romantic dinner on the beach at sunset? I didn't think you had it in you, Cooper. I love it."

My stomach swooped, and I wanted to pump my fist the way I had in high school when I'd aced an exam. But I played it cool and helped him cross the uneven sand to the table and pulled out his chair. I trailed my hand over his shoulders as I walked behind him to the chair beside his, and he shivered.

"You're not cold, are you?" A light breeze blew from the water.

"No, just...just happy." He grinned, and something clicked into place inside me. I grasped his hand and lifted it to my lips. I was happy, too.

"Señores, are you ready for the first course?" The waiter stepped up silently behind me.

"Sí, por favor."

He set our appetizers in front of us. Ben's eyes widened when he took in the food. "It's gorgeous. Too pretty to eat."

My gaze didn't leave his face. "No, it isn't."

Ben's cheeks went pink. "Why, Mr. Fallon. I believe that was sexual innuendo. Whatever am I going to do with you?"

I could think of a lot of things I'd let him do to me. But we had to talk first. And I wanted him to be in a good mood when we did.

I let one side of my mouth kick up. "Dinner first. And then we can talk about what you'll do with me."

His eyes sparkled golden in the sunset. He looked over his shoulder at the waiter, who'd busied himself with the contents of the chafing dish. Then I felt a slide of skin along my instep. His feet were sandy, and so were mine, but it made me imagine what our bodies might feel like, sliding against each other. The rough curls on his chest. My stubble scratching his inner thigh. I shivered. "Eat."

Ben went to work on the appetizer. My stomach was a hard lump, nerves wrapped with lust, so I offered my plate to him when he finished his.

"You aren't eating?"

I quirked my mouth again. "I'm hungry for something else."

He raised his eyebrows. "We're still on the first course."

"Maybe I'm waiting for dessert."

He raised his voice. "Señor, I think we're ready for the main course."

The waiter removed our appetizer plates and plated the main course. He set one in front of Ben and the other before me.

"Gracias, señor," Ben said. "I think we've got it from here."

The waiter looked at me, and I nodded. He stacked the appetizer plates on a tray and carried them away down the path toward the resort.

"Cooper, this is too good to pass up. Try a bite." Ben reached across the table and held his fork to my lips. Without looking, I closed my mouth around it. Some type of fish, light and flaky. Ben pulled the fork away. "Good, right?" His voice had gone breathy.

Maybe I didn't need to wait. Maybe this moment, sharing delicious food, the breeze ruffling our hair, the sound of the waves in the background, was the right one.

"Ben, I—I want to keep doing this."

"Having romantic meals together? I'm definitely on board with that." He winked and took another bite of the fish.

"Yes, and…and the rest of it. Going shopping together. Taking you on dates. And I want you to move into my bedroom."

He slipped his foot into my lap and pressed his heel into my groin. "You do? I like the sound of that."

I muttered a curse and took his teasing foot in my hand. I kneaded his sandy instep.

"I want you to"—I swallowed—"be part of my life."

His foot jerked out of my hand, and the languid haze cleared from his eyes. "Part of your life?"

I reached across the table, palm up, and he set his hand in mine. The touch reassured me, gave me courage to proceed. "I want you." I cleared my throat. "Permanently."

"Permanently?" He gripped my hand. "Like, forever?"

I took in a full breath, no longer constricted by a squeeze on my chest. "Forever."

He eased his grip and traced a circle on my wrist that made me shiver. "Even after you go back to work?"

The shiver turned into an icy rush through my body. Work? He wanted to talk about that now, when I was cutting myself open for him? "Fuck work. Fuck Synergy." *Fuck Jackson.* "I want you, Ben. Can't you see that?"

"Even if I don't work there anymore, I care about people who do. You can't give up on Synergy. Not for me."

Too late. "I've never felt free like I have here, on the island with you. I don't want to go back. Not anytime soon. Maybe not ever."

His eyes went soft, but his voice didn't. "They need you back at Synergy. Marlee. My sister, Mimi. And Jackson. Your friend."

I clenched my jaw. "Synergy—and Jackson—will survive if I'm there or not. If I sell down to my last fucking share. But I don't give a shit about anything back there. We don't have to go back to San Francisco. We could stay here. Aren't you happy here?" The island agreed with him. His olive skin had gone golden in the sun, and his dark hair had sunset-red streaks in it. But Ben was beautiful even under the fluorescents in the office.

He took away my lifeline and raked both hands through his hair. "I can't stay here. I have a life. Family. School."

"We can work through all that. Remote school. Visits to the mainland. Even bringing our families here." Mamá would love being back with family. Sometimes I thought I—and her church ladies—were the only things keeping her in the U.S.

"I don't know if you know this"—I gave him my winning smile—"but I'm rich as hell. Neither one of us has to work another day in our lives."

I'd expected his face to light up at that, at the thought of sharing everything I had, but his lips tightened. "I don't want to be dependent on you, Cooper. Not like that."

Cold whipped through me. "You used to rely on me for a paycheck. How would this be any different?"

He blinked down at his plate. "I—I don't know. Even when I hit bottom and my parents wanted to help, I wouldn't take their money. I guess I had to prove I could make it on my own. I've worked hard to build up a life for myself. Maybe it's not great, but it's mine, you know?"

The image of Ben alone in a homeless shelter made my blood go from icy cold to a full boil. "Why the fuck would you want that? I have everything, and I'm offering it to you!"

His eyes glittered in the setting sun. "You're not offering me everything, are you? I told you all about what happened to me growing up. But you haven't told me a single thing about your life before Jackson Jones."

My stomach churned. If I told him, those kind eyes of his would turn hard with judgment. Or worse, pity. "You don't want that."

"Of course I do," he snapped.

I stood, my hands shaking. "I've just opened my veins to you. I'm bleeding out for you. I'm offering you my fucking life!" I smashed the side of my fist against the fence, and it clanged like a bell.

Ben rose, slowly. "I don't think that's true. You haven't opened yourself at all. Not to me, not to anyone else. I like the glimpses you've given me this week. But I want it all."

"All?" I could feel my eyes bulging, and I didn't care. My voice ripped through my chest. "No one wants all of what's inside me." Someone as beautiful and perfect as Ben couldn't stand the ugliness I fought every day. I was used to hiding it. And for a moment, I had hoped that what I was willing to show him could be enough.

Ben's eyes went hard and glittery as topaz. "We need some time to cool off. We can talk when you're not like this." He turned on the bare sole of his foot and limped around the side of the fence to the path toward the resort.

"Wait." How had I fucked it up so badly? I sprinted to the corner of the fence and ran into a solid wall.

"Get out of my fucking way, Mateo," I growled.

"No, Lito. You can't talk to him when you're angry."

"Why the hell not?"

"Because you told me to protect him. And now I'm protecting him from you."

All the heat washed out of me like the receding tide. "I wouldn't—I'd never—"

He crossed his arms.

He was right.

The side of my palm twinged from where I'd slammed it into the metal fence. Shit. I scrubbed my other hand over my eyes. "Go after him, please. Make sure he's safe." I didn't add *from me.*

The next second, he was gone.

I turned back toward the table. The garish flowers. Ben's half-eaten dinner. My untouched plate. The cooler that held the too-sweet chocolate dessert he would've loved. I put my hands on top of my head and pulled at the roots of my hair. I'd fucked it all up. And now he was gone.

I wanted to kick the table. Shred the flowers with my bare hands. Smash the plates. It would feel good for a minute. Release all the tension that'd built in my muscles.

But it wouldn't bring him back.

I let go of my hair, and my hands flopped to my sides.

A whine came from below, and when I looked down, Coco gazed up at me, blinking his big, brown eyes.

"What the hell are you doing here? Why didn't you go with Ben?"

The dog yawned and then rubbed his face on my leg.

"Brainless animal. Everyone knows Ben is a better human than me. I'll probably forget to feed you. You should follow him. Go."

He plunked his ass on the sand and stared at me.

"Fine, then. Your mistake."

I set my plate of fish and vegetables onto the sand. While Coco scarfed it, I rinsed my feet in cold water from the spigot then trudged back into the house. I found a towel and wiped down Coco. When he was clean, I let him follow me into the house. I closed the bedroom door in his face—I had my limits—and crawled under the covers, alone.

25

BEN

I WOKE up to the scent of rich island coffee.

"Mmm, Cooper." I stretched, and when my hands hit the sofa cushion, my stomach jerked like I'd missed a step on the stairs.

I snapped my eyelids open and stared at the unfamiliar ceiling, which didn't dance with light reflected from Cooper's pool.

And a pair of brown eyes, not blue, watched me over the back of the sofa.

I sat up so fast that dark spots dotted my vision.

"Morning," Ramón said. "Coffee?" He held out a white mug.

"Please." I took it from him and sipped. He'd doctored it with cream and plenty of sugar, and I eased back against the sofa cushions. "Thanks for letting me crash here."

"No problem. But you're going back today, yes?"

"I don't know." Yesterday, walking through town, meeting Cooper's tío, had been pure joy. The future had opened up ahead of me, and I'd seen the two of us, Cooper and me, side by side, facing life's challenges and its rewards. Together.

Then when he'd tried to rearrange my life and, worse, when he held back that part of himself, the familiar feelings of doubt, of self-loathing, of jealousy had crept back in. Had he shared his truth with Jackson? Yet again, I was good enough for a fling but not for any of the serious stuff.

"Today." Ramón nodded, like we'd settled it. He didn't ask any questions last night when I'd knocked on his door. He just let me in and sat back down on the sofa to watch baseball. I got the feeling he would have listened if I wanted to talk. But he seemed to know what I hadn't said. That I couldn't give up Cooper Fallon any more than I could give up breathing.

"You're right. I should talk to him. I'm a grown-ass adult."

He chuckled. "Yeah, you are. Now go get your man."

I sucked down the last of the coffee and tried to make myself presentable in Ramón's bathroom. My eyes were puffy, and my button-down shirt was wrinkled from sleeping in it. But I didn't need to keep my rough night from Cooper. Let him see what he'd done. How he'd hurt me. So he wouldn't do it again.

Twenty minutes later, I took a deep breath and stepped off the path at Cooper's back gate. After walking out on him last night, using the keycard he'd given me didn't feel right. Neither did ringing the front bell.

A familiar bark came from the beach. I took two steps in that direction before Coco sprinted toward me, his floppy ears flying. Kneeling, I opened my arms, and he wiggled into them, licking every part of me he could reach.

"Stop, Coco," I said, laughing. "I missed you, too."

He paused for a moment to look back over his wagging tail. Cooper stood twenty feet away, holding a tennis ball.

When I stood, Coco trotted back to Cooper and sat at his feet.

"Hi," Cooper said. He wore the shorts and one of the guayaberas we'd bought on our shopping trip. Sunglasses reflected the overcast sky.

"Hi." I closed half the distance between us.

"I'm glad you're okay. Mateo said you went to Ramón's?"

"Yeah. We watched baseball, and I slept on his couch."

"He's a good man, Ramón."

"Yeah." I let a grin crack my face. "He makes better coffee than you do."

He shifted his jaw and stared at the waves that caressed the beach.

Slowly, I approached him until I was near enough to touch him. I reached for his hand and took the disgustingly damp tennis ball. I threw it toward the beach and wiped my hand on my jeans. Then I slipped my hand into his. I waited.

"Look, I'm sorry I blew up at you last night. If you feel safer at Ramón's—"

I squeezed his hand to stop him. "Your bark doesn't scare me. You should know that by now."

Coco raced across the sand and dropped the ball into Cooper's hand. He threw it right-handed, and Coco tore away.

I eased back my shoulders. "When you closed yourself off to me, it hit my soft spot, you know? I've had a lot of relationships, but no one sticks. I'm starting to think it's not them, it's me."

He stepped closer until our shoulders met. "Ben, it's not you. You're—"

"Just let me finish, okay?" I wished he wasn't wearing those sunglasses so I could look into his eyes. "Mimi—my sister—tells me all the time I wear my heart on the outside. I don't need you to do that, but I do need you to open up a little. To share what's going on inside you. When you're having feelings, talk about them instead of trying to distract me with one of your blowups. Okay?"

Under the sunglasses, his mouth pinched. After a few seconds of silence, he said, "I'm sorry, Ben. For blowing up at you and for holding myself back. I'll try to do better. Just—just stay."

I stepped closer, ready to take him into my arms, but he held up a palm and reached into his shorts pocket with his other hand. While he tapped at the phone, I tossed the ball down the beach again for Coco, who sprinted across the sand.

"Look." Cooper held out his phone to face me.

I scanned the screen. "A stock sell order?" I scrunched my

nose. "I thought we were having a moment here, and you're thinking about your portfolio?"

"Not a sell. A transfer. To you."

"To me? Is that Synergy stock?"

"Yes. Don't get too excited. It's only about five percent of my holdings."

I peered more closely at the number. That was a lot of zeroes. "For—for me? Are you sure?"

"I'm breaking up the partnership with Jackson. I want to be your partner."

I winced. "Cooper, that doesn't sound like the healthiest way to—"

"Shh. I'm all in, Ben. With you. Isn't that what you wanted?"

I gazed at the man standing on the sand, the sun caressing the golden waves of his hair and the tanned skin on his cheekbones. All in was exactly what I wanted. What I needed after the long string of men who'd never thought I was enough. I nodded.

He opened his arms, and I stepped into them, notching my face into the valley between his neck and his shoulder.

Snug in his embrace that felt like my parents' kitchen at Rosh Hashana, a warm sleeping bag on a chilly night, and a latte with just the right amount of foam, I never wanted to leave. If he was willing to try, to give me a peek at the real Cooper Fallon, the one that no one, not even Jackson Jones, ever saw, it'd be worth it.

"Okay," I said on a sigh.

He ducked his head to kiss me, his lips tugging at mine like he couldn't get close enough. I opened to him and let him pillage with his tongue. He needed to claim me, the way he claimed the power seat in front of a roomful of executives. *Mine,* his kiss said.

And because we were equal partners, I nipped his tongue. *Mine.*

When I couldn't breathe anymore, I pulled back. I let my lips curl up at the way his chest heaved, too, at the look of desperation on his face. "Care to take this inside?"

Wordlessly, he hustled me through the gate and into the house.

Straight down the hall to his bedroom. He closed the door. Coco whined once then thumped against it.

Cooper palmed the front of my pants as he delivered another punishing kiss. God, was he going to fuck me at last? I needed a shower first. I needed—

"Stop thinking. Let me take care of you here, at least," he growled against my lips. He lowered my zipper and shoved down my pants and underwear. Then he guided me to sit on the bed and knelt in front of me.

"Oh, God," I whispered.

Not breaking eye contact, he lowered his lips to my dick. He licked the tip. Then he opened his mouth and closed it around the head. Those blue eyes, shot through with lust, said, *You are mine. This is mine.*

I closed my eyes, overwhelmed by the intensity. Cooper Fallon had conquered me.

He sucked me down. It wasn't the most skilled blowjob I'd ever received, but he made up for it in eagerness. Pressure built in my balls, and the familiar tingle spilled down my spine. I touched his head, a warning. "Cooper, I—"

He stood, fumbled with his pants, and dropped them. Fuck, I almost came then, staring at his dick. It was longer and thicker than mine, with an upward curve. Uncut. And hard, just for me. It was going to feel incredible inside me. I leaned forward, eager to lick the glistening tip, but he yanked me up and took both of us in hand. He didn't bother with lube but used his thumb to gather our precum and slicked it across his palm.

His big hand engulfed us both, and he tugged us together. My dick slid against his. The tingle at my lower back intensified. I leaned toward him and captured his lower lip between my teeth. Then I cupped his balls, and he groaned, his hand moving faster.

I was about to erupt like a volcano, so I reached lower and ran a finger from his taint to his hole. Without lube, all I did was lay the pad of my finger over it. What could we do to each other later, when we weren't so desperate for connection, when the make-up sex was over? Did he like to be touched there?

He did. He jerked against me and splattered my shirt, his shirt, and my chin with his come. I shuddered and came, too, jetting onto us both. He gripped me tight through it all. Finally, I slumped into him. He released me and put a sticky hand on my back, holding me up.

I chuckled. "As much as I love make-up sex, let's not fight like that again, okay?"

His laugh ruffled my hair. "Okay. Though it was pretty amazing."

I kissed his cheek and then leaned back. "I'll show you amazing. After we clean up. And take a nap."

He blinked his bloodshot eyes. "I like how you think."

And, like we'd been doing it forever and not just ten days in paradise, he followed me to the bathroom and joined me in the shower.

26

COOPER

"LOOKS LIKE YOU TWO MADE UP."

I grunted, not letting my gaze leave the hacky sack Mateo kicked my way. I couldn't believe he'd found the old thing in tía Camelia's shed. I hadn't seen one since we were teenagers. I was a little rusty, but I couldn't let my cousin win. I caught it on my instep, dribbled it, and kicked it back to Mateo.

"When he went to Ramón's, I thought, eh, maybe you guys were done, and he was ready to move on to someone"—he nodded his chin behind me, and I heard Ramón's deep belly laugh and then Ben's higher one—"simpler."

My eyes burned to see what they were doing. Ben's laugh had its own key to my heart, and when he laughed with me—at me, more often—I wanted to hoard the sound like treasure.

I kicked the sack high, but Mateo easily headed it back to me. I caught it in the chest, let it drop to my toe, and sent it flying back at Mateo's groin.

He sidestepped, tapped it with his hip and then his heel, a rainbow over his shoulder, and toed it back to me. "I guess Ben's just naturally affectionate."

The sack caught me in the ass because I'd spun around to glare at Ben. But he was ruffling Coco's ears, and Ramón was six feet away, pouring another one of tía abuela Isobel's rum punches. If Ben drank too many of those, I'd have to carry him out. Mateo and I had puked our share of them into Camelia's bushes.

"Asshole," I growled.

"Can you blame me?" Mateo shrugged, palms up. "You're too much fun to rile up."

I picked up the hacky sack and slammed it into his palm. "I'm done. Go play with the other children."

He stuffed it into his shorts pocket. Then he laid his hand on my shoulder. "It's good to see you like this. I'm happy for you, primo."

An unfamiliar feeling, my cheeks stretching wide with a smile, tugged at muscles I hadn't used in a while. "I'm happy for me, too." I clapped a hand over his and held it there for a second. Then I flung his hand off me. "I'll find you when we're ready to go."

He saluted me with two fingers before he jogged off to join his nieces and nephews in their game of soccer on tía Camelia's small patch of lawn.

I turned back toward Ben, who sprawled in a low Adirondack chair and tipped back a cup of Isobel's pink punch. He was the one who'd dragged me to Sunday brunch with my family. And he seemed to be having a good time, devouring the simple food and practicing his rudimentary Spanish with my relatives. He was at home with my family. With me.

His happiness, his comfort, had become the most important thing to me.

He liked me as I was, ridiculous blow-ups and all. Though I hoped I wouldn't have as many blow-ups with Ben's calming influence in my life. And with the new freedom of being less invested in Synergy.

Once I resigned as COO and transitioned my responsibilities, I wouldn't have to be the perfect executive anymore. I wouldn't have to jet off to Singapore or Mumbai or London. Or Boston with a day's notice. I could focus on my family on the island. On helping them. I wouldn't have to worry about a global corporation's worth of people, plus all the shareholders and business partners. Only the people who cared about me.

Including Ben.

I could make him happy. He'd find a job, most likely back in California because his family—and his independence—was important to him. But we could visit the island as often as he liked. My family had already taken him in. One of my young cousins handed him a mantecadito, and he stuffed the buttery cookie into his mouth. The child laughed when Ben rolled his eyes back and pretended to swoon.

He'd never have to know the other side of my family. About my father with his alcoholism and his rage and his pummeling fists. I would tell him about Mick so he'd know the danger, both from Mick and from myself as his son. If Ben still wanted to be with me, I'd erect a firewall around him, the same as I'd done with Mamá.

Mamá would love him. She'd recognize his care, his kindness, his obliviousness that anyone could hurt him.

Our eyes met across the garden, and suddenly I wanted to taste the sweetness of the punch on his lips. I prowled toward him, winding my way along the path between Camelia's flowerbeds. His eyes widened, and a smile teased at the corners of his mouth.

My young cousin skipped away. I couldn't tell what Ramón was doing or if he was even still there with Ben. My gaze didn't leave those clear brown eyes of his. When I reached him, I bent at the waist and planted my hands on the wide handrests of the chair. The position put my face right in front of his. His breath came fast through his parted lips.

Slowly, I closed the distance until my lips met his, sticky with sugary punch. I licked away a cookie crumb and then delved my tongue into his mouth. One or two of my relatives hooted at us, but I didn't care. All I wanted was my Ben and the freedom to walk up and kiss him whenever the hell I wanted.

When I lifted away, his eyes fluttered open. "What was that for?"

"For? Nothing. I did it because I can." I let my gaze roam from his glazed eyes to his kiss-reddened mouth, all the way to the bulge in his shorts. I lingered there, and when I flicked my stare up to Ben's face, his eyes had sharpened.

He licked his lips. "Ready to go?"

"You bet your ass I am," I growled, too low for anyone else to hear.

He squirmed in the chair and surreptitiously ran his hand over his shorts before he held his arm out to me. "Help me out of this thing?"

I gripped his hand and tugged him out of the low chair, all the way up until his chest met mine. He wobbled, and I grasped his shoulders. "You all right?"

"Yeah." He blinked. "That punch is potent."

"Hell, yeah, it is. I almost got contact-drunk when I kissed you."

"Good thing we have a ride home."

Home. I smiled.

In my family, good-byes are never quick. Or sober. Almost an hour later, I tossed Ben's last cup of punch and followed him into the back seat of the SUV. Mateo looked over his shoulder to ensure we'd buckled our seat belts. I helped Ben with his.

He let his head loll against the headrest. "Did you have fun, Mateo?"

"Of course. It's always good to have my primo back home. I can tease him like I used to do when we were kids."

"Oh, really?" Ben gave me a wicked side-eye before he met Mateo's gaze in the rearview mirror. "What'd you used to tease him about?"

"Girls. And guys. And sports. Never school, though, because that was the one thing he kicked my ass at."

"One thing?" I raised an eyebrow.

"One thing. I just defeated you at hacky sack. And don't get me started on Isaac."

"Okay, okay." I held out my palms. "You win."

"I heard an interesting story today," Ben said. "From Luis."

"Oh?" I rubbed the face of my Rolex.

"He said you're part owner of the resort. That you gave him the seed money."

Luis. Get a cup of punch in him, and he sang like a kingbird. I squared my jaw. "It was a good investment."

"And Isobel said you funnel your share of the profits back into the community."

"I'm sure she didn't say that." Tía abuela wasn't a loose-lipped drunk.

"She said you're funding the new community center construction. And I remember that family friend of yours said you did the same thing with the school. Like, built it with your hands."

"Isobel loves the community center," I grumbled. "Dancing is good exercise for someone her age."

Mateo snorted. "We wish he'd stick to the fundraising. To keep him from hammering those money hands."

I glared at him in the mirror. "Everyone needed to pitch in after the hurricane. I wanted to help my family."

"Is everyone here on the island your family?" Ben turned his head to face me and blinked slowly.

"Not everyone. Not in the city. But in this part of it, just about. Mamá and I lived in the U.S., but she brought me back whenever she could." Whenever Mick would let her, or when he was too drunk to care. Though he usually cared when we got back. Still, those few days or weeks of peace had been worth it. And investing in the resort not only helped my friend but was a way of thanking the small community for what they'd done for me.

"Even the mayor is our third cousin twice removed. We're all family, and now you are, too, Ben." Mateo nodded at his own pronouncement as he threw the SUV into park in front of the bungalow.

"Wait here," he said. He unlocked the door and went inside. I hadn't thought he'd take his bodyguard duties so seriously. The cousin I remembered tended to laugh through life and let others handle responsibilities. It seemed that he'd changed. Could I change in the other direction, become more carefree and actually enjoy retirement?

I glanced at Ben. His eyes had drooped closed. I brushed an errant curl from his forehead, and he smiled. What had I done to deserve the right to have him here with me, and to have him like me enough to go to one of my family gatherings with me? To be willing to share a house with me, and a bed?

Nothing. I'd done nothing. Ben, with his heart on the outside, yearning for love, had done it all. And if he couldn't protect his own heart, I'd do it for him.

Mateo opened my door. "All clear."

I got out, circled the SUV, and opened Ben's door. After unlatching his seat belt, I ducked under his arm and half-lifted him from the car. He blinked his eyes open when his feet hit the driveway. "Home?"

"Yes. Home." I supported him to the door. "Thanks, Mateo. Good-night."

"Buenas noches, Lito. See you tomorrow."

I closed and locked the door and lumbered with Ben through my bedroom into the bathroom, where I propped him against the counter. "Do you need help?"

His eyelids still drooped, but he stood steadily enough. "I got this."

By the time I'd used the hall bathroom and changed into a pair of lightweight pajama pants, Ben emerged from the bathroom, still fully clothed but smelling toothpaste-minty.

"That punch really got to me," he said with an apologetic smile.

"I should have warned you. Isobel has annihilated larger men with it." I slipped an arm around his waist and supported him to the bed. "Did you have fun despite the punch?"

"Yeah. I liked being part of your family."

My knees wobbled, and I dropped him on the bed less gracefully than I'd planned. He laughed and bounced.

"You did?" I sank down beside him. I bent to slip off his shoes and socks.

He rubbed my back. "Yeah."

After tugging his shirt over his head, I eased him onto the mattress. I unzipped his shorts and tugged them off his legs, leaving him in his underwear. Then I folded his shirt and shorts and laid them on the bedside table before I circled to the other side of the bed and climbed under the covers.

Ben met me in the middle. He kissed me and then rotated to become the little spoon, shoving his ass against me. He might have had a case of whiskey dick, but I didn't. I shifted, trying to make my erection less obvious.

"I can see why you like it here." Ben's voice was slurry and slow.

"Do you now?" I kissed his shoulder. "What's not to like? Soft sheets, a gorgeous man in my arms—"

"I didn't mean me. Though I am both gorgeous and amazing." He yawned. "I mean here, the island. Your family."

I hummed an agreement. Now, while Ben was sleepy and drunk, wasn't the right time to revisit moving here permanently. But the possibility that he might not remember what I said made me bold. "My family—my island family—they're wonderful. But some of my family isn't."

"Yeah?" He shifted his weight, but I held him still. This conversation would be easier without looking into his beautiful eyes.

"I owe you some history." I rested my nose against his shoulder blade. "My father had a temper. No, I'm not going to sugarcoat it. He was abusive. First to my mother, and then to both of us."

"Cooper." He tried to roll over again, but I held him in place.

I squeezed my eyes shut. "And I'm—I'm like him. I'm even named after him. I'm Michael Cooper Fallon. That's why people around here call me Miguelito or Lito. It means little Michael."

"You're not like him. Cooper, let me—" When he squirmed to face me, one of his sharp elbows hit my stomach, and I grunted. "You're not."

I stared at the middle of his chest like I could see through it to his soft heart. "Don't you remember why I came here? I broke my fucking desk."

"The glass shattered because it wasn't the right kind of glass. One of those terrible temps you had before me must've ordered the wrong thing." He pierced me with his glare. "Yes, you have a temper. And you probably ought to work on it. But you're no abuser. You won't hurt me."

He didn't get it. He'd never been around an abuser before. "I slammed my hand into the fence the night you left."

"You hit the fence, not me. I left because we both needed to cool off. We did, and I came back."

"But I—"

"Shh." He kissed the center of my chest. "You won't hurt me."

He couldn't know that. Even I didn't know that. Mick had never been to the island, but that night, he was in my bedroom, hovering just behind me. The flashfire temper, the pounding fists, the remorse after. All my sessions with Dr. Pradhi hadn't convinced me he wasn't deep inside me, biding his time until he burst out and I hit someone I loved.

And despite my speech to Ben the other day about being all in, that was one risk I wouldn't take. I'd lock away that last piece of myself, the one that loved him.

Big emotions like love were dangerous. They hurt.

"Go to sleep," I whispered into his hair.

"Mm-hmm," he murmured against my sternum.

I rolled onto my back, pulling him with me so his head rested on my chest. His breaths evened out and slowed.

I could do this kind of intimacy. The romantic-dinner, meet-the-family, snuggle-in-bed stuff Ben loved. He didn't need that last part of me. If he knew how dangerous I was, he wouldn't want it.

Even if he wanted it, I could never give it to him.

27

COOPER

BEN WAS STILL ASLEEP, snoring softly, when I disentangled myself from him early the next morning. I ran to the neighboring town and back, the steamy air filling my lungs as the sun blazed into the sky, making me wish for the cool, foggy mornings in San Francisco.

I would miss the city I'd always called home. But I wouldn't miss Synergy. The restlessness that had stirred in me the last few days didn't mean that I missed the challenge, the sense of accomplishment at the end of a long day, or the people I used to call my work family. I had the community center to work on, and that was enough.

I had everything I needed on the island. Delicious food, a comfortable home, wifi when I wanted it, a loving—if a bit intrusive—family, and Ben. Ben made me happy. We'd develop a hobby to share. Golf. Pickup games of soccer with the neighborhood teens. Maybe I could brush up on my construction skills and be a real asset to the local community. There was more rebuilding to be done, even two years after the hurricane.

I just had to convince Ben to stay. That he needed me as much as I needed him.

As I pounded up the road toward home, I formulated a plan. With my support, Ben could attend school either remotely or by transferring to the university on the island. Going full-time, he could finish up his degree within a semester. There were plenty of kids who needed help on the island. He'd volunteer or else find a paid job at a local organization. And we'd work something out so he could see his friends and family in California as often as he liked. Satisfied with my arguments, I slowed and walked back to the house.

Still dripping sweat, I slipped off my sneakers and crept silently to the bedroom door. Ben had rolled onto his stomach, cradling my pillow. I watched his back rise and fall. I could've watched him the rest of the day, but I was sticky and rank with sweat.

As quietly as possible, I grabbed clean clothes and went to the hall bath to shower.

Twenty minutes later, I'd just poured myself a cup of coffee when my phone buzzed on the counter. When I leaned over to silence it, I saw a face that made my heart rocket into my throat. Jackson's.

I wasn't ready to talk to him. Not yet. I hadn't responded to his calls or texts for three weeks, since I slunk out of my office that day, my blood soaking Ben's handkerchief. We'd been best friends for fifteen years, and we'd never gone this long without checking in. Even when he was on his honeymoon, he texted me photos of the beach, of lizards and birds, a silly selfie holding a coconut next to his head.

The phone stopped buzzing. I could breathe again. I sucked in an air-conditioned breath and looked up when Coco's nails clicked on the tile.

The dog preceded Ben into the living room. Coco took up his post, guarding the slider. Ben's hair was rumpled, and one of my T-shirts hung off his leaner body. His cheeks were pink, one of them creased by the pillow. He walked up to me and rose on his toes to kiss my cheek.

"Morning." His breath smelled like toothpaste.

"M-morning." I tried to smile.

I didn't fool Ben. "What's wrong?"

"Nothing." But I couldn't keep from glancing at my phone.

Ben followed my gaze, and the banner on the lock screen gave away my secret.

"You should talk to him." He brushed past me on his way to the coffee pot. His stiff shoulders belied his casual words.

My stomach knotted. I didn't like this stony version of Ben. I caught his hand. "What is it?"

He was silent so long I thought he wouldn't answer. But after he poured himself a cup and lightened it with milk and sugar, he took my hand and led me to the sofa.

"How long have you been in love with him?" He didn't look at me when he asked, just stared out across the pool at the beach.

"What? I'm not—"

He turned, and a sad smile turned his mouth down in the center but up at the corners. "Of course you are. Anyone who's paid attention can see it. Too bad Jackson never does."

"Now wait a minute." My shoulders curled back, conditioned by too many years of defending my best friend.

"Don't get your hackles up. It's a fact. Jackson is too caught up in himself to ever think about you and what you need. And you've let him do it for years."

He was right. I'd defended Jackson, bullied him to do better, taken up his slack almost since the first day we'd met. But it wasn't until that last day in my office that I'd ever shown him how it made me feel.

"He's taking the first step." Ben tightened his grip on my hand. "You should listen to what he has to say."

I glanced back at my phone on the counter like it was actually Jackson. "I guess I could apologize."

Ben waited until I looked back at him. "Or you could hear him out."

I sucked in a deep breath and sighed it out. "Okay."

Ben pushed off the sofa. "I'll go—"

"Stay." I caught his hand. "It's not like that. Not anymore. Not for a while. I don't care about him the way I care about you. Stay. Please." I wasn't sure I could do it without him.

He smiled, not sad this time but reassuring. "Okay." He tugged out of my grip, circled the sofa, and handed me my phone. Then he sat beside me and turned so our knees touched.

The contact slowed my heartbeat. Eased the tingle in my fingertips. My hand didn't tremble when I hit the redial button and lifted the device to my ear.

"Coop." My name came out like a sigh, and my heart seized in my chest.

"Hi, Jay. What's up?"

"Don't fucking play this like it hasn't been three weeks since we talked. Are you okay?"

I'd thought I could bullshit my way through this call. I was wrong. "I'm fine."

"Jamila says Ben's on the island with you. I'm glad someone's looking out for you."

"Jamila called you?" I hadn't thought she'd rat me out.

"I called her, you asshole. Since you didn't call me."

"Look, I'm—"

"No. Listen." His voice was blunt like the end of a hammer. "I'm sorry. I'm having a hard time adjusting to…to everything. And I guess I took advantage of you. Of our friendship. I figured you'd always be available to pick up my slack. But that's not fair, and I'm sorry."

My breath stuck in my chest. He'd apologized for a lot, but never for that. "It's—thanks?" It wasn't okay. I'd had enough sessions with Dr. Pradhi to know that. But I could accept his apology.

"Yeah?" I could picture him, that hopeful expression on his face.

"Yeah." Ben laid a hand on my knee, and I covered it.

"Good, because I—I have a favor to ask. A big one."

The weight was back in my stomach. "What is it?"

"I hate to bother you while you're on vacation. Especially after you took care of things while I was on paternity leave. And for our honeymoon before that. Fuck, I'm such an ass…"

I snorted. "Agreed. And?"

"Things aren't good at the office. There've been people here. From Gurusoft."

I winced. Not Gurusoft. And Jackson had faced it alone. Fifteen years ago, they'd badgered his father to sell his startup. Jasper Jones had worked himself to the point of exhaustion and refused to sell it until the day he'd died. Then his widow had sold the company, his pride and joy, to Gurusoft. Jackson harbored a lot of complicated feelings about the company.

He rushed on. "Weston thought I wouldn't know them, but I do. I met one of the fuckers at that conference I went to last summer. Remember, I told you how he bought me drinks and tried to get me to take his assistant up to my room?"

Fuck, yeah, I remembered. Even though he'd been engaged, I'd been surprised the ploy hadn't worked. I grunted.

"Anyway, now Weston's called an emergency board meeting. I think they've offered to buy us out."

"What?"

"I guess neither one of you has been checking your email."

"Ah…no." We'd been much more enjoyably engaged. I'd turned off work notifications on my phone.

"Weston mentioned you sold some of your shares."

I bet he had, the asshole. Though who was a bigger asshole, Weston for spilling my secrets or me for not telling my friend? "Yeah, I—"

"Really? So it's true?" His voice cracked.

"It is. I've had—I've been thinking about the company." Ben

moved his hand up my forearm and stroked it. I breathed a little easier at his touch. "About how much of myself I give to it. About whether I want to keep going." He'd understand that. Especially given what had happened with his father.

"And you thought the best way to handle it was to divest without talking to me? We had an agreement, Coop."

Even Ben's touch couldn't counterbalance the weight that spread from my belly to my chest. "I—I couldn't talk to you. Not after—" My throat closed, and I struggled to swallow past it.

"Okay. Okay. But can you come back? The meeting's the day after tomorrow. If you could get here before, you could talk some sense into Weston. Maybe you don't give a fuck about Synergy anymore, but I do."

"You do? Weston said you were considering getting out."

"Goddammit. Weston would say fucking anything. Of course I care about Synergy. We built it together."

All the reasons why I couldn't—why I shouldn't—crowded into my brain. Jackson hadn't acted like he cared about our company. I shouldn't care about it. Or about him.

Plus, if I went back, what would happen between Ben and me? Our relationship was so new. I'd wanted to solidify it on the island before we returned to the pressures of San Francisco.

What if the anger came back? What if the stressors of work turned on the part of me Mick Fallon had created? What if it wasn't a desk or a table or a fence I hit but Ben?

I gazed into his eyes, full of steady support. Could I convince him to stay on the island, to wait for me to deal with this and return?

I tangled my fingers with his. I could ask.

And now my friend was asking for help. I never could tell him no.

"All right. I'll be there tomorrow."

His sigh crackled through the phone. "Thank you. And we'll talk after? About you and Synergy?"

We both knew he didn't mean Synergy and me. He meant we'd talk about the two of us.

"We will."

"Okay. See you tomorrow. Love you, man."

It was his standard good-bye. But this time, it didn't twist into my gut like a knife.

"Me, too."

28

BEN

COOPER HELD my fingers tight when all I wanted to do was run. He'd talked with his best friend, and he hadn't mentioned our relationship. And then he said he was going back to San Francisco. Not *we're* going back. *I'm* going back.

If Cooper Fallon thought he was leaving me on the island as a placeholder, he had another think coming.

He set his phone on the table and turned toward me so our knees touched. Then he looked up, apology in his eyes, and said, "I have to go back."

I tried to keep my tone light. "What disaster has Jackson gotten himself into now?"

"It's the entire company." He took my other hand. "Jay was light on details—he and Weston aren't exactly confidants—but Gurusoft people have been in the building, and Weston's called an emergency board meeting for the day after tomorrow. Maybe they've cobbled together a hostile takeover offer."

Poor Marlee. My phone had buzzed while Cooper talked to Jackson, but I'd been too engrossed in listening to Cooper to pick it up. "Do you think Weston supports a takeover?"

"No. He's a good guy. He probably got so caught up in doing work I should've been doing, he…" He frowned.

"It's not your fault, Cooper." I reached up and lightly touched the crease between his brows.

It didn't smooth out. "Actually, it is. I sold those shares."

"I guess we have to figure out what's going on and how to react. How would a buyout work?" I wished I could have made it all go away for him, but Cooper thrived on problem-solving. The best thing for him was to work through it. I could help with that.

He circled his thumb on the back of my hand, staring at it like it was one of his spreadsheets. "They couldn't have purchased enough stock to take over outright. I still have a good amount, and Jay has his. Weston has a strong position, too. It's possible they've accumulated a significant minority, enough to influence board decisions. I'm guessing Weston wants to bring the board together proactively to determine our response strategy."

I tightened my grip on his fingers. "I'm going with you."

"I promise I won't be gone long. A couple of days at most. And it'll be easier if you don't." He looked down at our joined hands.

My body went stiff. We hadn't figured out our future, but I thought we were on our way to something permanent. "Why would it be easier?"

"It's such a short trip. You wouldn't have to deal with the jet lag. You could stay right here and relax without any distractions." He leaned in for a kiss, but I turned so he caught only the corner of my mouth.

"And what about you?" This time, my tone turned snarky. "Is Jackson Jones going to be a distraction?"

He backed up, and even though I was pissed, I missed the connection with his hands. He smoothed down the legs of his shorts. "It's not like that. It's never been like that."

"You mean your attraction is one-sided? Because it's definitely like that."

"Jay is straight," he said, his voice flat. "He's never felt that way about me. And I never wanted to endanger our friendship by telling him how I felt. Dr. Pradhi said I had those feelings for him because he was safe. Unobtainable. Maybe she was right."

Safe? Jackson Jones was the farthest thing from safe. He was gorgeous and rich and Cooper's best friend since they'd been teenagers. The only thing Jackson could be relied on was to fuck things up, and this time, his fuck-up might destroy what Cooper and I were building together.

Jackson Jones had big, broad shoulders, and I felt them wedged between us. I could already feel Cooper's affection for me diminishing as he problem-solved his way back into Synergy.

I'd done exactly what I'd told Mimi I wouldn't do. I'd given him my heart. But now that I'd resigned, it would be Jackson in the office with Cooper instead of me. I'd known him only six months, and our relationship was less than two weeks old. He and Jackson had a whole history I'd never match. When he reconciled with his friend, would there still be space for me?

Not if I didn't tell him what I wanted. What I needed. We'd built something special, too. It might be new, but it was worth fighting for.

"Listen to me." I waited until he met my gaze. "We're going back together. I'm not your executive assistant anymore, but I want to help with this. Because I care about you. Because I—I love you." My heart stopped because I'd ripped it off the outside of my chest and laid it out in front of the man it beat for.

He blinked at me. "You do?"

Not the reaction I was going for. Still, I doubled down. "I do."

"Ben, I—"

"Shit." I leaped up from the sofa and stared out at the pool. I'd heard this script before. Many times. And it was better when I didn't look into their eyes when they tossed my heart on the ground and stomped it.

"No, Ben, I—"

I felt his bulk behind me, but he didn't touch me. "It's fine." I tried to make my voice breezy like I didn't care, but it cracked and betrayed me. I cleared my throat. "It's fine."

His big hand came down on my shoulder, and he tried to turn me to face him. I resisted.

He stepped around me, but I refused to look up into his beautiful face that would hold only pity for me and my ridiculous feelings.

"Ben." His voice broke, and finally, I looked up. His lip trembled. "Because of what my father did to my mom and me, I have some issues with love. With what it means. With opening myself to another person. After he hit her, my dad would always apologize to my mom and tell her how much he loved her."

"Holy shit." I traced the stiff line of his jaw. "That'd fuck anyone up."

"I'm working on it," he said. "In therapy. And I think I can get there. If you'll be patient."

My heart started beating again, and the warmth came back into my fingers. "I can give you time. Whatever you need. Would you rather I didn't say it to you again?"

"No." He stepped closer until our chests touched. "Say it again?"

"I love you."

He brushed away the rogue curl on my forehead. "I felt something for you the moment you walked into my office. The instant you shook my hand. An energy. Like the way I feel here on the island. Like belonging. Like we belong together." He smiled, one corner kicking higher than the other. "My words aren't coming out right. What I want to say is that I started to fall for you that first day, and I've fallen a little more for you every day since."

"Every day?" I laid my hands on his chest and felt his heart beating fast. "Even that day I was bitchy because you sprung that company-wide town hall on me with one day's notice?"

"Especially that day. You were a general, rallying the team, making it happen. And it went off without a hitch. I deserved every dirty look you threw at me. But it wasn't until you came here to the island and detoxed me and bought me shirts"—he plucked at the shell-printed shirt he wore—"that I thought…"

I was going to black out from the pressure building in my chest. "That you thought what?"

"That you might feel the same way. That we could be together. In a relationship. Boyfriends, though using that word makes me feel about fifteen years old."

Everything snapped into place like Mjölnir rocketing into Thor's hand. Cooper felt the way I did. He just couldn't say it yet. I leaned over and kissed him, a soft brush of lips. "I'll be your boyfriend, Cooper Fallon."

A flare in his blue eyes was the only warning I had before my back hit the sofa cushions, my wrists pinned against the arm of the sofa, his hips wedged between my legs. I gasped into his mouth. He kissed me, aggressive, punishing, desperate as a soldier leaving for the front. The abrasion of his shorts against the front of my boxers sparked a warm tingle that radiated to the tips of my toes, which I wrapped around his muscled calves.

Groaning, I kissed from his smooth jaw down to his neck.

He pulled back to crash his mouth onto mine, and I opened to him, let him invade my mouth like the strident executive he was. He tasted like power. And affection. I believed in him. He had the power to make things right for us. He'd stay when things got difficult.

I trailed my hand from his knee to the bulge in his shorts. "Bedroom."

"Jesus Christ, yes." He stood then reached out a hand and tugged me upright. Holding his hand, I led him to the bedroom and sat on the edge of the bed I hadn't made up. He joined me, his thigh pressed against mine. His kisses were gentler this time, almost sweet.

But I didn't want sweet. I wanted sweaty and dirty. To claim and be claimed. We were about to leave our island paradise and return to the cold city where things would be different. I wasn't about to let him return unmarked, unchanged. Maybe I couldn't go into the boardrooms with him, but he'd remember me when he was there.

Straddling him, I pushed him to his back. I lifted the hem of my shirt.

"No," he barked. "Leave it on. I fucking love seeing you in my shirt."

I lifted one corner of my mouth in a smirk. So he wanted to claim me, too. "Fine. But your shirt comes off."

He started unbuttoning at the top, and I worked from the bottom up until we exposed his chest. All those muscles. All mine. I traced a finger from the dip in his collarbone to his breastbone, where his hair sparkled golden in the early afternoon light. I ran my finger lower, across the bumps of his abs, which tensed at my touch. When I swirled my finger through his happy trail, he curled up, those abs bulging.

I pressed him down with one finger on his sternum. "I'm thinking about where I'm going to mark you. Not too high. I don't want to mess up that pretty neck of yours and make you hide it with your collar buttoned. Though I love seeing you in a tie." I ground against his pelvis. Someday, we'd make love while he was wearing one of his silky ties. Maybe I'd bind his wrists with it. Or he could bind mine.

"Mark me," he groaned, thrusting upward. "I'm yours."

I wanted to strip him right then and put my mouth somewhere I wouldn't mark. Not yet.

With my fingertip, I circled a spot just above his hip. "Here? Or here?" I traced around his navel. Then up his ribs, where his skin rippled, to just under his left pec. "Here?" I bumped my finger over his nipple to the fleshy part of his upper pec.

He thrust his hips again.

"There, I think." But I didn't do it yet. I kissed his hungry lips first, a bruising press and a slide of tongue. When he moaned, I moved down his jaw to his neck. His pulse throbbed, beckoning to me, but Cooper Fallon, COO, couldn't go back to the office with a hickey on his neck like a teenager. I trailed my lips down to his nipple and kissed it, then took the erect nub between my teeth and sucked.

He ground his hips into mine. "Please."

My skin fizzled with the power of his plea. At last, I drew a line up his pec with my tongue and circled my target once, twice, before I closed my lips over his skin and sucked. He bowed up under me, groaning.

I slid a hand between us and palmed the front of his shorts. He hissed. I licked to soothe the spot and then descended again, sucking and nibbling until I was satisfied he'd carry the reminder back to California. I kissed the spot, then I devoured his lips. When I lifted, he chased my kiss.

I dismounted from him and stood on the floor between his spread knees. I started at his neck, tracing a line down his chest, the center of his flat stomach, his navel. When I tugged off his shorts and underwear, his erection bobbed, flushed and desperate.

Descending to his balls, I inhaled the mix of soap and musk. Then I licked my way up, circling the head. His body strained, and he fisted the sheets.

I sucked him down as far as was comfortable and started to work him down farther when he clutched my hair. "No."

I backed off and held the base of him in my hand. "No?"

"I want—" He levered up onto his elbows and worked his mouth. "I want you to fuck me."

My heartbeat galloped. "You want to fuck me?" It was what I'd wanted all week. For months, actually. My asshole clenched.

He shook his head. "No. I want you to do it. Fuck me."

My eyes widened. I'd always taken Cooper for a top. His gruffness, his protectiveness, even his fucking title with "Chief" in it all pointed to a dominant man. I narrowed my eyes. "This isn't your first time with a man, is it?"

"No. Though it's the first time in a long time."

I sighed through my nose. "You mean, it's the first time since you met Jackson Jones?"

He looked away. "Yes."

Fucking broad-shouldered Jackson Jones. He didn't even want Cooper, not the way I did, and still his presence filled the bedroom.

"You sure about this? I mean, I'm not huge, but it's a lot to pop someone's cherry. Or repop it after so many years, I guess." I winced. Why was I being an ass about this? Jackson wasn't here. I was. And Cooper was asking me to fuck him.

"I use toys. I think you'll find I can take you." He stared right into my eyes, a challenge. "The things you need are in the bedside table."

I walked to the table and opened the top drawer. Sure enough, there was a bottle of lube, an unopened box of condoms, and an array of toys. A vibrator, a dildo, and a graduated set of butt plugs, one of them the biggest I'd ever seen in real life.

I pulled it out of the drawer. It was a monster, as big as my fist. "You've used this?"

"Yes."

"Hmm." Next time, we'd get out his toys and play.

But he didn't want a toy. He wanted me. At least, he thought he did. Penetrative sex changed things sometimes. And my relationship with Cooper rested on a knife's edge. He'd just proposed to leave me here while he went back to California. I didn't want an awkward first time to be another reason for him to close himself off again.

"You sure about this? We don't have to. I'm happy with what we've done so far."

"I want you, Ben. I'm fucking sure."

The tightness in my chest loosened. He'd said what he wanted, and I was going to give it to him. I opened the box of condoms and pulled one out. I set the bottle of lube on the bed.

I stepped back between his knees. Holding his gaze, I knotted the hem of his T-shirt to keep it out of the way, then, with as much swagger as I could muster, I shimmied out of my underwear.

This was it: the claiming I'd wanted. Whatever I'd said about not needing it, the caveman part of my brain insisted we did. A few drops of precum beaded at the tip of my cock.

"Ben, stop thinking and fuck me. I need you." Cooper set his hands behind his knees and lifted his legs, opening himself to me.

I ripped open the condom package and rolled on the latex. "You're sure."

"Dammit, Ben, don't fucking tease me."

I smiled. There he was. He might be bottoming for me physically, but he was still in charge.

I poured the lube into my hand and let it warm up for a few seconds. Then I slathered it over his dick, stroking it until he sighed and relaxed his tense muscles. At last, I smeared it across his hole, circling it with a slick finger. "Okay?"

"Mmm. Yes."

I worked a finger inside, then two, as I continued jacking him languidly with my other hand. "You want to come first? It might relax you."

"No, I want to come while you're inside me if I can."

"Such a romantic." I clucked my tongue. But that was what my romantic heart wanted, too. I squeezed a third finger inside him and found his prostate. Gently, I rubbed it, and he started to squirm. I stopped moving my fingers. "Feel okay?"

"Y-yeah. Don't stop."

"No, love." I worked my fingers inside him, watching his face. His lips parted, and his eyes closed. When I sped up my movement, his legs shook. That was my signal.

I removed my fingers, lubed myself up, and lined up at his entrance. "Look at me, love."

When he opened his eyes, I pushed in. He didn't clench, so I kept going until I was fully seated, the tight squeeze sending sparks straight to my spine. I paused. "Okay?"

He nodded, not breaking his stare. As I backed out and thrust in again, I drowned in the frost-blue pools of his eyes. I was so gone for this man. How could he think to go back to California without me? I wasn't sure I could even let him go to the office alone. I never wanted to break this connection, the electricity that coursed through me every time I touched him.

Heat sparked along my spine, urging me to go faster, but I kept a measured pace. My heart jackhammered in my chest as I watched him, his jaw slack and his eyes unfocused. Skin slapped against skin. A few drops of precum dripped onto his belly, and I dipped a finger into it and smeared the liquid over the head of his dick. "Is this okay?"

"God, yes, I'm—" He snapped his eyes shut as he full-body shuddered and come jetted across my hand and onto his abs.

I sped up my thrusts as I watched his dick jerk against his abdomen. My own orgasm rocketed toward me. I pulled out, ripped off the condom, and a couple of strokes later, my come splashed next to his on his chest.

I braced a hand on his knee, spots dancing in front of my eyes and my chest heaving.

When my vision cleared, I gazed down at Cooper. His eyes were open again, soft and hazy. He ran a finger across his sticky chest. "That was...incredible."

My chest expanded. The caveman inside me danced at seeing my lover coated in our pleasure. The softer, modern man was ready for a cuddle.

"I'll be right back." I nabbed a towel from the bathroom, cleaned us up, and tossed the towel in the hamper. Then Cooper and I nestled back into the bed and pulled up the covers. "Still good?" I murmured into his chest.

"So good." He kissed the top of my head and lay his heavy arm over my side. "You?"

I nudged my foot between his legs and hooked him closer. "Perfect."

And for that glorious hour, it was just the two of us in the bedroom. No Synergy, no Jackson Jones. Just me and my boyfriend.

29

BEN

COOPER STARED at the dog sitting between us in the back seat of the SUV. "I think he'd be happier staying on the island."

He thought I'd be happier staying behind, too. Not without him. And I knew Coco felt the same. I scooped Coco against my chest and held him tight. He licked my earlobe. "He goes where I go." *And I go where you go.*

Cooper's lips turned up in that neutral half-smile I'd gotten used to in California. "Okay. Whatever you want."

Mateo stopped the car right on the tarmac of a part of the airport I hadn't seen when I arrived. The Synergy corporate jet was parked a hundred feet away, bright white against dark clouds that churned offshore.

I'd seen the plane a couple of times before, when Cooper needed me to meet him at the airport to bring him something or to brief him before or after a flight but—I swallowed—I'd never flown in it. It wasn't any bigger than the tiny plane I'd flown in from Charlotte Amalie, the one where I'd lost my lunch. And we had to fly through those dense, turbulent clouds and then across the country in it. I clutched Coco tighter.

Like he could read my mind, Cooper said, "Don't worry. Emily will fly us around the storm. It's a good thing we're getting out ahead of it."

Mateo turned in the driver's seat. "You sure you don't need me, Lito?"

"I'm sure whoever jumped Ben has either given up or is staying on the island. I've got a security team in San Francisco. We'll be fine."

Mateo nodded, but his eyes didn't sparkle the way they usually did.

"Thank you." Cooper reached into the front seat and gripped his cousin's shoulder. "For protecting us. You can come visit us in San Francisco if we decide to stay."

From the tightness in his voice, the last thing Cooper wanted was to stay.

Mateo must not have heard it. He grinned. "I'd like that."

"We might be back before you get a chance to visit." Cooper's voice was gruff, the way it always sounded in California. I missed the easy melody I'd gotten too used to on the island.

I held Cooper's hand. "We'll talk about it once you've got things worked out at Synergy." We had a big talk in our future. But we could work through it. If I could get him to take more frequent vacations, he could soak up the sun and let go the pressures of home. Hell, he could retire if he wanted. I could never support us at the level Cooper was used to, but once I finished my degree, I could find a job that would keep food on the table. And Cooper's ample savings and investment income could take care of the rest.

"Let's go." Cooper opened the door and stepped out.

I released Coco. He jumped from the SUV and shook himself while I clambered out then braced myself against the gusting wind. I gripped the end of his leash and let the gale blow me to the back of the car to grab my suitcase.

Mateo hefted both suitcases as easily as I'd have lifted a couple of laptop bags. "I've got these. You go on up."

Cooper waited for me a few steps away, my laptop bag over his shoulder. The sun hid behind the threatening clouds that reflected dimly in his sunglasses. Without the bright sunlight I'd gotten used to, he looked duller, faded like he used to look in the office.

He held out his hand and, gratefully, I clasped it. Hardly bothered by the whipping wind, he walked briskly to the boarding stairs and ascended them. I trailed him, clinging to the railing as I climbed the steep steps. At the top, I sucked in my last breath of the fresh island air. Our paradise, where I'd fallen in love at last with a man who loved me back even if he couldn't say the words.

We ducked into the plane. Cool, dry air and a warm gray interior met us. On one side was a couch, complete with blue throw pillows. It faced a table with a big-screen television above it. Toward the back of the plane were groupings of squashy leather chairs, also in gray neutrals.

Cooper led the way past the couch to a pair of seats that faced each other on the left. He sat facing forward, and I took the seat across from him. Coco sniffed the seat then jumped up beside me.

The steward approached us. "Mr. Fallon. Mr. Levy-Walters. What can I get you? Bourbon? Juice?"

It wasn't yet nine in the morning. I raised an eyebrow at Cooper. Bourbon?

"Water for me, please. Ben?"

"Orange juice."

The steward said, "We have guava juice if you'd prefer it."

"Yes, please." I held it together just long enough for the steward to disappear into the galley before I turned wide eyes on Cooper. "You had them get me guava juice?"

"It's a private plane. They stock what I ask them to."

Cooper Fallon lived very differently from me. What else would I have to get used to?

The steward returned with our drinks. "Can I get you anything else?"

Cooper silently checked with me and then said, "No, thank you. And we're ready to depart when the pilot is."

"I'll let her know." The steward walked through a door at the front of the plane.

I buckled my seat belt. Across from me, Cooper scowled at his phone.

"Is everything okay at the office?"

He swiped something away, then set it on the table between us. "Weston scheduled a meeting early this afternoon. I'll have to go straight there."

"And Jackson?" I hated asking, but I needed to understand their relationship, too. The thought of Cooper and Jackson working together, hanging out—goddammit, drinking together—while Cooper fell back under Jackson Jones's spell stabbed me right in the heart. Would he still care about me with Jackson around?

"What about Jackson?"

"Don't you think you should clear the air?" I held my breath.

"It doesn't matter anymore. He's with Alicia. And I'm with you."

My lips wanted to curl up. *I'm with you.* But—

"You should tell him how you feel. Felt. You're best friends, and it's not fair to hold something like that back."

"I"—he scrunched his eyebrows together—"okay. Maybe not today, but sometime soon."

I had to accept it. It was his friendship. His relationship. And I had to work on my own relationship.

"So if you're going to the office, I'll..." Shit. I hadn't thought that far ahead.

"I'll get another car to take you...ah."

I couldn't tell if the shiver that went up my neck was joy that he'd almost said the car would take me home to his place or a warning that we were moving too fast, that he was trying to grab control. "No, I'll go to the office with you. I'll check in with Marlee. There's probably a few things I should deal with before I

—before I clear out my desk." I'd miss Synergy, but being with Cooper was worth giving up my job.

"And after that?"

I should've known better than to think he'd let me push that conversation to later.

"I think I should go back to my sister's. Don't you?" My voice was Mickey-Mouse high. I gulped my juice.

"If you need to get your things. Or I can send someone to get them for you."

"High-handed much?" But I spoiled my snarky comment by gripping the armrests when the plane started to move. My heart raced.

"I am, and you'd better get used to it."

Fuck. I needed a fan. And a Dramamine. I swallowed. The plane juddered as it lifted off the runway. Cold tingles ran across my skin.

"Are you all right?" Cooper wedged himself into the seat beside me and dumped Coco into his vacated seat.

"Aren't you supposed to be wearing a seatbelt?" I clutched his hand and fixed my gaze on the table, anywhere but outside the window where the jet tore through the black clouds.

"You didn't tell me you were a nervous flyer." He chafed my hand.

"I guess I didn't know. The first time I ever flew was when I came here." The front of my shirt trembled with the force of my heartbeat.

He slipped his hand out of my grip. "I'll be right back."

"No, you're not supposed to move around the cabin!"

But he was already gone. A moment later, he was back with a bottle of vodka. He poured a glug into my glass of juice. "Drink up."

My fingers trembled as I reached for the glass. But I did as he asked, sucking back the sweet juice that masked the alcohol flavor.

When I'd drunk it down to the ice cubes, he put his arm

around me and eased my head onto his shoulder. "Everything's going to be fine. Emily makes this trip all the time. Look outside. We're away from the storm. Do you feel how steady it is now that we've leveled out? It'll be like that all the way to California."

I rubbed my chest, hoping I could slow my racing heart. "Promise?"

"I promise. It'll be smooth flying until California."

I breathed out. In. "And then?"

"Maybe a bump or two on the way down." He kissed the top of my head. "But we'll be fine."

"I love you, Cooper." I turned my face up to him.

He kissed me, a reassuring press of his lips. But he didn't say it back. That was okay. For now.

The steward cleared his throat. "More juice?"

"Please." Cooper kissed me again, a little more tenderly.

The steward swept my glass off the table and left.

"You just kissed me in front of a Synergy employee, you know," I murmured against his lips.

"Did I?" The corner of his mouth quirked up. "You'd better get used to me kissing you everywhere."

"Everywhere, Mr. Fallon?" My lips felt numb and loose.

"Everywhere." He bent his head and pressed a sucking kiss just below my jaw.

I shuddered. "I could get used to that."

30

COOPER

WE WERE RUNNING LATE because I'd forgotten about the dog.

I hadn't actually forgotten about him; he was with us the entire flight. With the help of one of Sara's friends, a veterinarian, I'd scrambled for shots and papers to get Coco into the U.S. The trouble and adding another favor to my ledger with Sara had all been worth it for the radiant look on Ben's face when he snuggled into the airplane seat with Coco.

After Ben fell asleep on my shoulder, Coco jumped up, half on the seat and half on Ben, and gave me a baleful look I'd never seen on him. Those brown eyes never left me, not even to close in sleep, until we landed in San Francisco.

That was when I realized we needed a separate car. For the dog. Because we might be a progressive company, but we didn't allow dogs in the office.

The car never made it because of the snarl of San Francisco traffic, so we drove with Coco to the office.

When Ben sat on one of the chartreuse chairs in the lobby, Coco plunked down at his feet. "Don't worry about us," Ben said.

"We'll wait for you here." He had his phone out, ready to text his sister or one of his many friends at Synergy.

"Why don't you just go—" I cleared my throat. I wanted to say *home*. My home. But Ben had slept through the flight, and we hadn't had time to work through our living arrangements. I eyed the dog. Maybe he would be an asset in those negotiations. Did his sister's apartment complex allow dogs? Of course, it would be just my luck if Ben wasn't ready to move in with me and I somehow got custody of a dog I didn't want.

"We'll wait. I'll see if Marlee can come down here."

"All right. I'll text you if I'm going to be a while." Weston had been short on details of our meeting. I shouldn't have been surprised. He always held his cards close. His ego was even bigger than mine.

Upstairs, I went straight to Weston's office on the sunny side of the office at the opposite end of the floor from Jackson. I didn't have time to pop into Jackson's office even if I wanted to.

Did I want to? Since we'd talked, it didn't seem so terrible. Until I remembered what Ben thought I should confess.

I'd worry about that later when I wasn't late for a meeting with the CEO.

Julie looked up from her screen. Glancing at the clock, she tightened her lips. "He's expecting you."

I hated being late. But there was nothing I could do about it. So I rapped on the door, turned the handle, and walked in.

"Cooper." Weston sat at his desk, his white dress shirt open at the collar to show a neck almost as tanned as mine. He must have gotten out on his boat recently. As usual, his hair was perfectly trimmed, not rumpled like mine often was from running my fingers through it or smashed down like Jackson's from his headphones.

"Harris." I crossed the plush silk rug and shook his hand. It was cool, like usual. But his smile was warm like always, and the tension between my shoulder blades eased.

"Have a seat." He beckoned at the studded leather chairs in front of his desk.

I perched on the stiff cushion and leaned forward, resting my elbows on my knees. "What's this I hear about—"

He spoke over me. "Vacation looks good on you. Did you enjoy yourself on the island?"

"I did." Usually, Weston preferred to get down to business like I did, but it made sense to catch up since I hadn't seen him in three weeks. "What's not to like? A little sun, sand, and umbrella drinks." I'd never revealed to him that my family lived there. It wasn't something I usually shared. Let everyone think I was a tourist there, one who came from a suburban, white, wealthy background like most of the tech executives I encountered. Like Weston himself.

"I worry about you, Cooper." His eyebrows lowered although his forehead didn't crease. He might have let the gray show at his temples, but I'd never seen a line on Harris Weston's face. "For the past year or two, you haven't seemed as happy as when I first met you and Jones."

Maybe Botox would've made it easier for me to keep my face expressionless. By this time last year, I'd known Jackson would never love me the way I'd loved him. But none of that mattered now. Not when Ben waited for me downstairs.

"I'm doing better now. The time away gave me perspective."

"Clearly, you needed it after the incident in your office. Is your hand all right?"

Julie must have told him. Heat started at the top of my head and consumed my face. I flashed him a tight smile and held up my right hand. Only a few red marks crossed it. "It was just a scratch. No cause for alarm."

He tilted his head. With his Roman nose, he reminded me of a hawk. "I think people around here were very alarmed. Especially Jones. And even more so when you sold your Synergy shares."

The heat burned down to my chest. I wanted to unbutton my

collar, but I couldn't, not under his hawk's stare. I remained still as a field mouse.

"Fortunately, I had some funds available and was able to secure them. So they've stayed within the Synergy family." He opened his palms in a benevolent gesture.

Cool relief flowed through my veins. My shares hadn't wound up in Gurusoft's clutches. I hadn't made the company a takeover target. Weston originally had a smaller holding than Jackson or I did, but now he and I would hold roughly equal amounts of the company, with Jackson owning the largest part. Together, the three of us still held a healthy majority. I leaned back in the chair. "I'm glad you did that. I wasn't thinking clearly when I initiated the sale, or I would have spoken to you about it."

"Interesting that you didn't talk to Jones about it, either. He seemed unaware that you were divesting."

I winced. "I, ah. Like I said, I wasn't thinking clearly." Although I'd been drunk off my ass when I'd initiated that sale, I'd been clear-headed, thinking about retirement with Ben, when I'd gifted him the next chunk. Once we got past this, I'd make a rational decision about the rest of my holdings. If I decided to sell, I'd offer them to Jackson or Weston.

"I suppose good things can come of rash decisions." But he curled his lip. I doubted Weston had ever made a rash decision. And I'd never, ever seen him drunk. Not even the night after the company went public and we all became instant multimillionaires.

"Yes. They can." If I hadn't lost my mind and run to the island, Ben wouldn't have followed me. We'd have remained boss and employee, never touching, never feeling the fire that sparked between us, the pull I felt right then to him, five floors below.

"And a very good thing came from your decision to sell your shares." Weston leaned back in his chair and steepled his fingers over his chest. "We've received a buyout offer from Gurusoft. And Jones doesn't have enough shares to block it."

A chill ran across my skin. "A…what?"

"An extraordinarily attractive buyout offer. Cash plus equity. You'll be a very wealthy man." He chuckled. "An even wealthier man."

Bile rose into my throat. I'd promised Jackson I'd keep our majority bloc for just this reason. And now I'd fucked up, and Synergy would land in Gurusoft's clutches. Everything we'd built together consumed by the larger company, the software—Jackson's brainchild—broken up and built into theirs or else retired completely. Exactly what had happened to his father's company. The employees, from Marlee to Ben's sister to the newest, most junior developer, given severance packages and tossed out on the street. Only a few star developers, like Jackson's protégé, Tyler Young, would be valuable enough for Gurusoft to keep. I swallowed.

"Don't worry." He flashed me an avuncular smile. "You'll enjoy retirement. And if you don't, you can start a new company, as long as it doesn't violate the noncompete clause."

A fucking noncompete. Gurusoft would bring out the legal power to enforce it, too. They'd never let us start a new software company from the ashes of Synergy. Jackson would be furious. And I deserved it. My selfishness had just destroyed everything we'd built together. When I'd sold the stock, I'd wanted to be done with Synergy. But not like this. The familiar anger boiled in my gut.

"No!" I leaped out of the chair and stood. "I—I don't want that. Not now."

His eyebrows lifted a fraction. "It's what's best for you. And the company. You and Jones can be friends again without all this" —he waved his hand—"unpleasantness between you."

Unpleasantness. That's what he called Jackson's and my stormy—though highly effective—partnership. Synergy, the multibillion-dollar company we'd built in our dorm room, had become *unpleasantness.*

I took a deep breath like I'd practiced with Dr. Pradhi. But despite my mentor's betrayal, the anger that usually boiled just below the surface wasn't there. Sure, there was heat and hurt, but my infamous temper was still on vacation.

"No," I said again, more steadily. "Jackson and I'll fight this. We'll talk to the board—"

"Cooper, be reasonable. It's what's best for all of us." He lifted his arms to encompass his office, the sixth floor, the historic building. "We'll all take our payouts and go on to the next venture. You'll have more time to spend with your loved ones. We all will." He let his gaze drift to the framed photo on his desk, the one of himself, his daughter, Phoebe, and her horse.

The people I loved depended on Synergy. Even if Ben wasn't my assistant anymore, I couldn't leave any of them, especially not his sister, jobless. I paced a few steps away from his desk and then back to stand in front of him. "I can't. I can't let you."

Weston squared his jaw. "You will. It's the right thing to do."

My rage stayed curled up in a ball inside me, like Coco when he napped. I propped my hands on my hips, taking advantage of my size. But I kept my voice soft. "I won't."

He shook his head, and an expression almost like regret crossed his face. "You will. I have quite a few incentives to make you see my way of thinking."

"Incentives?" What could he possibly offer that would change my mind?

"You've heard of carrots and sticks. I believe you already have a carrot. You don't want to see my stick."

"A carrot?"

A slight smile lifted his lips. "Surely you consider your handsome young man a carrot? He seemed to make you quite happy."

A chill juddered down my spine. I shoved my numb fingers into my trouser pockets. "W-what?"

"I was sent a video documenting how you spent your spring break." He tapped a key sequence on his keyboard and turned his monitor to face me. The video was silent and grainy, but my face was easy to make out, my mouth gaping in ecstasy as Ben, his back to the camera, pounded into me.

My breath caught in my chest. That beautiful moment we'd shared, the closeness we'd experienced, the vulnerability I'd worked so hard to give Ben, all of it there in crude black and white for Weston to examine and judge.

"Mr. Levy-Walters is your assistant, is he not?" He craned his neck to watch the video, his face impassive. "I wonder what the board will think of your arguments when they see this."

"He resigned. Before that." I waved a trembling hand at the screen then tore my eyes away from it. How the fuck had he gotten that video? No one ever went into my place, not even housekeeping. Had Ben—? I swallowed. No. Ben wouldn't have planted cameras in the bungalow. Not ever. But who?

Weston watched the screen for a few more seconds. "Does it really matter?"

It didn't. In that video, I was a privileged man, taking advantage of a subordinate, regardless of whether I was still his employer. "Are you—are you blackmailing me?" I sank into the chair. Without the steel of my anger, I had nothing to prop me up.

He tilted his head again. "I'm simply sharing all the facts with you."

It was blackmail, pure and simple. But if I called him out on it, the video would become public. And he probably had more. Weston never came to a negotiation unprepared.

It didn't matter. What mattered was how I responded to his threat. Slowly, I rose to my feet. "I'm in love with Ben. I'm proud of our relationship."

Weston pursed his lips. "You're the Chief Operating Officer, overseeing human resources at this company. Banging your secretary—or being banged by him—is not a good look."

"You're right." I swallowed. I thought after Ben resigned, our relationship was acceptable. But the black-and-white video proved me wrong. I had all the power. I'd practically forced Ben to resign. It wasn't a good look for the COO, in charge of employee relations.

"I'll make a statement to the employees," I said. "The board will decide on the consequences for my actions. If they decide to remove me, so be it." It was what I deserved. And not so different from what I wanted. Though Ben would be pissed off about the violation of our privacy. Hell, I was, too. "How did you get that video?"

He paused the playback and speared me with a hard stare. "Does it matter?"

It didn't. Ben would be even more upset if Synergy was sold to Gurusoft and everyone he cared about lost their jobs.

I'd been wrong, so wrong about Weston. Jackson had been right all along. No one who cared about me, who respected me, would use a video like that to get what he wanted.

I'd thought of him as a father figure. But like my actual father, he didn't give a shit about me.

I leaned a hand on the back of the chair for support. "Release it if you must. I'm not budging on my position."

He tightened his jaw. "I have another card to play. I didn't want to do this, but you leave me no choice." Looking almost regretful, he picked up his desk phone and hit a button. "Julie, please send in our new security guard."

"Security guard? What the fuck, Weston?" Was he going to have me escorted out of my own building? For having consensual sex? For disagreeing with him? The anger, hot and familiar, finally woke and stirred in my stomach. My fist curled, wanting to smash something. I pinned it to my thigh.

The office door opened, and the last person I expected to see slithered through it. He wore a faded navy polo shirt. His khaki pants hadn't ever met an iron, and they were too short for his long legs, showing a couple of inches of dingy gray tube sock. He was still wiry and fit like he'd kept up with his boxing regimen, but his hair and the stubble on his jaw had gone completely white, and his face was more lined than when I'd last seen him.

He was unmistakably my father.

He scowled, and the expression replaced my anger with a wash of cold fear, even all these years later.

I retreated until the backs of my thighs hit Weston's desk. "What—?"

Weston stood, and his voice sounded at my ear. "Isn't it a coincidence that his last name is Fallon, too? I thought it was interesting enough to bring him up here to meet you."

"Mikey. It's been a while. How's your ma?"

Mamá. If Weston had found my father, he probably knew about my mother, too. All it'd take was a tiny slip—intentional or otherwise—and Mick would know where she lived. And if he knew where she lived, it wouldn't matter that I had a small army protecting her. He'd weasel his way in and hurt her.

I pushed myself off Weston's desk and took a step toward my father. "What the hell are you doing here, Mick?"

He leered at me. "Is that any way to talk to your dear old da?"

A gasp came from outside the door. Sure enough, Mick had left it open, and three people, Julie, Marlee, and—fuck—Ben, gathered around Julie's desk, their mouths gaping like Mamá's in front of one of her telenovelas.

Through gritted teeth, I muttered, "Shut the door."

He ignored me and stepped further into the office. "Is that porn?" He pointed at the screen beside me. "Gay porn? What the fuck is going on here?"

"It's security footage of your son and his assistant." I'd forgotten Weston was still there.

"Former assistant," I growled. My hands curled into fists. What if Mick thought to threaten Ben, too?

Mick chuckled. "You're diddling your assistant?" He cocked his head. "Or he's diddling you. I shoulda known you'd turn out that way. Soft. Like your ma."

"Shut your goddamned mouth." My voice was so low I almost didn't recognize it. "I'm not soft, and neither is she."

"I guess not." He snorted at the video behind me. "Not when it comes to your boyfriend."

Fuck, if he hurt Ben, the way that man had hurt him on the island—no. I couldn't give him that leverage. I couldn't let him anywhere near Ben. Couldn't let him know how special Ben was to me.

My rage scuttled back into the place it had always hidden when my father threatened me. My fists uncurled, and my hands flopped at my sides. "He's not my boyfriend."

Another gasp from the other side of the open door. I kept my wince on the inside. I'd explain later. If he'd let me.

"What the hell kinda place is this, Weston?" When Mick took a step closer, I smelled the scotch. Was he drunk in my building? I couldn't allow Mick Fallon to endanger my other employees, either. When we'd been a family, I'd never been able to protect Mamá. But I was older now, and I had the power of my position and my wealth. I'd do whatever it took to protect my Synergy family, especially Ben.

"No." I turned to face Weston, keeping my father in sight. I'd learned a long time ago never to turn my back to him. "No."

Weston's smile was tight, like the whole drama playing out here was too much even for him. "I'm sorry it came to this. But I'm glad you're seeing reason, Cooper."

Footsteps stomped away, and when I glanced past my father, only Marlee and Julie remained, staring at the ruin I'd made of my happiness.

31

BEN

NOT HIS FUCKING BOYFRIEND. I'd feared our relationship wouldn't survive the pressure of corporate boardrooms, but I hadn't predicted it'd take less than an hour for Cooper to crumble.

I threw my tissue box into the cardboard moving container on my desk. I wouldn't need it. My eyes were dry, blazing with the fire of my anger. Anger at Cooper, but also at myself. I'd hoped he'd seen me and loved what he saw. But that was all it was: hope.

Heels tapped on the floor, and I caught the scent of Marlee's perfume. "Don't do this, Ben. Stay and talk to him."

"Oh, I'll talk to him, all right." I stared at Weston's office door, which someone had finally had the sense to shut.

"So it's true? You guys are together?"

I froze, my hand reaching for the tiny cactus I kept on my desk. Fuck, I'd forgotten her old crush on my boss. And their kiss. Slowly, I turned to face her. "We were."

"Oh, Ben." Her eyes filled with tears. "Stay. Work it out."

"You heard him. He's not my boyfriend. There's nothing left to work out." I whirled around and grabbed for the cactus but missed. Pain shot through my finger, and a drop of blood welled where the spine had stuck me.

A pair of sneakers creaked, and then Jackson's voice boomed through the silent floor. "Wow, you can cut the tension here with a knife. Coop must be back."

"Not now, Jackson." Marlee put a hand on mine. "Put the box away."

"Wait, what's going on?" Jackson's gaze fixed on the packing crate. "Ben, you're not leaving, are you? You can't. Cooper will lose his mind."

"Really, Jackson, not now. Go back to your office. I'll explain it all later." Marlee's voice was gentle as a wave at the beach with the power of the ocean behind it.

"But Ben can't—"

"I can." I nestled the cactus next to the tissue box and wedged the other side with my emergency stash of granola bars. "And I will." I'd grab Coco from José in the lobby and then sneak him back into Mimi's place. I wouldn't be going to Cooper's opulent home, the one I'd fantasized about sharing with him and our dog. He had failed the very first test of our relationship. He didn't love me. He never would.

"Ben." Like I'd summoned him with the thought, he was there, crowding between Marlee and Jackson. "Stop."

I reached into the drawer, but it was empty. I slammed it shut. "No."

"Coop, what the hell is going on?" Jackson puffed up, big and bristly. "You can't bully Ben like those other assistants. You need him."

"That's just the thing, Jackson," I said. "I already resigned. So I'm leaving." A fleeting regret about the tuition program, my paycheck, and sleeping on Mimi's couch for the remainder of my twenties flitted through my brain. But I'd left my heart unprotected again, and now Cooper had shattered it like the glass on his desk. I couldn't stay.

"I need you, Ben." Cooper's voice was low, and his blue eyes were softer than I'd ever seen them. "I love you."

Jackson's mouth dropped open.

I stared into Cooper's eyes. "You're saying it *now?* After you denied me?" I'd fucking overreached again. He'd said the words, but his actions said something different. Cooper Fallon could never love me the way I needed to be loved.

"Let me explain."

"What the fuck is going on?" Jackson said in a harsh whisper. "Cooper, are you…gay?"

"Shut it, Jackson." Marlee's whisper was sharp. "Cooper, Ben, take your drama into your office. The whole floor is listening."

It didn't matter to me; I was leaving. But for Synergy's sake, Cooper needed to save face. Without a word, I pivoted and stormed into his office.

Cooper trailed me. Slowly, he shut the door, and then he took a minute to open the blinds over the interior windows.

"Don't worry. I'm not planning on touching you ever again." I flopped into the chair I usually sat in, on the other side of his desk, when I gave him his daily download and took his instructions. Then I jumped up. There was nothing normal about this situation. And I was no longer his assistant. He'd said so himself. I crossed to his seating area and eased myself into a wing chair.

When he finished fiddling with the blinds, he turned. Like he carried the weight of the building on his shoulders, he plodded to the seating area and dropped into the loveseat next to my chair.

Running both hands through his sandy waves, those waves I once had the right to touch, he stared up at the ceiling. "I fucked everything up."

I snorted. "Isn't that the truth." Righteous anger straightened my spine, and I glared at him. "How did you not know there was a security camera in your bedroom? You have to destroy that recording."

"Of course." He scrubbed his scalp. "I've put the company at risk. I've broken my promise to Jackson…"

He went on, but I stopped listening when he said Jackson's name. A red haze clouded my vision. He told everyone I wasn't his boyfriend. The beautiful thing between us was reduced to a fucking sex tape. After everything we'd said on the island, his tenderness on the jet just this morning, it meant nothing to him. His *I love you* was meaningless. I was the fool who'd mistaken it for more. Who'd given up my goddamned *job* for him.

Although he was still talking, I stood. "I don't need to hear any more."

"But I told you I love you, Ben. Doesn't that mean anything?" He stood, towering over me as usual, and all I wanted to do was lean into him.

But I couldn't. "You keep saying that. I'm not sure you and I have the same understanding of what it means."

"It means I'll take care of you. Always. Go to my house. Take a swim in the pool. Or a nice, long soak in the tub. Norma will make you something to eat. Coco, too. And when I've finished damage control here, I'll come home, and we'll talk."

"Damage control?" He winced at how high and loud my voice had gone. "I'm damage control to you? No, thanks. You take care of the fucking recording. I told you, I can take care of myself." I squared up my chin and glared at him.

His hands curled into fists. "I know you can, but that's what I do for people I love."

"People who love me are willing to admit it in public."

Cooper's face went red, but his voice was controlled. "You have to give me another chance."

"No. I don't." I brushed past him and opened the door. I picked up my box and, head high, strode toward the elevators.

I paused when I got to Marlee's desk. She and Jackson were in his office, their voices low murmurs. I reached into my box and pulled out the carton of granola bars. She'd know what to do with them when Cooper got too busy and forgot to eat.

I turned and flung open the door to the stairs. I wasn't waiting for the elevator today. I was done with Synergy. Done with Cooper Fallon.

I knew the drill. I'd go home, cry, and eat my feelings. Just like always. The only complication this time was that now I was jobless, too.

$$32$$

COOPER

SHERBET-COLORED rays streamed into my office window, making my heart ache for the many sunsets Ben and I had watched from the bungalow's deck. But I couldn't go after him. Not yet. First, I had to figure out what the hell I was going to do about my company because if I let Gurusoft take over and lay off all his friends, Ben would never forgive me. He'd gotten in a fucking airplane—twice—to prevent it. I couldn't let him down on that, too.

I bit my lip and stared at the rosy-pink clouds. On the island, Ben had worn a golf shirt in that color. It was the first time I saw his bare arms. Would I ever see them again? Maybe not, after I'd done exactly what I'd been afraid I'd do. I'd hurt him.

A rap startled me, and my best friend poked his head into my office. "You ready to talk about"—he waved his hand—"everything?"

I flashed him a grim, closed-mouthed smile that hid the emptiness inside. "I'm not sure about everything. But we do need to talk."

That furrow he always got in his forehead when his feelings

were hurt appeared. He shut the door. "We're best friends. We used to talk about everything."

I circled my desk and sat, not on the loveseat where I'd been when Ben froze me out, but across the coffee table in the corner of the chaise. I ran a hand over my face. "Jay, I've never told you everything." I'd never been open, not even with my best friend.

Not until Ben. And I hadn't been honest enough with him.

He flopped down on the end of the chaise. "You never told me you were gay."

I sighed out a breath. "I'm bisexual. Always have been."

"Why didn't you tell me?" The furrow deepened.

"Because I—it was complicated."

"Complicated how?"

Fuck, I'd just been outed in front of the CEO, my homophobic father, and half the sixth floor. Why hold this back from him?

"Because I was in love with you. And I didn't want to make you uncomfortable. I didn't want to endanger our friendship." The confession, so long in coming, didn't make me feel any lighter. I braced for his reaction.

The furrow disappeared. He opened his mouth and took a breath. Then he closed it.

Say something. Now that it was too late, I wanted him to see me. See what I'd gone through.

Finally, he spoke. "In love with *me?* But you were always yelling at me."

I sank further into the corner. "My therapist thinks I displaced my inappropriate affection with anger. And that I thought I was in love with you because you were safe. You'd never return my feelings, so I would never have to make myself vulnerable. Classic sublimation."

He scrunched his brow. "You've thought about this a lot. You've talked about it with your therapist. And yet you never said a word to me. You could've given me a fucking chance."

"Jay." I softened the edges of my voice. "I appreciate that you think our friendship is strong enough to withstand a confession of love, but you never could have returned it. What good would it have done?"

He reached for my hand and sandwiched it between his rough palms. "You know I love you, man—"

I stacked my hand on top of his. "I know. But I let all of that go when Valentine was born. I knew you had what you needed. You were complete. You were so happy. You are so happy."

He gripped my hand and then pulled back. "So you sold your shares."

Regret twanged through me, cold and sharp. "I didn't say I wasn't jealous. Hurt. And angry."

"Don't you want to work with me anymore? I thought this—Synergy"—he waved his hands at the office—"was what you cared most about."

"I cared about you. And what we built together. And then, then it was too much. When it seemed you didn't care about it anymore."

"Fuck, Cooper." He rubbed his chest. "It's not that I didn't care about it. I just had to shuffle my priorities for a minute."

I clasped a hand around my fist, easing the tension out of it. "And it felt like our friendship—I—was the lowest priority."

"Way to keep lobbing the grenades, Coop. Let it all out."

I glared at him. "Are you fucking kidding me right now?"

"No, I'm fucking serious. I'm glad you're finally telling me how you really feel. I may be a pulverized pile of emotions after this, but it'll be worth it."

"Okay." I rubbed at my knuckles. "Okay."

"This might be easier with alcohol. You want to go somewhere?"

"No, I—" I rolled back my shoulders. "I quit drinking."

He blinked his eyes wide. "You what, now?"

"I was a mess when I got to the island. I got blitzed and stayed that way. Until Ben made me stop. And I—I like who I am better without it. Want to go for a run instead?"

"Yeah. Okay. Meet you in the hall in five?"

"You sure you have time? Don't you have a wife and kids you should be going home to?"

"Coop." He reached out again and gripped my hand. "You need me. You're my top priority right now."

My eyes burned. "Five minutes."

"Sure thing." He turned to go.

I grabbed his wrist. "Wait. One more thing. Weston has that… that recording. Of Ben and me. I need it gone."

A gleam came into his brown eyes, and he cracked his knuckles. "I may have just the bit of code to take care of that. Give me ten minutes to set it up. It can do its job while we run."

The fewer questions I asked about why he had this code lying around, the better. "Thank you. You're the best."

"It's true, I'm the best coder. I'm still working on the best friend thing."

My voice was hoarse, straining through my closed-up throat. "That makes two of us. Now get the fuck out of here."

––––––––

OUR SNEAKERS POUNDED THE PAVEMENT, our steps synchronized, as we left downtown behind and headed for the trail that skirted the bay.

"So what do you want to do about the company?" Jackson shot me a glance.

"What do you want to do about it? Let it go, or are you all in?"

The furrow was back. "Of course I'm all in."

"Really? Weston said you…" Fuck. Weston.

"Weston? After what that asshat did to you today, how can you believe anything he'd say?"

"You're right. I'm sorry. I should have talked to you."

Jackson stared at the path ahead. I was glad he didn't say what was on his mind.

I lengthened my stride. "This is going to take a fuck-ton of work. And some groveling."

"Groveling? You're the jerk who sold your shares to Weston."

I winced. "Not to me. To the board."

"Oh. Then I guess I'm in." He dodged an ambling pair of Yorkies on a double leash. "You think we can grovel enough to sway them to our side at the meeting tomorrow?"

If we hadn't been practically sprinting, I'd have sighed. But, ever the competitor, I'd set the pace too fast, and I didn't have breath for that. "All we can do at tomorrow's board meeting is delay the decision. I'll call it a victory if we can get a week to work our magic."

"Maybe Gurusoft's offer isn't great." Jackson turned hopeful eyes on me. "Maybe it'll be easy to turn down."

"I doubt it. Weston called it extraordinary. He'll have gotten them to put out their best number."

"Weston." Jackson spat on the grass beside the running path. "What he did to you was low. We have to get him out now."

"If we push him out, it'll be just the two of us until we can hire someone else. That's a lot of work to take on. I can't do it myself. You'll have to shoulder your share."

"I'll hire more help. In another month, after school is out in Texas, we can ask Alicia's moms to spend the summer with us and the kids." He stared down the path. "But if I fuck up—and I will—you won't quietly pick up my slack. You'll tell me, yeah? And we'll do the work together. Or delegate it." He shot me a quick glance.

I relaxed my shoulders and shook out my hands. "Yeah."

"Okay, then. We plead our case to the board. Then what?"

I accelerated to pass a slower pair of joggers. "Pray they see it our way."

"You know I'm an atheist."

"Then you'd better grovel your ass off."

"Speaking of groveling"—he side-eyed me—"what are you going to do about Ben?"

"I don't know. I fucked it up pretty bad." I could still see the shock and hurt on his face, hear his gasp when I'd denied our relationship. "I tried to call him before we left, but he didn't pick up. I'm not sure he thinks I'm worth it."

Ben was smart not to pick up. Not to want anything to do with me. Not to give me another chance to hurt him.

I wished I was smart enough not to want him back.

Jay veered right to nudge my shoulder. "You're worth it. If I were gay, I'd totally be all over that." He waved his hand from my sweaty face to my shirt, which stuck to my chest and smelled like angst and despair.

"You would, would you." I chuckled for the first time since I'd walked into Synergy earlier. "I think Ben has higher standards."

"Seriously. He wouldn't have been so hurt if he didn't care."

My lungs seized. Confronted by Mick Fallon, I'd only wanted to protect Ben—and myself. Like all those other times, I'd frozen. I should have stood up for myself. For Ben. I didn't deserve him.

"You know what you've got to do now, right?" Thankfully, he toned down his smirk.

I sped up, and he matched my footsteps. I grunted.

"A grand gesture, baby. Marlee has this stack of books." He gestured above his head.

"No." I sliced my hand through the air. "No fucking romance novels."

He shrugged. "Your loss. Some of them are pretty hot. And she's got some with just guys that"—he cleared his throat—"they're not so bad."

"This grand gesture. Sum it up for me."

"On your left!" A bicycle whizzed past us.

Jackson slowed, and I did, too. "The point is, you have to make yourself vulnerable. Sacrifice some of that"—he waved his hand over me again—"that pride. That self-control. Show him you love him. Because after what you did, words aren't enough."

I squeezed my eyes shut for a moment. "When did you get so fucking smart?"

"After I figured my shit out with Alicia. You'll get there. It just takes practice."

"Practice? You mean I have to do multiple grand gestures?" I didn't know how to do one. How could I do more?

"No, you big nerd." He tapped the back of my head with his palm. "A relationship is fucking hard work. You're always doing something you have to apologize for. And you learn to suck it up and apologize."

If our time on the island was any indicator, he was right. How many times had I apologized to Ben? Still, he'd stayed. Until I'd denied our relationship in public.

And that proved I wasn't the best thing for him.

I didn't deserve Ben. The smart thing—the kind thing—to do was stay far away from him.

"No grand gestures," I huffed. "Let's work on our strategy to save our company."

"You mean you'll take care of Synergy first, right? And then Ben?"

"I mean, fuck right out of my love life. We have work to do."

33

BEN

"Honey, we're home."

I closed the door behind me and set down the wiggling duffel bag I'd used to smuggle Coco back into Mimi's building. He leaped from the bag, shook himself, and started snuffling along the perimeter of the room.

I sniffed hopefully, but no food smells came from the kitchen. I should've picked something up, but with no job and next semester's tuition due in a few months—and no paycheck, much less a company program to pay for it—I hated the thought of spending money for expensive take-out.

Tossing my backpack on the couch—also known as my bed—I turned toward the kitchen. Mimi stood at the sink, throwing back an allergy pill. Illuminated by the vent hood light, she looked just as drained as I felt.

"Did you work late?" I walked into the kitchen and poured fresh water into Coco's bowl.

"Yeah. They're making us pull all sorts of extra reports. I assume for the buyout."

"You didn't tell anyone about it, did you?" I'd signed a

nondisclosure when I'd hired on at Synergy. We all did. Telling Mimi anything I heard on the sixth floor was verboten, but it had all come pouring out of me last night when I'd walked in with my box. And my dog. And a bottle of Benadryl for my sister.

Coco trotted into the kitchen and loudly lapped up water from his bowl.

"Of course not. I'm being a good little accountant and keeping my nose out of business that doesn't concern me." She set the glass in the sink and gave me a flat look. Of course the buyout concerned her. Overhead departments like accounting and marketing were usually the first to be laid off.

"Jackson and C-Cooper are going to fight it. I know they will." If he didn't plan to resist the buyout, he wouldn't have bothered to say I wasn't his boyfriend. He could've taken his payout and walked out of there with his secrets intact. With our relationship intact.

Not that our relationship was more important than Synergy. My friends' jobs depended on keeping the company intact. I guessed he knew that, too. Even though he'd crushed my heart to dust, I still had to admire him a little.

"You didn't see him today, did you?" The question exploded out of me before I could stop it.

"No. Today was the board meeting. I'm sure he was sequestered up on the sixth floor." She crossed to the far counter where we kept the mail and plucked a large, stiff envelope from the bottom of the pile. "This came for you while you were gone."

She handed it to me, and I looked at the return address. Synergy. I supposed it could be paperwork about my termination. Better to deal with it while I felt like crap. What was one more stab in my empty chest? I slid my finger under the flap and pulled out a couple of sheets of paper with a cardboard backing. A cover letter. And a stock certificate. For an eyepopping number of shares.

"Shit." He'd told me about the stock transfer, but seeing those engraved certificates made it real. I shoved the papers back in the envelope. I hated the thought of accepting them. I should shred them and mail them back to Cooper in ribbons. But I'd need the money if I didn't find a job soon.

"What is it?" Mimi asked.

"A gift."

My sister raised her eyebrows.

"We were together when he did it. It doesn't mean anything now."

She beckoned for the envelope and slipped out the certificate. She whistled, low. "I'd take a meaningless gift like this anytime. This is, like, condo money. *And* European sportscar money." Ever the practical-minded accountant, she narrowed her eyes at me. "I mean, retirement money. And now Cooper needs you."

"He doesn't need me." I was just a toy to him, something to play with when it pleased him and toss aside when it didn't.

"Synergy needs you. *I* need you. If it comes down to a shareholder vote, you have to vote against the sale."

"My vote won't matter. The executives hold so many shares, it'll come down to them."

"Benny, this is going to be highly contested. Every single vote counts. Do it for the company. Do it for me."

She was right. She, Marlee, and all my other friends needed me. "For you. But not for him."

"Okay. We'll open an account for you to put those in. And then you won't be tempted to deface them."

"You mean, oops, they happened to fall into the shredder?"

"Exactly. That's a nice chunk of cash right there. You'll need it if…"

"Yeah." Without a recommendation from my former employer, with another weird gap in my work experience, finding a new job was going to be a challenge. "Now that I've taken my final exam, I'm going to start looking tomorrow."

She smiled at me, grim. "I might start, too. Just in case."

My chest tightened. "Mimi, I'm sorry."

"It's okay. At least I have advance notice. I've been wanting to do something different for a while."

"Something different? Why haven't we talked about this?"

She shrugged. "You've had your hands full. And I didn't want Mom to worry."

That made me smile a little. "Mom always worries."

"Yeah."

"Something different?" I poked her arm.

"A nonprofit, I think. Your volunteer work has always inspired me."

"A nonprofit? Mom will be worried."

"It'll be fine," she said. "You know how cautious I am."

"Yeah." If only I had a whisper of her caution, I'd never have fallen for my boss. Then I could've convinced Cooper to return to the office sooner so Weston wouldn't have had so much time to put together his scheme. If I were like Mimi, I'd have done my job and not lost my heart.

"Let's celebrate," she said. "Pizza?"

"What the hell are we celebrating?" I swallowed, but the lump remained in my throat.

"You have a little cushion." She waved the envelope. "Okay, it's not so little. A nice, fat cushion. And as of today, I have a job. We're both healthy, we have a roof over our heads"—we both looked up at the yellow water stain on the ceiling; was it spreading?—"and we have a fruity Chianti to go with it."

So, despite my low bank account balance and that tuition payment looming, we ordered pizza. And, sitting on my bed-slash-couch, we drank the Chianti. After too much wine and not enough pizza, I said, "Mimi. Mimi. Look at me."

She blinked bloodshot eyes at me. Low alcohol tolerance was a family trait. "Yeah, Benny?"

"I'm done with love. You hear me? No more. You're going to find someone and have a couple of kids, and I'll be the cool uncle and live next door."

"You know that won't make you happy, sweetie. If anyone ever needed love and a couple kids, it's you."

"Need love?" I laughed, bitter. "Not anymore. I love this dog." I scratched Coco between the ears. "I love you. And I'll love your man. Like a brother, I mean, not like a weird love triangle. And I'll love your kids. And Mom and Dad. That'll be enough."

It had to be. Because I had a feeling this time, my heart wouldn't stitch itself back together, not like it had after I'd broken up with Trey.

"But what about"—she waved her slice toward my groin—"companionship?"

"Oh, I'll fuck anyone who'll have me. But no more love. I promise. In fact, I'll find someone to fuck right now." I stood, but it was too fast. I swayed and plopped back down on the couch, and the glass of wine in my hand sloshed, splashing me and the couch. "Fuck, I'm sorry." I grabbed a napkin from the stack on the coffee table and dabbed at it.

"Don't worry about it. The fabric's dark. It won't show. It's a shit couch anyway."

"Believe me, I know."

We laughed, the way I hadn't since I'd left the island. Since he'd broken my heart. And the laughter gave me hope that I could move past Cooper Fallon. That I could live my life with my heart on the inside where it belonged and not let everyone I met break off a piece of it.

Coco seemed to know what I needed. He curled up next to me, his head propped on my knee, watching me with his soulful brown eyes. *Cooper's gone,* he seemed to tell me, *but you still have me.*

It would have to be enough.

34

COOPER

"SIT."

One word was all it took for me to know how my conversation with Jamila would go. I lowered myself into the cushioned wicker chair on her veranda overlooking the ocean. She perched on the chair beside me and poured me a hot cup of the chamomile tea she liked. It smelled like dirt and the wrong kind of flowers, pale and small.

Lifting her own mug to her lips, she said, "I assume this visit is for business, not personal?"

"Yes." Jackson and I had split up the board of directors. He'd taken his stepfather, Charles, who was also the chairman, and the half most likely to listen to him. He thought he could sway Charles to our side.

I'd taken Jamila and the other half. The difficult half. None of my other visits had been successful. Either Weston had gotten there first or they'd lost faith in Jackson and me. Maybe both. I assumed Jamila would be an easy win, so I'd left her for last. She should have agreed with me, considering our longstanding friendship. But the frown on her deep purple lips tightened my chest.

"Listen, Jamila—"

"Don't you 'listen, Jamila' me. I'm a member of Synergy's board of directors. I have to vote for what's best for the shareholders. Weston, asshole that he is, presented a strong argument the other day. And I'm not so sure keeping Synergy independent is the best move for you, my friend."

"What?" I set down the scalding tea. Despite the chill morning air, my body heated. "I built this company. Why would I want it broken apart by Gurusoft?"

She sipped her tea and set down her mug. Her eyebrows arched. "I seem to remember sitting on a different veranda and talking about your future with the company. The Cooper I spoke to then was burned out. Hurting. Done with Jackson. And Synergy. You sang a different tune."

Shit, I remembered it, too. The pain. The exhaustion. The hopelessness. What had changed? For one, I'd taken three weeks off work. And I'd had a good conversation with Jackson. He was pulling his weight so far, having exactly the kinds of interactions he hated with the board members, schmoozing and talking numbers, when all he wanted to do was write code.

But the biggest difference was Ben. He'd reminded me the company wasn't only mine and Jackson's. It was bigger than the two of us. People I cared about depended on it, believed in it. I'd been selfish to consider only myself.

"I can't—we can't—let our employees down. If Gurusoft takes over, it'll be the lucky ones they lay off. You know how toxic their work environment is."

She bit her lip. "I've heard things. Everyone has. But are you sure you're willing to stay, take back control from Weston, and act like the company founder they need you to be?"

My reply was automatic. "I am."

"Not so fast, Coop." She leaned across the end table that separated us. "It's not just the shareholders. I care about you, too. Have you talked to your therapist since you've been back?"

"I've been back five days, and most of that has been hustling to meet with shareholders. When would I have time to talk to her?"

"Make the time. You won't have my vote until you do. And what about Ben?"

His name on her lips made me want to curl around the hole in my chest. I told her what happened in the office on Tuesday. The recording Weston showed me. How he dragged my father into it and the old fear had rushed back until I said things I didn't mean.

"That snake!" Jamila exploded. "I wish I'd known that at the board meeting. Weston's so low he has to look up to see hell." She brushed her hand against her pearl-colored slacks like she could wipe off his handshake. "Do you need help erasing that recording?"

"Jay took care of it. But it was just the physical proof. I never should have slept with my assistant."

"Technically—"

"Technically nothing. As the COO, I was wrong to take advantage of him like that. I'm supposed to set an example. Once we're on the other side of this, I'll make a statement to the employees."

"Cooper." Her voice was gentle. "You can't be the COO all the time. You have to be a human, too. Humans fall in love."

"I didn't think I could. Let myself love anyone who could love me back. But in the end, I was a better person with Ben. Because of Ben."

"In the end? The Cooper Fallon I know doesn't give up."

"Mila, he walked out with his shit and didn't look back. Besides, I'm toxic. He's better off without me."

"Toxic? Dramatic, much?" She smirked. "I admit, it's going to take some hard work to get your man back after you pulled that shit. But I've never known you to shy away from hard work."

Jackson had told me the same thing. But I didn't know how to do that kind of work. Give me a stack of spreadsheets, and I'd crank through them. Presentations? I could compose them on the spot. But I'd never had a good look at people putting work into a relationship. I shuddered, remembering my parents' marriage. The constant fear in my mother's eyes.

"What if I—what if he doesn't want me back?" I picked up the mug of tea and sipped it to hide the tremor in my lips. The tea was revolting, and I spat half of it back into the mug and coughed the other half into my elbow.

She laughed. At me. But the anger didn't rise into my chest the way it usually did on the rare occasions someone—usually Jackson—mocked me. My heart hurt too much.

"Of course he wants you back. He was over the moon for you when I saw you on the island. He needs you to prove you care about him."

"Jay said I need to make a grand gesture."

She snorted. "I don't know about that. You have to prove you're serious about him."

"I'm plenty serious. But I need to think about what's best for him, too. What if that's not me?"

She waved her hand like my shortcomings were light enough to waft away on the ocean breeze. I knew better. They were massive. Heavy. They'd weighed me down for years. I couldn't let them crush Ben, too. What I did in the office last week flattened him. He didn't deserve that.

"We're going inside." Jamila stood. "We'll get you something to drink, something to eat. You'll think better then. And we'll make a plan for Synergy and for Ben. If you carry it through, if you promise to take more vacations and see your therapist regularly, I'll vote against the merger."

With Jamila's vote, we might have a majority. I was less confident about her help with Ben. She'd had even more meaningless relationships than I had. "No more chamomile."

She stood and pulled me to my feet. Her arms went around me, and I relaxed into her hug. I hadn't felt that safe since I'd eased out from under Ben our last morning on the island. "Okay."

I let her lead me inside. Because one thing I'd learned through all this was that the only way I could regain control of my life was by giving up control.

———

THAT AFTERNOON, I tracked down my mother. If I'd remembered it was Sunday, I wouldn't have bothered calling her security detail. There was only one place she'd be.

Even though Mass had been over for hours, the scent of incense clung to the building like vines on the trees on the island. Bitterly, I turned away from the doors to the sanctuary. God hadn't saved us from Mick Fallon. His Church hadn't saved us. I'd saved us both.

I found her in the donation closet. A skinny young Latina clutching a swaddled baby to her chest stood nearby, her wide eyes on my mother as she dug through plastic bags of clothing. A black eye swelled on the woman's tan skin.

Mamá emerged from the bag and held up a pair of black pants and a garish floral blouse like she'd found the cure to cancer. "Pruébate estos, querida." She extended them to the young woman.

Then she saw me.

"Lito! You're here!"

She knew I'd come back; I'd called her the night we'd returned.

"Don't get excited. I'm not looking for salvation. I'm looking for you."

She held up a finger to me. Gently, she took the baby from the woman and handed her the outfit. "Pruébate estos." She nodded at the clothes the woman clutched.

The baby in her arms, Mamá stepped into the hall outside, and I followed her. Pictures of Mary Magdalene rolling back the stone from Jesus's tomb, brightly crayon-colored by the kids in CCD, fluttered on the walls.

Mamá tilted her head at me the way Coco used to do some-times. "You don't look happy. Isobel said you were happy."

"Jesus, Mamá. Hello to you, too."

She covered the sleeping baby's ear with one hand. "You take the Lord's name in vain in church, Miguel? I raised you better."

My skin heated the way it always did when I remembered the man she'd named me for. "He hasn't bothered you, has he?" The security guys reported that he hadn't tried to see her, but they weren't monitoring her phone. She wouldn't let me do that.

"No. Has he tried to see you?"

"Not since Tuesday, when I saw him at work." I wished I hadn't had to tell her, but I'd done it for her own safety.

"Good. But tell me, why aren't you happy? Is it because of him?"

I leaned against the white-painted cinder block wall. "Nah. Work and…other things."

"Ah. Isobel told me about tu novio. Ben. What happened?"

"I—the CEO confronted me with a—a video. Of Ben and me. Then he brought in Da—Mick. It was a lot, and I reacted badly."

"Did you talk to your therapist about it?"

"Je—" I choked it back. She sounded just like Jamila. "I have an appointment this week."

"Good. I wish…" She looked down into the sleeping baby's face and fussed with his blanket.

I touched her shoulder. "What do you wish, Mamá?"

"That I'd been stronger when you were little. That I'd stood up to him."

The incense-soaked air was too heavy to breathe. "Mamá, no. You did the best you could."

"And so did you, Lito. I'm proud of you."

"I never stood up to him. Not the way I should." All those times I'd heard them in their room, I should have stormed in there. Done something. Done anything. But I never had the courage.

"No, no. What I needed you to do was grow bigger than him. And you did."

"That's just genes—"

"No." She laid her hand over her heart. "Bigger here."

My own blackened heart thumped. "I'm not, though."

The young woman stepped into the doorway. The blouse, eye-searing as it was, fit her well and brought out the red highlights in her hair.

Mamá handed her the baby. "Un minuto, querida."

When the woman returned to the closet, Mamá stared me hard in the eye. "You're a good man."

I scuffed my dress shoe against the dingy linoleum tile. "Am I, though?" I ticked off items on my fingers. "I nearly hit my best friend. I sold my stock even though I'd promised Jay I wouldn't, and that endangered my company and every one of my employees. And then, when things got difficult, I said Ben wasn't my boyfriend. Even though I wanted him to be. I didn't tell him I loved him until it was too late." I squeezed my eyes shut so I couldn't see the disgust on her face.

"Lito." She reached up to tip my chin so I'd look her in the eye. "Everyone makes mistakes. Sometimes they make a lot of them, all in a row. But listen, you're not like your father. I knew him at his best and at his worst. And even on your worst day, you're better than he was on his best."

"Really? Because when I smashed my desk, I felt a whole lot like him."

"Really." She put her work-roughened palm on my cheek. "You care about doing the right thing for other people. For your family. For people you love."

"But I didn't, Mamá. I fu—I screwed everything up."

"But you're working to make it better, aren't you?"

I sighed. "I apologized to Jay. And I'm doing everything I can to save the company."

"And Ben?"

"He's better off without me."

"From what you said, he doesn't think so. He loves you. And who are you to make that decision for him?"

I squeezed my eyes shut. "Stop being so wise."

"Lito. I earned this wisdom. By making many, many mistakes." She patted my cheek. "I want you to make better choices. Apologize to him. Show him you love him. If he still loves you, that's all it will take. You deserve happiness."

"Mamá. It's not that easy." According to Jackson and Jamila, I needed something more to win back Ben. Jackson's grand gesture ideas were shit. And Jamila might be great at planning app development, but her get-back-Ben plan verged into stalking and kidnapping and was more likely to land me in jail than to soften Ben's heart.

"For you? No, it's not easy." She patted my cheek. "You have to let down those walls of yours first. For you, that's the hardest part."

The ice-cold chill in my stomach told me she was right. "And then?"

She smiled. "Then you show him the kind of man you are. In here." She laid a hand over my heart.

Show him sounded a lot like Jackson's fucking grand gesture. And I knew the expert to guide me.

35

COOPER

COFFEE SLOSHED over the rim of my cup and splashed onto the counter in the sixth-floor employee break room.

Jackson leaped to help with a wad of paper towels. "Stay back! You can't walk into the board meeting with coffee on your suit."

"Goddammit, I know that," I growled, stepping away from the cascade of coffee over the counter while trying to hide how my hands shook. "More paper towels."

"Guys! Back away from the spill," Marlee barked from behind us. She sighed, the weight of the world in it. "I'll clean that up. Here." She handed me a green smoothie. "Drink this instead."

"Thanks." I gave her a weak smile.

"We can't have our star player missing his antioxidants or whatever." Her tone was joking, but her concern showed in the tightness in her mouth. Her job was riding on my performance in the boardroom this morning. If Gurusoft took over, Jay and I— and his assistant—would be the first to go.

"I'll do my best." I wished I could say I wouldn't let them down, but I wasn't sure we had the votes. Since I hadn't followed Jamila's win-back-Ben plan, she hadn't committed to voting against the buyout. And at least one of Charles's bloc of two voters would be swayed if she didn't. Weston had three board members firmly on his side.

If only Jay were still on the board, I'd feel better. But Weston's first power grab a few years ago had been to vote him out after Jackson had missed too many board meetings. Fine, he'd missed every single one, but I'd argued hard for my friend.

Jay clapped me on the shoulder. "I know you can do it. Now drink up and let's go."

I poked the straw into the lid and took a deep swallow of the green smoothie. Like the others Marlee had gotten me this week, it tasted like grass and dirt. Ben must have possessed some kind of smoothie magic mere mortals couldn't replicate. Thinking of him widened the hole in my gut. I put my hand over it.

"How's the smoothie?" Marlee asked, tossing the coffee-soaked paper towels into the compost bin.

"Delicious. Thank you." She'd be all right. I'd ensure she and Ben had jobs after this, even if there was no longer a Synergy to employ them. *Ben.* "Did you, ah—?"

"I invited him to lunch. We're going to eat in the cafeteria downstairs, so you'll be able to find us. You *do* know where the employee cafeteria is?" She arched an eyebrow.

"I do. I just don't eat there. Our employees have a shockingly poor idea of nutrition. But I'll see you there. After."

"Come on. I'll walk you to the door." Jay crooked an elbow.

I eyed it with distaste.

He winked, a habit he'd picked up last year in Texas. "Too soon?"

"It will always be too soon for that, asshole."

He grinned. "There's my Cooper Fallon. But seriously, walk with me."

He led the way out of the break room, and we walked side by side toward the boardroom, for possibly the last time. The board-room was slightly more opulent than the other conference rooms, with our cushiest chairs and best videoconference gear. I knew for a fact our cleaning crew toiled after every meeting to wipe the fingerprints off the sleek glass table. Weston had chosen it, I suspected because he wanted to be able to scrutinize every part of a person's body, from their sweaty hands clasped under the table to their nervously tapping toes.

At the door, I straightened my spine. Jay flicked a phantom fiber of lint off the shoulder of my jacket. "Go get 'em."

He didn't need to say anything more. I knew from the stiffness in his posture, the tightness in his voice, that what happened in the boardroom mattered to him. And I wasn't about to let down my friend.

I nodded and walked through the door. The other board members were already inside. Some sat at the table, scanning the papers Julie had set at each place. Others stood at the credenza, filling their plates with pastries or topping up their coffees. Weston sat alone at the head of the table. He caught my gaze and smiled. Before, I'd have said his smile was self-assured. Confidence-inspiring. Since that fiasco in his office, when he'd thrown all my demons in my face, his smile looked secretive. Smug.

I turned back for one more reassuring glance at Jackson, but that wasn't who stood at the door. The man was bulky. And familiar-looking. How did I know him? The way the too-small Synergy security shirt bulged at the buttons reminded me of another ill-fitting uniform. I sucked in a breath. The housekeeper in my bungalow. I knew it for certain when he turned and limped away.

What the fuck was he doing in my building? I strode through the door. I'd confront him. Get his ID. "Jay, grab—"

My voice evaporated in my suddenly dry throat. The last person I ever wanted to see again stood in the hallway. I swore under my breath, and my heart hammered.

Unlike the other man's, his Synergy-logo button-down fit his lean, muscular frame. But his dark pants, lacking a belt, sagged at the waist. And his black shoes were scuffed and worn at the toes.

"Going somewhere, son?" My father crossed his arms.

Jackson was heading toward his office, but at the sound of my father's voice, he whirled to face him. "What the hell? What are you doing here?"

"Security." Mick Fallon sucked his teeth.

My hand curled into a fist, but Jackson stepped between us. "You're going to need fucking security up here when I—"

"Is there a problem?" Weston glided out of the conference room, a smirk on his face.

"What the hell, Weston?" Jackson burst out. "You can't bring him here."

My father bristled, and I flinched. I was as tall as he was, and heavier, but a dozen years of being his punching bag had trained me too well.

His smile broadening, Weston leaned in the doorway. "I think I can."

"Leave it, Jay," I muttered.

"But—"

"It's fine." It was anything but fine, and Jackson knew it. Weston had brought my father here again to fuck with my head. As a threat, too. He'd out me as the son of an abusive drunk, a poor one, so different from most of the wealthy board members. I winced. Would the board members we'd swayed to our side change their minds when they knew I wasn't one of them? If they knew that if it weren't for my mother's encouragement and a hell of a lot of scholarship money, I could've ended up as their gardener or their driver?

The scents of sour sweat and whiskey flooded my nose. I tossed my plastic smoothie cup in the trash. "It's fine," I said more to myself than anyone else.

"I think it's time for you to go back to work, Jones." Weston put his hands on his hips.

My best friend stared into my eyes. "Coop, are you—"

"I'll be okay. I'll let you know what happens."

He glared at my father, then at Weston. Then he strode off toward his office.

"You can wait out here, Mr. Fallon," Weston said to my father. "I'll call you if we need you."

Did he mean if things got rowdy in the boardroom, or if he needed to throw my father in my face again? I squared my shoulders. It didn't matter. Or it shouldn't. I had a job to do. *Focus.*

"Wait," I said.

Weston turned and raised his eyebrows.

"There was another man out here. A man with a limp. Who was he?"

"I have no idea." Weston's face was a mask. But those deep blue eyes of his flicked to the side so quickly that if I hadn't been closely watching him, I would have missed it. He knew the man. Why was he now a security guard at Synergy?

But before I could press him, Weston said, "It's time for the meeting to start. You know how we are about punctuality."

He was right. I was already at a disadvantage. The last thing I needed was for the board to have another reason to vote against me.

Numb, I followed Weston into the room. The board members had settled into their usual seats around the table. Charles Hayes sat at the head, and the seats to his right and left were reserved for Weston and me. Jamila sat in the leather chair to the left of mine; the secretary, Rod Sanchez, bent over his laptop at the foot of the table, and the rest were arranged along the sides.

Weston closed the door behind me. The click of the latch felt like I'd been locked into a cage to fight for my life. I froze a smile on my face and greeted each of the board members, who suddenly felt less like my team and more like my opponents. Even Jamila, who didn't miss the tremble in my fingers when she shook my hand.

"Are you okay?" she asked, her big, brown eyes widening with concern.

"I'm fine. I talked to Dr. Pradhi yesterday," I whispered. She hadn't made me feel any better, but at least it had been an hour that I wasn't concerned about the fate of my company. I'd had bigger demons to confront.

And now one of those demons, my father, menaced me from outside the boardroom. And the mystery man—Weston's man, who'd been *in my home*—roamed freely in the halls.

She whispered, "What about—"

I shook my head. I had to wait until the meeting ended to make my hail-Mary pass. If Ben wouldn't listen to me that afternoon, I was done. No more chances.

I took my seat and, while Charles called us to order and ran through the agenda, I jiggled my knee under the table. Weston smirked at it through the glass, but I couldn't stop. I wanted to shake each board member. They wouldn't be here if not for Jay and me. They had to see that we were worthy of another opportunity to make the shareholders—and each of them—millions of dollars richer. I glanced at the clock. Would we finish in time for me to race downstairs and meet Ben? And would I have good news or bad to share with him and Marlee?

Finally, Charles turned to the main event. "First item. As we discussed in last week's meeting, we received a buyout offer from Gurusoft. We agreed to meet today to vote on whether to accept or reject the offer. If we accept, we call a shareholder vote to confirm. Now I'll open the floor to discussion. Harris, I believe you asked to go first?"

Weston stood. "Thank you, Charles." He slowly circled the table. "I believe some of you have been approached to ask for your vote against the merger. I understand that emotional arguments have been made to encourage you to side with Mr. Fallon, who seems to have recently changed his mind about the company.

"You see, Mr. Fallon"—I winced every time he used my last name, remembering that I shared it with the despicable human on the other side of the door—"recently sold a significant number of his Class A shares in the company with the intention to exit his position. Now, suddenly, he's regained interest in keeping the company independent. Why?" Weston spread his hands. "Maybe he'll tell us when it's his turn to speak. Maybe it has to do with what Mr. Fallon got up to during his leave of absence."

Frosty recognition gushed through my veins. That was it.

Weston's man, the pretend housekeeper and now pretend security guard, had planted cameras in my house and reported to Weston what I'd *gotten up to*. My brain clouded with rage, but I fought through it to think clearly. Where else had I seen him? Perhaps in the bar, but I'd been too drunk to trust my memory. At the restaurant with Ben that night? There had been a man eating alone, and he'd had a similar build. The day we went shopping? I couldn't be sure. I had eyes only for Ben that day. And I'd been worried about his ankle.

His ankle.

Ben said a burly guy had jumped him and Coco bit him. Was that why he was limping? Was he the guy who attacked Ben?

My vision hazed in red.

Beside me, Jamila cleared her throat. She narrowed her eyes at the pen in my fist. I'd bent it with the force of my grip, and crimson ink dribbled over the back of my hand. I snatched up a napkin and blotted it.

Focus.

"Regardless, Mr. Fallon's"—Weston hesitated and spat out the next word like it tasted bad—"instability should be a cause for concern to this company and this board. We've all observed founders with emotional attachments to their companies who fail to see what's in the shareholders' best interest. I'm afraid we're in that situation now. Mr. Fallon appears to have an emotional entanglement"—his blue-eyed gaze caught mine and held it—"that may prevent him from seeing clearly that a sale is what's best for Synergy."

Beside me, Jamila shifted. Despite the clear signs I was cracking—I swiped at more red ink—she couldn't agree with him, could she? I glanced at her, but she kept her gaze on Weston.

He continued, "I urge you all to consider this generous offer from Gurusoft. It might mean the end of an era for some, but it will surely bring new opportunities for success to the company and new wealth to its shareholders."

There were murmurs of agreement on Weston's side of the table. After Weston took his seat, Charles turned to me. "Cooper, I believe you'd like to say a few words?"

"I would." I stood and paced behind my chair, willing my emotions to settle. No matter how much I loved Synergy, today was about logic, not emotions. "Harris is correct that a few weeks ago, I was burned out. Discouraged. Ready to leave Synergy behind me. I left abruptly, leaving Harris and others behind to clean up the mess. And I apologize for that.

"I also sold a significant part of my stake in the company, fully intending to exit Synergy as Harris said." More murmurs erupted on the other end of the table. I paced around that side to quiet them.

"However, in my time away from Synergy, I learned some things about myself." On this side of the table, I could see Jamila's face, but she kept her expression blank. "I've always been a hard worker. Not many of you know this, but I came from poverty. We never had much, but my mother encouraged me to study and to work hard so I could raise myself above what I'd always known."

Weston's shoulders stiffened, but he didn't turn around.

"My hard work and Jackson Jones's brilliance created this company. We gave it everything we had: our money, our effort, our time. I'll always be grateful to Jackson, to our early employees, and to this board, who have helped shape Synergy into a success beyond anything that boy who lived hand to mouth, who was lucky to be tall and strong enough to get his first job in construction at fourteen, could have imagined.

"I was so proud of what we'd built, so invested in its success, that I hardly took a break from the time we founded the company a decade and a half ago to now." I glanced at Jamila. "I know now that was a mistake. That I disregarded my own mental health for the sake of the company's success.

"When I had an unexpected reaction to a disagreement with Jackson, I realized I needed a break. And in my emotional state, I thought I needed to make that break permanent. I was unsure that I could contribute to the company in a positive way after that.

"But while I was away, a good friend"—I caught Jamila's gaze and held it—"talked to me about balance. I don't always have to be the one running the show. I have strong partners in Jackson, in the board, and in the many strong employees we've hired to share the load. I intend to take regular vacations going forward. Stepping away from time to time will make me a better leader."

I continued my circuit around the table. "Someone I care about told me how much the company means to him. Other employees have approached me in the halls this week to do the same. Over the years, we've worked hard to make Synergy a place where everyone feels welcome. Where our diverse workforce feels connected to the company while maintaining a healthy work-life balance. Well"—I chuckled—"except for its COO, and as I told you, I'm taking steps to change that."

Jamila's stony expression cracked into a grin.

"I think we're all aware that Gurusoft doesn't share our company values. Article after article has highlighted their toxic work culture. From mandatory overtime to bullying and harassment, to a disappointingly homogeneous board, Gurusoft runs their business very differently from what we're trying to do at Synergy." Sure, Synergy could be more diverse, but we were trying. Gurusoft didn't appear to be doing that. "We all agree that diversity of employees and leaders leads to diversity of ideas and innovation. I think that separately, Synergy can surpass Gurusoft in the next five years.

"But we'll never know that if we vote today to let Gurusoft take over. Synergy's products, our innovative culture, and our brilliant ideas will die a slow death inside our competitor. I hope you'll all join me in voting against the buyout."

I was still standing, but Weston rose from his seat, his expression no longer avuncular but angry. "This is a financial decision. I encourage you all to consider your fiduciary responsibility to the organization, rather than your emotions." He pursed his lips. "Mr. Fallon, while talking about Synergy's *values,* has entangled himself with his secretary. He's not as noble as he'd have you believe."

Leather creaked as the board members turned in their seats. A few gasped. All eyes turned to me.

Well, fuck. I'd hoped to keep the board out of my bedroom, but Weston had opened the door and flipped on the lights.

"It's true that I've embarked on a romantic relationship with my former assistant. I love him. And I'll do whatever it takes to be with him.

"I love this company, too. Ben resigned before we started our relationship. He was an asset to the company, and if he ever decides to come back to work at Synergy, Human Resources and I will work together to ensure there's no impropriety with his employment, that we set a good example for other intracompany relationships. I think I owe it to Ben and the other Synergy employees to be honest about who I am and who I love."

The other end of the table grumbled.

"But my personal relationships aren't what's up for debate today. The acquisition of Synergy is. Synergy will be stronger without the weight of Gurusoft and its pernicious business practices. I hope you agree with me and vote no today."

I sat down, and after a long moment, Weston did, too. I looked around the table. Charles gave me a subtle nod. Like he was proud of me. On my other side, Jamila patted my shoulder. The two board members to her left kept their expressions blank, but their eyes bounced between Charles and me. At the end of the table, Sanchez typed the notes furiously into his laptop while Weston's cohort frowned. Weston himself glared at me, his sapphire eyes blazing and his jaw grinding under his gray goatee.

"Would anyone else care to speak?" Charles asked. When no one spoke, he said, "All right, then. Who moves to vote on the matter of Gurusoft's offer to purchase Synergy?"

36

BEN

THE FLUORESCENT-YELLOW VISITOR'S badge clipped to my shirt pocket annihilated my appetite. Sitting in the Synergy employee cafeteria, I picked at my salad as my former coworkers came to our table, sometimes individually, sometimes in groups. Some of them were surprised I wasn't working there. Others had heard I quit—no one seemed surprised I'd left notoriously demanding Cooper Fallon—and asked where I was working. *Still considering my options,* I told them, like I had a half-dozen offers and not zero. *Taking some time to think about my next steps,* I said, which was closer to the truth.

The one good thing about agreeing to meet Marlee for lunch at the cafeteria was that there was no chance I'd run into Cooper there. The employees voted on the menus, and they liked fat and carbs. If you knew to pass by the deliciously greasy burger grill, there were plenty of healthy options. But Cooper avoided the cafeteria like if he looked at it, he'd gain ten pounds.

"Ben." Marlee said my name loudly, like it wasn't the first time. "Earth to Ben."

"Sorry." I speared a bit of lettuce and a blueberry. "It's just strange to be here again."

"I know. I miss you."

"I miss you, too." I missed my job and my former coworkers. Updating my résumé and spamming it out to every job board I could find was more painful than I'd expected. Especially when I had to enter an end date on my employment with Synergy. I could imagine the questions they'd ask me about it. *Why did you leave after six months?* And the answer I couldn't give: *I fell in love with my boss. Too bad he didn't feel the same way.*

"I heard you haven't answered his calls or texts?"

I swirled a piece of lettuce through a puddle of vinaigrette. "I blocked his number."

"Oh, honey." Her voice was full of sympathy.

It felt good when I did it. The final severing of communication. I'd been tempted to listen to his voice mail messages, but I deleted those, too. If he couldn't acknowledge me in public, I wouldn't listen to him in private. "It's okay. I'll be okay. I know better now."

"You know better?" She pushed her own salad around on her plate.

"Better than to fall in love again."

"You deserve love, you know."

Ah, Marlee and her romantic ideas. "Deserving love and being willing to break myself open again are two entirely different things." I set down my fork.

I glanced across the table at Marlee and her still-full salad bowl. Shit, I was a self-centered asshole. Something was bothering her, too. "Marlee, what's up with you? Everything okay with Tyler?"

"Oh." Her eyes went soft at that. "Yeah, we're good. In fact, we're going away together this weekend. Some sort of big surprise." She made jazz hands.

"And your dad?"

Her smile dimmed. "He's good. About the same. But same is better than worse, I guess."

I reached across the table and patted her hand. "You're getting him excellent care. Same is good. Is that what's bothering you?"

She turned over her hand and squeezed. "Not exactly. Today is the day"—she lowered her voice to a whisper—"they're voting."

"That's today?" I shouldn't have cared. It didn't affect me at all anymore. But my breath caught in my chest. Would Cooper be able to save his company, everything he'd worked so hard for? Or would he get what he said he wanted, an extended break, retirement? As idyllic as our time on the island had been, I couldn't picture him lying on the beach, day after day. Though lying on the beach—and in bed—with him had been something I'd wanted once upon a time. I'd been back from the island for seven days, but it seemed like a lifetime separated me from those perfect weeks with Cooper.

I sensed it before I heard it. A prickle along my arms made the hair stand up. Then the hum in the cafeteria lowered.

Marlee, who faced the entrance, looked up and blinked her eyes wide. I swiveled in my chair.

Cooper stood a few feet inside the entrance, scanning the faces in the cafeteria.

"Shit!" I whirled around, my back to him. Of all days for Cooper to make a state visit to the cafeteria, I had to be sitting there like a stalker.

Marlee waved her arm at him.

"No! Don't do that!" I whispered.

She arched an eyebrow and continued to wave. "I want to find out how the vote went. And you two need to talk."

Fuck. Me. It had all been a ruse. "Our friendship is over. I will not be the loving gay uncle to your adorable children."

Her cheeks pinked. "Be reasonable. You love him. You can't avoid him forever."

She lowered her hand, and I sensed him, tall and inflexible, standing next to us. "Mind if I join you?"

Unnatural silence surrounded us like still water in a lagoon. I nodded. He certainly wouldn't say anything here, in the middle of the busy cafeteria, surrounded by employees trying to figure out why the COO had suddenly developed a taste for the sloppy joe special.

He lowered his tall frame into the chair next to me, but he didn't look at me. He looked at Marlee and said, "It went our way. No sale."

Some of the tension left me, and I slumped against the plastic back of my chair.

She squealed and clapped her hands. "I knew you'd do it! You told Jackson?"

"He was lurking outside the boardroom."

"And Weston?" she whispered.

"He's out. And his lackeys with him. Including my father." His lips tightened. "I told the board about Weston's behavior to persuade me to support the sale. They took away his seat on the board. He wasn't pleased."

It was probably an understatement. I could imagine Weston, all cold fury and dastardly plans for revenge. I shivered. At least I wouldn't bear the brunt of that.

He turned to me. "I took his ace. I told them how I feel about you."

"You didn't," I said, my voice flat and unbelieving. He'd denied our relationship to Weston. No way would he reveal it to the board, who could fire him like they'd fired Jackson.

"I did. Ben, I'm sorry for denying it when we came back. When I saw my father, I panicked. He hurt me for so long, and I didn't want him to think he could hurt me by hurting you."

I melted like cheddar on the hamburger special. "Cooper, that's—that's—"

"It was cowardly, and I'm sorry. I wish I could do it over, but I can't. I want to win you back if you'll let me." He smiled. "Charles congratulated me after. He, ah." Those sharp cheekbones went pink. "He thinks it'll be easy. That you'll just fall into my arms. I know you won't."

"Oh. Um." Marlee scooted back her chair. "I think I should give you guys—"

"It's fine, Marlee. I don't care who hears." Those steely blue eyes of his cut me open. "I love you, Ben," he said, in a voice just loud enough for me to hear.

Cooper Fallon, COO, told me he loved me in a crowded cafeteria. The closest tables probably read the words on his lips. My heart pitter-pattered, trying to leap across the table toward him. I flashed him a flirty smile. "Care to say it a little louder so the rest of the class can hear?"

He grinned, showing that gorgeous left-cheek dimple. "Okay, Ben."

He scraped back his chair, the metal legs screeching against the tile. He stood.

"Shit, wait." I fluttered my hand, trying to get him to sit down again like a reasonable person.

He ignored it. In the carrying voice he used to project to the very back of our all-employee meetings, one that could be heard even by the cafeteria workers as they rattled dishes and threw food onto the sizzling grill, he said, "Ben Levy-Walters, I love you. I know you're angry with me right now because I hurt you. I was wrong. I was a coward, and I'm sorry. I'll do my best never to hurt you again."

If I thought the cafeteria was quiet before, it was nothing to the silence that descended over the large room. Even the grill seemed to go quiet. Someone shouted in the back room of the kitchen, and he was shushed.

"I—what?" I was lost in the blue pools of his eyes.

He smiled with both sides of his mouth. Not quite the easy grin he'd given me on the island, but a fond smile that connected with the warmth of his eyes. "Ben, I love you. Will you forgive me and consider taking me back?" He held out his hand.

I took it and let him raise me to my feet. I took a second to look around at the employees who were no longer pretending to eat but stared at us, eyes and mouths open.

"You didn't have to do *this*," I whispered. "All I wanted was for you to say you love me and call me your boyfriend. In private. Not in the fucking employee cafeteria."

"Ben," he said, still projecting to the back of the kitchen. "I'll declare my love everywhere. Because I love you, and I want the world to know it."

I squeezed my eyes shut. "You're not even drunk. You'll regret this tomorrow."

"I don't think I could ever regret anything about you. Except what I did to hurt you. Will you take me back?"

The cafeteria was silent. I don't think anyone dared to chew. Or to breathe. Could they hear my heart thudding in my chest? For Cooper. It beat for him.

I bit my lip and nodded. Softly, I said, "I love you, Cooper Fallon."

"What's that?" He cupped his ear. "I don't think they heard you in the far corner."

I sucked in a deep breath and projected my voice, not as well as Cooper had done, but as loud as I could go. "I love you, you big jerk. I'll take you back."

Murmurs spread across the cafeteria. One person clapped.

Cooper gave me a full-on, two-dimple grin that almost knocked me back a step.

"Now what?" If I could've broken our stare, I'd have looked down at Marlee for the post grand–gesture game plan.

"I'm going to kiss you now, Ben," he growled, lowering his voice to a register that I could hear in the backs of my molars and in my belly.

"What, here?"

His lips landed on mine. Even over my pulse banging in my ears, I heard the whoops all around us. Cooper Fallon was kissing me. In public.

I looped my arms over his shoulders and held on tight. But when he opened his mouth to tease my lips with his tongue, I leaned back, breathless. "Hey, now. None of that. We're at work, for God's sake."

His cheeks were red, and his chest heaved, too. "Maybe we could find a supply closet so I can show you how much I missed you?"

I was glad I'd worn my looser jeans that wouldn't show how much that idea appealed to me. "After work, you can show me somewhere private. Like your bedroom."

"I like the sound of that. But first, we'll go on a date. Dinner and a movie."

"A date in San Francisco with Cooper Fallon? What will the tabloids say?"

"Does it matter?"

"Fine. Dinner. Pick me up at seven. But I won't have the patience for a movie. I'd rather check out your bedroom."

He pecked my lips. "I'll pick you up at six. Wear the tight jeans." He didn't slap my ass, but his hot gaze said he'd do it later.

I licked my lips. "Okay. I don't care what you wear. I'll be taking it off as soon as I can."

"Guys?" I'd forgotten Marlee was right across the table from us. "Maybe save it for your date."

He reached for my hand and squeezed it. "I've got to get back upstairs and approve the response to Gurusoft."

"Don't forget to eat." I gripped his hand and released it. "See you at six."

With one last, gas-flame glance, he turned and walked out. Yes, I watched his ass. So did half the cafeteria.

When I turned back to Marlee, she was standing. Her cheeks were pink. "Come on. I'll walk you out. Then I'm going to find Tyler. And a supply closet."

37

BEN

GOING on a date with Cooper Fallon was more complicated than I predicted. He picked me up promptly at six. That wasn't the complicated part, although Mimi gave him one of her patented menacing, big-sister glares when he came to the door. He drove us in his sleek gray electric Porsche to one of the fancy restaurants overlooking the bay.

What was complicated were the stares and the camera flashes. Cooper was the face of Synergy, and people knew those high cheekbones, those piercing blue eyes. Even if they didn't know his face, no one was fooled into thinking his clothes came off the rack. His slacks had that expensive sheen, and his shirt flowed effortlessly over his toned torso. He dripped power and wealth, and heads turned when we passed.

He held my hand as we walked into the restaurant, and the whispers started. When I heard someone say his name, I turned— he didn't—and that's when someone's camera caught me gaping, looking like an unruly child Cooper was towing. The photo made it to a local celebrity blog the next day, where I was labeled "Cooper Fallon's Naughty Boy Toy."

I didn't hate it.

The host seated us on a private balcony overlooking the water. It would've reminded me of the meals we ate on Cooper's deck on the island, but the breeze off the water raised goosebumps on my arms—or maybe that was being so close to Cooper. Regardless, I wore my jacket, and so did Cooper. I missed seeing his skin.

Later, Ben.

The dinner itself was amazing. The menu had no prices, and when I tried to skip the obviously a la carte appetizer and salad courses, Cooper told me to stop being ridiculous or he'd order my food. That sent a thrill up my spine, but then I remembered the healthy food Cooper preferred, and I ordered everything that sounded delicious.

Finally, over the main course—fish for both of us, but mine was fried, and his was broiled, no butter—I got up the courage to ask about Synergy.

"How mad was Weston? Did security walk him out?"

"Mad? It's hard to tell. He's always in control. He walked out voluntarily. Calmly. I wish I could be like that."

"No." I pictured Cooper the way he sometimes was before you got to know him, icy and aloof. So what if he got a little hot sometimes? I could handle it. He could, too. "I love you just the way you are."

He cleared his throat. "I did have security walk my father out. I got a bit…heated over that. And it was a good thing I didn't find that guy who attacked you on the island. Who hid video cameras in our bedroom."

I blinked. "Wait, what?"

"I saw him in the building before the board meeting. The housekeeper we saw that day we came back from town. I confronted Weston after the meeting, and he admitted he hired him to follow me. He said the guy wasn't supposed to jump you. Only send intel back. Weston said it was because he was concerned for my mental health." He gripped his fork with a force that would have bent one of Mimi's flimsy ones.

I wanted to break something, too. "That asshole."

"I let my security guys know he's in San Francisco. They'll find him if they can."

"Oh, my God. All that, plus Weston threw your father in your face again. Are you okay?"

He set his fork on his plate and reached across the white tablecloth to hold my hand. "I am now."

I leaned over and kissed his cheek. "So, the buyout?"

"Not happening. But I don't think we've heard the last of the merger conversation. Some of the board, not only Weston, thought it was the best path for Synergy's future. For our security. We'll prove him wrong." He looked up, his eyes blazing.

I swallowed. "I'll support you all the way."

He knew without my having to say it that I wouldn't go back to Synergy. Not as his assistant. Not even in marketing after I got my degree. "And what about you? What will you do?"

"Keep looking for a job. At least I can pay my tuition now, thanks to your gift."

"You can't sell that stock to pay your tuition. The price is going to soar. Just you wait." His cheeks glowed with confidence. I shivered.

"Listen to me, Ben. Really listen." He waited until I met his gaze. "I know you don't want to be dependent on anyone, but let me do this for you. Let me pay your tuition. Go to school full time. How long would your degree take if you did that?"

"A-assuming I could get the classes I need, just one more semester. But I pay by the class, so—"

"Don't worry about the money," he growled. "I know the value of a good education. I also have connections at a number of foundations that help kids. Isn't that what you're interested in?"

Shit, he remembered. I blinked back the burn in my eyes. "Yeah."

"I could get you a part-time internship at one of them while you go to school. It could turn into a permanent job after you graduate."

"You—I—you can't."

"Why not? You're an excellent employee. Consider it an investment in San Francisco's youth. In Synergy's future workforce."

"Wow." I set down my fork. "Way to make your very generous offer sound unromantic." But it was a lie. Cooper took care of those he loved, and now I was in the group of loved ones he cared for.

He leaned back in his chair, his blue eyes shining. "I haven't even started the romantic part. You asked about business, so I gave you business. Will you consider my offer?"

"Yes." I'd be a fool to pass it up. And once I had a job in my field, I could pay him back the tuition money.

"All right, then." He shoved his plate a little away from himself, and our observant waiter whisked it away, along with mine. "I'd like you to come home with me tonight."

I flashed him a wicked smile. "I think I already agreed to do that. Remember, we're doing Netflix and chill without the Netflix?"

He gave me a *look,* and I shivered. I could imagine him looking at me like that as I knelt before him, lowering his zipper.

"I'd like you to come home with me and stay. I've got more space in that house than I could ever need. Seven bedrooms, and you'd get your choice. Though I hope"—he picked a crumb off the tablecloth—"you'll choose mine."

"What, and give up Mimi's ratty sofa?" I waited for a smile that didn't come. Okay, I guessed some things you didn't joke about with Cooper Fallon. "I'm kidding. Yes, let's do it. On a trial basis, anyway. You might hate how I throw my socks on the floor."

His left eye twitched. He would definitely hate how I threw my socks on the floor. I'd have to stop that...eventually.

"But I need to pay for some things." Cooper had probably paid cash for his mansion, so he wouldn't have a mortgage I could split with him—not that I'd ever be able to afford *that.* "Groceries. Nights out. Though nothing as swanky as tonight." I glanced inside at the crystal chandelier that dominated the main dining room.

"I'll let you buy my smoothies. They weren't the same when you weren't there."

Blueberries was on the tip of my tongue. But I held it in. Better to keep some secrets so he still needed me.

"And"—he looked at me through his lashes, and my heart gave a giant thump—"I'll let you pay for half of our engagement party. Well, half less the value of the time you'll put into planning it."

"En-engagement?" My lips were too numb to function properly. "Are you proposing? Tonight?"

"No." He leaned back in his chair, all smug ease. "Not tonight. But soon."

"We've been dating for less than a month. We can't get married."

"Of course we can. I've been in love with you for months." He raised his eyebrows.

"Months? Since I started working for you?"

"Well." He looked down at the tablecloth. "Since I pulled my head out of my ass over—" He shook his head. "I can tell from the way your eyebrows are scrunching that it's too much for right now. I can be patient." He leaned forward and put his lips right next to my ear. "In some things."

He leaned back to smirk at me just as the waiter approached with the dessert menus.

"Would you gentlemen care to—"

"Just the check, please." My voice was too high, and my cheeks flamed.

"Of course." He disappeared.

"No dessert?" Cooper's hand landed on my knee under the table.

"I'll wait until we get home."

"I like the sound of that. Home." And he kissed me, closed-mouth and sweet. But it held the promise of more. More nights like this, the two of us holding hands and kissing in public. And more nights alone, the sheets tangling around us. More years together after I learned to pick up my socks and after he learned to like seeing my socks on his floor.

That kiss on the veranda meant forever.

COOPER

I COULDN'T HAVE BEEN prouder.

Ben still wore his graduation cap from the ceremony earlier, the tassel hanging over the left side. He stood sandwiched between his parents in front of the gazebo while his sister, Mimi, snapped a photo with her phone.

Clutching my glass of seltzer, I strode over. Mimi should be in the picture, too.

"Cooper, c'mere, c'mere." Ben took off the cap, shoved it onto Mimi's head, and tugged me in close. "Engagement photo time." A few hours into the party that spilled out from a heated tent in our back yard, his breath smelled like beer.

"I thought I'd get a picture of the four of you together." But I ran my fingers through his hair, fluffing it up where the cap had flattened it.

"Oh. That too. But this first." He tucked an arm around my waist and turned us to face Mimi.

"One, two, three." Mimi clicked the shutter. "You two look great. I didn't even have to remind you to smile, Cooper. Mom and Dad, you get in, too." It had taken a few months of proving myself, but Mimi had finally accepted me into their lives.

It may have had something to do with my introducing her to the foundation director. It seemed that Ben wasn't the only Levy-Walters who wanted to support children's causes.

"Wait. I'll get Mamá. It'll be a family portrait." I scanned the guests scattered across our lawn. My mother and Mateo leaned on the bridge over the koi pond. Coco sat at their feet. "Mamá! Mateo!" I beckoned them over. I'd invited Mateo to live with us and coordinate security. With Weston's former spy and Mick Fallon on the loose, I couldn't be too careful.

I shoved thoughts of my father out of my brain. He had no place in our happy occasion.

When my cousin led my mother to us, Coco yapping and dancing beside them, I said, "Mateo, you take the picture. Mimi, come around here."

"Careful," Mimi snapped when Mateo bobbled her phone. Always so smooth and suave, since he'd joined us in the States, he'd become clumsy. Especially around Mimi.

His face went red. "I've got it now."

Ben scooped up Coco. I put my hands on my mother's shoulders and positioned her in front of me. Ben's parents flanked us, and Mimi stuck off on the end. Mateo motioned us closer, and I put my arm around Ben and turned toward him.

The shutter clicked, but all I saw was Ben's handsome face. Now that all the stresses of school were behind him, now that his internship at the foundation had turned into a full-time job just as I'd predicted, he looked relaxed, the lines around his eyes smoothed out. I bent and kissed him, softly. He tasted sharply acidic from the IPA he'd been drinking. Coco squirmed and leaped to the ground.

"Good day so far?" I asked my fiancé as the group started to break apart.

He threw his arms around my neck. "The best."

"You don't regret having to share your big day with me?" I'd tried to convince him to have separate parties for his graduation and our engagement. But, ever mindful of finances, he said it'd be more efficient to combine them. And he was right: planning and scheduling one party had been easier than two. I was doing better at work-life balance, but I still traveled a lot for Synergy.

"My graduation is as much your milestone as mine. I wouldn't be here if not for you."

"Of course you would. It just would have taken you longer." I ran a hand down his back just because I could.

"No." He shook his head. "Having the Cooper Fallon scholarship was one thing. But I've always looked up to you. Even before I met you. You're a fucking inspiration, love."

I hid my hot face in his shoulder. "Thanks."

He kissed my cheek and gently pulled away. "Hey, Marlee. Tyler."

Ben's parents had walked off with my mother. Mimi and Mateo had disappeared. And standing in front of us were Marlee and Tyler, holding hands.

"Congratulations, Ben. Congrats to you both." Marlee leaned in and hugged Ben, then me. "Let's hear it."

"Hear what?" I asked, shaking Tyler's hand.

"Your romantic engagement story."

"I told you about it at work right after we got back. Don't you remember?"

She rolled her eyes. "I want to hear it from Ben. Your version wasn't romantic enough."

I blinked. I thought I'd been very romantic in my proposal. And I'd told her the story and answered most of her questions.

"Besides, Tyler wants to hear it, too. Don't you, honey?"

After I'd gotten together with Ben, Tyler had finally stopped glaring at me.

"Sure," he said, grinning. "I'd love to hear it, Ben."

"Okay, so we went to the island for Thanksgiving. We took Rosa, too, to see the family. So I wasn't expecting anything, right?

I figured if he hadn't asked by New Year's Eve, I'd propose to him then."

"You were going to propose to me?" I interrupted him.

"Didn't you notice me trying to find out your ring size?"

"I thought that was to replace the larimar ring I cracked."

He tapped his temple. "Sly as a fox. But you beat me to it. Anyway"—he turned to Tyler, like Tyler cared at all about the story—"Rosa stayed with tía abuela Isobel after dinner one night, and Cooper and I went back to our place alone. He asked me what I wanted to do, and I said walk on the beach. The moon was full that night, and it was so beautiful on the water."

I remembered how the moonlight glinted on his dark hair, too. I touched a glossy curl that sparkled burgundy in the afternoon sunlight.

"We were walking, and I was telling him about something I'd learned in my psych class. What was it?"

"Behavioral genetics," I murmured.

"That's right. And all of a sudden, he stopped, and I turned, and he was down on one knee."

"Holy Frank Kameny! I didn't think you had a romantic bone in your body, Cooper Fallon." Marlee smacked my arm.

"I guess I do." I shrugged. "That's what you wanted, right, Ben?"

"Moonlight and my man on his knees. Exactly what I wanted. And then, *then,* he made a speech."

"Wait, Cooper Fallon on his knees in the sand, making a speech? I told you, you left out all the good parts, Cooper."

"The speech was personal." I glared at Ben, but I couldn't help smiling, too. Tears had glittered silver on his cheeks.

"It was the most romantic thing ever." Ben put his arm around my waist, and my hand landed on the small of his back, right where it belonged.

"See? I knew there was a better story than what you told me." Marlee lowered her voice in an imitation of mine. "'We went to the island and got engaged.'" She rolled her eyes. "I'm glad you get me." She kissed Tyler on the cheek. "You'd never tell me a story like that."

Ben tugged me tighter and gave me a secret smile. He understood that I saved my romantic moments for when it counted, just for him.

"Congratulations, guys," Tyler said. "And thanks for inviting us. I think Marlee needs another drink."

"Or a makeout session behind the garage," Ben muttered. I hadn't missed the way her lips had lingered a hair's breadth from her fiancé's.

"Benny!" Mimi fluttered into Ben's shoulder, her dark curls wild. "Sorry, gotta go. Congratulations, you two."

"Where are you going?" Ben asked. I hadn't realized it during the photos, but Mimi was weaving on her feet, her eyes unfocused.

"Girls' night! I told you, Benny, remember?"

"I remember. Are you sure you want to go out? Looks like you've had plenty to drink already."

She smiled at him, but it didn't reach her eyes. "I promised. And I'll be fine. A water for every drink."

Even that wouldn't sober her up. "Be careful, okay? You have a ride?"

"Yes—" She bit back whatever else she was going to say. She did that a lot in front of me. I wished she could think of me as her brother's fiancé and not her boss, several levels up.

"Have fun. And be safe." Ben hugged her, and she minced away, taking those too-careful steps I remembered from my drinking days.

"Want me to—?"

"Yes, please." He bit his lip.

"Mateo!" I barked.

Surprisingly, he was at my side in a moment. "Yeah, Lito?"

"You know Ben's sister, Mimi?"

He nodded, an inscrutable expression on his face.

"Keep an eye on her, please. From a distance. Make sure she makes it home safely. And alone."

"Got it." He slapped Ben on the back. "Congratulations, Benny. And I'll keep your sister safe."

"Thanks." He hugged my cousin's shoulder. Mateo prowled off in that catlike way he moved.

"Alone at last." Ben sighed.

"We're at a party with a hundred of our closest friends and relatives, and you expected to be alone?" But I pulled him up against me, not caring who saw.

"Not really. But that's the best part of combining my graduation party with our engagement party."

"What is?"

"That I can do this." He balanced on his toes and kissed me, and I let him in to slide his tongue against mine. There were whistles and clinks of glasses all around us, but I didn't care. All I cared about was that this man, Ben, was mine to kiss. That he wanted to kiss only me for the rest of his life.

"I guess there's no tongue at a graduation party?" I murmured against his lips.

"Not nearly as much as at an engagement party." He lowered to his heels, ensuring that he rubbed against me as he descended.

I held him close to hide the bulge in my dress slacks. "What else can we get away with at an engagement party?" I whispered, my lips brushing the shell of his ear.

He shivered. "I think a brief disappearance by the engaged couple wouldn't be out of line."

"Lead the way, love. I'm right behind you."

Our disappearance wasn't as brief as it should have been. But the party went on without us. And later, when we returned, our clothes rumpled and our lips kiss-swollen, everyone understood. Everyone, that is, who knew what it was like to have met the love of your life and to be looking forward to forever with him.

———

Thank you so much for reading *Boss Me!* Please consider posting a review on your favorite retailer, BookBub, or Goodreads. Reviews help other readers find new authors like me.

Need another sexy scene with Cooper and Ben? And a cameo by Coco (of course)? Join my newsletter at michellemccraw.com/Cooper or use your phone's camera to take a picture of the QR code below to download a bonus epilogue!

Did you catch the sparks between Mimi and Mateo in the epilogue? The next book in the series, *Forget Me,* is a fake-dating, opposites-attract romantic comedy with a fun spin on the amnesia trope. It features an uptight accountant and a himbo who can't keep it together around her. It can be read as a standalone and is the fifth book in the Synergy Workplace Romance series. Read on for a sneak peek.

FORGET ME (SYNERGY BOOK 5)
CHAPTER 1

MIMI

I'D FORGOTTEN EVERYTHING. Except his pretty eyes.

Blue and round, though the tequila had dulled the details. I couldn't recall the exact shade or if they had flecks in them. Just blue. And glasses. Clark Kent glasses. The pendant light that hung over our heads glinted off the lenses.

The shape and color of the frames were fuzzy in my memory, but I was ninety-two percent certain they weren't round and metal like Byron's. Even as drunk as I was, I'd have run the other direction.

How long had I stared into his eyes while we sat at that Divisadero Street bar? It felt like hours, but the tequila. So much tequila.

A flash of memory: blue eyes crinkled in concern and a big hand gripping my arm to steady me on the stool. And another flash, though this one flitted away from me, just out of reach. His gaze burning into me, serious and intense. Something pressed into my hand.

I looked down at my palm like it would still be there. But there was nothing except an ugly plastic ring, the light-up fake diamond as big as a walnut. When I tapped it, it flickered weakly in neon pink. As Bree's maid of honor, I'd laid down the rule: no vulgar swag at her bachelorette party. But one of Bree's other friends had brought a sack full of plastic crap. And after a couple shots of tequila, I didn't care about the rules. I wrenched the ring off my finger and dropped it onto the counter.

Damned hangover. I rubbed my temple, but that did nothing to soothe the tightness around my brain.

Although I didn't remember much about his appearance, I remembered how last night's mystery man made me feel. Interesting. Cared-for. Safe. And I'd laughed so hard my stomach muscles were still a little sore.

Actually, that might have been from the puking.

The buzz of my phone against my kitchen counter set off a new pain somewhere in the vicinity of my molars.

I plucked the cheap fuchsia sash off of it—the script on it read, "Hot Mess," and hadn't *that* turned out to be true?—and tossed it aside. I scraped the phone off the counter and squinted one eye at the display. Bree. I stabbed the answer button.

"Why are you up so early?"

She groaned, and her voice came out hoarse. "Had to hug the throne. You drank as much as me. How are you?"

"Same." How was my breath? I couldn't show up to my presentation smelling like regurgitated tequila. I cupped my hand over my mouth, breathed out, and sniffed. Minty fresh. I jammed a pod into the coffeemaker and hit the brew button.

"Mimi," my best friend whined, "wasn't this easier in our twenties?"

"The drinking part or the hangover part?"

"Both. I remember going out on Saturday night and then drinking mimosas at Sunday brunch. Now just thinking about champagne—or orange juice—makes me want to hurl."

"I guess a lot of things are different now that we're over thirty." Like the weird rash around my mouth I'd had to cover up with an extra layer of foundation. The one that looked suspiciously like beard burn, though I definitely didn't remember kissing anyone. "Hey, do you remember much from last night?"

"Ugh, not really. Especially after the third round of tequila shots."

Third round? I strained my sluggish memory, but it was a blur of Bree's head thrown back in laughter, the other girls' giggles, and those glasses framing a pair of twinkling blue eyes.

The coffeemaker light blinked off, and I picked up my mug. The bitter scent of it made my stomach seize. I set it back on the counter. "Did you have a good time?"

"Yeah. Thanks for coming out. I know you had a lot going on with your brother's engagement party yesterday."

"I wouldn't have missed your bachelorette party for the world. We've been friends too long for that." We'd been best friends since we'd met in the theater showing *The Incredibles*. Both our families had refused to watch it with us. It was the third time for me, the fifth time for her. We'd bonded over how much we identified with Violet, though we hadn't known how to express it then. As our friendship deepened, we'd obsessed over Spider-Man, Henry Cavill's Superman, and every one of the Avengers.

So even though I didn't usually waste time at parties, I'd rearranged my entire weekend to fit in both Ben's party and hers, working late on Friday night to finish up my presentation.

"Thank God we have a day to recover before we have to go back to work," she said.

I hummed and pulled my presentation out of my satchel, just to check it one last time. The crisp pie charts, the line graphs showing my projections. There was nothing for perfect Larissa to find fault with, and we were going to wow her boss, Jackson Jones. Who also happened to be an executive at Synergy, where I worked.

"Oh, no," Bree said. "That's not an I'm-going-back-to-bed *hmm*. That's an I'm-going-for-a-ten-mile-run *hmm*."

I chuckled. "You know I hate running. Actually, I have to work today."

"On a Sunday?"

"It's for the foundation. We have a brunch meeting in the Mission in half an hour, and I'm presenting next year's budget to Jackson Jones."

"Wait, you're not even getting *paid* for this?"

"No." Though someday if I copied my little brother and turned my passion into a paid job, I could have an occasional day off. "Hustle culture, you know."

"Ugh, don't give me that bullshit. You're a mensch. You're doing it for—for the kids."

I knew she'd almost said *for me*. It was true that I'd started volunteering for the foundation for my best friend. For the time I'd heard that jerk, Anthony Anker, call her Blinky Barbie on our first day of seventh grade. I'd wanted to get up in his face, try out the punch my brother had taught me the summer before, *definitely* make sure Anthony never made fun of my friend's tic again, but Bree had held me back, told me he wasn't worth getting detention over. But all these years later, I'd kept up my volunteer work because I truly loved the work the foundation did for kids with Tourette's. Kids like Bree had been.

I'd just opened my mouth to break up the tension with a joke when she said, "Did you think about what we talked about last night?"

Staring at my poster of Doctor Strange, I scanned back for a memory of anything other than tequila and screams of laughter and dancing. Dancing? "You're going to have to refresh my memory."

"You don't remember?" Shit, she sounded hurt. "We talked about how you're the last single person in our friend group. You promised to try to—"

"Doubtful." I twisted my mug on the counter until its handle was at a precise 45-degree angle. "You know how focused I am on my career now. And on the foundation. I don't have time for distractions."

"A distraction like Byron, you mean? That guy was a douche

canoe. There are tons of good guys out there, Mimi. Guys who'll help you and won't steal your promotion."

"I don't need help. I can succeed all on my own." The words came out sharper than I'd intended.

"I know, I know. All you need is smarts, drive…"

"And confidence," we finished together. My mother had said those words about a million times.

"Your mom got married," Bree said.

"She's the top environmental lawyer in the state. I'd never compare myself to her. And just because you're a week from saying 'I do' doesn't mean it's right for everyone. I want to establish myself in my career first."

"And scratch that itch with one-night stands?"

I lifted my chin even though she couldn't see me. "There's nothing wrong with my no-strings hookups. I get all the benefits, none of the arguing over whose work function we have to go to and where we spend the holidays."

"It's kind of nice to have someone to spend the holidays with, you know."

I eased a hip against the counter. I hadn't missed the way Mom's eyes had gone soft when my brother showed up at her Hanukkah party with his fiancé. They'd worn matching ugly Hanukkah sweaters. Even my cold, black heart had melted a little at how adorable they were together.

Me? I couldn't exactly ask one of my hookups to come to my parents' party after I'd slipped out of his apartment before dawn and stopped replying to his texts.

"What, you want me to show up to your wedding with a plus-one?"

"No!" Her laugh was high and strained. "We already gave the final count to the caterer. But you're deflecting. Even Ben—"

The intercom dinged, saving me from my best friend's speech about how even my little brother had finally found lasting love. She was right about all the coupling-up. A week never went by without the arrival of an invitation to a wedding or a bridal shower or an engagement party. If someone sent me a birth announcement, I was going to puke. Again.

"Sorry, Bree. Someone's at the door." It was probably Ben dropping by to check on me. Though last I'd seen him at his engagement party yesterday afternoon, he'd been pretty tipsy himself.

"Good luck with your big presentation. I know you'll rock it. Call me after?" She made a kissing sound before I disconnected.

I walked to the intercom. It was just like Ben to bring me a sack of breakfast pastries to soak up the alcohol. My stomach gurgled.

"Hey," I said into the speaker as I buzzed him up.

I opened the door a crack and headed back toward the kitchen to tuck my presentation into my satchel. Then I froze. Ben still had a key. Why would he use the buzzer?

When I whirled back around, the answer filled my doorway. Six-foot-something of tanned skin, blond hair, a clean-shaven jaw that could cut glass, and eyes the color of the Pacific Ocean on a rare sunny day. Ben's friend, and his fiancé's cousin, Mateo. I stared at his muscle-rounded shoulder where his too-tight black T-shirt clung to it. Looking at his face was like staring into the sun. Eye-searingly bright and beautiful. Too handsome to be real. And today I didn't need a distraction that came in the shape of a flirty Thor look-alike.

"Good morning, bella," he said, stepping into my apartment.

I wrinkled my nose at the faint scent of cigarette smoke that wafted in with him. I'd known Mateo long enough not to feel any flutters in my belly. Everyone in his world—male, female, old, young—got a flirtatious nickname. He was an equal-opportunity player, and it meant nothing.

Case in point: at Ben's party yesterday, he'd chatted up Marlee, Ben's work-bestie. She was the most beautiful woman I'd ever met, all smooth honey hair and fashion sense. But she was taken, and Mateo knew it. Still, I'd caught him looking at me over her head a couple of times. Like he wanted me to notice that

Marlee was the kind of person he spent time with. Never someone like me. With me, he was silent and aloof.

In fact, why had he come here this morning? He'd never been to my place, not even with Ben.

"Why are you here?" I crossed my arms. "Fresh out of swimsuit models to seduce?"

His sparkling grin drooped. He looked…hurt? "I came to check on you. Are you feeling all right this morning?"

"Fine," I said. "Though I'm actually in a—wait. What do you know about last night?"

His dark-blond eyebrows scrunched down. "Don't you remember?"

I thought back to yesterday. I'd been buzzed already when I'd dashed from Ben's engagement party to join Bree's bachelorette party in progress. Had Ben noticed and sent Mateo to watch over me? It was the kind of thing my little brother would do.

I didn't remember seeing Mateo at the first bar. Or the second one. I remembered the booth, the round table spread with shot glasses, Bree snort-laughing, sparkling plastic tiaras, holiday lights blinking around the window, and the room spinning around me as the drinks kept coming.

"No. Why? Were you there?"

The corners of his mouth turned down. "You don't remember?"

"Should I?" I'd definitely have remembered if he'd been at the bar. Bree's friends would have made him the king of their court. They'd have flattered him, touched him, flirted with him in a way that made me itch. They didn't know Mateo like I did. He might be fitness-model gorgeous, but he was about as deep as a puddle.

He seemed to deflate. Then he pasted on a shadow of his usual teasing smile and held out a white bakery bag. "I brought you breakfast."

My stomach roiled. "No, thanks. Hangover. I need coffee."

"No." He brushed past me. "You need carbs. Sugar. Do you have any ginger tea?"

I scurried to catch up with him, but his broad shoulders and the stink of cigarettes filled my entire galley kitchen. My throat burned. I didn't have time for another visit to the toilet. I waved my hand in front of my face. "Sorry, but you smell like smoke, and"—I swallowed—"I'm afraid my stomach isn't settled enough for that. Thanks for dropping by, but…"

His face fell, but he set the bag on the counter before he shoved open the kitchen window. Huh. I'd thought it was painted shut.

"Better now?" He stood beside it for a moment as if he could air himself out.

I took a deep breath of the cold, fresh air. "Better. Thanks."

"Now, for your stomach." He opened an upper cabinet. "You need something with ginger. Or prickly pear?"

Prickly pear? "No. I live in the real world where we drink coffee when we're hungover. Thanks for coming, but I need to get ready."

"Ready?" He shut the cabinet and turned toward me. "You look perfect."

"Thank you." The words came out flat, automatic. He said that kind of shit to everyone. In my oversize black sweater and jeans, I wasn't anything approaching perfect, not compared to a demigod like Mateo. Obviously, he kept up his physique with daily work-outs. He was the kind of guy who'd drink kale smoothies with his equally hot underwear-model partner. Who talked about supple-ments and reps and flipping prickly pear.

Not that there was anything wrong with that. It was just differ-ent. I preferred to work out my brain with spreadsheets, fueled by a bag of salt-and-vinegar chips. Hard pass on kale.

"I need to go. To a meeting. I'll eat there." I squeezed around him into the kitchen to shoo him out.

"Yes, your meeting with Larissa and Jackson. Shouldn't you eat first?"

"My—my what? How do you know about that?"

He looked down at the bag and mumbled something.

Right. Ben must have mentioned it at the party yesterday. Get a couple drinks into him, and nothing was a secret. Not that my foundation meeting was a secret, but it definitely wasn't any of Mateo's business.

"Okay, so, good chat, but I'm sure you've got some muscles that need sculpting." He didn't. They were absolutely perfect, but his ego didn't need any stroking from me. "And I've got to leave."

"You'll deal with Larissa's bullshit better if you don't show up hangry. Try these. They're delicious." He reached for the bakery bag, but when his arm brushed mine, he jolted. The bag knocked against my cup of coffee and tipped it. Dark-brown liquid gushed across the counter, straight toward my papers.

"No!" I leaped to pick them up, but Mateo's solid body blocked my way. Coffee soaked into the papers, melting my perfect pie charts and smearing my lovely line graphs. "Shit, Mateo. That's my presentation for"—I checked the clock on the wall—"for my meeting that starts in fifteen minutes!"

"Can you print new ones?" He grabbed the kitchen towel and blotted at the papers, but all that did was transfer the stain to my pristine ecru towel. Panic tightened my throat.

"Don't! Stop." When I grabbed his arm, he flinched. The wet paper ripped.

Even if I could magically dry the paper in fifteen minutes, a pie chart held together with Scotch tape wasn't going to impress anyone. My presentation, and my chance to impress Jackson Jones, was ruined.

"I—I'm sorry, Miriam."

My body heated, and my anger boiled over. "Dammit, Mateo. I'm going to be late, and now I have no presentation. Get out of my way." I tossed the papers in the trash. I didn't have time to go to the office and reprint them. I'd have to show them on screen. Except—

Horror dawning, I looked down at the coffee. It had breached my satchel. With my laptop inside. When I yanked it out, coffee dripped from the corner.

"Shit!" I snatched the ruined towel from Mateo and blotted at the edge. *Please, please,* please, *start.* I set my laptop on a dry part of the counter, flipped it open, and pressed the power button. A few pixels lit, then the screen went black.

I mashed the power button, and this time, nothing happened at all. "Goddammit!"

His face was paler than my kitchen towel. "Can I do anything?"

I ground my molars. "Get. Out."

"I—I can ask Lito—I mean Cooper—to get you a new laptop—"

"No!" He might be Mateo's favorite cousin Miguelito, but to me, he was Cooper Fallon, my boss's boss's boss. No way could he learn that I'd ruined my Synergy laptop. His temper was legendary, and even his soon-to-be sister-in-law might not be safe from one of his infamous tongue-lashings. "Just go."

"But I—"

"Go!" I pointed at the door.

He folded into himself and shuffled away. My apartment door clicked shut as I stuffed my deceased laptop into my soggy satchel.

Despairing, I glanced at the clock again. I'd definitely be late. Neither Larissa nor Jackson Jones would be impressed. And tomorrow, I'd have to ask my boss for a new laptop.

Thanks, Mateo.

———

Forget Me is available in paperback from your favorite retailer.

———

She doesn't remember their night together. He can't forget it.

When accountant Mimi wakes up after a night of fun with her

girlfriends, she remembers the hot guy in glasses she flirted with at the bar but not much else. With no way to contact him—no phone number, not even a selfie—she'll do her best to forget him. Because nothing, not even a sexy mystery man, will keep her from winning her dream job.

Except…Mateo.

Her brother's friend is everywhere—spilling coffee on her presentation, bringing apology flowers to her at work, even wowing her new boss at her project meeting.

Mateo has never struggled to be the fun, cool, suave guy—except around Mimi. She's found his Awkward switch, and now it's stuck in the ON position.

After screwing up Mimi's presentation, the least Mateo can do is help her. He charms her boss, who pushes them to attend the foundation's upcoming gala together. If helping Mimi means being her fake date at her big work event, he's more than up for the job. And if he can convince Mimi he's good enough to be her real boyfriend, he'll have all he's ever wanted since he met her that night in the bar.

Forget Me is a fake-dating, opposites attract romantic comedy with a lighthearted spin on the amnesia trope. It features an uptight accountant and a himbo who can't keep it together around her. It can be read as a standalone and is the fifth book in the Synergy Workplace Romance series.

ACKNOWLEDGMENTS

First off, thank you, my reader, for coming on this journey with me. I never anticipated that less than a year after publishing my first novel, I'd have so many kind people who send me emails telling me you like my books. Your support makes a huge difference, and I'm forever grateful. (I'll say it again: I love y'all!)

Thanks to my ARC team who gave me a chance and who cheer me on with each new release. I hope you've enjoyed this one!

Thanks to my indie pub squad, Tiffany, Brandy, Liz, Carla, and Kristin, for your encouragement and advice. You've made my writing life more fun!

And thanks to my beta readers, Lauren Accardo, Carla Luna, Ofelia Martinez, and Becca Taylor, for your thoughtful feedback and reassurance. And Carla, I know I owe you a hero you'll actually like—just wait for Mateo!

CREDITS

Edits

Heart Full of Ink

Proofreading

April Bennett, The Editing Soprano

Cover Design

Qamber Designs

ABOUT MICHELLE

Michelle McCraw loves reading kissing books and working in tech. One day, she decided to combine her two interests, and now she writes steamy, nerdy contemporary romance that just might make you laugh. Her books feature characters who unashamedly love science, engineering, and technology.

A native Texan, Michelle has shoveled snow during nor'easters and knows the proper response when someone yells, "O-H." She now calls Georgia home, where she doesn't miss snow AT ALL. She enjoys reading, travel, drinking bourbon, and spoiling her extraordinarily ill-behaved but adorable dog. She has been a finalist in the RWA Vivian Contest, the Contemporary Romance Writers' Stiletto Contest, and the Windy City Romance Writers' Four Seasons Contest.

For updates about upcoming books and more free reads—plus guaranteed puppy pics—subscribe to Michelle's newsletter at michellemccraw.com. You can also follow the author on Facebook and Instagram.

facebook.com/MichelleMcCrawAuthor

instagram.com/MMOWriter

amazon.com/author/michellemccraw

goodreads.com/MichelleMcCraw

bookbub.com/authors/michelle-mccraw

Work with Me

She's got a checklist for every occasion. He's never met a bad decision he didn't make. Can straitlaced single mom Alicia find a way to work with billionaire tech genius Jackson and save her business—without falling for him first?

"Slow burn magic!" (5-star review)

Friend Me

Romance-obsessed executive assistant Marlee has a plan to woo her crush, icy and aloof San Francisco tech executive Cooper Fallon. But it all goes wrong when her fake date, instead of making her crush jealous, sparks more-than-friends feelings. Kissing the wrong guy? Not in her plan. Neither is falling for her best friend.

"Un-put-down-able" (5-star review)

Trip Me Up

Nerdy computer scientist Samantha Jones didn't mean to end up on a book tour trying to pass off her artificial intelligence-written novel as one written the old-fashioned way. And she certainly didn't mean to fall for her flannel-wearing, poetic tour partner. Opposites attract in this road-trip romance.

"This book had me hooked right from the start and up until the wee hours devouring their story!" (5-star review)

Boss Me

Frosty billionaire philanthropist Cooper Fallon would never start a fling with his off-limits assistant, Ben…or would he?

"OMG…If you like forbidden romance this is the book for you!!!" (5-star review)

Forget Me

She doesn't remember their night together. He can't forget it. When Mimi's prospective boss mistakes Mateo for her boyfriend, she's shocked when he rolls with it. But when their fake romance becomes real, will buttoned-up Mimi let down her guard for love?

"I absolutely love this twist on the grumpy sunshine trope." (5-star review)

Tempt Me

When a gaffe caught on camera threatens her company, a no-nonsense tech CEO calls on her bestie's little sister for help. But falling for her sunshiny public relations assistant could get her into even more hot water.

"THIS WAS FUN!!" (5-star review)

Fashion and Passion

After a disastrous self-help seminar, Carly finds friendship, empowerment, and maybe love with a younger admirer. Get swept away by sparkling banter, new besties, and spicy seduction, perfect for a bubbly escape.

Frenemies and Lovers

When Carly needs a date to her ex's wedding, she agrees to a deal with Andrew, a devilishly handsome younger man. Her frenemy's son. Who happens to be her one-night stand. What could go wrong? Who says you can't be fabulous over forty?

"Total catnip" (5-star review)

Books and Hookups

Writer Lucie's life is looking up: she has a new book deal, fabulous friends, and a bar where everyone knows her name. The last thing she needs is a surprise (geriatric?) pregnancy with her much-younger neighbor.

Conspiracies and Chemistry

Secretive billionaire Tessa seeks redemption from the biggest mistake of her life by betting it all on a groundbreaking biotechnology company, which happens to be run by her younger nemesis. Who knew lab coats were so sexy?

Advances and Retreats

When Bridget and her nemesis, Cole, are temporarily assigned as co-CEOs and given the chance to compete for the solo job at a corporate retreat in Costa Rica, they encounter crocodiles, sabotage, and—possibly—love.